The Smile

Book 1 of "The Beautiful Life Trilogy"

KM LOWE

Order this book online at www.trafford.com
or email orders@trafford.com

Most Trafford titles are also available at major online book retailers.

Printed in the United States of America.

ISBN: 978-1-4907-3557-3 (sc)
ISBN: 978-1-4907-3559-7 (hc)
ISBN: 978-1-4907-3558-0 (e)

Library of Congress Control Number: 2014908472

Trafford rev. 05/06/2014

 www.trafford.com

North America & international
toll-free: 1 888 232 4444 (USA & Canada)
fax: 812 355 4082

ACKNOWLEDGEMENTS

First of all, I would like to thank Yza Gomez at Trafford for helping to publish my novel. You have made the process so much easier, and I don't know how to thank you all enough.

Second, I would like to thank my family and friends for putting up with me over the last several months. My husband will, maybe, get some sense out of me now.

Third, to my children, I love you dearly and you mean so much to me. I hope that one day you will be able to read mummy's work.

Finally, to my readers, thank you all for purchasing my novel. It means a lot to see so many of you reading what I write.

DEDICATIONS

I would like to dedicate this novel to my late mum and dad. I know that they would be very proud of me if they were here today. xx

ASHLEY'S STORY

CHAPTER 1

New Beginnings

Today is the day that we have been waiting on for so long. So much time has passed, since we started university four years ago, that I haven't had any time to think about the future. My room-mate Christine and I moved into halls together to study business and economics, and we had had a blast together. We had been through exams, break-ups, make-ups, and so much fun together, that nothing would ever make us fall out. Now it was time for the real world, and we were moving from the halls here in Florida to the beautiful town of Anchorage in Alaska. We had both secured placements within Black's Enterprise, one of Alaska's biggest companies buying and selling businesses and property all around the globe.

'Oh, this is so exciting.' Christine came running through to tell me she was all packed and ready to go. She was loud and very excited, just like she always is when something is happening. I didn't know how we had been friends for so long because we were as different as chalk and cheese.

'I can't believe we are now entering the real world.' It all still seemed so unreal. Time had flown by so quickly over the years that I swore I didn't know how we got here. I, sometimes, looked back on my life and wondered where the time had gone. I had been through so much in my short life that I wouldn't wish it on my worst enemy. But when I thought about it, everything that had happened to me had made me the person I was today.

'I know it is going to be early mornings and late nights for all the opposite reasons.' We had had four years of parties and lectures; now it had all got to be hit on the head with a hammer. We were going to be wrapped up in work and meetings for the next X amount of years. My heart was pounding in my chest. I felt as though I could pass out with the thought of everything going on in my head. I was all packed and ready to turn the page into a new chapter, but I still wasn't sure that I was ready for all this change. We were leaving our comfort zone and entering the big bad world.

'Ashley, you look as though you have seen a ghost, babe.' Christine had her two hands on my shoulders, pushing me towards the door. This flat had been our security net for so long, and now we had to stand on our own two feet. I knew that I had a few years without my parents, and I had no choice but to stand on my feet. But now it seemed like we were being thrown in at the deep end. It was amazing to think how much security school could give you. When I lost my parents in the car accident, I would have fallen into pieces if it wasn't for Christine and school. They were my rock when I felt like I had nothing and no one.

'I just can't believe that this is finally happening.' Tears welled up in my eyes as I took my last look around. Everything that we have achieved over the last few years happened here, and I was sad to leave it all behind. It was like one door was closing and a whole world of opportunities was opening up to us. We closed the door and walked down the path slowly. It was like a force was holding me back. I might have had a lot of heartache here, but it has made me the strong and independent person that I am today. We both looked back at the very same time. Even if Christine seemed happy about moving, she was still sad about leaving everything behind; she had a lot more to give up than me. I don't think that I could have walked away so easy if my parents were still alive. I would have still had a connection here.

'Alaska might hold a lot more pathways for us, Ash. It has been too long since we have been in a stable relationship.' I looked at my friend through sarcastic eyes. We hadn't even got away from halls, and she was looking for Mr Right. She was torture.

'Let's move and settle into our new home and job before you decide to jump into the arms of the first person who comes along.'

'Ha ha.' I really did hate when she thought that I was joking especially when I was being serious. I just wanted to move to Alaska and have a normal life. I wasn't interested much in the whole falling-in-love scenario. I thought that I was going to stay single for the rest of my life; I wasn't into the whole break-up thing at the end.

'I mean it, Christine. Haven't you learned your lesson?' As usual she didn't listen and skipped off to the car. My friend had more relationships than I had hot dinners, and she drove me daft. I loved her to pieces, but I just wished that she would listen to me at times. I cared about her like a sister, and I didn't like to see her get hurt. Our long journey was now in progress, and we had the music on in the background while we were reminiscing all our fond memories. The last four years were the happiest four years of our lives, and we had lived life to the max. We never had to answer to anyone apart from ourselves. We had the taste of the good life, and things could only get better. Christine was always trying to spice things up and get me on blind dates, but I really wanted to wait for my Mr Right. I wanted someone to love me, care for me, and treat me right. I had this perfect picture in my mind, and I had hoped Alaska would hold my key to Mr Right. Florida only brought me idiots and self-centred pricks, and I had enough of them all. I had come to the conclusion that I would be better off alone than to put myself through any more stupid relationships. If there was someone out there for me, then I would meet him one day.

The journey to Alaska was horrendous. The long winding roads had my heart in my mouth. You could tell when we reached the Alaskan borders because the scenery changed, and it was just beautiful. I had always been used to the fast track of busy Florida, and it was going to take a lot of getting used to out here. Everything was so calm and peaceful.

'Ash . . . Ashley.' I heard Christine practically shouting my name, and I realised I was daydreaming again. It was kind of hard to concentrate when you were out in the wilderness. There was always something that was taking my attention and making me daydream.

'Sorry, I was just thinking.' Christine had that big smile on her face like she was up to something. She always made me nervous with this look. This was the look that I got when I was least expecting something to pop up.

'When we get unpacked, we can go out and get a feel for the area and see what Anchorage is like.' We weren't even at our new home, but she was thinking of going out. All I wanted to do was curl up and sleep for the full weekend.

'Yeah, yeah, Christine, just spit it out. You just want to see who you can get a feel of.' I had my witty face on so that she could see that I knew what she was up to. She was so predictable. I didn't know why I seemed surprised. My friend was the queen of partying, and Anchorage wasn't going to stop her.

'You know me too well . . .' That was an understatement. I knew her better than she knew herself. 'Ashley, you need to get out more before you turn into a grandma before your time.' I could always rely on my friend to tell it how it was, even if it wasn't what I wanted to here.

'How can we be very good friends, yet we are so very different?' I laughed and so did Christine. That was why we were meant to be best friends because we could bounce off one another no matter what was going on in our personal lives. I was more of the laid-back girl, whereas Christine was the party animal.

'BFFs.' Christine was grinning like a happy child, for once I didn't want to burst her bubble. I thought carefully about what she had said, and it hit me right between my eyes. I didn't want to come across old before my time, but I was comfortable in myself. Maybe that was the problem. I was getting stuck in a rut, and I needed to get out of it somehow.

'BFFs forever.' Christine and I had been friends for years, and we never got tired of one another. God knew what we would do when we moved on with husbands and kids. We probably still won't be far away from one another. It would have been easier if we were homosexual and married each other. We wouldn't need to bother about the whole separation when it arrived. We had been travelling for what seemed like an eternity, but really, it was only eight hours. We had just entered our hometown of Anchorage in Alaska, and it really was beautiful. Our car was the quietest it had been all day. We were both gobsmacked at the scenery; it was truly beautiful. I had noticed how beautiful everything was for about two hours, but it had just suddenly hit Christine when we hit our hometown. We turned into this driveway of a typical Alaskan cottage. I couldn't believe that this was my new life. I truly was happy. Our home was stunning. It didn't look old, but it was traditional. It was out of this world.

It was surrounded by trees and water, and it looked better in real life. I didn't notice half of the features from the pictures that were sent to us. It was like a dream come true.

'Come on, Ash, let's get this party started.' I followed my friend and got the car unpacked. We were like two school children excited about a birthday or Christmas. I stupidly let my friend talk me into getting ready to go out tonight. I didn't know why I seemed surprised. She always gets her own way. We had the whole weekend to get ready for our new start at work on Monday morning. But I knew that the time would fly in, and we would be left running about like headless chickens. But there was no talking to Christine when she got something into that head of hers. It seemed like we were getting a feel for the cottage and we were getting ready for a night out, all in the same breath. It was madness. I hated getting ready to go out when you didn't know what to wear. Christine was always beautiful, and she didn't even have to try to look stunning. She was a blonde beauty, whereas I always felt under pressure to look gorgeous. I hated everything about myself. I would love to find some self-confidence and forget about everyone else. That was my problem: I care too much about what everyone else thinks and forget about what really matters. Maybe when I find my prince charming, it will all fall into place.

'Come on, Ash, I am waiting. I am starved and thirsty.' I sniggered to myself at my friend's comments. She really could amuse me at her childish outbursts. I immediately thought hungry and thirsty for what? She never just had food and drink on the agenda, and anyone who knew her well enough would know that. I was all ready, and walking along the hall, I felt crazy to be going out tonight, but I gave in just for the peaceful life. I really could see the back of tonight. 'Wow. Ash, you are looking lovely tonight. I am so jealous of you.'

'Eh, why? You're thin, and I am curvy. You're blonde, and I have brown hair. You have a great personality, and me there isn't a word to describe.' I didn't mean to sound so negative, but by God, there was nothing to be jealous of me for.

'Come on, Mrs Negative, let's go.' Her arm linked mine just like she had done for years, and it was nice to share this whole experience with someone who knew me so well. I would have been a nervous wreck if I had to come out here on my own. It was a very true saying that 'two was company'. I couldn't imagine life on my own now.

We took a walk into the village, and we still couldn't believe that we were here in Anchorage. Everything looked like the picture on a postcard; the trees, the buildings, and everything was breathtaking. We went down to a lovely restaurant at the dock called 'Maggie May's'. It was lovely. I really didn't know what to expect, but it wasn't any different to what I was used to. We were made to feel very welcome the minute we walked in, and it felt like we belonged here. Our waiter took us to our table. It was a nice quiet booth, dimly lit like candlelight. It would have been perfect for a romantic night out, with no one to interrupt you. But instead, I was here with my obnoxious friend.

'Can I get you both a drink?'

'We will have a bottle of your finest white wine, please.' Christine was very polite; I had wondered what came over her. She was usually a very bubbly and in-your-face kind of person. But I smiled over at her as I was very grateful to see this side of her for a change. We sat for a few minutes and studied the menu. It was very nice and authentic. You could just tell that the food was going to be gorgeous. Our waiter was very nice and polite, and he seemed very good at his job. He had the perfect personality for a job like this. Everything seemed too good to be true.

'Your wine, ladies.' He was very quick of the mark, which was always a good sign. He seemed pretty feminine for a guy, not that it bothered me though. I preferred the gay community. At least you know where you stood with them. I felt that we could be good friends if we got to hang out together. I had a good sense of judgement when it came to people, except when they were boyfriends or potential boyfriends. Then I would go as blind as a bat.

'Thank you.' Christine was being very well behaved tonight, and I was impressed. But usually it was that calm before the storm, unless Anchorage was the making of her.

'Ash, something smells lovely in here. I could eat a scabby horse.'

'That would be our speciality, honey, the Alaskan salmon.' I never even noticed our waiter clearing the booth behind us. But obviously, he heard Christine's comments. 'Hmm, I will try that. Thank you. What are you having, Ash?' I didn't know what to pick for the best. Everything sounded delicious and too good to eat.

'There is too much to choose from . . . I think I will have the same. It smells divine.' We handed our menus to the waiter, and I was glad to be sitting here now. It had given me the perfect feel for the place. It made me feel right at home and forget about this being our first night here.

'Good choice, ladies. You will be eating here every night of your vacation.'

'O, this isn't a vacation. We have just moved here from sunny Florida. We have moved into Anchorage, and we start work on Monday morning at Black's Enterprise.' Christine had a flirtatious look on her face, and I knew right away that she was wasting her breath. I don't think that the waiter wanted our life history in one conversation. All I could do was smile because it was clearly obvious that this waiter was gay. She always wore rose-tinted glasses when it came to the opposite sex. She had a one-track mind. But in all honesty, she was just as bad as I was at finding a decent man.

'Well, I hope to get to know you two better. You seem like two lovely girls. Anchorage is a lovely place to live. You will love it. My name is Christian. If I can get you anything, please let me know.'

'Thank you, Christian. My name is Ashley, and this is my best friend Christine.' I felt like I had known this man for years. He was so easy to get along with.

'Christian, can you tell me where the ladies' room is, please?' I rolled my eyes at my friend because she always spent most of her night in the bathroom. The alcohol would go straight to her bladder.

'Sure, sweetie, just over there.' Christian pointed over to the corner where the bathroom was, and he headed off to place our order. I was sitting on my own now, enjoying my glass of wine; it was sweet and cold, just how I like it. I looked around myself to take in the whole restaurant, and I caught sight of this group of people in the middle of the room at a large round table. They looked like they were working at a business meeting. But there was one man doing the very same as me—looking around the room. I couldn't help but notice how bored he looked. He caught me watching and shot me a smile and a nod of his head. I could feel the heat in my cheeks rise quicker than any mercury could, and I quickly sent a smile and a courteous nod of my head back. I wasn't really in the mood for any male attention tonight, but I wasn't the sort of person who could have been rude and ignored him.

'What have I missed?' Christine was back, and I never even noticed her return. My attention had been otherwise engaged, and I wasn't even sure why I was bothering about it.

'Nothing, I am just being nosey.' I thought that she knew something was wrong, because she grinned at me and sipped away at her wine. Her eyes never left my face, and it just made me more nervous.

'Here we are, ladies. Enjoy.' I was glad when our food arrived because it would take the attention off me and it would give her something else to concentrate on.

'Thanks, Christian.'

'Can I get you anything else?'

'No, thank you. This is perfect.' I couldn't think of a better word at the top of my head. The food looked and smelt delicious.

'I am starved.' Christine said that like a child who hadn't eaten for a week. I just laughed as Christian walked away. There was one good thing about having a friend like Christine, and that was life was never dull. We ate our meal in silence like it was the last supper. It was as I thought it was going to be: delicious. I was glad that I picked the special now. It let us see what their types of food would be like, and I thought that I would put on ten stone in my first year staying here. I wasn't lucky enough to be one of those women who could eat anything they liked. I just had to look at a sweet, and it went right to my hips.

'I could go home to bed now.' I knew that Christine wasn't going to let me off that lightly. I would be made to party until I dropped. We were walking up to the bar, and I felt dead on my feet. I was going to need a miracle to get me through tonight.

'I don't think so chick. The night is still young.' I would love a bit of her energy; she was non-stop on the go.

'I knew you were going to say that. I can read you better than you can read yourself.' I dropped my bag on the counter and just waited for her witty response.

'Yeah, yeah, you only live once, Ash. C'mon.' Christine gave me her pathetic, pleading, puppy dog eyes, and I wished that I could say grow up, but I knew that she would get her own way. She was just like a princess, and everyone pussyfooted around her.

'You ladies, head along the main walk, and you will find lots of nightlife. Give me a shout one weekend, and I will show you all the sights.'

'Thanks, hun. That will be a date.' Both Christine and Christian exchanged numbers, and we headed for the door. I couldn't believe my luck. The man in front of us holding the door open was my Mr Smiler. I felt my cheeks heat up already, and he hadn't even spoken to me yet.

'Good evening, ladies, enjoy your night.' His voice made me blush even more. I had no idea why I was feeling like this. Christine and I kept walking. I really wanted the ground to open up and swallow me.

'Thank you.' I was glad that my friend answered because my mouth was stuck shut. We kept walking until we were out of sight, and it was just me and my friend again. But I had no idea what made me feel like this. This kind of thing never happened to me, not with any man. 'OK, Ash, let's make it a night to remember.' I followed on linking arms like we were school kids again. The last time Christine said something along the same lines, I was ill for a week. We reached a few bars were we could hear music and laughter, and for a small town, it sounded like they knew how to have fun. 'Cocktails are shouting my name, Ash.'

'Now there is a surprise.' I let out a laugh as we walked inside towards the bar. It was another beautiful place, and it was quite busy, again not what I expected. But I spotted a table and went to get it while Christine was getting our drinks. She was a drinks' queen. She knew what I liked and didn't like, so she was the best one to go to the bar. I took a look around, admiring everything when suddenly someone knocked into my back. I quickly glanced around, and I was speechless. There standing in front of me was Mr Smiler, again.

'I am so sorry about that. I kicked the leg of that table. I didn't hurt you, did I?' I was in a daydream when something inside me suddenly said, 'Snap out of it, Ashley.'

'No, you are OK. I am fine.' I didn't want to come across as all stuttery, but I don't think I was succeeding very well.

'I think we are following each other, Ashley. My name is Dale. Pleased to meet you.' His arm stretched out to me to shake my hand, and I couldn't be impolite; I had to shake his hand back.

'Likewise, Dale.' His hand was so soft and warm. I could tell that he was well groomed with a hand like that.

'Can I get you a drink, Ashley?' I smiled and looked directly into his eyes. I felt an immediate connection with this man, and I didn't want to feel like this tonight. They were dark and striking. There was something appealing about his whole presence.

'My friend is already at the bar . . . Thank you though.' Dale nodded his head at me with a sexy smile on his face. My heart was beating so fast that I thought he would hear it.

'Some other time maybe?' It just dawned on me that he knew my name, and I never even told him. Now I was feeling very cautious and alarmed.

'How do you know my name? I mean, I never told you.' I could hear the curiosity in my own voice, so I was hoping that he could pick up on it as well.

'I heard your friend in the restaurant, and I thought it was a lovely name for a lovely girl. So it stuck in my mind.' Just then Christine came over with our drinks. I was saved just in the nick of time.

'Are you going to introduce me, Ash?' With a flirtatious grin on her face, I could see that she was smitten already.

'Dale, this is my friend Christine. Christine, this is Dale.' Christine stretched over me to shake his hand. She couldn't be any more in your face if she tried.

'Nice to meet you, Dale.' Dale had everything Christine would love in a man: tall, dark, handsome, and very fashionable. But Dale didn't even take a second look at her. I could tell that she wasn't amused. She sat on her high stool and took a sip of her drink. I was blushing at the fact he thought I was lovely.

'It was nice to meet you, Ashley . . . Christine. I must go and get my friends before they kill each other.' We both smiled at each other like there was a magnet holding us together. I watched him carefully as he walked over to get his friends, and I sat back in my chair, taking the last five minutes in. I could feel Christine looking at me in a funny way; she could never hide what she was thinking.

'I leave you for five minutes and you're chatting up with the local talent.' I couldn't help but laugh at my friend's comment because this wasn't like me at all. She had the cheek to even say something like that to me.

'It makes a change . . . You are only jealous because it isn't you.' Christine made a face at me, and we were both laughing like a couple of teenage girls. The rest of the night was a blur. The drinks kept flowing, and Christine danced and sang on the karaoke. My mind flickered to and from Dale, and I really was enjoying myself. There was something about him that made me act like an irrational, hormonal teen. I thought that I secretly liked that feeling, but I would never in a million years admit this to my friend. Besides, Anchorage wasn't a huge town. I was sure that I would find out who this man was and what he was doing. My mom always drilled into my head 'what is meant for you won't go past you', and I had always kept that in my mind. Moms always know what's best.

CHAPTER 2

Settling into Anchorage

O h my God was my first thought as my eyes fluttered open. My head was spinning, and I thought that it was going to fall off. I hated feeling hung-over. It was the worst feeling in the world. My door was pushed open, and there stood my friend bright as a button, like she hadn't touched a drop of alcohol last night. 'Good morning, Ash. I thought that you would need these pills.' I knew that I was going to need some help to shift this feeling, but I wasn't sure if pills would be enough.

'Thanks. You are such a bad influence on me. You know that I can't handle too much alcohol.'

'Oh, stop being a baby and shake it off. We have so much to do between now and Monday.' I could see my friend laughing under her breath as she galloped out of my room. She was such a big character that I had no idea why we got on so well. I was so jealous of her. Why did she have to be so fresh? It didn't seem fair. My mind flickered to and from last night and this Mr Smiler. *What is wrong with me? I never get like this, not just after speaking with someone I don't even know.* My last relationship lasted nearly two years, and he never made me feel like that. There was something about Dale that was very appealing. I managed to get up and get showered and had something to eat. Toast was all I could stretch to this morning, and I didn't know how I kept that down. I immediately thought that I needed to do a shopping trip to stock up the cupboards, but I didn't think that it would be any time soon. I was always the organiser and mother-hen figure in this household, whereas Christine was so laid-back that she should be horizontal. I glanced over to see her singing away while she unpacked her boxes. I was so envious of her this morning. I needed air and plenty of it. The house was too lively for me this morning. I needed some peace and quiet to recover.

'I am going to go for a walk in the woods to see if it will clear my head.' I just wanted to see the area, and it would hopefully clear this hangover as well. I wasn't good at feeling ill. It was a good job that I was never ill. I must have an immune system that is like steel.

'OK. Ash, don't get lost. I don't fancy sending out a search party on our first day here.' I sent my friend a sarcastic look. I was sure she thought she was my mom at times. I put my boots and jacket on and headed for the door. It was like I was in a dream; everything was beautiful.

I couldn't get enough of it. Surely, the fresh air would make me feel human again, or that is what I was hoping for. Everything that I passed was gorgeous, even down to the smell of the wild flowers growing. I just kept walking. I didn't really want to stop or turn around. The unpacking would still be there later. I was relaxed out here; it was so quiet and peaceful. I can't remember ever feeling so calm and collected. Anchorage certainly was good for the blood pressure. I had never felt nervous once since I arrived here.

I looked at my watch and realised that I had been walking for nearly two hours. Christine would be having kittens. But I really didn't care.

I was enjoying the scenery, too much to think about life in general. I heard sticks break behind me, and I quickly turned around to see who was there. But I found this dog hurtling towards me so fast that I couldn't think straight. I was too slow to get out of the way, and I was knocked flying on to my behind.

'I am so sorry, Miss. Did he hurt you?' I was startled, pulling myself on to my feet, rubbing my legs down. I was just about to give the owner a piece of my mind when I looked up to find the man from last night standing in front of me.

'No . . . I . . . am fine.' I stuttered and stammered with nerves. I didn't know where to look or what to say. The cat had stolen my tongue, and I was speechless.

'Are you sure? He is just a big softy. He just loves to meet people.' I smiled at the dog and rubbed his head. I finally managed to look up at Dale and find the confidence to start a conversation. I didn't want to be angry at him for the dog. It was only a bit of dirt.

'Are you clearing your head as well?' I realised it was a lame attempt to make a conversation, but his smile made me feel a little bit more relaxed.

'No, I was looking for Rufus. When he gets out of the house, he just runs, especially if he can see another animal.' Dale pointed up the hill towards this big house. It looked gorgeous.

'Is that your house? I am sorry if this is private property. I just came out for a walk.' I felt really stupid now. How could I not know that this was probably private land.

'Don't be silly. You can walk here. It isn't often that a beautiful woman walks on my land.' I blushed again and looked down at the dog.

I was speechless yet again, and the dog was the best place to look right now. The dog couldn't make me talk or make a fool of me. I should just stick to canine company. I couldn't help but wonder what made this man so special?

'Please, come and have a coffee with us. Warm up before you go home.' I managed a nod without even thinking. His charm was certainly rubbing off on me. I wondered what harm a coffee could do as I walked alongside him. I heard the negative side chant on my shoulder, but I chose to live a little and ignore it. This was another first for me. I never had coffee with men I didn't even know. He could be a mass murderer for all I knew. Life here was certainly different to what I was used to.

'I can't believe you live here. Do you live with family?' The house was out of this world. It was like something out of a movie.

'No, just myself and the hired help.' I didn't want to sound so nosey so I tried to keep it casual. Besides, we didn't know a thing about one another, so the conversation shouldn't run dry.

'Sorry, you just look so young.' I really needed to get this blushing sorted out; he was going to think I was some kind of nervous wreck.

'Don't be sorry. I get that a lot from people who don't know me.' We entered his house, and everything looked like something from a magazine or something like that. I was frightened to move in case I broke anything. I saw this small lady with beautiful skin and long dark hair walk towards us. I shrugged off my jacket, and Dale handed them to her. I thought it showed that I wasn't used to all the fuss.

'Rosa, can you bring us coffee through, please?' I couldn't help but notice how polite he was to her. It was nice to see that he wasn't an arrogant prick to his staff. That was a good start.

'Yes, Dale.' She quickly moved away from us just like there was some kind of emergency, but I was in no hurry for a coffee. We walked into a nice room which looked like a study. It was stacked from floor to ceiling with books on shelves. I felt at home here since I loved reading so much. We sat at a lovely seating area; it was so comfortable, and the smell was lovely.

'You like books?' I thought before speaking, *What a silly question that was, but that was me all over.*

'Yes. I don't read a lot now, though. Work takes up too much time.' His voice was so soft and gentle, and I realised that I could listen to him all day.

His smile was infectious, and there was a twinkle in his eyes. For the first time in my life, I thought I knew what 'love at first sight' meant now.

Rosa came in with a tray full and placed it on the table in front of us. 'Thank you, Rosa. That will be all.' I felt my fingers twitching with the fabric on my trousers. I felt comfortable, but I felt so nervous inside. Men usually did that to me, and I generally wanted to run in the opposite direction.

But something was holding me here, and I was intrigued to find out what it was.

'So, what do you think of Anchorage, Ashley?' *Where was I supposed to start?*

'It is lovely. The people, the scenery, I can't get enough of it.' Our conversation went on for well over an hour. We spoke about everything that entered our heads. It flowed so well until I looked at my watch. 'Oh God, look at the time. I must get home. I have so much to do before I start work on Monday.'

'I will give you a run home.' Before I could turn down his offer, he had the jackets and car keys in his hand. I really wished that I hadn't looked at my watch. I really wanted to say who cares about time? But that wasn't me. I always cared about the time, and I couldn't ignore everything that I had to do.

'Thank you.' It was the only two words that I could say. We headed out of the house, and there was a black Mercedes waiting for us. I didn't notice it when we first came in, which meant either I wasn't paying attention or it had just pulled up.

'Thank you, Carlos.' Dale had exchanged words with another hired help, and he closed my door behind me. I couldn't believe that I was sitting here in this luxurious car. It was also lovely and comfortable inside. Dale jumped into the driver's seat, and he looked really comfortable behind the wheel, although I got the feeling that he didn't have to drive very often. 'Do you like, Ashley?'

'Yes, it is lovely.' I managed to shuffle back in my seat and take in the whole situation. My mind still managed to wander. My first thought was, this was all too good to be true. This lovely man had it all, but what was wrong? Why did I have a doubt in my mind? This wasn't my luck. I took in all the different sights as I got chauffeured home. I hadn't seen any of them before today, and it was nice to see them. We pulled up outside my house, and I spotted Christine, looking out of the window. My heart skipped a beat because I knew I was going to get a Spanish inquisition when I got inside. 'Thank you.' As much as I was sitting outside my house, I didn't want this moment to end.

'No thank you, Ashley. You brightened up my afternoon.' I couldn't speak. All I could do was sit and look good. I couldn't find any words to say. I really had to overcome my shyness before he run a mile. 'Can I see you again?' I really didn't know what to say. My hands were sweaty, and my heart was racing. I wanted to see him again, but I wasn't sure that it was for the best.

'Yes, maybe. I am going to be very busy over the next couple of days, but I am sure with my track record I will bump into you at some point.' I opened the door and got out slowly. I was still hoping that time would freeze. I couldn't believe that I had said 'track record'. What was he going to think about me? I should have been blonde.

'I look forward to it, Ashley.'

'Thanks for going out of your way to bring me home.' I was really grateful to him for his hospitality. It saved me a long walk home.

'No worries.' I walked away from the car and into the house. I didn't even look back. Dale must think that I am a right ignorant bitch. I could kick myself sometimes. I heard the car drift off, and I knew that my biggest problem was walking right towards me.

'What have you been up to, Ash? I was getting worried.' I really tried to figure out what to say to her. I didn't want to sound too keen. Christine always sounded like my mother at these kind of situations. Where have you been? What have you been doing? She drove me insane at times.

'I went walking and bumped into Dale and his dog, Rufus. He offered me a lift home.' Christine's eyes were huge in amazement, and I couldn't really blame her.

'What have you done to the real, Ashley?' I couldn't help but smile at her because she was right; I would never have done anything like this back home. The air here had really gone to my head.

'Oh, ha ha, Mrs Sarcasm.' She was right though this was out of character for me. My Mr Smiler could be my Mr Right, and I was feeling excited about the whole thing. I spent the rest of the weekend making the house into a home and getting everything organised for work. Our first weekend in Anchorage had been fantastic, and we hadn't even tried to make any friends or have any fun. It just found us. If this is what life was going to be like here, I had no complaints so far. It should continue for long time.

CHAPTER 3

First Days

My alarm woke me up, and already the nerves had kicked in. I stumbled out of my room and banged on Christine's door because she was not a morning person. She would never have made it through school without me waking her up. I made it to the bathroom without being sick, so that was a bonus. I really hated being a nervous person, but I knew that today would be a challenge. I ran the shower and turned to look in the mirror. My heart was racing. I could feel it pounding in my chest. The butterflies were back with a vengeance, and I really felt sick as a pig. I could hear Christine getting up so I knew I had to get a grip; she would find me rather amusing. I took my toothbrush out and brushed my teeth. My morning routine never seemed to change; even though we were in a new town, it all stayed the same. I took my shower and washed my hair. Nothing beats a nice shower in the morning to make you feel refreshed. But this morning I really didn't know what was wrong. I just had this feeling in my gut that something was going to get wrong, and normally, my feelings were not far wrong. I headed back into my room, with just a towel wrapped around me. I would do anything to skip today. I hated starting new jobs because the first days were always the hardest.

'I have just made coffee, Ash.' Christine made me jump out of my skin as she shouted through from the kitchen. I was a woman on edge this morning, and anything could make me blow.

'Thanks, I will be through shortly.' Coffee was just what I needed. That would fix my nerves one way or another. I had my clothes already laid out waiting for me. I went for smart and business like since it was my first day, a plum two-piece skirt and jacket with a cream shirt.

I looked in the mirror and immediately thought someone might get the wrong impression because my shirt was quite revealing. But it was about time that I forgot about other people and their opinions. I was fully dressed and ready to face the day, and I approved of my look.

'Wow. You look stunning, Ash.' I got a fright because I was too busy worrying about my image that I never even heard my door open.

'Don't you know how to knock?' I didn't even know why I am surprised and why change a habit of a lifetime.

'Since when do we knock, babe? Come and get breakfast. That will settle your nerves.' I knew that my friend was right, but nothing was going to shift my nerves today. I went through to the kitchen and took a slice of toast and poured a cup of coffee. I didn't think I would manage much more this morning. My mom used to tell me that a good breakfast would set anyone up for a day at the office, and I knew if she was here, I wouldn't have got out the door without a full breakfast. But if I ate too much, I would be sick, without a doubt. This morning had gone by so quickly that I felt like I was on a different planet. It was like we were in a time machine and we had no control of what was going on. Before I knew what I was doing, Christine and I were driving to work together. The car was so silent. There wasn't even any music on the radio. We didn't have a clue who we were working for until we arrived at the office, and we would get pointed in the right direction. My nerves were in full swing right now, and that was all because of the unknown. I would probably be calmer if I knew who my boss was going to be. We pulled into the car park and found a space. The building looked huge. It looked different from all the pictures I had seen. But now it was reality, and we were here in front of it. There was no going back now. This was it.

'I hope that we are working close together.' I sounded as if I was going to burst into tears at any minute.

'Don't worry, Ash. I will meet you at lunchtime anyway. Enjoy it. We are living our dream.' After all the years Christine and I had known each other, I just felt that today would be so much easier if we were working together. We walked into the building, and it was like someone had waved a magic wand. The whole space seemed to open up once you stepped in the door. I tried to take it all in, but I didn't think I could see straight. We walked up to the desk to receive our passes, and the young girl behind the desk looked very nice. We didn't even have to tell her our names, and she directed us to a seating area. Unless she had magic powers, I did wonder how she knew who we were. Christine and I sat down beside each other in silence. I thought that my friend was just as nervous as I was, not that she would ever admit that. Five minutes had passed without anyone coming for us. I thought that they had forgotten all about us. Maybe that was wishful thinking on my part. Christine and I sat very professional, waiting patiently. I really wanted the ground to open up and eat me or the fire alarm to go off so we didn't need to be introduced to our new boss. I was sounding pathetic. I did realise that, but my mind does wonders when I am nervous.

'Miss Morgan.' Christine stood up and shook the man's hand. Though she was nervous, she didn't show any signs. I wish that I could be more like her.

'Hello, sir. Please call me Christine.' Now there was a first for everything . . . Christine was very calm and ladylike. I wished that I had a video recorder because I was never going to see that again.

'Hi, Christine, I am Rupert Grant. I am your new boss. I work under Mr Black to help make things run smooth . . . Miss Malone.' I stood up quickly as Mr Grant addressed me. 'Mr Black will be down for you shortly. Please make yourself comfortable.'

'Thank you, sir.' I was gobsmacked as I sat back down on my seat. *Why did I have to work with the boss? The owner of the whole company. Why me?* I had every right to be nervous now. I knew that today was going to be a tough one, and now I knew why.

'Have a good day, Ash.' Christine trotted alongside Rupert Grant, like a child doing as she was told. I looked away towards the door and thought how easy it would be to make a run for it. Christine didn't seem fazed by any of this. I really wished that I could have her confidence.

'Miss Malone.' This pure, passionate voice broke my chain of thoughts. I looked up and couldn't believe my eyes.

'Hi, Dale. I didn't expect to bump into you here. I am waiting for Mr Black.' Of all the days that I had to bump into this man, it had to be on my first day at work. I was nervous enough without having to deal with him as well. Dale laughed slightly, and I did want to know what I said that was so amusing.

'I know why you are here . . . I am Mr Black, Ashley.' My body froze, and I felt numb from head to toe. If the ground could open, now would be the best time.

'Of course, you are . . . Why did I think any different? Why else would you be calling me Miss Malone? I am sorry.' I looked down to the ground, hoping to wake up from this nightmare. This could happen only to me; it was just my luck.

'Don't be. It is an easy mistake to make. Come and follow me.' I picked my bags up and followed him. My head was all mush. What were the chances of my boss being the man whom I found rather appealing? Before I had time to think about anything, we were on the top floor in front of a lot of people. I felt like all eyes were on me, and it just made me feel worse.

'Good morning, everyone. This is my new assistant, Ashley. I hope that you will all make her feel very welcome.' I smiled at all the faces, and Dale took my hand and led me into his office. I couldn't believe that he took my hand. I wasn't complaining, though; I kind of liked it.

'Did you know at the weekend that I was going to be working for you?' I didn't know what I wanted to hear right now. I tried to see the answer in his face, but it was straight.

'No, love, I didn't. I only found out when I was pointed in your direction this morning. I am sorry. I couldn't help but let you think I was just a worker here.' He wasn't sorry at all. I could see the snigger on his face. He was a typical male who thought he was funny.

'You really had no idea who I was at the weekend?' I wish that if I did know, maybe today wouldn't have been so nerve-wracking.

'No, not at all.' Why would I know who he was? I had never crossed paths with him before. I feel kind of stupid now, though, because all the signs were there, and I just never seen them at the time.

'Would you have done anything different if I had told you I was your multimillionaire boss?' Now, what kind of question was that? How on earth could I answer that question properly?

'Probably.' I had to think about this one. I didn't want to sound fussy, and I didn't want to let him know that I really liked him. 'I wouldn't have had coffee with you, and I wouldn't have let you drive me home.' I now sounded like an arrogant bitch. I knew I wouldn't want anything to do with me, never mind him.

'Well, I am glad you didn't know, Miss Malone, because I enjoyed your company.' I blushed and looked to the floor. I was new at this, but I still knew that my boss was flirting with me. My cheeks felt on fire, and my heart was racing.

'We will have to do something about your nerves, Miss Malone. My clients will eat you up and spit the remains out.' I looked at him in amazement. He could spot that I am nervous. But who am I trying to kid anyone a million miles away could spot my nerves or feel the heat rise from me.

'I am not nervous when it comes to business, Mr Black. Just . . .' I thought it was better to stop before I said something that I would regret later.

'I make you nervous, Ashley . . . Please, relax. We are going to get along just fine, and please call me Dale. I can't be doing with formal talk from close employees.'

'OK, Dale.' It felt weird calling my boss by his first name. But it was nice to know that he wasn't like any other millionaires and the money and status went right to his head.

'Come with me, and I will show you to your office.'

'Office.' The shock in my voice must have been noticeable because I could see the amusement in his face again.

'Yes, it is right next door . . .' He stopped and turned back towards me, and I really wished that he wouldn't look at me. 'What did you expect?'

'A desk with everyone else.' His laugh was just as sexy as he was, and I had a feeling that he knew what he was doing to me. He was going to love working with me. He would just laugh his way through the day.

'Sorry for laughing at you, love. You are just so impressionable.' I followed him through to my office, and I couldn't help but smile now. Could this day get any better? I intended to enjoy every moment and just take it all in. Never did I expect to be a personal assistant in my first role. The rest of the morning went by in a blur; it was like a flash. If I hadn't been here, I would never have believed it. I guessed that I was going to enjoy coming to work, and it wasn't going to be because I enjoyed what I was doing. A certain Mr Black was going to make my day a little less boring.

Lunchtime was fast approaching today, and I went to meet Christine at the cafeteria. I was so excited. I couldn't wait to tell her all about my morning. I still thought that I was dreaming and I was going to wake up at any moment. As I entered the busy room, I saw Christine, sitting at a table, and waved over to her to acknowledge her sitting waiting. I knew that she was probably on a tighter schedule compared to me, so I joined the queue for a coffee and picked up a sandwich on my way. I knew right away that my friend would find it all hard to believe; she wasn't a person who believes in the whole 'something happens for a reason'. Finally, I got everything I wanted and headed over to my friend. I felt like I was floating over to her. 'Hey, Christine, how has your day been so far?' I wasn't even sitting when I started our conversation. I just wanted her to be quick so that I could share my day. I felt like I was on cloud nine, and no one was going to spoil it for me.

'Fab. Lovely boss. Great desk overlooking the water. What more could a girl ask for? What about your day?' This was the bit I had been waiting for. I didn't want to sound too bright and bubbly, but I couldn't contain myself any longer.

'Where do I start? Can you remember Dale from the other night? Well, he is Mr Black.' I saw her take it in piece by piece, and the shock soon registered on her face.

'Oh my God, really.' Christine was all excited. I thought the whole cafeteria heard her response. I tried not to laugh at her, but it was kind of hard.

'Keep your voice down . . . I am working for him as his personal assistant.' Even sitting here and saying it out loud made me cringe.

'You should have a marble desk then, Ash.' I heard a sarcastic tone in Christine's voice, and I should have known that she would be like this.

The good stuff should always happen to her and not me; no a wonder she was feeling a tad jealous.

'Ha ha.' I did think about leaving the conversation, but I was happy, and if I couldn't share it with my friend, then whom could I share it with? 'I have an office right next door to his. It is huge.' I thought I was overenthusiastic on the 'huge'. I was getting to be the drama queen for once.

'Oh my God, Ash, you have certainly landed on your feet.'

'I know. No words can explain how I feel.' We spent our lunch hour talking about work and bosses and comparing the differences. Again, the time seemed to fly in. Our lunch break came to an end, and we said our goodbyes and headed our own separate ways. Walking up to my office, I still felt like I was floating. Things like this didn't happen to girls like me. Christine was always the fortunate one. I spent many nights hearing all her good stories. I reached my office, and for the first time in my life, I felt like I belonged. Like this was meant to be. I sat at my desk just as my laptop pinged. I knew immediately that I had mail, but I was very curious to know who it would be on my first day.

To: Miss Ashley Malone
From: Mr Dale Black
Msg: Dinner date

Hi, Ashley, I have a works dinner meeting tonight, and I was wondering if my assistant can join me?
I will pick you up at 7 p.m. sharp.

Yours sincerely
Dale Black

I looked at my mail in shock. Could today get any better? I hit reply and sat for a moment thinking about my reply. I was flattered that he was asking me to join him, but I didn't have a clue about any of his clients. *Would I be of any use?* Surely, he would be better asking someone who knew what they were talking about.

To: Mr Dale Black
From: Miss Ashley Malone
Msg: Dinner date

That wasn't a question, Mr Black. That was you telling me to be ready at 7 p.m. sharp. I would love to join you.
I will be ready and waiting.

Yours Sincerely
Ashley Malone

I closed my mail and got back to my deadlines for today. I didn't know why I was so nervous this morning; today couldn't have gone any better. The work was easy. The people were nice. Maybe this was just away to edge me into everything, and tomorrow would start with a bang. I didn't really care any more. I was happy with my work, and nothing and no one was going to burst my bubble. My deadlines were all complete for today, and I looked at the clock, which read 4.30 p.m. I started shutting down my laptop and doing a quick tidy-up when a knock on the door startled me. 'Come in.' I wondered, *Who would be knocking on my door? Why don't they just come in?* It was going to take me a while to see that I was quite important and people just don't walk into somewhere unannounced.

'Wow. You can just tell there is a woman in this office now. It smells and looks really good.' His comment took me by surprise and so did the fact that he knocked before being told to come in.

'Thank you, Dale. Was there something that I could do for you?'

'No, I was just checking to see if you were OK.' He was kind as well as considerate. This man was like a God. There weren't many of them around nowadays. I walked over to my desk and perched on the front of it. I was so comfortable with him that I didn't feel the need to sit on a seat.

'Yes, thank you. Everything is all done. I am just going to do a quick tidy-up before I leave.' As usual, Dale found something that I said very amusing.

'Get yourself home, honey. We have a cleaner for that.' I knew that there would be a cleaner, but I didn't want to leave a mess or important things lying around. That was just me; my parents always used to say that I had OCD because I was always so tidy. Nothing was ever out of place.

'Thank you.' I watched as Dale turned to walk towards the door, and he turned his head round slightly so that I could see his face. I really didn't feel as nervous now; he was a big pussy cat.

'I will pick you up at 7 p.m.'

'OK, thank you. I will be ready.' *Is this my boss or my friend?* I felt so relaxed around him that I really thought that I had known him years. My mom used to give me a hard time when I was growing up. She would always tell me to let my guard down, 'Let people see the real you, and they will find it hard not to fall in love with you.' I always kept my guard up. But with Dale, I didn't feel like I needed to block him out. I was trying to keep my feelings hidden because he was my boss, and I didn't really like mixing business with pleasure. But there was something about him that appealed to me in every way possible.

I was waiting in the car when Christine came out. It never crossed my mind that I would have been out before her, but it gave time for me to clear my head of what happened today. 'Skiving already, Ash?' I gave my friend a snide look; I didn't really need her sarcasm today.

'No, actually, I got finished at 4.30. I have a dinner meeting at 7 p.m., so it gives me extra time to get ready.' Christine's smile was enough. I didn't want to hear her pep talk. I got away a little bit early to get ready and relax, not to have her terrorising me with questions.

'Someone is smitten.' Her childish, teasing tone would drive me crazy tonight.

'Oh, don't be daft. It is just work.' Was she right, though? Something inside me had changed, and I didn't want her to know that she could be right. I would never hear the end of it.

'Yeah, yeah, sweetie. I believe you thousands wouldn't.' We drove the rest of the way in silence, and that suited me tonight. We were both exhausted after our first day at work, and it was only going to get worse as the week went on. My excitement kept me from falling asleep before we even got home. I am so glad that we are only minutes away from work because I was going to need more than two hours to get ready. I felt really nervous again, but it wasn't about meeting Dale, 'that ship had sailed'. I thought it was more about meeting clients that I had no idea who they were or what they specialised in. I really needed to get a grip. I was only going on a business dinner, and by the look of things, there would be plenty more to come. I thought that I was just showing up to look good, to smile, and to nod in all the right places. The car came to a stop outside our home, and we both got out and took our bags from the back seat.

'What are you going to do tonight, Christine?'

'Don't worry about me, Ash . . . A bubble bath has got my name on it, and I will probably be sleeping by the time you are ready to leave.' We both knew that her nose would bother her too much to fall asleep. She would have to be around to see what was going on.

'Cool, I am going to go and attempt to sort myself out. At this rate, I will be ready for a trailer park.'

'Stop being so negative. You will look lovely no matter what you wear.' I always relied on Christine to boost my confidence. I really didn't know what I would do without her. I took my things and rushed along to my room. I really was no good at this kind of thing. I would go for jeans and a top any day, but I thought that wouldn't be appropriate tonight. I went to my closet and pulled out a knee-length black dress, silver shoes, and matching bag. Then I spent the next half an hour picking all the faults with this outfit. I went to run a shower and get freshened up. I hoped that tonight wouldn't run on too long. I was exhausted. I did hope that the clients wouldn't notice how tired I felt. I felt dead on my feet. I really was envious of my friend tonight. I could just jump in a nice hot bath with a glass of wine, but instead, I was going back out to work.

I stepped out of my clothes and into the steamy hot shower. I stood in the centre of the water for five minutes, letting it cascade down my back and breasts. It felt so good after the day I had. I really could go a relaxing bath, but I knew if I had a bath, I wouldn't be at any dinner meeting. I heard a knock on the door, and I obviously knew that it was Christine. 'Ash, do you want a cup of coffee?'

'No, thanks.' I could see me having coffee and spilling it or burning myself. I was very accident-prone, so tonight, I was staying away from any accident waiting to happen. I didn't want to get out of the water. I could have stood here all night and forgotten all about the dinner meeting.

Where did the time go? It was now 6 p.m., and to say that I was a nervous wreck was an understatement. I had an hour before Dale would pick me up, and I only had jewellery to put on. I was well on target, but it didn't make me feel any easier. I headed along to get Christine, to help me put my necklace on. I just hope that she thought I looked OK. *Clip-clop*, along I went. She heard me coming obviously and jumped up into my line of vision. Her face was a picture. I didn't know what she was going to say, and I wasn't sure that I wanted to know either.

'OMG, Ash. Are you going to see royalty? You look stunning. You are going to knock Mr Black and his clients into next week.' I really didn't think I was that nice looking. I only took the first thing that came to my hand. There was no planning that went into this look whatsoever.

'Can you help me put this on?' I handed Christine my necklace and bracelet to put on. It was one of my mother's. She gave it to me before she died. It was a white-gold chain with one simple diamond on the end. I knew that she would have approved of Dale, and it felt appropriate to wear something that belonged to her.

'Where are you going for dinner?'

'I don't know. He never said. What if it is too much?' I never even thought about where we were going. I just thought that you couldn't go wrong with a little black dress.

'Too much is better than not enough, babe. Calm down. You look perfect.' I was always good at making people feel good about themselves, but when it came to myself, I was useless.

'I could go a stiff drink.' I was just becoming nonsense now. I could sense that I was annoying my friend. But I couldn't help it at all.

'You don't need one. You look stunning, you smell gorgeous, and you sound like an angel.' I really didn't know where my lack of confidence came from. I was always popular in school, and my parents praised me to the highest level, and I had always done the best that I could. I was just very bad at taking compliments. 'Ash, he is here.'

'He is early . . . I am not ready.' I was needing to get a grip; I was being pathetic. I knew exactly what Dale was like, and I knew that he would do anything to keep me right. But I just couldn't shift this feeling in my stomach.

'Ash, get a grip. I will go and let him in, and you compose yourself.' I was a nervous wreck as usual. *Why did he have to be early?* I watched Christine as she left the room to go and let Dale in. I closed my eyes and counted to ten. I did hope that when I opened my eyes, the night would be over with.

'Hello, Mr Black, Come in.'

'Thank you, Christine. But please call me Dale.' I forgot to tell Christine that he didn't like all the formal talk.

'Well, come through, Dale. Ashley is through in the living room.' I heard the footsteps coming through into the living room, and I picked my bag up just as Dale walked in. He looked radiant in his black suit and white shirt. I could just picture him with no shirt on, and my cheeks must have been red at the thought. I needed to clear my mind of any sexual thoughts. He was my boss, and nothing was ever going to happen between us.

'Hi, Mr . . . Dale.' I was about to call him Mr Black when I quickly realised that he hated it.

'Hi, Ashley, you certainly know how to get a man's pulse racing.' I did wonder how long it would be until he had me blushing. He must have been a record-breaker. I was just relieved that he liked what I had on.

'Are you ready?'

'Yes, I think so.' I walked in front of him, heading for the door, hoping that I didn't fall over in these shoes. I wasn't good with heals at any time, never mind when I was nervous.

'Have a good night, you two.' Following the voice, I could tell that Christine was in the study when we were leaving. I really wished it was me curled up with a glass of wine and a book. At least, books didn't make me feel uncomfortable. I noticed a chauffeur standing with the door open to the Mercedes, and I could briefly remember his face from my brief visit at the weekend.

'Sir. Madam.'

'Please, Carlos, call us Dale and Ashley.' Carlos nodded, and we got into the car. The door shut behind us, and I could feel Dale's body sitting close to me. His aftershave caught my nose, and it got all my senses racing. Everything about this man got every inch of my body tingling.

'Why don't you like all the formalities?' I didn't know where my courage came from to start the conversation, but deep inside, I felt proud of myself. It dawned on me that my nerves had disappeared and I felt like a strong person for a change.

'I don't see myself any better than anyone else, and I don't see the need to get people to call me anything other than Dale.' I smiled and looked down to my hands. *Why did he have to be so nice all the time?* It would be better if he was a horrible pig. I wouldn't feel as smitten over him. He seemed too good to be true. 'What did I say to amuse you, Miss Malone?' He turned his body on his side so he was looking right at me. His face was as sexy as his smile, and a male model sprung to my mind.

'Nothing. It is just that most company directors are too far up themselves to even care about their workers.' I was being truthful because I didn't want him to think I was something I wasn't.

'What can I say? I am not like other people. I am a nice guy.'

'It would appear so.' I felt so comfortable sitting here talking with my boss, and that tonight had went right out of my mind. He was just like my friend rather than someone who paid my wages. 'So are you going to fill me in on these clients that we are meeting?'

'No.' I looked at him wide-eyed and bushy-tailed. I didn't know what to think. 'I think when they take one look at you, the deal will be done. You have made this one easy for us all.' I really didn't think that it was a big deal how I looked, but I was going to accept his compliments and smile back at him. I have waited a long time to be around a man who appreciates me for who I am, and whether he was my boss or not, I was going to enjoy it. Carlos opened our door, and I followed Dale out. 'Thank you, Carlos. I will call when we are ready to be picked up.'

'No problem, Dale.' Carlos seemed to be getting the hang of the name thing. I wished I could say the same about me. I looked around us, and I couldn't believe how beautiful the building was. I didn't know what I expected, but it certainly wasn't this. It was gorgeous.

'Everything is so close by. You blink and your there.' In Florida, I was always used to cars piled up in queues and always being late for things.

'A pity it wasn't further away. I was enjoying our conversation.' As we walked into the building, I couldn't help but notice how beautiful everything was. It seemed like every place I went to was bigger and better than the last. I was enjoying our conversation as well, but all good things had to come to an end. Every time I was with him, I found out something more about him or his lifestyle.

'Welcome, Mr Black. Please follow me, and I will show you to your table. Your guests have just arrived five minutes before you.' We were early, and our guests were still here before us. *That was commitment*, I thought.

'Thank you, Natalie.' It got me curious how the waiter knew Dale very well and how he knew of her. I did wonder if they had, maybe, been an item at one time. She was very beautiful and certainly had eyes for him.

'Robert, Renee, a pleasure to be here with you again. This is my assistant, Ashley Malone.' Renee and Robert kissed both of my cheeks, and they seemed very warm and friendly. They were not what I was expecting.

'Nice to meet you, Ashley.'

'Likewise, Renee.' They both made me feel very welcome. They both were old enough to be our parents, and they showed a lot of respect to Dale and me. We were all seated at the table, and I couldn't help but notice the waiter filling up our glasses. She couldn't take her eyes off Dale, for more than a second. However, Dale and Robert were so wrapped up in their conversation that he wouldn't have even noticed.

It was nice to see how at ease the two men were getting along. It didn't feel like a nitty-gritty business meeting. I felt a bit stupid being so uptight earlier.

'Well, Dale, I have gone over the plans for building down at the nature reserve, and I think that it is a win-win situation for everyone. I will get my assistant to get the ball rolling tomorrow.' Dale had a smile on his face, but if he was being honest, he knew that it was a done deal before we arrived.

'That is fantastic. We will get everything cleared up at our end, and everything will be good to go.'

'Great stuff.' The waiter appeared at our table to take our order, and I decided to listen what Dale was having first.

'Are you all ready to order?'

'Can I get my usual, please, Natalie?' Natalie didn't even need to ask what that was, and that could be for one of two reasons: either she knew him too well, or he eats here a lot of time. I really hoped that it was my second thought.

'One smoked salmon.'

'Can I have the same, please?' I thought that was the safe option.

'Sure, sweetie, coming right up.' I didn't know why I felt so jealous of this waiter. Dale was my boss at the end of the day, and there was nothing else to it. I was too busy with my thoughts that I never heard what Robert and Renee ordered. When I was with Dale, I tuned out of character.

I was not quiet Ashley Malone. I turned into a feisty young woman. I knew that if my parents were here, they would be proud of me because they were always at me to be the person that they knew I could be and not who someone else wanted me to be.

The evening had been really nice, considering that it was a business meeting. I thought of my first dinner meeting; it had been a success, and now it had set the standards high for the rest of them.

'This has been a lovely evening, guys, but I am afraid I have to call it a night.' Robert and Renee stood to leave, and Dale and I stood to say goodbye. They had been such a lovely couple, and I hoped to see them again sometime. The waiter came over to show them the way to their jackets, but I wasn't sure that they needed any assistance; they knew this place inside and out.

'It was very nice to meet you, Ashley. I hope that you can keep Black on his toes.' I had laughed and smiled more tonight than I had done in years; it had all been perfect.

'Thank you for a nice night.' They kissed my cheek and shook Dale's hand, and they swiftly followed the waiter out. I could feel eyes peering through me, and I turned my head around to look at my boss. I was beginning to feel relaxed when he looked directly at me tonight. I didn't feel like some circus entertainer any more.

'Come with me. We can finish these drinks off in the snug before I call Carlos to come and pick us up.' I didn't even open my mouth. I picked up my drink and followed behind him like a naughty school child. The snug was tiny. It only had a couple of small tables surrounded by dim light and calm music in the background. It was very dark compared to the restaurant, but it was just as perfect.

'I told you that we would have them eating out of our hands.' We lifted our glasses at the same time. It felt like we were reading each other's mind.

'To us.'

'Thank you for coming at such short notice.' I didn't know why I was being thanked. It was work at the end of the day. I couldn't exactly turn down the experience.

'You're welcome, Dale. I have enjoyed myself.' I couldn't imagine not coming now. After all the fuss I made beforehand, I felt so stupid now.

'Good, that is what I like to hear.' I took a sip of my drink and sat in silence for a few moments.

'You know, Ashley, you have only been here a day, and already you are the best assistant I have had in a long time.' I didn't know what to say to that. I was speechless. It was the first tonight that I was blushing, and surprise, surprise the business meeting had ended and we now in our own personal time.

'Thanks. I guess we work well together. Not that I have had much to do today. Your last assistant has everything up to date.'

'I haven't had any assistant for a few weeks.' I was shocked. I thought that every director had an assistant at all times.

'What happened to your last assistant?' Dale's eyes never left mine. Normally, eye contact would give me goosebumps and make me nervous, but it was strange tonight. I had no nerves or goosebumps. I was enjoying the conversation.

'He was too slow. He didn't take anything on board that I said, and I was just fed up of keeping him floating.' I didn't expect him to say 'he'. I honestly thought that all of Dale's personal assistants were all beautiful young women. But I guess that nothing would shock me now. My boss wasn't normal. 'I bet I can guess what you are thinking right now . . .' He had me smiling again because I knew that he would be able to guess what I was thinking. 'Why do I have men assistants? Well, to answer that quickly, you are the first female assistant I have ever had. I wanted a change, and I had no luck with the assistants whom I had hired. So I said to human resources that I wanted a lady this time around.'

'And they sent me to you. They must need their head checked.' I wouldn't have classed me as a lady, but I should have been honoured that someone thought I was.

'You are perfect. My office has never run smoother as to what it did today.' Confusion blurred my mind. *What made him so sure that I was perfect?* This just put added pressure on me now. I had to be great at my job!

'I will always give 110 per cent, Dale . . . This is my first role as a PA, but I think that I have got a good teacher.' I didn't want to come across as too keen, but I wanted him to know that it was all new to me.

'I think that we will get on just fine. You just need some time to settle in.' He was sitting here talking to me, and the fact that he was my boss hadn't really entered my mind. 'Come on, Ashley, let's go. Carlos is waiting for us.' He must have magic powers because I had never even seen him phone Carlos. We got up and headed out of the snug. I was looking forward to getting home to my bed. The waiter was standing by the door as we went through to the lobby, and I couldn't help but notice her. I felt very honoured to be here with Mr Black, even if tonight was a one-off, and I wasn't letting a waiter get in the way of tonight.

'Good night, Mr Black.'

'Good night, Natalie.' We didn't stop; we just kept walking out of this grand hotel. I would come back here any day. It was lovely. I caught a glimpse of Carlos standing by the car. He opened the door when he had seen us coming, and his smile was just as inviting as before. 'Good evening.'

'Good evening, Carlos.' We climbed into the car, and the leather interior immediately sent chills through my body. It had got rather chilly since we left this evening. 'Here, take this. You look freezing.' Dale wrapped his jacket around my shoulders like the perfect gentleman. He was so kind and considerate to other's thoughts and feelings. I could get used to be around him after tonight.

'Thanks.' The car was silent, and I had lots that I had to ask, but I didn't want to sound pushy or nosey. 'What is it with that waiter and you?' I could have been a bit more subtle, but now I just sounded like a jealous assistant who wanted to know too much.

'Natalie.' I didn't expect him to answer me, and he had every right to ignore a personal question. 'She tried to kiss me at last New Year's party we held in the hotel. But I wasn't interested, and I am still not interested . . . No one has ever noticed before. It is a good sign that you are observant.' If that was his polite way of saying, I was a nosey cow, then he really was too nice.

'Sorry, it has nothing to do with me.' Curiosity killed the cat, and one day it was going to kill me.

'No, don't be silly. You have every right to know who you are working with. I like that we can be open with one another.'

'Thank you for everything. Tonight, the jacket, and making me feel so welcome. I have had fun.' I didn't expect to have fun, but it had surprised me how nice Dale and his clients were.

'You're welcome, hun. There are plenty more of these nights if you want them.' I glanced up into Dale's eyes, and my look said it all. I was exhausted and needed sleep and lots of it. 'Don't come in until 9 a.m. tomorrow. I will send Carlos for you. Catch up on some sleep.' It was like this man was a mind-reader; he seemed to know everything I need before I knew myself.

'Are you sure?'

'Of course, I am sure. You have worked around the clock for me today. You can't run on empty.'

'Thank you.' Just as I spoke my last word, Carlos was jumping out of the car, and I suddenly realised that I was home. I couldn't believe how lucky I had been to get a boss like Mr Black. Never did I expect to find myself so high up in the company. I leant over and opened my door. I really didn't want this night to be over, but it had to be very soon. Dale lifted my hand and placed a kiss across my knuckles; as much as I knew, I should be saying 'stop'. I couldn't bring myself to refuse.

'Good night, Ashley. Thank you for a lovely night.' I was like a school child looking at my hand. I didn't know where to look.

'You're welcome, Dale. I will see you tomorrow.' My body was leaving the car before my mind was. I spotted Carlos, waiting to help me out, but somehow I managed myself.

'Good night, Ashley.'

'Good night, Carlos. I will see you in the morning.' I walked away towards the house, and I could see that Christine was in bed. This was the best thing that could come out of tonight. There would be no interrogations. I could get right in and go right to bed. I heard the car pull away as I was through the door, and I felt like I was in a daydream again. My first day was like a dream come true. What more could a girl ask for? I couldn't help but think that something was going to be terribly wrong. This kind of scenario didn't happen to me. I had secretly got used to my dull life. I had got into my room and stripped into my pyjamas in the quickest time ever. My bed was my sanctuary right now, and it wasn't going to take me long to drift off into dreamland.

CHAPTER 4

Continuing the Dream

My alarm woke me up, and I felt like I had been sleeping for weeks. The house was quiet, and I suddenly realised that I was going into work later today. I got up and went through to the kitchen, still feeling like I was dreaming. There was a note on the breakfast bar for me, and I read it quickly.

Hey Ash,

Hope you had a good night. Black left me a message to say you were going in later this morning. Meet you at lunch, and I want all the glory details.

Christine xx

My boss thought of everything. I completely forgot all about letting Christine know about this morning's arrangements. I poured a cup of coffee that my friend had kindly made before she left for work. The smell was mind-blowing. I took it through to the bathroom with me and ran a shower. I really loved a bath, but since moving to Anchorage, I have never had the time to soak. I needed to make myself presentable for another day at the office, and now I didn't worry about my appearance. The rest of my morning went by in a flash, and I was a lot happier and at ease with myself today. I didn't even have time for breakfast with the way I had been dotting around. By the time I knew what I was doing, I only had ten minutes to wait before Carlos came for me, and surprise, surprise, my mind started playing tricks on me. *What if Dale forgot to send Carlos for me? What if I am late? Will he be angry at me?* But all my 'what ifs' were not needed as I heard the horn from Carlos. Of course, he wouldn't forget to send Carlos. What was I thinking? I lifted my bags and headed out to the car, where I could see Carlos standing with the door open, waiting for me. I felt like a princess since we moved here, and it was only the beginning.

'Morning, honey.'

'Morning, Ashley. You look a lot livelier this morning.' I couldn't believe that everyone realised how tired I was last night. I didn't think that I was so predictable, but I was clearly wrong.

'I feel fresh as a daisy, honey.' It was weird how well I got on with Carlos. He was just so down-to-earth. I would never have classed him as a chauffeur. He was like a breath of fresh air. I felt at home sitting in the back of Dale's car now. It didn't feel weird to me at all. I was just looking forward to getting on with my work today. It was always a good start when you were happy to go out to work. My dad always used to tell me that the day you didn't want to get up or you weren't happy at going to your job, then that was the day that you needed a change. But I had a funny feeling that I was going to be at Black's until I was cashing in on my pension.

We arrived at the office, and I went to open the door just as Carlos was opening it for me. I really needed to get used to the hired help. I thought that I was just used to getting on with my life myself. I haven't had any help for the last few years since my parents had died. My life was my own, and I didn't have anyone to answer to. I should be lucky that I have landed on my feet and I have got a boss who was going to be a very good friend of mine. Things were finally looking up for me.

'Sorry, Miss . . . Ashley.' I could see that Carlos was really trying, but he didn't need to be any different for my benefit; we were both workers at the end of the day.

'You're OK, Carlos. It looks like we both have a lot to learn in our new jobs.' We were getting along just fine. Carlos seemed like the kind of person whom I could be friends with. It was just a pity that he worked around the clock for my boss. I was walking up the steps to the main building, and I suddenly knew what it was like to be happy in your work. I had seen that it was my lucky morning because there was no one waiting for the elevator. It suddenly pinged open, and I looked up to see Dale on his cell.

'Yes, Mom, I know. Don't worry. Hold on, Mom.' His bored-looking face looked directly at me. 'Ashley, can you come with me?' I really didn't know why he asked me things like that because obviously I was going to do what he said. 'Mom, I will see you in a couple of weeks when you arrive in town. But at the moment, I have work to do . . . I love you.' Dale hung up his cell and looked at me. He seemed harassed this morning, not like his usual self. 'I am going to show you around a few of my properties today just so that you can get a feel for what we do.' He sounded exasperated this morning, and it was only 9.15 a.m. He told me to start later this morning so that I could catch up with my sleep. I thought that he needed to have a day off to recuperate after working so hard.

'Good. A field trip.' I could see that harassed look fading as his smile crept back on his face. I was glad that I had that effect on him. I didn't like to see anyone looking tired or unhappy.

'If that is what you want to call it.' Poor Carlos was still waiting by the steps when we left the building. I could see that Dale was pleased with the way Carlos had been dealing with his demands over the last couple of days. 'Hey, thanks, Carlos. We are heading out to the reserve.' I recognised the sound of 'the reserve' from last night. I was intrigued to see what the fuss was all about. We all got in the car, and everything was silent for a few moments. I didn't really want to start the conversation again, but I didn't want to sit in silence either.

'So, your mom is coming to town.' I thought that it was a casual-enough question, but I felt that it was going to be an awkward subject for him.

Was this the reason he was harassed this morning? He turned on to his side to talk to me face to face, which I was beginning to like looking into his gorgeous eyes.

'Yes, in three weeks.' He almost said it in a whisper.

'You don't seem too pleased about it.'

'They are my adoptive parents. They come to visit twice a year. They enjoy all the outdoor activities at this time of year: hunting, fishing, and skiing further on in the winter.' His head shook slightly as if he had said too much already. But me being me, I kept the conversation going. I wanted to know more about him.

'They like to hunt . . . My dad used to take me and my mom on his boat to go fishing. It was one of the most boring things that I have ever done. I used to go for the peace to read and to get all the goodies on board.' I could see him concentrating on every word that I spoke. It was nice to be sitting with a man who was interested in me and my life.

'One thing that we have in common, I don't like fishing either. This is one of the best times to hunt and fish in Alaska.' I guessed that is why it was all fishy dishes that were specials on the menus. Now it made sense.

'Do you have any siblings?'

'I have a brother and sister. We used to be close, but over the last few years, we have grown further apart.'

'I am sorry. I didn't mean to pry.' Although I was asking normal questions, I felt like I was prying into his business that had nothing to do with me.

'Don't be silly, Ashley. I don't mind talking about my family. It is just they are different to me, and I would prefer to get to know you better before we get to my family.' *Did he say different? Was I going to be surprised as to what was to come? Who needs to hunt nowadays?* My mind could go on all day trying to pick negative signs, but I was just going to ignore it for a change and enjoy my day. 'I would much rather get to know you.' A smile spread across my face, and I bit my lip, which was normally a nervous thing, but I wasn't nervous at all.

'What do you want to know?' We both sat back comfortable in our seats and looked at each other with big grins on our faces. I was giving him the reins to ask me whatever he liked. I could regret this later on.

'What brings you to Anchorage? I mean there is a whole world to choose from and you choose here.' That was a good question for someone who didn't know me and my past life.

'There were too many memories in Florida. I lost my parents in a car crash when I was seventeen, and it haunted me every day. These two placements came up with your company, and I and my friend jumped at the chance to start afresh. It is a new chapter for me.' For the first time since I met Dale, he actually looked speechless. I didn't want to stop talking to him. He was so easy to talk to.

'I am so sorry to hear about your parents.'

'Please, don't feel sorry for me. I moved here to get away from everyone and their constant pity. I have moved on. It is hard, but they wanted the best for me, and here, I am living my dream.' Dale placed his hand on mine, and my heart was going crazy.

'If you ever need anything, time off or a holiday to be with family, you just have to say.' I went to interrupt him, but he put a finger up to his lips as if to say, I am not finished yet be quiet. 'I lost my parents twelve years ago, and although I was lucky enough to be adopted into a loving family, there isn't a week that goes by without me thinking what if?' I knew exactly what he was talking about, and all I could do was sit and smile. It was nice to see that a man could have a sensitive side.

'Thank you for understanding. But on a positive note, my past has brought me to a brighter future here in Anchorage. I have a nice home, good job, sensitive boss, and reliable friends.'

'And that I am eternally grateful for.' I had goosebumps on my arms from the way the conversation had turned out. I had never had a conversation with a man like that before. I must be getting soft in my old age.

'How long have we been here?' It dawned on me that we were at our destination and the car had stopped.

'One of the perks of working for the boss is that you don't have to worry about time. There is never too late or too early.'

'So I see, Mr Black.' I truly felt like I was flirting with my boss. As much as I wanted to, I didn't want to come across as desperate.

'Come on, Miss Malone, I will show you around and let you get to grips with the plans. I would like a woman's perspective.' I was honoured that he wanted to know what I thought about the plans. I could tell that I was going to enjoy working here because two days were never the same.

'I will see what I can do.' We got out of the car, and I followed Dale round to the trunk of the car, and I watched curiously as to what was inside. I saw waterproof jackets and waterproof boots. I looked at Dale with a look of confusion. He surely didn't want me to put those on, did he?

'Would you like to walk around in mud with your Louis Vuitton shoes on?' When he put it like that, he had a valid point. My confused look turned into a sarcastic smile. He really did think of everything.

'How did you know my size?'

'Your friend, Christine, helped me.' Sure she did; wait till I see her. I leant against the car and took off my shoes one by one and replaced them with bright pink boots. I let out a laugh as I looked down at my feet. If anyone saw me, they would think I was daft.

'And I bet she told you my favourite colour was pink.'

'How did you guess?'

'I hate pink.' Even Carlos was laughing now. Dale had been played just as much as I had.

'They suit you, Ashley.'

'Yeah, yeah, sure they do.'

I really wanted to hit Dale and Carlos for finding the whole situation so amusing. I was glad I had been entertainment for them this morning. Then there was the jacket, bright yellow and knee-length. Dale had the cheek to help me into it. He was matching me, with yellow jacket and yellow boots. But me, I was like something out of the funny farm.

'Do you expect bad weather?'

'No, it just gets quite cold out in the reserve.' I was really going to need to think before I opened my mouth. We were in Alaska; of course, it would get cold.

'You really do think of everything, don't you?'

'I sure do. I don't fancy losing you to illness, Miss Malone.' I felt very flattered that he was thinking of me in that way. No one has ever been that considerate to me apart from my parents. 'We will be back in about an hour, Carlos.' We both walked away from the car, and I could see the need for the boots now. It was very muddy and wet, certainly not for a girlie girl.

'So, is this the reserve that was getting discussed last night with Robert?'

'Yes . . . This reserve has caused a major stir in Anchorage over the last year. There were property developers all over the world who wanted to knock it all down and build a brand new housing scheme. But the people of Anchorage love this reserve. It is their lives and their homes. So Robert and I came together with this one. Robert is the builder and the planner, and I am the investor.' I was taking it all in piece by piece. It was lovely really old-style Alaska.

'But I thought that the town didn't want anything to happen on this land.'

'I am impressed that you are listening.' I always took my job seriously and listened carefully. 'They don't, but we came up with plans that let the reserve stay in its natural state. We won't be knocking anything down. We just agreed that we would improve the area. We will not take anything away from it.' I thought my look said it all because Dale took my hand and led me to a patch of land that was bare. 'This piece of land, for instance, is bare. There isn't much happening on it. But we haven't quite decided whether to turn it into a campsite or a nature spot. We are not destroying anything as there is nothing to destroy. We are improving it for the better.' I was looking around myself like I was in a whirlwind. Although the land was bare, the scenery was gorgeous. I could see why the people of Anchorage didn't want it destroyed.

'What are you thinking about, Ashley?' I walked on in front a little bit, admiring the whole land, trying to picture what I could see.

'I am just trying to picture it all. It is beautiful. Why would anyone want to destroy it?'

'You get some people out there who are only in this line of business to make big bucks. But me personally, I don't need to kill the heart of Anchorage to achieve that.'

'So, you bought this land so no one else could.' I was overwhelmed by everything that I was hearing. This man was fantastic.

'Yes.' I was so impressed at everything that I had already heard today and that I wasn't bothered about anything else. This man was a legend. I really wanted a man like that in my life, but as it stood, Dale was the only man that I knew who fitted this bill. Was it wrong that I wanted my boss to be more than just my boss? Why did this man bring this side of me out of the closet?

'You look shocked, Ashley?'

'It is just that you seem so different from any other man that I have ever met. You are smart and considerate, and you don't use your millions to get what you want. Are you really Mr Black?' He moved over to me laughing, looking at the ground. This was the only occasion that he hadn't looked me directly in the eyes.

'So, because I own millions, I should be an arrogant ass.' That was the general idea that I had in my mind, and I couldn't help but feel a little bit stupid now.

'Most millionaires are. My last boss was a major ass. I was glad I had only done two shifts a week while studying. He thought that he was God's gift.' I had classed all millionaires like my last boss, and it was clear to me now that all bosses were not as arrogant.

'Well, doll, my lifestyle doesn't change me. I am me, and anyone who doesn't like that can take the high road.' I liked his thinking. I wished that I could follow his footsteps and think the same. But I cared too much as to what people think about me.

'What's not to like?' *Did I just say that out loud?* Judging by the smug look on Dale's face, I could see that my mouth had got the better of me.

'Glad you think so, Miss Malone.' He gently took my hand and helped me back to the path. I could feel my feet slipping so I was glad of his hand for support. I didn't want to let go. 'Come through here and I will show you how people of Anchorage live.' I followed him through bushes and wondered where we were going. I didn't quite understand what I was going to see. But the minute I stopped, I saw all these old-style hut-style houses. Again, it was like looking at a book. I didn't think that this style of living was still normal for people. Everyone was going about their day-to-day life, and they all looked happy. 'You look a little bit shocked, Ashley.'

'I didn't think that people still lived in this type of houses. But now I can see why they didn't want anything destroyed . . . It is their home.' I could see the rustic-style buildings that were built following traditional building techniques and natural materials.

'This style of housing has been around from roughly 1916 . . . It was widely used during the Great Depression that hit Alaska . . .'

'How has it survived so long?'

'It is still commonly found in rural areas of the country . . . The people of Anchorage have fought hard to keep their homes in its natural state, and who are we to come along and take it from them. Generation after generation has lived in these huts, and it means a lot to them.' When I was growing up, I lived in a tight-knit community, and this just reminded me of that. I was just glad that they had Dale and Robert on their side to help them maintain it.

'I am glad that you showed me this side. It makes everything clear now.'

'I am glad that you approve, Miss Malone . . .' I still couldn't take my eyes off the whole area. It was magnificent to see how people still live like this.

'Let's get back to the car for a heat.' I managed to follow alongside him, never letting his hand go. It was mid-September so it was very damp and cold, yet his hand was very soft and warm. I was glad I was going back to a nice warm car because I could now feel the cold hitting me.

'See, it is a good job that I think of everything, or you would be Baltic right now with no jacket on.' I rolled my eyes at him because although I knew he was right, I didn't want to admit it to him.

'Are you this nice to everyone you know?'

'I try to be. But if I don't like someone, I really can't hide that fact.' I felt that cold now, and I didn't want to speak any more because my teeth would chatter and my voice would be all shaky. I saw Carlos get out of the car, and he headed around to the trunk.

'Thank you, Carlos.' One thing that I had noticed about Dale was that he was always polite to every member of staff, no matter what their job was. We sat back on the edge of the car again and slipped the boots off. Carlos had a bag out ready to put them in, and if it was left to me, I would put them straight in the trash. I felt even colder now that the boots were off, and I couldn't help but think how a nice hot bath would go down a treat right about now. I slipped out of the jacket, and Carlos had my door open, waiting for me. Dale opened his own door, and we met each other in the back seat. I was glad that he was close to me because I could feel his body heat next to me.

'Thank you for showing me the reserve. It was beautiful.' Dale let his head rest back against the headrest and let it flop to look at me. He looked so at ease with everything, and I admired him for everything that he has worked to achieve.

'You're welcome, Ashley. You need to see everything that I do, so we are as well starting as we mean to go on.'

'So, is all the paperwork on my desk?'

'God, you are quick. Yes, it is. It will all be done quickly because I have done most of it last week when I didn't have an assistant.'

'You are good to me. When does the real work start? I mean the last two days have just been a breeze.' I realised that I sounded like I was complaining, but I was just being a bit sarcastic.

'Are you complaining now, Miss Malone?' It was nice to have a boss whom I could have a laugh and joke with. The days would drag in if no one spoke in the office.

'No, not at all, Mr Black. I am not one to complain.' We headed back to the office to get the paperwork sent off to Robert, and I sat in amazement. This dream was getting better and better as the days went on, and I expected someone to come along and wake me up at any moment.

Sitting at my desk finalising the paperwork for the reserve was one of the best jobs I had done in the two days that I had been here. I felt like I knew what was behind the paperwork, what was coming, and what the people of Anchorage were getting out of the whole thing. I have had so much enjoyment in the last couple of days that I realised that the last few years I was miserable, and I got by because I had to. But here, I was happy and I was getting through each day because I wanted to. My laptop pinged to let me know I had mail, and for the first time in my adult life, I was excited to see what was in my inbox.

To: Miss Ashley Malone
From: Mr Dale Black
Msg: Thank you

Thank you for joining me today. It meant a lot. I am very grateful to have an assistant who takes an interest in the business as a whole.
I have never shared much about my family to anyone, let alone my assistant.
It was nice to get to know you a bit better and break the ice.
Will you join me for dinner tomorrow night?

yours sincerely
Mr Dale Black

I couldn't believe what I was reading. Maybe I brought the best out of him as well. Another dinner date sounded nice. I couldn't possibly refuse.

I hit reply and stared at the screen for a few seconds. I debated whether to be serious or be casual, and I was just going to be myself and see where that got me.

> To: Mr Dale Black
> From: Miss Ashley Black
> Msg: Thank you
>
> Mr Black, do you not have any work to do? You are next door to me. Can you not come through here to me?
> Thank you for having me today. It was nice to get a feel for the company and the area. Should I take that as a compliment about being a good PA? It was good hearing about your family. I look forward to meeting them when they are in town.
> Who are we meeting tomorrow for dinner? You are going to get fed up seeing me before too long.
>
> Yours Sincerely
> Miss Ashley Malone

I hit reply before I could change any of my response. I had hoped that he took the funny side to my reply. He seemed to be laid-back so there was no need to worry about how he would take it. I was getting ready to leave my office to fax the paperwork to Robert, before I went for lunch, when my laptop pinged again. I was in two minds to ignore the mail and carry on with what I was doing, but my curiosity took over, and I rushed back to my desk to open it.

> To: Miss Ashley Malone
> From: Mr Dale Black
> Msg: Thank you
>
> Miss Malone, I am the boss. I can choose when to work. I can't help but want to talk to you. You are distracting me from my work. Also, I don't like you calling yourself my PA! You are equal to me, not my skivvy. Assistant will do nicely.
> You don't want to meet my family, as I said they are different. They spend all their time here out in the wilderness.

We are not meeting any one tomorrow night. I thought you could come by for dinner apart from work. I would understand if you had other plans.

Ps. Anything I say that is nice to you is a compliment.

Yours Sincerely
Mr Dale Black

I quickly read the email, and it was beginning to annoy me how he always treated his family differently to us. What did he mean that they were different? I was flattered at the fact that he wanted to spend time with me apart from work. How could I refuse his offer? I couldn't get enough of him. He was like ecstasy to a drug addict, and he was starting to become my drug.

To: Mr Dale Black
From: Miss Ashley Malone
Msg: Thank you

Why do you keep saying that your family are different? They can't be that bad! Will you stop being so nice to me? I am your PA. It is just a word.
I would love to come to dinner tomorrow night, if you promise to stop treating me like a fragile flower that is going to snap.
I have to go now to fax this paperwork and meet my friend for lunch. I wouldn't want to tell Robert that it is late because you were distracting me. :-)

Yours sincerely
Ashley
x

It was like I was having a conversation with one of my friends back home on a social network site. I had to keep reminding myself that I was in fact at work speaking to my boss. This day had to go on, and I had things to do and people to see. I would get nothing done if I sat speaking to my boss through a wall on a computer.

CHAPTER 5

The Dream

The sun was splitting the trees as I was galloping happily through the forest. Dale was running behind me, trying to catch me. We were so happy, enjoying each other's company. I couldn't run straight for laughing so hard. I suddenly came to a stop when I spotted a large blanket on the ground with a picnic basket laid on top of it. It was like a movie scene.

Dale's arms wrapped around my waist, and he kissed me passionately on the neck. My body was tingling from his touch. I had never felt this magic from anyone before. I turned slightly to take his mouth with mine. His lips were so soft and warm against mine, and the electricity soared through my body. We were in this embrace for what felt like forever. I didn't want to let him go.

'I could stay in this position all day with you, Ashley.' That made two of us because I had never felt so compatible with someone in my life.

'What have you stopped for? We have all day.' Dale picked me up and placed me on the blanket. The soft screams escaped my mouth as I felt like *a teenager all over again. He was very careful with me just like I was a China doll. It was a nice sunny day, and we kissed and kissed and kissed. He slid his hand up my shirt, and the feel of his hand on my bare skin made me hungry for more. My body wanted him and so did I. We were both hot and bothered, and I completely forgot that we were in the forest and that anyone could be watching us. I undid the buttons on his shirt and slid my hands down his chest. He felt so warm, and his heartbeat was pumping hard against my hand. I could touch him all day. He sat me up and slipped my top over my head. My breasts were calling out to be touched and to be sucked by his mouth. I slid his shirt off and undid the belt on his jeans. I popped the buttons open on his jeans as his hand slipped around my back and unclipped my bra. He carefully lowered me back down on to the blanket and caressed my breasts with his mouth. I was lying oblivious to the outside world around about us. I could feel his package rub against me through his jeans, and I couldn't take any more. I wanted him here and now. My body was screaming for him.*

'We have all day as you reminded me.' His whisper in my ear sent my body into overdrive. I turned to look at his face, those sexy twinkling eyes. I couldn't wait all day. My heart was beating so fast, and my breathing was out of control. I needed him now.

'I can't wait any longer.' He smiled at me and pulled my trousers off. All I was laying in was my black lace pants. I didn't know that it was this possible to want someone as much as I wanted him. He slipped out of his trousers and underwear and was lying on top of me naked. He was just teasing me now. His hands slipped my pants down, and I felt his mouth kiss every inch of my legs on his way back up. My sex was crying out for him. His mouth was on my thigh and slowly on to my sex. His mouth was so warm and wet, and my body was on fire. I couldn't control the electricity flowing through me as I was on fire. The groans escaped from my mouth as my whole body climaxed. I felt him move up my body kissing my torso all the way up until he bit my breasts. His mouth on my lips took my breath away. I felt him put his hand on my thigh as he slowly entered my body with his long, hard penis. A cry escaped me as I felt every thrust. My body climaxed over and over again. His whole body shuddered as he climaxed. We lay tangled within each other, and I could feel him still inside me. The world felt like it was moving, and I never wanted to move another muscle.

I woke up soaking with sweat, and my breathing was out of control. *What had just happened?* I had just had this raunchy love-making session with my boss, in a forest. I quickly swung my legs out of bed and sat with my head in my hands. I couldn't believe that I had let this happen. I never had dreams. I never let someone get under my skin the way Dale has got under mine. I got up and looked in the mirror, and I looked like I had been dragged through a hedge backwards. I opened my door and bumped into Christine, the one person whom I could do without today.

'Hey, Ash, did you sleep at all last night?' *'O' dear, what had she heard?* I didn't want to look into her eyes because she would just know something was wrong. I just wanted to go for a shower and forget all about what had happened in my dreams.

'Not much. I had a restless night.'

'I know. I heard you thrashing about in your sleep. Is everything OK?'

'Yeah, just one weird night.' I continued my walk into the bathroom without even thinking too much about it. 'I will be through soon.' I felt confused. My head was throbbing, and I couldn't think straight. I ran the shower and slipped out of my pyjamas. The bathroom was filling up with steam, and I felt really woozy. How was I ever going to look Dale in the face again? This was the quickest shower I had ever had. I stepped out of the cubical and wrapped a towel around me. I looked in the mirror and felt and looked a lot more fresher, but my insides were still all over the place. Just as I opened the bathroom door, I remembered that I hadn't brushed my teeth. I could sense that it was going to be one of those days. It was a good job that I set my clothes out the night before, or I could be going into work today like a multicolour swap shop. I went for a navy suit and cream shirt. I really didn't fancy feeling sexy today. If this day got over quickly, it would be for the better. There was a knock on my door that made me jump. I really could do without Christine this morning.

'Come in.'

'I have made you a coffee.' I needed this right now. It was like another drug for me. It would set me up for the whole day. I was very grateful for it.

'Thanks, hun, you must have read my mind.'

'What are friends for? Are you sure you are OK? You still don't look too hot!' I could always count on my friend for telling me like that, even when her opinion wasn't needed.

'Thanks for that, love. You have really boosted my confidence this morning.'

'I only notice these things because I know every inch of you, inside and out. No one in the office will notice.' I really hoped that they wouldn't notice because I could do without their fussing over me. I managed to get my shoes on, lift my bag, and follow Christine through to the kitchen to finish my coffee. I could sense that today was going to be a nightmare. I was normally stuck to a routine in the morning, and it had gone out of the window. That was recipe for disaster.

I arrived at the office over an hour ago, and I found my to-do list on my desk. But the rest of the office was very quiet today. Luck was on my side after all because the main bonus was that there was no Dale either. I did wonder where he was because he was normally in before everyone else. I wasn't complaining him for being not today. The space between us was just what I needed. There was a loud knock on my door that made me jump. *What is it with everyone today?* My heart couldn't take many more frights.

'Come in.' The words stumbled off my tongue naturally, but I couldn't contain my nerves as the door opened slowly.

'Good morning, Ashley. Mr Black has just phoned and asked me to ask you if you will meet him out front. Carlos will be waiting.'

'Thank you for that.' I felt really rude because I couldn't remember the girl's name. She nodded to me with a courteous smile and left my office. I collected my things and headed for the elevator. I really thought that I was going to get away from Mr Black today, but who was I kidding? The time seemed to stop since I received Mr Black's message. I was worried why he couldn't tell me himself, but I tried not to let it get to me. The elevator opened, and I walked in, for once I was hoping that the elevator broke down with me in it; it would bide me some time. The nerves in the pit of my stomach were very intense right now. But was there any wonder after my adventurous night? The elevator stopped, and I made for the exit. I could see the black Mercedes waiting for me. Carlos saw me coming and opened my door for me.

'Good morning, Ashley.'

'Good morning, Carlos.' I climbed into the car very slowly and hoped that it was empty. But that wasn't going to happen any time soon.

'Good morning, hun.' I glanced over at Dale and could see him studying me. I just knew that he was going to say something that I didn't want to hear.

'Good morning.'

'Ashley, are you OK? I know we don't know each other very well, but you don't seem yourself.' I was amazed that he even noticed how I looked, but I made no plea to lie to him.

'I just had a restless night. I saw every hour on the clock.'

'I hope that I am not working you too hard.' He really did look concerned about me, but there was no need. I would survive.

'No, not at all. I have hardly done anything.'

'Well, it is a good job that I have a nice, quiet, chilled out day planned.' I didn't quite follow him, but I wasn't in any mood to argue.

'Where are we going?'

'I have planned lunch in one of my cottages up in the mountains . . . Carlos is going to drop us off.' I couldn't believe that I was hearing this today of all days. I had a full list of things to do. Could I really afford to be out having fun?

'What about work?' I really needed to stop asking silly questions. It was not like the boss minds.

'I am the boss, sweetie. I make the rules, and everything that was on your list has been done. I typed it up this morning so that I could get you to myself for the day.' I was shocked that he would go to so much effort. *Why would he do that?* I was sitting here like the cat had stolen my tongue.

'Why?'

'Why do I want to spend the day with you?' All I could manage was a nod of my head.

'Well, Ashley, you intrigue me. I haven't dated anyone in a very long time, never mind someone I work with. But from the very first moment that I have seen you . . . you lit up the room. Since then, I thought something was telling us that we were destined to be together . . . All the times we bumped into one another and then you turn out to be my assistant . . .' He suddenly stopped talking, and we were both sitting looking at one another like lovesick puppies. I had never really thought about all the coincidences. I just knew how I felt.

'But you are my boss.'

'And does that make a difference? I will transfer you to another department if that is all that is going to stop us . . .' This was coming as a shock to me today, but if I was honest, I saw it coming. 'If you turn around now and tell me that you don't feel anything . . . I will get Carlos to turn around, and we will go back to a business relationship.' As much as I wanted to lie and say I didn't feel anything, I couldn't. I shook my head and watched Dale's eyes rise, wondering what I was going to say.

'I . . .' I couldn't quite find the words that I wanted to say. 'Feel different when I am with you. I don't feel like Ashley.'

'Is that a bad thing?'

'No, it's not. You make me feel alive. No one has ever made me feel like you do.' He moved closer to me and took my hands in his. He looked directly into my eyes, and my body felt like a nervous wreck.

'Let's give it a shot, Ashley. We can take things as slow or as fast as you like.' What was I waiting for? My head and mouth felt disconnected, and I couldn't say what I actually wanted to.

'This is a first for me, Dale . . . I never date, especially not my boss.' I haven't lied to him before, and I wasn't going to start today.

'It's a first for both of us then because I never date full stop.'

'Why?' Of all the times that we had shared a conversation, it had flowed nicely. But today, I felt all over the place.

'Why don't I date . . . ? I have never found anyone whom I would sacrifice work for. I mean I would work around the clock if I could, and it wouldn't be fair on the relationship.' I wasn't sure that I wanted to hear that response, but I couldn't fault him for telling me straight.

'So, why am I any different?'

'I don't know.' He shrugged his shoulders and looked down at our hands. 'I have never left work to its own devices before. I have never wanted to be with someone as much as I have wanted to be with you.' I felt the car stop, and Dale's words had stopped as well. I felt like I was in another dream.

'I don't know how we can work this or even if it will work. But based on how I feel and listening to your feelings, what harm can it do to try?' The old, quiet Ashley had been flung into a box, and the new confident Ashley was in full swing.

'You have no idea how happy I am to hear you say that.' My door opened, and I was startled. I forgot that Carlos was with us. I let Dale's hands go and shuffled out of the car. I felt like I was drunk. My legs felt like jelly, and my head felt fuzzy. But I couldn't be happier.

'Thank you, Carlos. I will give you a call when we need you.'

'Have a nice day.' Carlos moved away from us and got back into the car. We both watched as the car pulled away. The morning was perfect.

The sun was shining, and the views were stunning. I walked over to the edge of the mountain, and my breath was taken away. You could see right over Anchorage from this spot. I felt Dale walk up behind me, and he placed his arms around my waist, just like he had done in my dream. I felt so alive. It was like déjàvu.

'It is beautiful, isn't it?'

'There isn't a word that I can use to describe it.' I had never seen anything as beautiful as this in my life.

'This cottage came up for sale two years ago, and I was supposed to be selling it for someone. I came up to take a look at it and immediately fell in love with it.' I could understand why because I had just done the same thing.

'So you bought it yourself.'

'I always pictured myself standing here with the woman I marry . . . sharing our life together. But I lost hope up until now.' I turned my head slightly to glance over at him, and I could feel a smile appear on my face. My body felt like a quivering wreck because I was so cold.

'I had Carlos come up early this morning to put a fire on. The cottage will be warm as toast.' He took me by the hand, and I followed behind him. The cottage looked stunning just as much as the scenery did. How much more could my body take today? The heat hit me the minute we entered the cottage. It was lovely. I had to take my jacket off before I melted.

'It is really nice in here. Did you do it all yourself?' The cottage had been restored to its natural state. It was all wooden beams and antique furniture. I caught sight of the fire burning, and I just wanted to melt in front of it.

'I haven't really done much to it, if I am being honest. It needs a woman's touch.'

'I wouldn't change it.'

'Not a thing?' I thought Dale was surprised with my answer, but it was gorgeous. I looked around again and thought carefully about what I was going to say.

'I would change the drapes and add some flowers just to make it homely. But honestly, it is beautiful.' Dale seemed satisfied that I was happy with everything.

'Can I get you a drink?'

'Whatever you are having will be fine.' I wasn't a fussy person. I would go with the flow whenever I could.

'Coffee?'

'Perfect.' Dale went through to the kitchen area, and I went for a seat in front of the fire. It had been calling my name since we arrived, and I couldn't resist any more. I sat and made myself comfortable, and it was the worst thing that I could have done because I felt so tired now.

'Here we go, honey.'

'Hmm, it smells lovely.'

'Only the best for you.' Dale sat down beside me on the couch, and he pulled my feet up on to his legs. Why did he have to do that? My body just got even more at home. Why was I so at ease with this man? It just didn't make any sense. But one thing was for sure, I had never felt happier. 'Do you want to go for a lie-down? You look exhausted.' I could quite easily sleep for a week, but I didn't want to admit it.

'That wouldn't be very nice of me. You want to spend the day with me, and I go for a lie-down. I wouldn't be much company sleeping.'

'I have you here with me. It wouldn't bother me if you were sleeping or dancing. The fact that you chose to be here has made my day.' Dale leant forward and rubbed his hand on my cheek. My heart knew what was coming because it was pounding in my chest. 'Do you mind if I kiss you, love?' I couldn't speak, but I managed to shake my head and give him the go-ahead to kiss me. I felt flattered that he cared so much to ask my permission first. He reached over and took my cup out of my hands and placed it on the table. I was glad that he thought about the hot coffee because I would probably scald myself with excitement. His soft hand returned to my cheek, and my cheekbone felt like it had a pulse. Then when his lips slowly touched mine, I was alive. I could feel the electricity move through my body as his lips caressed mine. His warm tongue would enter my mouth at any opportunity it got. Our breathing was out of control as we stopped and looked each other in the eyes. I thought that we were both as shocked at how we reacted to one another.

'I have never felt like this about anyone before . . . I am aching for you, Ashley.' I couldn't think about what to say. My breathing was still out of control. I managed to scramble up on to my knees and took his face with my hands. I kissed him like there was no tomorrow. I needed to feel him just as much as he needed me. 'Are you sure about this, babe?'

'Just shut up and make love to me, Mr Black.' Our mouths became one again as our hands became familiar with each other. I took out the buttons on his shirt and rubbed my hands down his chest, feeling every inch of him. As he took my shirt off, I laughed as he tickled my back with his hands. We were entwined together like we had known each other for years. He loosened my skirt, and I raised myself up so that it would fall down. We were semi-naked, but it was so hot, and not just with the heat of the fire. I was fidgeting to loosen his belt when he smiled at me and did it for me. He lowered my back down on to the couch, and with one hand behind me, he loosened my bra. My body was on fire, and my breathing was erratic. My body was getting caressed with his hands and his mouth. I didn't know that it was possible to feel as much pleasure. The cries escaped my mouth with the pleasure of his touch. I needed him now. His hand slipped into my pants, and it felt so good. Like his hand was meant to be touching my sex. I climaxed with just his hand. My mind had died and gone to heaven. He slipped my pants down and then took his off. He lay on top of me, and I could feel every inch of him rubbing against me. My body was close to a peak again. He inserted his large package slowly inside of me, and the pleasure escaped both of our mouths. He slipped in and out of me as I cried out with ecstasy. His body felt like a temple as I climaxed over again. I felt him pound inside me with one harder push as his body shuddered on top of me. We were both lying there hot and bothered, to breathless and limp to move. He rolled beside me so he was facing me, and I felt his eyes on me as his hand caressed my cheek.

'Are you OK, sweetie?' I lay still and tilted my head around to look at him. Why was he asking me this question? Didn't my body speak for itself?

'Of course, I am . . . I am better than OK.' I felt like the luckiest person alive lying here with one of the most kindest men I had ever come across.

'I just want you to know that I don't make a habit of seducing beautiful young woman.' I laughed. Not even thinking about what I was laughing at. I could see that Dale was wondering what I was so amused at.

'What is so funny, Miss Malone?'

'This . . . Everything . . . Us . . . You are my boss, and I am your employee, and we have just had sex together in the middle of the morning. We should actually be in the office working.' He leant up on his arm and stroked my cheek with a very tender look on his face.

'First of all, Miss Malone, I can decide if and when we work. Second, I did not just have sex with you. I made love to you.' His lips touched mine with a gentle peck, enough to let me know that he meant in every word. 'Do you have any regrets, honey?'

'Of course, not. This has been one of the best mornings that I have ever spent with someone.'

'But?' I was going to have to get used to having a man who took notice of me as a person, and he knew me better than I knew myself.

'But how are we going to be able to work together and see each other in a personal way?' Mixing business and pleasure was never an easy task for anyone, let alone me.

'If we really want this to work, it will, honey. We can keep it to ourselves if that is what you want.'

'No, I don't want to sneak around to see you. We are not doing anything wrong. Unless, this is where you tell me you have a wife and kids.' I couldn't help but get that last sarcastic comment in.

'Nope, no wife and kids. Not yet any way.' Dale lay back down beside me, and I turned on to my side to cuddle into his bare body. He pulled a fur blanket from the back of the couch over the both of us, and I closed my eyes. My day started off in a dream, and it has finished off in a nice blur. I didn't want it to end. The heat of the fire and the warmth of the blanket made me cuddle into his body. I had never felt as relaxed as this in my whole life.

CHAPTER 6

Work and Play

M y first week in Anchorage had gone by so quickly. I never thought for one second that I would have jumped into a serious relationship so quickly. But I was a firm believer of things happening for a reason, and I believed that Dale and I could be soulmates. I couldn't remember what life was like before we moved here, and maybe that was all for the best. I really was taking the bull by the horns and living life like a princess. I was lying in bed curled up in the covers, taking advantage of a Sunday morning long lie. Dale was picking me up at 11 a.m., and I couldn't wait. I didn't even feel guilty about leaving Christine because she was going to meet people from work for a Sunday session of fun. But my priorities were changing every day. My idea of fun now was spending as much time as I could with Dale. I got up out of bed and went through to the kitchen for a coffee. It was a cold morning, and I could just do with Dale's arms wrapped around me. The coffee machine was taking its time this morning, and I never had patience for waiting.

'Morning, Ash.'

'Morning. Coffee is brewing. It won't be long.' I really hoped that she could stay in this bubbly mood because I really couldn't be doing with any pep talks right now.

'Thanks. You're up early this morning.' I was and really hoped that she wouldn't have noticed. I couldn't sleep because I was too excited about meeting Dale. I hadn't seen him since Friday night, and it felt like an eternity. Of course, we had spoken on the phone and sent lots of messages to one another, but that distance between us had been torture.

'I can't sleep long past that darn alarm. My body clock is set already.' I was moving around the kitchen just like I had been there for years. Christine was slumped at the breakfast bar, looking kind of rough from the night before, and for once I wasn't out with her, so I was fresh as a daisy.

'Do you want to come out for drinks and some lunch this afternoon?' I felt like screaming at her 'don't you listen'.

'I told you I am meeting Dale. He is picking me up at eleven.' I didn't know what I had to do around here to get someone to listen to me. I could have sworn we spoke a different language at times.

'So you did . . . Sorry I forgot.' She had that look on her face like she had something else to say, and I debated whether to ask her or not, but there was no point her beating about the bush.

'Spit it out, Christine. What is wrong?'

'What is going on with you and Dale?' I really wanted to tell her to mind her own business, but I couldn't be bothered arguing with her at this time in the morning.

'We are just having some fun. Aren't you always telling me to live a little?' I was trying to outsmart her using her advice, but her face said it all.

'Yes, but not to sleep with your boss.' I threw Christine a look as if to say get a life and leave mine alone. What was it to do with her anyway? I enjoyed his company, and we had fun together. But most importantly, I could be myself around him.

'I beg your pardon. Yes, we are dating. Yes, we are having some fun. Who are we hurting?'

'You will be hurting yourself if it goes pear-shaped.' I could always depend on my friend to burst my bubble.

'Well, that is a chance I am willing to take. I have never felt like this with anyone else before . . .' I really didn't think that I needed to explain myself, but I wasn't hiding anything from anyone. 'Thank you for your support, Christine.' I lifted my coffee and walked out of the kitchen. I heard her shout out my name, but at this moment, I was too angry to even talk to her. I couldn't win with her. She moaned at me when I worked round the clock, and then when I found someone whom I want to be with, she still moaned. I went to run a shower to try and forget about my obnoxious friend, but she had gone too far today. My morning routine was getting a bit boring now: shower, hair, teeth, and clothes. I was glad that I had my afternoon set out with Dale, who always sparked new things. I had a one-track mind right now, and it was Dale all the way. Five minutes didn't pass without me thinking of him. I debated what to wear today, but I was going for the casual look. I dressed to impress all week, and today, I was going for my jeans and a top. I had wanted to jump into my jeans for days and now that I had a chance I wasn't going to let it slid past me. I was taking my time to get ready because I didn't want any more confrontation with Christine. I picked up my phone and decided to text Dale.

To: Dale
Msg: Hi, sweetie, are you busy? I need to get out of this house.
Ash xx

I threw my phone back on to my bed and slumped down. I thought that he would take a while to reply, but instead, he was super fast. I didn't think sixty seconds had went past.

From: Dale
Msg: What's wrong? I will be there in ten minutes. You sound
    pissed off. Hope you are OK.
Love Dale xx

I was glad that he was coming to get me early because I could feel myself ready to crack up. I quickly got ready and slipped my feet into a pair of shoes. I grabbed my bag and light jacket and headed back through to face the pack of wolves. Hopefully, she was away getting ready or found something else to annoy. I felt like I was in a secret service going along the hall, trying not to stumble across her, but she was my friend; she should just be happy for me for once.

'Ash.' Who was I kidding? Of course, she was still in the kitchen.

'Yeah.'

'I am sorry. You know I just care about you.'

'Save it, Christine. I am happy, and I feel human for the first time in my life, and I am not going to let you ruin that for me.' She had really pissed me off this morning and wasn't getting away from it that easy. All my life, I had tiptoed around her, and I wasn't going to do that any more. This was a fresh start for us, and I was planning on using to my advantage.

'Where are you off to? I thought Dale was coming at eleven.'

'I texted him to come and get me. So he is on his way over.' Even ten minutes was too long, but it was better than spending time with Christine.

'Am I that bad that you can't spend another minute with me?' I was glad that she said and not me.

'I just don't want to argue with you.' I was saved by the horn of Dale's car. I wanted to run, but I didn't want to be childish. 'Have a nice day, Christine.'

'Yeah, you too.' I left the house quite quickly before any more arguing happened. I spotted Dale standing beside the car, and I could sense that Christine was watching us. She just couldn't help herself. I practically ran to him, and he wrapped his arms around my waist and kissed me softly on the lips. Already, my hellish morning had been forgotten.

'What is wrong, honey? Are you OK?'

'Can we just get away from here? And I will explain everything.'

'Sure get in.' I realised that I was walking round to the passenger's seat. It felt really weird getting into the front of the car with no Carlos driving.

'No Carlos today?'

'I give him a Sunday off, especially if there is no work to be done.' Of course, he did. Why did I expect Carlos to be the only one working on a Sunday.

'I forgot how generous you can be.' We both smiled at one another as I noted how weird it was watching Dale drive for a change. I had only seen him drive once, and that was when he took me home after my walk. We had come a long way in just a short space of time; it was so unbelievable.

'So what is wrong? You had me worried when I received your message.'

'Would you believe me if I said that I just missed you?' I really didn't want to talk about it, but I knew that he wouldn't just drop it like that. If something was upsetting me, then it was upsetting him too.

'No. It sounded worse than that.' How do you tell someone that you were bickering over them?

'Well . . . my friend doesn't entirely approve of us. She thinks that we are playing with fire.' The car was silent for a short time, and I hated silence between us.

'I see.' I didn't think that he was surprised at what I was saying. He didn't show it anyway.

'But I don't care what she thinks. We knew there would be people trying to butt in . . . She was doing my head in, and I just had to get out of there.'

'I don't want to break your friendship up, babe.' I might have guessed that he would think of my friendship first, but I wasn't so he didn't have to bother.

'Stop it. If she can't be happy for me, then that is her problem. She will come round . . . Can we forget about it and have a nice day?' Dale reached over and placed his hand in mine. His slightest touch made everything disappear, and I was alive again. I would never get fed up feeling like this.

'Do you mind what we do?'

'Nope, as long as it is with you. What do you have in mind?'

'A surprise.' I really didn't like surprises, but I was with Dale, so it really didn't matter what we were going to do. Although he was driving, I could sense that he kept looking at me, just like I kept looking at him.

'Are you not going to give me a clue?'

'Nope.' His teasing voice was very sexy. It was a good job he was driving or we wouldn't have made it anywhere.

'You are just a tease, Mr Black.' I had amused him with my comment. It was good to be here for a full day with him, without work in mind. We were driving for a while, and I was getting restless. I just wanted to know where we were going. I saw a sign for a docking arena, and we were getting closer and closer to water. But I had no idea where or what we were going to do.

'Are you getting any hints yet, Ash?' That was the first time he had ever called me Ash. I glanced over at him with a surprised look on my face. It was nice to feel comfortable enough with him to express feelings. 'What? What did I say?'

'Nothing. You haven't ever called me Ash before.'

'Sorry, don't you like it?'

'No, it isn't that. It was just weird hearing you call me it.' My Mr Smiler was becoming more and more mine every day.

'Back to my question. Do you have any idea where we are going yet?'

'No, not really. Unless we are going in the water.' I laughed at myself. *What a stupid response to come up with.* Dale had a cheeky grin on his face as we pulled into a car park, and I caught a glimpse of a big white boat floating in the water, and it never crossed my mind what we were going to be doing.

'We are not exactly going in the water. But we are going on the water.'

'You have lost me now.' We got out of the car and walked towards the boat. It was beautiful.

'We are going on my boat.' I never thought for one minute that the boat floating on the water was for us. I was gobsmacked. 'I haven't been here in months, and I wanted to do something nice with you. I couldn't think of a better way to spend my Sunday . . . Here with you.' I used to love sailing on my dad's boat, and today would be perfect.

'I haven't been on a boat for years. My father owned his own boat, and we used to go sailing. My dad loved fishing, but it wasn't my thing.' I had a flashback of going fishing with my dad. It was a hot sunny day in Florida, and we set sail early in the morning. The boat was packed full of our favourite food and drinks. We always had so much fun together.

'Ashley, sweetie, are you OK?'

'Yeah, I was just thinking. Sailing brings back some good memories.'

'I am so sorry, sweetie. I never thought. We can abort the boat and do something else.' He was so sweet about everything, but I wanted to take the boat out.

'No, not at all. I want to take the boat out.' He leant across me and placed a loving kiss on my lips. It was a feeling that I was getting, too, used to now.

'Let's get going then.' We both climbed on to the boat, and I stood beside him, looking around at the views.

'Is there anything you don't own?'

'I don't own a castle . . . yet.' It felt so natural to be here laughing along with him. I really did feel like a princess now. 'Welcome aboard, Mhairi.'

'Where did the name come from?' I expected him to say an ex-girlfriend or surprise me and say ex-wife. But that was my negativity trying to jump back in full view.

'I named her after my mother.' Of course, it was his mother. I was just looking for the worst possible answer.

'She is beautiful.'

'My mother fell in love with her as well. Both of you have the same taste.' He pulled me into his arms and touched my cheek with his hand. 'Apart from my mother, you are the only other female to board Mhairi.' I leant over and kissed him with everything that I had to give, and he kissed me back so passionately that he was holding my body standing. He was always so gentle with me.

'Do you want to have a tour before we sail off into the sunset?' Sailing off to the sunset sounded blissful, especially on a Sunday.

'Sounds like a plan, Mr Black.'   ·

I followed behind him holding his hands. I didn't want to let him go even for one second.

'Did you choose all the decor?'

'No, my mom did it for me. She has a good eye for fashion. She was over the moon when I gave her the reins to do whatever she wanted.' He seemed really proud to talk about his mom, and I got a feeling that he really wanted to talk about her.

'You seem really close to your mom.'

'I am I guess. I had a big wake-up call, and it made me realise that you never know what is round the corner. I don't see them much, but when I do, it is special.'

'They sound lovely. Just like you.' I couldn't imagine any of his family being any different from him.

'I am nicer, of course.'

'I can't agree with that yet because I haven't met your parents.'

'Cheeky.' As we went downstairs into the living quarters, I felt that the mood had changed slightly. Did I say something? Or was family a tricky subject for him? One way or another, I was going to find out.

'Is everything OK? Did I say something?'

'No, of course, you didn't, sweetie . . .' His face had suddenly looked like he was in pain from something. 'There is too much that I would love to share with you, but I don't know how to, without scaring you away.' I felt nervous now. Of course, there had to be something that was going to shock me as everything was going so smoothly.

'What can possibly be so bad, Dale? I have never felt like this before, about anyone. Nothing is going to scare me away.' I tried to reassure him, but I didn't think that it was working too well.

'I wouldn't be so sure about that. Can we change the subject for today? I promise that I will tell you all about it one day.' If his face didn't look as though he was in pain, I would have changed the subject. But it killed me to see him so upset.

'Is it about you?' I didn't want to push him into anything, but I wanted him to know that it was him I loved.

'No, nothing at all to do with me.'

'Well, why would it scare me away then? It is you that I love.' Did I really just have to say that? He was going to be the one scared off now. I couldn't read his thoughts as he walked over to me, and my stomach was doing somersaults.

'Can you say that again?' I got all shy and looked down to the floor, and he tilted my face up with his hand and looked directly into my eyes.

'It is you that I love.' I found the courage to repeat my words and felt like I was going to pass out. I was so overwhelmed by it all.

'Ashley . . . I love you too. I just didn't want to frighten you off so quickly by saying it out loud.'

'So, I bet you to it.' My nerves made me laugh. I could quite easily freeze this moment and never move on.

'Come with me, and I will get you a drink.' We walked through the boat until we came to a seating area. I felt very at home here. There was a hostess trolley in the corner that held lots of different drinks, perfect for a minibar. Dale walked over to it with a sprint in his step, and I was glad that I told him how I felt because it had opened up new pathways for us.

'Make yourself at home, Ash.' He came back over and sat beside me with a bottle of red wine. I couldn't pronounce the name, but I accepted a glass any way. I thought that I was going to need it by the time he finished telling me what was so bad. I wasn't usually good with shocks, but as long as I had him beside me, I would be fine.

CHAPTER 7

The Truth

My wine was going down a treat. There was nice music playing in the background, and I had goosebumps from it. Or was it with my mind playing tricks on me? What was the big secret? I was lying on the sofa with my back perched up against Dale's chest, and the silence was golden. It felt like forever, but it was only a few minutes. I felt Dale reach over and put his glass down on the table, and his body was tense in a way that I had never felt before. I put my glass down beside his and swung around so that I could see him. I wanted to see his expression with whatever was going to come out of his mouth.

'Dale, whatever you have to tell me, please remember that I love you.' His hand grasped mine, and he took a deep breath. He looked terrified.

'Will you let me finish everything I have to say before you ask any questions?' He made me promise before he would continue, and now I was nervous for him.

'Of course. I promise.' I had to try and sit still. My mind and body was a wreck just thinking about what was to come.

'Can you remember how I told you that I was adopted?'

'Yeah.'

'Well, that isn't entirely true. My parents did die twelve years ago . . . They were on a camping trip in Canada, and they got lost. They were looking for their camp for hours when they came across two bears. They froze on the spot . . . They didn't know whether to run or stand still, but my dad managed to whisper to my mum, "Don't move a muscle." These bears were not in a playful mood, and they made a charge at my parents. They certainly didn't have much of a chance against two of them. They left my parents for dead . . .' I felt cold from this story, but I was confused in more ways than one.

'I don't understand. How do you know this story like you were there?' He was telling the story like he was a spectator. I wasn't grasping what he was trying to tell me. I touched his face as I had seen the tears well up in his eyes, and I was close to tears myself. I hated seeing the man I loved in so much pain.

'Please, Ash, let me finish.'

'My mum and dad knew that they were going to die . . . They didn't think that there would be a cure or that anyone could save them in time . . . They heard the trees move, and their first thought was that the bears had come back to finish them off . . .' I had chills down my spine hearing of this horror story, and I hated watching Dale go through the whole story. 'But two people came towards them . . . My dad always said he thought that he had already died and gone to heaven. They were beautiful. One man and one woman . . . They were very pale skinned, and when they touched my mom and dad, they were very cold. My mom pleaded with them to help. She could only think about me, Callum, and Nikki . . . The two strangers started talking amongst themselves, and the next thing that my parents could recall was these two things . . . Biting their neck . . . It sounded like a horror story . . . It still is when I relive it. I was at home with the nanny and my brother and sister. We can remember getting told that our parents were missing, and the authorities thought that they had been attacked by bears. My grandparents were there to take care of us . . . I can remember it like it was yesterday. The police never found any bodies so we couldn't have a funeral, but we did hold a memorial service for them.' I was crying now, pretty hard. Dale put his arms around me to console me, and I sunk my face in his chest. Although I didn't know his parents, I felt the pain in his story. I also knew what it was like to lose your parents. I wouldn't wish it on my worst enemy.

'I don't understand how you know the whole story if they went missing.' My head was all over the place, and I didn't know what I had missed.

'My parents showed up three months later. There was only me, my brother, and my sister at home. We couldn't believe our eyes at first. My dad sat us down and explained the whole story from start to finish.'

'Am I being so stupid? Have I missed something?' I could be a dizzy blonde at the best of times, but put me into a riddle, and I couldn't help but be dumb.

'No, Ashley, you haven't missed anything. I thought the same after I had heard the story . . . They were . . . bitten by vampires.' I shot my head up very quickly. I thought that I wasn't hearing this story right. *Vampires didn't exist, did they?*

'Vampires.' I managed to stumble the word out, but something inside me thought that he was joking. I couldn't believe that he was telling me this story.

'I know that this is too much to take in. I was the same when I found out. I would understand if you get up and run.' Reality hit me now. This was no joke. It was the truth. Every last detail was the truth.

'So they are not dead?'

'Technically they are, but they are still around.' I had watched films and read books about vampires, but I always thought that they were made up. I would never have guessed this in a million years.

'How do they live? I mean what do they eat?' I knew all the mythical answers, but I also knew that something was going to shock me.

'That is why they stayed away for a few months . . . The two vampires that changed them were trained vampires. They can live without human blood. They don't kill people for fun, and they taught my parents everything that they know.'

'So they live a normal life?' What was normal? I had to ask the stupidest questions of all. But I was dumbfounded that my lover had got to live with this every day and that he had trusted me enough to share it with me.

'That is why we moved from sunny Florida. We started afresh in Canada, and when I graduated, I moved here to Anchorage. No one knows anything, and no one suspects a thing when they come to visit.'

'That is why they like hunting.' The penny was starting to drop now, and I was finally catching on to everything.

'Yes . . . you seem to be taking this a lot better than I expected.' I felt like I was dumb on the whole subject of vampires, but I would pick it up quickly. This was his parents not him. I couldn't possibly blame him for any of this.

'I am not going to lie. I am shocked beyond belief. But as I said, it is you that I love, no matter what your family are . . . What about your brother and sister?'

'My brother lives in New York. He gets on with life just like me. We have accepted it. But Nikki lives with my mom and dad. She has never quite accepted it. She wants to be changed.'

'So that she can be like them.'

'I guess so. But if she was being honest, I think she would probably tell us it was to see what it was like . . . To accept it all and move on. But my mom and dad have told her that they would never change someone unless it was totally necessary.' If this was the only skeleton that was going to come out of his closet, then I could live with it. I wanted to live with it, with him.

'What are you thinking, Ash?'

'I really don't know.' I really didn't know. My mind was totally blank, and no matter what I was thinking, it didn't make sense.

'Do you want me to take you home?' He thought that I was going to run and never come back. That was never going to happen, especially over this.

'No, of course, I don't. I am very grateful that you told me, but it is going to take a lot more than your horror story to get rid of me.' I threw my arms around his neck. I never wanted to let go. I could feel all the tension ease away from his body, like someone had taken a huge weight off his shoulders.

'This wasn't the response that I expected, babe. I have never shared any of this with a single person before.' Dale placed a kiss on my lips, so soft and tender. He looked at me with so much passion, that it made my heart skip a beat.

'Why? I mean, why did you share it with me?'

'I just feel that what we have is forever. I didn't want to let months go by keeping a secret from you . . . As I said, I thought that you would run a mile, and I couldn't bear to hurt you . . . I have fallen head over heels in love with you, Ash . . . When I told my dad about you, he said that you were a keeper, and we couldn't start a relationship based on lies or secrets.' Every word hit me like a bullet to the chest. No one had ever said anything so nice to me, and no one had ever cared for me the way he had before.

'Mr Black, you could never hurt me. You don't have a bad bone in your body.' My whole body was aching for his touch and his kiss. I stood up and took his hand until he was standing beside me. 'Are you going to lead the way to the bedroom?' I had never taken the lead before, but with Dale, I didn't need my shell to hide behind. I could be the person that I have always wanted to be.

'Are you sure?'

'Of course, I am sure that I want to make love to you. Nothing has changed the way I feel about you.' I followed behind Dale, along the corridor and into the small bedroom. There was a bed and a dressing table, but nothing much else. He took me by the waist and kissed my neck. I felt like I was going to fall, but he had most of my weight.

'Ashley, a lot of years have passed, and I never thought I was ever going to fall in love with someone like you . . .'

'Shh.' I placed my finger over his lips. I knew exactly how he felt about me, and right now, I wanted him inside me. My hands slipped his buttons open on his shirt as he kissed every inch of my mouth and neck. I could feel how swollen my lips were; they were hungry for him. He pulled my tunic over my head to reveal my white-lace bra. I was normally so self-conscious about my body, but when I was with him, I felt like a model.

'You are so beautiful, Ash.' His breathing was out of control. I heard the words, but I didn't want to acknowledge them. I didn't even feel him loosen my jeans. It was like he was invisible. My breasts were swollen, and my body was a quivering wreck. He undid his jeans and slipped them off as I sat on the bed and edged my way back slightly. I couldn't stop staring at his muscular body. He leant over me in just his boxers; his kiss was so sweet and tender. I rubbed my hands down his body and around his back as he kissed every inch of my body. I was like electric. I arched my back as he loosened my bra. His mouth took my breasts, and he bit my nipples softly. The groans escaped my mouth as he moved down and took my pants off. *Was it possible to climax from just his touch?* I felt him kiss my thighs up into my sex. I couldn't breathe.

His tongue on my clitoris sent my body into spasms. His mouth kissed my body all the way back up to my neck 'I love you, Ash.'

'I love you too.' My breathing was erratic, and my heart was racing as I felt his package rub against me. His hand lifted my leg as I felt him enter my sex soft and slow. Our love making was just mind-blowing. I wanted him over and over again. He slid in and out of me as my body climaxed over again. My nails were embedded into his back like a wild animal, and his final thrust made him shudder on top of me. We lay on the bed not moving. Our breathing was just as fast as each other. I could stay in this embrace forever.

'Are you OK, hun?' His voice was so passionate and caring.

'Of course . . . why do you ask me that every time after . . . ?' Dale lifted his head to look at me, and I had never seen him look so sensitive.

'I just don't want to hurt you.'

'Why are you going to hurt me? Do you have any other secrets?' His head shook softly as a slight smile crept up on his lips.

'I wish that we could stay in this position forever.'

'Well, I don't know about forever, but we can lie here for as long as you like.'

'Sounds good.' Dale reached down and pulled a fur blanket over the two of us. I didn't know what it was with all the fur blankets, but my skin was becoming accustomed to it. I placed my cheek on his chest and lay oblivious to everything that had happened today. I was exhausted. My eyes closed as I felt myself drift off to sleep. The boat was going to be kept stationed today, but I was glad that he had showed me one of his hot spots. It was just what we needed.

One month later . . .

Chapter 8

Surprises

Our drive to work always seemed to drag in. I was sitting admiring the cold winter's morning, and the crisp leaves were all blowing off the trees. Who would have thought that bare trees could be so beautiful. I always took for granted what we had before, but it wasn't until you moved to somewhere like Alaska that you would appreciate what you had around you.

'Can you believe that we have been here a whole month?' It was hard to believe that a month had passed. It was one of those months that you had to keep nipping yourself, to make sure that you were not dreaming.

'I know, Christine. It has been amazing.' Christine took her eyes off the road to look at me, and I wondered what was coming next. I really wished I could be a mind-reader so that I could tell what was coming.

'Are you happy, Ash?' I had wondered when this subject was going to come back up. She had let the whole me and Dale subject drop lately.

'I honestly couldn't be happier, babe.' I really wanted her to accept me and Dale together as a couple, and by the smile on her face, it looked like today could be the day.

'I am happy for you, Ash. You deserve it.' Finally, I could see that she really did mean everything. I felt a huge weight lift from my shoulders. It meant so much having her on board.

'Thank you, honey, it really does mean a lot.' Christine was my best friend, my flatmate, and my family. I loved her dearly, and I wouldn't want to choose between her and Dale. The rest of the journey was completed in silence, and already, my day couldn't get any better. As we pulled into the car park, I noticed that it was very busy. I wondered if there was something on that I had forgotten about.

'Why is it so busy today?'

'I can't think of anything. Besides, it is too late if we have forgotten about something, Ash.' Christine always knew how to make a joke out of a bad situation. I never normally forgot about anything, but there could be a first for everything. We managed to find a car space and got out to gather up all our belongings. It was one of the coldest mornings that I had felt in Anchorage, and I couldn't wait to get inside for a heat. We got inside the building, and it didn't seem any busier. It certainly didn't explain all the cars outside.

'Meet you at lunch, if you are in the building.' Why did she just say that? Did she know something that I didn't?

'Where else am I going to be?' We both stopped and looked at each other, and Christine smiled as she walked in her direction. For the first time in weeks, I felt nervous. What was she up to? It had been a strange morning, and Christine wasn't a good liar. Standing waiting on the elevator to ping was like watching the kettle boil. But when it finally pinged open, it was empty; now that was a first. I got in and waited to reach my floor, and it was taking forever this morning. I got to the tenth floor eventually, and I wasn't sure if I was huffed or chuffed about it. The office was very quiet, only Steph, the receptionist, was on the floor.

'Good morning, Ashley.' She was her usual happy self. Everyone who worked on this floor was happy at work.

'Morning, Steph, It is very quiet this morning.'

'I know. There aren't many people in. They must be out meeting clients.' I knew that she was probably right. I just had a feeling in my stomach that something was going on, and they were normally right instincts.

'Can you bring me a coffee, please, honey?' I didn't like sending people to do chores for me, but I was running a little bit late already.

'Sure.' I moved into my office and threw my bags down on the couch. It looked the same. Nothing had changed that I could see of. I noticed an envelope on my desk that was addressed to me, and I opened it slowly and took out the note.

Ashley,

Can you meet me in the conference suite, please?

Dale

xx

I looked at the note and looked at the door. It took a few seconds to register what I had read in the note. I left my bags as they were and moved out of my office towards the conference suite. The door was closed, and I quickly thought that I was late. That would just be my luck. I didn't want to interrupt, but I knew that I was going to have to. I knocked on the door and listened for an answer, but there was nothing. I turned the handle and walked in slowly. The room was in complete darkness. I felt the wall for the switch and turned the light on. I got the fright of my life. Everyone I knew was standing at the top of the table smiling at me. I could feel my face go scarlet. The heat was rising in my cheeks. I spotted Dale walking towards me with a huge smile on his face. I could have run in the opposite direction. He took my hands and looked into my eyes. It was probably better that he took my hands. I couldn't run away that easily.

'What is going on?' His smile was infectious, and now I was smiling with him. 'Ashley, I know we haven't been together long, but when I am with you, I feel complete. I can't imagine my life without you.' A few seconds went silent, and I wanted to know what was coming next. He bent down on to one knee and held a box open in front of me. I was speechless. 'Will you do me the honour of becoming my wife?' Did I hear him right? Everyone was smiling at us, and I knew what I wanted to say, but my mouth was stuck shut. 'Ashley.' I snapped out of my daze and looked into his eyes and managed to whisper 'Yes.'

'Was that a yes?' He was looking at me for confirmation.

'Yes, yes, yes.' Dale took the beautiful diamond ring out of the box and placed it on my finger. I was so happy that tears escaped my eyes. He got up and threw his arms around me, and everyone cheered and clapped as I clung to my husband-to-be. Christine interrupted our embrace by giving us both a glass of champagne.

'Congratulations to both of you.' Everyone took it in turns to congratulate us, and I was still in shock. I couldn't get my head around the fact that I was going to be Mrs Dale Black.

'You have made me the happiest man alive.'

'You certainly know how to do things in style.'

'For you nothing is too much. I would go to the end of the earth and back for you, my love.' He kissed me so gently in front of everybody, and normally, I would be so embarrassed, but I couldn't care today. Everybody seemed invisible. 'I have another surprise for you.' I didn't know how many more surprises I could take this morning.

'What is it?' Dale tapped his glass to get everyone's attention, and all eyes peered on towards us, and he put his arm around me. I could take anything if his arm was wrapped around me.

'Thank you everyone for helping me to arrange this surprise for my wife-to-be . . . I would like you to carry on the celebration on our behalf, but I am going to whisk my fiancée away for a couple more surprises.' Dale looked down at me to see how I was bearing up. Everyone was cheering at us as Dale took my hand and guided us out of the room.

'Do you need anything out of your office?'

'Yes, my bag.' We walked to my office, and I quickly grabbed my bag. Before I could even catch my breath, I was being whisked away to the elevator. Everything was happening so quickly.

'Where are we going?' I was very inquisitive. I was like a child going somewhere that they didn't know about.

'All will be revealed, honey.' He knew that I didn't like surprises. He was just playing with me. We got out of the elevator on the ground floor and walked out of the building. I couldn't spot Carlos anywhere. I thought that he maybe forgot about us, but that wasn't like him either. Dale pulled me off towards this lovely black sports car, and it had a pink bow placed on the top. I was that stupid that I still didn't catch on to what was happening. Dale could hardly contain his excitement.

'Surprise number one, honey.' I was in shock. Had he bought me a sports car?

'I don't understand.'

'It is yours, Ash. An engagement present.' He handed me the keys, and I didn't know what to say. I couldn't believe that he bought me a car. I walked towards it and put my hand on it, like it was going to disappear.

'Don't you like it, Ash?' I didn't know how to say what I had to without feeling or sounding horrible.

'It is lovely.'

'But?'

'It is too much . . . I mean I never drive anywhere. If Carlos doesn't drive, then you drive.'

'Well, now is your chance, babe.' He really wanted me to accept this gift, but I didn't know if I could. 'Please let me shower you with gifts, hun.'

Deep down I knew how much this meant to him, and I couldn't possibly hurt his feelings. I held out my hand to take the keys, and his face lit up. He was so happy that I accepted the keys from him.

'Where are we going?'

'Just get in, and I will give you directions.' *How much happier can we get?* I never thought that it would ever be possible for me to be so happy.

'No more gifts!' I realised that I was sounding very ungrateful, but I had the one and only gift that I ever needed: him.

'Not really a gift as such, more of a surprise.' We both got in the car and sat and looked at each other. He leant over and kissed me so delicately that I didn't want him to stop. 'Miss Malone, can you remember how to get to the cottage in the mountains?'

'My attention is never on the road when we get chauffeured.'

'I will give you directions.' If anyone was reading our body language right now, they would sense that we were flirting with one another. I entered the office as normal and left as an engaged woman. I had a smile from ear to ear, and my happiness was displayed all over my face. My mind wondered what we were going to the cottage for? What was the surprise? I followed all the directions very carefully. I was frightened to death of doing something silly. The road up the mountains was very narrow, and I was cautious about being so close to the edge.

'We are on the last hurdle now, just another minute.' I recognised this bit of the road, and I could remember the branch off bit for the cottage. 'Take the road that forks off to the right.' I could see the black Mercedes already parked in front of us. *Why would Carlos be here?*

'You have done well, babe.' He was just being sarcastic now. I could drive. I just chose not to.

'You mean that I got us here in one piece.'

'I didn't doubt you for one minute.' He sounded very tense, just like he did the day he shared his family secret with me. Why did he look like he had seen a ghost?

'If you are not ready for this, we can turn around now.' I was puzzled. What could I possibly not be ready for? He looked at the cottage and twisted towards me, his hand grasped mine. 'I got Carlos to pick my family up.' In my mind I knew that this day would come. But I never expected it right this second.

'Family . . . Your parents . . . Your brother and sister . . .'

'Just my parents and Nikki. My brother is going to join us later.' I was ready for this; of course, I was.

'They won't hurt me?' I actually laughed at my own question, but Dale didn't laugh with me. He obviously knew that I was nervous. It isn't every day that you get to meet vampires.

'They won't hurt you. I am human as well, remember, and so is Nikki.'

'Let's do it. Of course, I want to meet them.' Dale kissed my hand and got out of the car. I sat still. As much as I wanted to get out, something made me stay put. Dale came around and opened my door, and he took my hand and helped me to get out of the car. A little bit of encouragement was all I needed.

'It is OK. They are looking forward to meeting you.' I followed Dale to the cottage, and we entered through the front door. Something was cooking, and it smelt delicious.

'It is OK.' Dale's encouraging voice reassured me. I was just overreacting as usual.

'Mom . . . Dad.' The first person who came towards me was a young teenage girl. She was very like Dale. I assumed that this was Nikki.

'Hey, Ashley, I am Nikki. It is very nice to meet you, eventually.' Nikki wrapped her arms around my neck; she was very nice and friendly.

'It is nice to meet you too, Nikki. I have heard so much about you.'

'All good, I hope.' We were all smiling like we had known each other for years. I felt honoured to be amongst people like them.

'Ashley, this is my mom Mhairi and my dad Jake.' They looked so young and very pale skin, but unless Dale had told me about their secret, I would never have guessed. 'Mom, Dad, I would like you to meet my fiancée, Ashley.' I could see their surprise in their faces. They only thought that they were meeting his girlfriend. Was this surprise for me or for them? Jake walked towards me, and my heart sank. I didn't know how to act.

'Ashley dear, it is so nice to meet you. Welcome to our family. It is nice to finally see our son settle down with a lovely girl.' I looked at this man standing in front of me. Why was I being so protective? Anyone could see that Jake was as kind and gentle as Dale. I stepped forward and shook his hand, and he placed a kiss on my cheek. We were both as shocked as each other. 'It is nice to meet you, Jake.' Mhairi then stepped forward to be beside Jake. She seemed quite frightened of me.

'It is nice to meet you, dear.' I really didn't know how to react to her. She wasn't as welcoming as Jake and Nikki.

'Mhairi, it is nice to meet you too.'

'Why don't you two get a drink? We will finish off with brunch, and congratulations on your engagement.' Everyone seemed very welcoming towards me, and I was very grateful for their hospitality. It couldn't be easy for them either. Nikki had come back in towards us with her jacket on.

'Dale, do you mind if I use your car?'

'No, but get Carlos to drive you.'

'Nikki, get Carlos to take mine. It will save me moving it.' I wasn't into the whole reversing just yet. I would probably go over the cliff.

'Thanks, sis.' The room went very quiet as Dale and I stood all on our lonesome. 'Thank you, honey . . .'

'Is that your convertible?' Dale was interrupted as his sister came rushing back in. We immediately thought that something was wrong with her.

'Yeah, it is. Why?' She ran over and gave me a hug. I really didn't know what all the fuss was about. It was only a car. 'You are going to be the best big sister, ever.' Dale and I watched as she run back out the door. What was that all about?

'OK. Now that she has got that out of her system, what were you going to say?'

'I can't remember, but I do know that you have just made her day.'

'How good it must be to be a teenager!' I was still looking at the door in amazement at Nikki's response to my car.

'Thank you for making me the happiest man alive and for being here meeting my parents. I really didn't know what you were going to say today, so I guess I am relieved to be standing here with my bride-to-be.'

'Did you think I would say no today?' 'No' never even crossed my mind this morning. I could vaguely remember all the faces. I was very surprised that I managed to say anything.

'I expected to be picking you up off the floor after you saw all the faces gazing at you . . . I didn't think you would say "no", but I wasn't sure if you would say yes.'

'Why? Isn't that what two people do when they are in love.'

'I can't explain what was going through my head this morning. For once I was the nervous wreck. But here we are with a long and happy future ahead of us.' Dale's voice was so flirtatious that my mind had forgotten all about vampires. As grateful as I was to be here meeting his family, I just wanted to be alone with him. 'I didn't think that I would ever introduce my parents to anyone, so thank you. Today seeing you with my dad was one moment that I will never forget . . . Apart from you coming into my life and agreeing to be my wife.' I couldn't resist myself any longer. The urge to kiss him was so strong. I leant forward in his arms and placed a kiss on his lips. Why did he have to kiss me back? Now I only wanted more. His tongue invaded my mouth so passionately that my heart was beating so fast.

'Sorry, you two.' I pulled away from Dale, with an embarrassed look on my face. How could we be caught in an embrace like that, by his dad of all people? I thought if vampires could blush, then Jake would be the same colour as me.

'Dad, it's OK. Let me help you.' Dale walked over to Jake and took the plates off him.

'Where did you get your manners from, Son?' Dale and I looked as guilty as each other. What was Mr Black going to come out with next? 'You haven't got your lovely wife a drink yet.' I sighed with relief. I honestly thought that we were going to get a lecture on the birds and the bees. We were all laughing together. It was a special moment that would probably live with me forever.

'We were too busy talking, Dad.'

'Tonsil talking, that is a new one.' Jake was certainly the joker. It was nice to have someone like him around to break the ice. My cheeks would probably be able to heat the room up, now though.

'You will get used to my dad's humour, babe. He thinks that he is funny.'

'A bit of humour is always good.' We were both ganging up on Dale right now, and I just knew that he would get his own back at some point. He was taking it in his stride just like he did with everything. He obviously took that from his dad. It was nearly lunchtime, and I couldn't believe how much fun I was having. It was nice to have an extended family around, even if they weren't human. After losing my parents, my extended family dwindled away over time, and I got used to it being me and Christine.

'You will regret encouraging him, Ash.' Jake walked back into the kitchen, looking all pleased with his actions.

'Your dad is lovely.'

'Yeah, he tries his best.' Dale took me by the waist and looked at me, like something was bothering him. I knew him only too well now. He can't hide his feelings or emotions from me. 'I am sorry about my mom. It is not like her.'

'Don't be. It must be just as strange for her as it is me.' I tried to sound reasonable because none of this was Dale's fault. I knew how I felt sitting in the car, so I could only imagine what was going through Mhairi's mind.

'She is around humans all the time, Ash. There is no excuse.' I was worried that she didn't like me now. Why was she being off with me? I never thought about her being around humans a lot; that was me acting blonde again.

'Excuse me the now. Make yourself comfortable, doll. I will bring you a drink back.' That was kind of hard now. How could I be comfortable when I knew that he was going to confront his mother on my behalf? I moved over to the couch and sat down. That wasn't such a good idea either because all my mind could do was flicker back to my encounters with Dale on this very couch. I felt hot and bothered at this precise moment. I wanted Dale enough without thinking about it.

'Ashley dear.' I glanced up at Mhairi as she came and sat beside me, and her cold hand took mine. I couldn't believe how cold she felt. 'I need to apologise . . . I wasn't very sociable when you arrived . . .' I went to interrupt her, but she somehow managed to stop me from talking. 'I am over the moon that my son has found love. I thought that he was going to let it bypass him because of what we were . . . I guess I got scared of how you would react to us in person, and I wanted to give you some space. I really didn't mean to be so blunt with you.' I tightened my grip on her hand as I took everything in.

'First of all, you don't need to give me any apology. You were nicer than I expected. Second of all, Dale is going to get a row from me. I never even noticed your bluntness towards me until he pointed it out. But finally, I am glad that you came over to speak with me. It has cleared the air.' I leant forward and placed a kiss on Mhairi's cheek and gave her a hug. I really didn't want to be the daughter-in-law who didn't get along with her mother-in-law. I spotted Dale coming back through from the kitchen, and Mhairi stood up. 'I better get back to the kitchen before they burn it down.' Mhairi placed a kiss on Dale's cheek like any loving mother would do. 'I hope that you two will be very happy together. Ashley is a keeper.' I felt very honoured to hear Mhairi say such a thing about me. It meant a lot. Dale sat down beside me and handed me a glass of champagne.

'I should be mad at you, Mr Black, but since I love you, I will let you off.'

'I did it because I love you, babe. Everything I do is with love.' I loved this man more than words could explain, but right now, I suddenly felt really weird. I curled in beside him and placed my head on his chest. I really wanted this sickly feeling to pass, but it was getting worse. I handed him my glass to put on the table. I really didn't know what was wrong with me. I felt fine five minutes ago.

'Are you OK, Ash?'

'I think I have had too much champagne on an empty stomach.' I got up quickly and rushed to the bathroom. Of all the days I had to catch a bug, it had to be today. I just made the toilet and no more. I really hated being sick. My stomach felt on fire. Dale's hand rubbed my back as he perched down beside me. He must have run behind me to get here just as quick.

'Ashley, sweetheart, are you OK?' I didn't want him to see me like this. I really wished I could be invisible.

'Hmm, I will be fine. I haven't eaten this morning, and I think all the wine has bubbled in my tummy.' He pulled my hair out of my face and sat down beside me. I pulled the toilet seat down and flushed before I cuddled into Dale's chest. 'You don't have to be here, you know.' I was giving him the get-up-and-go card. I didn't want him to think that he had to stay beside me because he was my fiancé.

'In sickness and in health, babe, I am not going anywhere.' I felt so comfortable here in his arms that I could quite easily fall asleep. A knock on the bathroom door made me look up, and I could see two faces stood staring down at us.

'Ashley dear, are you OK?' Mhairi sounded very concerned. I guessed that was her maternal side kicking in.

'I think it is just a bug. I will be fine.' I tried to be reassuring, but they could see past my brave face.

'You have gone very pale, dear.' Even Jake was showing his concerned father routine.

'I hope you don't mind, Mom, but I am going to get Ashley home for some rest.' I felt that all the fuss was really not needed. I would be fine.

'Of course, Son . . . Take some soup with you, and let me know how Ashley is in the morning.' Dale stood up first and helped me up on to my feet, but I felt very faint. Dale grabbed my arm as I stumbled. This sickness bug had really floored me. 'Do you not want to get a doctor?'

'I will be fine, Mhairi. Honestly, some sleep will do me the world of good.' Dale bent down and picked me up, and I was cradled in his arms like a baby. This concerned husband routine was going to suit him to a 'T'.

'Mom, I am going to take the Merc. Will you tell Carlos to drive back with Ashley's car? And I will send him back up here for you.' I seemed to be flying through the cottage. Dale was very fast and very strong, and if I had my eyes open, I could have been sick again. I could sense that he was worried, but he needed to calm down; it wasn't like I was dying.

'Dale, I will take you home, and then I can bring the car back for Carlos.' It really wasn't like Dale, not to have the best plan, but his mind was elsewhere today.

'Perfect, Dad. Thank you.' We were in the car before I could blink. I curled up into Dale on the back seat, and I felt secure, just like a baby would in its mother's womb. My eyes couldn't stay open, no matter how hard I tried. I had never ever felt this exhausted in my life. I was just glad that I had my rock beside me. I could get through anything as long as he was around to catch me.

CHAPTER 9

My Care

I could feel my eyelids flicker open. The room was warm and still and quite dark. All I could see was a dim light coming from the desk in the corner of the room. I managed to sit myself up without making a sound, and I could see the outline of Dale, sitting at the desk with his laptop in deep concentration. I didn't want to startle him, so I just sat looking at him, taking it all in. I couldn't believe that he had stuck around while I was sleeping. I did hope that he hadn't sat there too long. I didn't want his life to stop because I had a bug.

'Hey.' I spoke one word, and my husband-to-be was dropping everything to be by my side. He never failed to amaze me.

'Hey, sweetheart, how are you feeling?' His warm hand on my cheek soothed me back into relaxation.

'I am fine. How long have I been asleep?'

'Since we came home yesterday.'

'What time is it?' Did I even want to know the answer to that question?

'Just after 11 a.m.' I was shocked. I never slept for hours and hours like that. My body was obviously needing it, though, and who was I to complain about it.

'Why didn't you wake me? I have to go to work.' I jumped out of bed and stumbled on my feet. Thank God that Dale caught me or I would have ended up on my backside.

'Please get back into bed, babe. Work is covered for today. I am doing what I can from home, and you, my dear, are going to take things easy.' I got back under the covers and sat with my head in my hands. I still felt very weak. I couldn't remember ever feeling as ill in my life. I thought that I was immune to bugs and viruses because I never got ill.

'My mom has got us well stocked up on soup.' They had been over here, and I was sleeping—typical for me to be unwell when people visit.

'Why didn't you wake me?' I felt really unsociable at the best of times, and I didn't want his family to think I wasn't nice.

'Do you think that my mom would have let me wake you? Her motto is plenty of bed rest when you are ill. Sleep is the best cure apparently. Besides, they have decided to stick around for a few weeks. You should be honoured that they never stick around for me.' Dale moved closer to me and placed a kiss on my cheek. I didn't care about anything when I had him close to me. It was like he could erase everything bad from my mind. 'I am going to heat you up some soup. Mhairi's orders.' I lay back in bed as he pulled the covers back up on me. I was going to have to get used to him fussing over me. 'Don't move.' His voice was stern with me for the first time ever, and it was quite amusing hearing him.

'Yes, sir.' Dale seemed to be on automatic lately; he rushed out of the room and down to the kitchen in a second. What was the rush? I really liked that he had a nice caring side to him, not many men showed that side. His mom was lovely for bringing me soup. Her cooking smelt delicious yesterday. Since our rocky start yesterday, hopefully things were back on track. I just knew that we all would get along just fine. They had a very nice aura about them. His bed was just so comfortable, and I could get used to days like this, just minus the ill bit.

'Here we go, sweetie. It smells delicious. My mom always was good at making soup.' Dale placed a tray on my knee and sat down beside me.

The soup did smell delicious. I just hoped that I could keep it down. The orange juice was my first stop. My mouth felt like sandpaper.

'It does smell good, but the orange juice will take a lot of beating.'

'There is plenty more where that came from. My mom squeezed a full jug before she left.' I couldn't believe how sweet everyone was being to me right now. I was lucky to have a nice family behind me.

'That was nice of her. She is very sweet. Your parents seem so normal for their way of living . . . I feel so lucky to be a part of it.' Listen to me rambling on, it was a good job I was feeling ill. At least I had an excuse for feeling sentimental.

'My mom has her moments. You two will get along just fine. I cannot be happier to see my whole family get along . . .' I could see the relief in his eyes as he spoke to me. It was a big thing for him. 'Yesterday was the best day of my life, until you got sick, of course. I would rather take any illness for you.' The way I was feeling today, I could quite easily cry at how nice he was. It was scary to think that I had given up on ever finding the man of my dreams and now here I was in the perfect relationship.

'Even though I caught this bug . . . yesterday was just perfect. Thank you.'

'No thank you, honey. Now less talking and more eating. I want you back on the mend so that we can finish our celebrations.'

'That sounds like a plan. I will be right as rain tomorrow for work.' As soon as I said work, I knew that Dale would have something to say about that.

'We will see about that in the morning, soon-to-be Mrs Black.' I didn't answer him back because I was too busy actually enjoying my soup, and I liked to keep him guessing.

'It is good to see you eat. I was worried about you sleeping all that time without food or drink. I will have to get my mom to stock our freezer up with this soup.'

'It is delicious. It is weird hearing you say "ours" as opposed to "mine" or "yours".' That had to be the quickest that I had ever eaten anything. I felt full and satisfied with my light lunch. But I wasn't satisfied at how quiet my fiancé had gone. 'What is wrong, Dale?' I propped my pillows up and lay back to look at him.

'I was going to get to that part, just not today with you being ill. But since it has come up . . .' I didn't realise what I had said or what was going to come next, but I was curious.

'What? Spit it out.' I took his hand to reassure him that whatever he was going to say, it would be fine.

'Well, I know that you haven't long moved here with Christine, but I was going to ask you to move in with me. We can stay here until we find somewhere new that we both like. Obviously here in Anchorage or close to . . .' I don't know why I didn't know what to say because I knew him now, and nothing that he ever said to me was going to make me run away. 'I just thought that since we were getting married, it would be the next obvious step forward.' His sweet face made my body feel all weak and tender. Of course, it was the next step; why wouldn't it be?

'I haven't even thought about it . . . I guess that we have been having too much fun, for me to think about the serious stuff. I don't want to leave Christine in the lurch. She is like my sister.' My head sank to my knees. I didn't want him to see me upset again. I felt Dale's hand on my shoulder as my comfort blanket, and I realised that Christine and I were going to move on at some point in our lives.

'Look at me, Ash.' Sitting still was the easy part, but raising my head to look at the man I love was the tricky bit. We needed to face all these hurdles together as one, and my hiding wasn't going to solve anything. I looked up and wiped my tears away. I was like a hormonal blubbering wreck for no reason at all.

'What is wrong, Ash? You can tell me anything. I want us to be open with one another.' We both wanted to be truthful with one another, and I couldn't ask for any more. His honesty was just what I needed.

'Honestly, it is nothing. I am just being silly. I just don't know how to break this to Christine.' I didn't know why I bothered so much about Christine because I knew if the tables were turned, then she would be off like a shot. It just didn't make me feel any easier about the whole thing.

'Ash, we are getting married. Christine is a clever woman. She probably knows that this next step is on the horizon.' He was right, but the strong feelings that I had for Christine was like a motherly love. How could I break the news to her without tearing us apart?

'I know that you are right. I will think of a way to break it to her gently . . .' I just needed to grow a pair and put myself first for a change. Everyone who mattered would stand by me, no matter what I decided to do. 'By the way . . . I like here Mr Black. Don't you like this house?'

I was all over the place today. I couldn't understand myself so how was Dale meant to? I didn't know that he would give this house up for me, and I didn't want him to think that he had to.

'I like this house, Ash. But I am not sure I can picture us here as husband and wife, raising a family.' Dale climbed into bed beside me and lay us both down so that our eyes met each other. It was so nice to be lying here with my man, discussing our future.

'I like how you can see our future planned out. It sounds nice. Two point four children and a long and happy life together. What more could we ask for . . . ?' Everything felt complete when we were together, and nothing was going to break how we felt. 'Can I say something?'

'Anything, Ash. I want you to be open with me.' Every time this man opened his mouth, I fell in more love with him. I didn't even know why I asked because I knew that he would listen to anything that I had to say.

'I really love the cottage in the mountains as our getaway. We could, maybe, find somewhere similar but bigger and child-friendly for future sake.'

'So you would like somewhere like the cottage?' I stroked his cheek and rubbed his lips with my thumb.

'That cottage will be ours until the last one of us is standing. I fell in love with the cottage the very same way that I fell in love with you.'

'We will have a long and happy life together, Ash, and the cottage will be sick of seeing us.'

'Sounds good.'

'Enough of this today. We have plenty of planning time when you are better. Let's just use this time to vegetate, and hopefully tomorrow you are feeling better.' Dale turned on to his back, and I placed my head on his chest. His heartbeat against my face was so soothing, and his hand tilted my head back so that he could place the gentlest kiss on my lips. My lips were tingling from it, and they wanted more. But today he wasn't going to give in to our sexual tension.

'I love you, Ash.'

'I love you, Mr Black.' I lay very still. My eyes were getting heavier and heavier, and I really didn't want to sleep. Sleeping would block out this magical morning, and I didn't want to ever block out the memories that we shared together.

My eyes felt very refreshed as I sat up in bed, and the room was light and empty. How long had I been sleeping this time was the first thing that crept into my mind. The house sounded so quiet, and I could hear the birds outside chirping away. I climbed out of bed and put my dressing gown on. My body still felt very weak, considering that I had slept the clock round over the last couple of days. I walked down the stairs and headed for the kitchen because I could hear someone cluttering around. I really wanted it to be Dale and not the hired help. I did hope and pray that I haven't missed him already. My luck was changing when I looked in to the kitchen, and there pottering around was my husband-to-be.

'Hey, good morning, Ash.'

'Morning, honey. Something smells good.' I was getting my appetite back because I could stomach strong smells.

'Come and sit down. I have made you some pancakes.' I could see him pay careful attention to what I was like this morning, but I felt a lot better today. There was no reason for him to be worrying about me now. 'You still look very pale, Ash.'

'Lack of air is making me pale. I feel fine this morning. I am hungry, so that is a good sign.'

'Coffee?'

'That is a silly question.' Dale placed my breakfast and coffee in front of me and joined me at the table. He was a perfect gentleman every minute of every day. 'You do know how to spoil me, Mr Black. I could get used to this.'

'Please do get used to it, Ash. You deserve it.'

'What is on the cards today?' I thought that I would chance my luck and see what he said to me. I had a funny feeling that I wouldn't like it though.

'You don't waste any time, do you?' My first lecture was brewing. It was weird how I could read him like a book. I had never been interested in anyone enough to get to know what they thought.

'I need to get back to work, Dale. We will go crazy if we stuck in the house another day. I need fresh air, and I will be 110 per cent. If I feel ill at work, I will phone Carlos to pick me up.' I was laying everything down on the table and playing every trick in the book to get my own way.

'You are one stubborn lady.' This was one conversation that he wasn't going to win. He could argue his point until he was blue in the face. I was going back to work today.

'You must have a lot to catch up on. You have been out of the office for two full days.'

'I wanted to be here with you, Ash. It wasn't a chore for me to be here. I do have a couple of clients to see today, but that doesn't mean you have to go back.'

'I know that I don't need to go back in today, but I want to. These pancakes will set me up for the day. They are delicious.' My taste buds were working this morning. Every mouthful was making my mouth water. My poor stomach must have thought that my throat was cut over the last couple of days.

'It is good to see you with an appetite, babe.'

'I know, I would never normally eat a big breakfast, but I need it this morning.' Dale got up and started putting his dishes over to the sink.

'Good morning.' Rosa came through very fresh and bubbly, and I was glad of the distraction.

'Good morning, Rosa.'

'How are you feeling this morning, Ashley?' Rosa had become like a mother figure in my life. She was always very nice towards me. Her smile melted my heart every time. She was just like Dale in many ways.

'I feel a lot better. Thank you, Rosa.'

'Good. If you need anything, please just ask me.'

'Thank you, Rosa.'

'Dale, leave all your dishes. I will sort the kitchen out.' She was a godsend to Dale, and I, I can't remember the last time that I had to lift a finger.

'Thank you, Rosa.' Rosa's hand rubbed across my shoulder as she walked past me. My mom always used to do that to me when she passed me sitting at the breakfast bar. It was weird how the older generation all had the same characteristics. I did hope that I could be like them one day.

'What would I do without you, Rosa?' Dale kissed Rosa on the cheek. He was very sweet with her as well. 'Now I am going to leave this touchy-feely kitchen to go and get a shower.'

'I will be up behind you, so don't go hoggin' it all morning, Mr Black.'

'Can you see what I have to put up with, Rosa?' It was really nice to see this side of Dale. His eyes winked at me as he left the kitchen, and I died and went to heaven. I moved off my seat to go and help Rosa clear up. I didn't like sitting doing nothing, especially when someone was clearing up our mess.

'You know, Ashley, I have never seen Dale look so happy. You two are a match made in heaven. I am glad that you have found one another.' It was nice to see that it wasn't just me who noticed Dale's happiness. It must be true if other people could notice as well.

'I have never been happier, Rosa. I am glad that we found one another.' Every day when I wake up, I realise how lucky I am. Not many people out there could say that they had a perfect life. But I was one of the lucky ones; everything was more than perfect.

'Ashley, go and get ready. I will take care of the kitchen.'

'Thank you, honey.' I headed out of the kitchen and walked up the stairs. I could hear the shower running, and immediately, I contemplated joining my fiancé. I reached the bathroom door and turned the handle, and of course, it opened. Who else would be walking into the bathroom? Dale probably knew that I couldn't resist the temptation. The room was all steamy, and I stripped off my pyjamas piece by piece. By the time I got to the shower, I was naked. I stepped in behind Dale, and my cold hands touched his back.

'Jesus, babe . . .' I couldn't stop myself from laughing at his jumpy body. 'Do you have a death wish?' Dale's heart was racing. He clearly never heard me coming in. We were both in fits of laughter, and it certainly cheered us both up.

'Your heart works any way.'

'You are funny, Miss Malone.'

'I wanted to surprise you.' Surprise was an understatement. I nearly killed him.

'You certainly know how to do that, babe.' He pulled my naked body close to his, and I could feel myself melt in front of him. I had longed for this moment for two days. We had been away from each other too long.

'I have missed you.'

'Me too, Ash. It has killed me the last couple of days seeing you ill.' I pulled his face down to me and took his mouth. His lips were mine, all mine. I felt every inch of his naked body tense around me. 'God, Ash, you are going to be the death of me. I have a meeting at 9.15 a.m.' I let my kisses trail off down to his nipples in a teasing motion. His hands pulled my head up to look at him. The water cascading down his muscles made my body go weak inside. 'Ash, I hate the term "quickie", but that is what this would be . . .' I placed my finger on his lips to silence him. I didn't care how long it took. I just needed to feel him close to me.

'Shh. Stop overthinking things, Mr Black. It can be our quick and steamy love-making session.'

'When you put it like that?' Dale backed my back up to the wall, and my body screamed from the cold tiles. If I was still half sleeping, I was fully awake now. He lifted me on top of him, and I cried out with pleasure as I felt him slide inside of me. His hands tangled in my hair as we were devouring each other's body. His long, hard package teased my clitoris every time he eased me back down on to him. My body felt hotter than the water as a climax quivered through my body. My cries of pleasure continued as he slid in and out of me, harder and harder, until his body shuddered against me. My head leant against his shoulder as we both caught our breath. 'I hope that lived up to your expectations of a "quick and steamy love-making session".' Anything with him lived up to my expectations. I didn't know why he was always so hard on himself.

'Anything with you would live up to my expectations.' My voice was still shaky, but this man made me feel things that I never thought was possible.

'I really hate myself for breaking this moment up. I just want to take you to bed and forget about work. I am sorry that I have to get ready for work.'

'Don't apologise. We can carry on where we left off tonight. There is plenty more moments like these.' I knew that I was teasing him more with my words, and I was just tantalising myself now.

'I love you, Ash.'

'I love you too . . .' I pulled his mouth down to meet mine, and it the electricity was going to start all over again. 'Will you get washed and go and get ready for work?' I knew if we stayed together any longer, there would be no work getting done at the office.

'Used and abused springs to my mind.' Dale had a cheeky grin on his face as he leant over to reach for the shower gel. I slapped his backside as he turned away from me, and I must say I quite enjoyed it.

'You are cheeky this morning. Has that bug went to your head?' I was beginning to ask myself the same question. I didn't know what was coming over me lately.

'No, you have gone to my head, Mr Black.'

'Enjoy your shower, Miss Malone.' I stood alone in this big shower and shook my head. Dale certainly knew how to drive me wild. I finished my shower off on my lonesome. I really did feel refreshed as I stepped out of the shower. My mind was clear to face the day, whatever it might bring.

CHAPTER 10

Misunderstandings

I felt really weird sitting here in the cafeteria. It felt like I had been away for weeks and not just three days. I had spent the first full morning on my own in the office and really hated it. I was missing Dale like crazy, and I was counting the hours down until home time.

'Hey, Ash, how are you feeling?' Christine broke my chain of thought as she threw her arms around me. She always had to be melodramatic. 'I have been so worried about you.' If she would shut up for a minute, I would be able to answer the questions that she asked me.

'I am fine. Feeling much better today . . . It was just a bug.' I didn't like all the fuss from everyone. I was better to just get on with it.

'Are you sure? You still look quite rough.' I couldn't help but laugh at my friend. She always knew how to make me feel like rubbish.

'You still know how to make people feel good about themselves, don't you?'

'Sorry, babe, I just tell you the truth. What are you doing back?' Christine was like Dale, in so many ways. They were sensitive, caring, and protective, and they always had to get their opinions across.

'I will tell you the same as I told Dale. I had a bug. I am fine. I just needed to get out of the house and get back to some normality.' I wasn't used to be stuck in the house for any reason, and it was worse here because I enjoyed getting out and about in the scenery.

'OK, if you say so. Are you not eating any more?'

'Had enough . . .' I just wanted everyone to forget about being ill yesterday. It wasn't necessary all this fussing. 'Dale made me a big breakfast this morning.' My mother hen was back on full form, and I could scream. I felt smothered. Between Dale and Christine, I would never come to much harm.

'OK. Enough of my fussing. How did the rest of your engagement go?' Now this was a conversation that I could talk about all day. She would, maybe, get fed up of listening to me.

'It was lovely. I still have to pinch myself to see if it is all real.' Christine was sitting smiling at me like a Cheshire cat. She knew me to well, and it was easy to tell that I was so happy and in love.

'What?'

'Nothing. It is just nice to see you so happy. Did Dale get you anything nice?' I was surprised that she didn't already know.

'He took me outside after the proposal to show me my present . . .' Christine couldn't take the suspense any longer. 'A brand new convertible.' Christine's mouth couldn't have dropped any further if she tried.

'Oh my God, Ash. You will be taking me for a spin in that.' What was everyone's problem? They heard sports car and they went crazy. It was only a nice car to me.

'Then we went up to the cottage in the mountains, where I met his parents and younger sister. It was all lovely until I took sick.' It was just my luck to take sick on the day that I got engaged.

'It all sounds so romantic.' Christine would love a nice romantic story; she was like a princess herself. It was really nice to see her so happy for me. Everything was complete when Dale and Christine were in my life.

'This will be you one day, Christine.' I had faith in love again, and I knew that my friend would make someone happy.

'Yeah, maybe. I am just happy that you have found happiness. You deserve it, babe.' Christine and I spent our lunch hour putting the world to rights. I had missed our lunchtime chats.

'You know, Ash, when I heard that you were sick, I immediately thought "OMG" my best friend is pregnant and she hasn't even told me.' I didn't know why I was surprised that she thought the worst of me; she was always the same.

'Don't be silly. You would be the first to know any big news, especially baby news.'

'You're not saying you're not.'

'Christine, I am not pregnant. It was a bug.' If my best friend was putting two and two together, what was the rest of the building thinking?

'OK, I am sorry for jumping to conclusions. This has been a quick lunch today. Are you going to Dale's after work?' I hadn't thought that far ahead, but I guessed it would make sense.

'I think so. But don't quote me. He is out of the office most of today, but I will get a message to you.'

'That is cool. Don't worry about having to let me know. If you are home, great, but if you get a better offer, have fun. I am having Christian over for dinner and drinks so you can join us if you are home.' I was glad that Christine wasn't being funny about me and Dale, and I was glad that she had good friends around her.

'Waiter Christian?'

'Yeah. Oh, and you were right, he is a gay. He is great company.' It didn't take an idiot to know that Christian was gay; he was a typical gay person. I was so happy that Christine and Christian were getting along.

'I knew he was gay. All the good ones are.'

'Tell me about it, Ash. Christian and I are like two peas in a pod. I was going to ask if you minded me offering him our spare room? He is looking for somewhere new, and it seems a shame to waste our spare room.' I was so glad that my friend was bringing this conversation up. It would make my job easier.

'I am glad this conversation has come up. I wasn't going to say anything just now, but Dale has asked me to move in with him. We agreed that we were going to look for a house together at our own leisure. But . . .' Christine's hand reached out to mine and squeezed it tightly. I was surprised that she was taking it so well.

'Ash, I knew that you would be moving in with Dale. You wouldn't be starting married life living apart, and honestly, I am so happy that you have found someone like Dale . . . He will look after you. We will just have to have plenty of girls days and nights.' I knew that parties would come into my friend's response. She couldn't help herself.

'Sounds good, honey.' Christine looked up and away from me. Her face had dropped. She seemed scared or concerned about something. I had never seen her look so scared before. 'What is wrong, Christine?'

'Damn, I am late.' I didn't know that we were late, and I certainly wouldn't be getting that nervous or worked up over it.

'Excuse me, ladies . . .' I looked up to see Christine's boss looking at us both. 'Sorry to break up this chit-chat, but don't you have work to do?'

'Sorry, sir, we are just on our way.' I felt really nervous now. What was his problem?

'Christine, just get back to your desk.' I couldn't believe Rupert came all the way down here to speak to Christine like that. What had rattled his cage?

'Excuse me, sir, there is five minutes left to our lunch break, and I had Christine here confirming numbers for the charity ball.' Was I really standing here answering back the man second in charge of this company?

'Well, excuse me, Miss Malone, but this has nothing to do with you. You work for the boss man.' I couldn't believe that his attitude was so bad. 'Christine, make sure you are back at your desk in five minutes.'

'Yes, sir.' Rupert turned and walked away from us. I didn't know what had just happened. Christine was gathering her things up, just like that bully had told her to.

'Christine, what is going on?' I needed to ask the question, but I wasn't sure that I wanted to know.

'That man . . .' Christine was wiping her eyes with her hanky. She never cried. Now I was worried about her. 'He is a pig.'

'Why was he so horrible to you . . . to us?'

'I need to get back, but we will continue this conversation tonight or tomorrow. Thank you for sticking up for me, Ash.' Christine gave me a hug and walked away. In all the years that I had known her, she had never looked so unhappy. My head was pickled, and I didn't know what to do for the best. I got up and walked away, like I was a defeated challenger. I felt so hurt and humiliated. I needed to get back to my office before I cracked up with some innocent bystander. My feet moved quicker than they had all day, and the elevator pinged as I got up to it. Perfect timing for a change, I didn't have time to wait around. I was like a ticking bomb. All I wanted to do was close my office door and block out the last half an hour. I got out of the elevator and noticed straightaway that Dale's name was still marked as 'out'. I walked through to my office and slammed my door shut. My bags were thrown on to the couch with the force that I could have punched Rupert.

'What did that door do to you, babe?' I jumped out of my skin. I didn't even notice Dale in the corner of my room. This was just perfect. How the hell was I going to get out of this one? I burst into tears before I could compose myself. I just couldn't answer him right now.

'Ash, what is wrong? This isn't like you, sweetie.' He put his coffee down on the table and wrapped his arms around me. I immediately felt secure in his arms. He sat me down on the couch and lifted my head up with his hands. I had never felt so upset in my life. I needed to start speaking, but I couldn't stop sobbing long enough. 'Ashley, you are worrying me now. I have been out of the office one day and come back to find you in a state.'

'It is nothing. Don't worry about it.'

'Yeah, right, Ash, I will crack the jokes. Something has got you like this and I want to know.'

'I don't want to get anyone into trouble.' I felt so silly, sitting here sobbing like a baby. What had got into me lately?

'Let me be the judge of that, honey. Just tell me.' I put my head on his chest, and he held me so possessively. He was all mine, and I had to tell him what had happened.

'I was in the cafeteria with Christine, like we do most lunchtimes. We had a lot to talk about, and there was five minutes left of our lunch hour . . . Christine froze . . . I have never seen her look so scared . . . What has he done to her?' I just couldn't get her out my head.

'Ash, you are scaring me now. What the hell happened?' His voice was harsh, and he was scaring me more.

'Rupert came down, and he was really horrible to her. I tried to make an excuse that she was helping me with numbers for the charity ball, but he was really horrible to me. He told me to mind my own business and get on with my own work. I work for the boss man.' I felt like a snitch, telling tales on his second in command, but I still couldn't believe the cheek of that man. I was relieved when he threw his arms back around me. I wished that I had stayed at home now.

'I will sort this out. Rupert doesn't get away with speaking to you like that, and he certainly doesn't address employees like that in their lunch hour.'

'Please . . . I don't want to make things worse for Christine. She really seemed scared of him.' I couldn't care what he done or said to me, but Christine had to carry on working for him.

'Don't worry, babe. It won't make anything worse for Christine. Go and get a coffee from the kitchen. I will be back soon.' Dale kissed me and walked through to his office. I needed to straighten myself up before I left this room. My bag was at easy reach to straighten my hair and make up out, but I wouldn't be right until I got a coffee. I left my office, and immediately, I saw Rupert come out of the elevator. Surely, it was too soon for Dale to do anything, so why was he here?

'Ashley.' I turned and looked over to him. I was petrified of this man and didn't even know him.

'What is it?' I wasn't in any mood for small chat with him, and I had made it clear that I didn't like him much.

'The next time you ever feel the need to undermine me, please remember who you are talking to.' I actually couldn't believe the cheek of him. How dare he came up here to have a go at me?

'Excuse me, Rupert, but you were out of order and you know it. I would have done the same for any member of staff if they were in the right.' I tried to edge around him so that no one would notice anything, but his presence was making a scene. He turned to follow me, and I was really nervous, but there was no way that I was going to let him see my fear.

'You think that because you are marrying the boss, you get to be all miss high and mighty.' He pulled my arm really hard, and I stumbled into the wall. I was more in shock that he had just assaulted me in front of everyone.

'Get your hands off me.' Something had snapped inside of me, and all I wanted to do was punch him. I felt so angry and humiliated.

'Or what?'

'Is that a threat, Rupert?' I didn't know where my confidence had came from, but I wasn't going to back down to a bully.

'Wouldn't you like to find out, Miss Malone?'

'Get your hands off my fiancée now.' Dale's voice was very angry. I had never heard him angry before.

'Eh, Dale . . . This is just a misunderstanding.' Dale walked past him to come and stand by my side. His arm securely went around my waist, and I was glad of his support.

'Are you OK, Ash?' All I could do was nod slightly. I was still in shock. Why did this have to happen to me?

'Can you tell me why you are here, Rupert? Better still don't bother. I have heard all about you today, and I want you in my office now . . .' I felt my body freeze as Dale spoke to this horrible man. 'For the record, Rupert, Ashley doesn't have to remember who you are. I own this company, and she is going to be my wife, which means that she owns this company as well. You should remember whom *you* are talking to.' I was in shock at everything today. I had never given it a thought that this company was going to be half mine when we were married.

'I came up to clear things with Ashley.'

'You ever touch my fiancée or threaten her again and you won't be walking out of this office . . . Do you understand me?'

'Of course, Dale.'

'Now get into my office before any more people are dragged into your scene.' I sighed with relief as this man walked into Dale's office. I was mortified at the whole altercation.

'Ash, go and get that coffee, babe. I will sort this out.' Dale was very sweet to me, but I didn't want to leave his side.

'Are you sure?'

'Yes, go, hun.' He placed a soft and gentle kiss on my lips to reassure me that everything was going to be OK. I walked away to the kitchen and heard his door bang shut. I would love to be a fly on the wall right now.

'Are you OK, Ash?' Steph made me jump as she walked up behind me in the kitchen.

'Yeah, thanks, Steph, I will live.' I wasn't OK, but it was the best that I could come up with right now.

'I will get you a cold pack out for your arm. It is bruising already.' I looked down at my arm and noticed that Steph was right. The pig had really bruised my arm. Steph placed the pack of blue gel on my arm, and I felt really rotten. I should have punched him, and that would have made me feel better.

'Here, hun, this will help.'

'Thanks, Steph.' I burst into tears again. What was wrong with me today? I was an emotional wreck and never cried. This creep had certainly got under my skin. The comfort of Steph sitting beside was nice, but I just wanted Dale.

'Listen, Ash, don't let him get to you. He is an arrogant ass, who gets a kick out of scaring women. I don't know how he has got away with it for so long. I hope Dale kicks his ass out this time.' It just showed that you couldn't always read a book by its cover; he never came across like that to me until today.

'He has done this before?' Steph got up to make me that coffee, and I had my questioning head on now.

'Yeah, not up here though. Always on his own floor, but he was good at covering his tracks. Today is a different story. He has left witnesses.'

Thank God, he finally got what was coming to him. After all the time I was feeling bad for telling Dale about him, and he has been ruling woman all the time.

'Here, hun, strong and sweet. It will calm you down.' I thought that I was going to need more than a coffee, but it was a good start.

'Thanks.' I sipped away at my coffee when I heard Dale come in. Relief swept over me as he came and sat beside me.

'Thanks for looking after her, Steph.'

'No worries, Dale. Ashley, keep that ice pack on for a while. It will calm the bruising down.' The room went silent as I sat with one arm across my knee with an ice pack and a hot coffee in the other. Could this day get any worse? Dale's hands lifted my hurt arm to loosen the elastic on the pack so that he could examine the damage.

'Are you OK, babe?' His voice sounded like he was holding back tears. How was I actually feeling? That was a good question.

'I really wish people would stop asking me that.' I snapped his head off for caring, for being my fiancé. 'I am sorry. I didn't mean to snap at you.'

'Ash, you are OK. Has he hurt you anywhere else?'

'Just my side where I banged off the wall, but I am fine.' Dale fastened the pack back on my arm and wiped my tears away with his hand.

'I wanted to punch that bastard, and now I want to kill him.'

'Shh, I am fine.' I didn't know what shocked me more, Dale's anger or his language. 'What happened when you went into the office?'

'I have suspended him with no salary. A full hearing will take place, and based on evidence and witnesses, he will be fired.' I hated myself for getting someone fired. Why did he have to do this to me? 'Ash, he will never hurt you again.'

'Thank you.'

'For what?'

'The way you handled everything today and not blaming me.'

'Baby girl, none of this is your fault. Come on, let's get you home. I want to take care of you.' It really was an honour to have someone like Dale looking after me.

'What about your meetings?'

'They are all done. It is time for us to have time together.' I really needed to be with him right now. I was shaky and exhausted, and his existence was just what the doctor ordered. 'I will go and get your bag and jacket, and I will fill the office in on what needs to be done, and we will be good to go. Stay and finish your coffee.'

'OK.' The minute he left the room, my mind went into overdrive. My man has gone from never taking a day off to having days off all the time. My mind was muddled; how could I possibly keep working here now? Would it be fair on me or Dale to keep this working relationship going? Today just proved that living and working together might not be the best answer. I got up and walked over to the sink to wash my cup out. I wish I could wash my head out the same way.

'Are you ready, babe?' I leapt out of my skin. I never heard him come back in, and the way I was feeling right now, anything would make me jump. 'I am sorry. I didn't mean to frighten you. Let's get out of here.'

'Dale, wait.' I needed to get this off my mind now before it buried me knee-deep and while it was all fresh in my mind.

'Ash. What is wrong?'

'I can't do this. I really thought that we working together would work, but today has proved otherwise. I can't have you as my boss and my husband.' I said it without even breathing. I didn't want to beat about the bush. I just wanted to be honest and straight with him.

'What are you saying, Ash?' He sounded hurt and in pain, and I hated myself to be the cause of it. I couldn't even look him in the eye right now.

'Are you saying that you don't want to marry me?'

'No, of course, I am not. I said I couldn't have you as my boss and my husband, and I meant that I wasn't losing you for work. I will work till you find another assistant, and I will look for work elsewhere.' I couldn't believe that he thought I could just walk away from him like that.

'I am not your boss, Ash. If this is all to do with what that prick said, ignore him. I want to run this company with you as Mr and Mrs. Not Mr Black and his assistant. Everyone in this office loves you. They treat you like me when I am out, and that is what it should be.' I knew that this office was fab with me, but the rest of the building didn't know me from Adam, and I was out of my depth with it all. It was easier to walk away.

'But that doesn't stop things like this happening again. Who is to say that the next time isn't worse?'

'Rupert is the only one who would ever be brave enough to do something like this. He isn't coming back. I want you to run things with me, but if you want to leave, then I will support your decision as your husband and not your boss.' I was relieved that he wasn't going to change my mind. It meant a lot to me to have his support.

'I feel like it doesn't matter what we do, someone is going to be talking about us.' It was always going to be the same in an organisation like this, and I didn't like to have my dirty laundry aired in public.

'Where has this come from, Ash?'

'Christine today. She is my best friend, but her first thought when you told her I was ill was that I was pregnant. If she can think that, what is everyone else thinking?' I was getting everything off my chest now; he would be wishing that he stayed out of the office all day today.

'And does it really bother you? I mean would it be the worst thing if you were pregnant?'

'That isn't what I mean, Dale. Of course, it wouldn't be a bad thing. I just mean that whatever goes on between us is going to be office talk.' I was stressing over everything, and I was giving myself a sorehead.

'Well, can we walk and talk before everyone thinks something is wrong in here?' Sarcasm really wasn't what we needed right now, but he did have a point. I put my jacket on and took my bag off him. We headed out of the kitchen towards the elevator, and I was glad to be going home away from it all.

'See you guys later.'

'Bye, hun.' Steph was coming out of the elevator as we were going in. I had met a lot of nice people here; everyone had made me feel very welcome, and I would miss them all very much.

'Are you coming with me or is Carlos waiting?'

'Carlos is doing something up at the cottage for my parents, so it's me and you, hun.' I didn't even want to know what Carlos was doing. It was nice to know that it was just me and him for a change.

'Do you want to drive?'

'Sure, hun.' We got out of the elevator and headed for the door. I was never so glad to see daylight and get some fresh air. My car was sitting in the executive spot since Carlos always parked up front. I handed Dale my keys and climbed into the passenger's seat. I had never felt so deflated before. Dale jumped into the driver's seat, and without a word, he started the car and drove out of the car park. The next ten minute's drive was done in silence, and that was a first. That had never happened before. Either Dale hoped that the silence would make me forget everything that I had said, or he hoped that it would make me see sense and retract everything that I had said. We pulled up outside the house, and I just got out of the car and walked in. I passed Carlos and Rosa, without even acknowledging them. What was my problem? It wasn't their fault. I headed right up the stairs as I heard Dale close the front door. I just wanted to hibernate and get today out of my head.

'Dale, is everything OK with Ashley?' My actions even concerned the staff. They seemed to know me so well.

'It will be, Carlos. I will explain later, but just now I need to be with her.'

'Sure go.' I heard Dale run up the stairs and suddenly stop. I was glad that I was getting a minute's breathing space.

'How did it go at the cottage?'

'Yeah, fine, Dale. Your mom was on her best behaviour.' I heard Dale trip up the last few stairs, and normally, I would have found it funny, but I couldn't be bothered now.

'Ash, where are you?'

I was already in the closet pulling out a T-shirt that belonged to Dale. I stripped out of these clothes in record time. I didn't want to feel like a used-and-abused assistant right now. My clothes got thrown over the chair as I walked back into the room, and Dale pulled the bottom of his

T-shirt so that I was close to him. We sat on the bottom of the bed like two little lost sheep. We weren't even this quiet on our first date.

'Ash, you are OK. I will never let anyone hurt you again.'

'You can't protect me from everything.' I was being snappy again, and I could kick myself for it. The last thing I wanted was to push him away.

'I will try, hun. You are my life now, and when you are unhappy, so am I. If you want me to go downstairs to give you some space, just say, babe. I will understand.' I stroked his face gently. He was my helpless hero sitting doe-eyed.

'I don't need space from you, Dale. I want you to hold me.'

'I will hold you every minute of every day if that is what you want, Ash. Just don't push me away, babe. I can't bear to see you like this.' I cuddled into Dale like he was my rock; nothing could break through his shield. I sobbed into his shoulder until no more tears could come out.

'I am sorry if you thought I was pushing you away.' That was the last thing that I wanted to do to him.

'Don't apologise, Ash. Do you want to finish off our conversation where we left it at work?'

'What about? Me being pregnant or me resigning?' I didn't know what I wanted to say or do. But I was fed up of crying and being serious; it just wasn't me.

'Are you pregnant?' He sounded shocked. His voice went high pitched, and he studied me for any information that I was going to share with him.

'No, that is what we were talking about in the office. What the staff thought.' Typical man having cloth ears.

'Sorry, I know that is what we were talking about, but just when you said there . . . I jumped to conclusions.'

'And you wonder where your staff get it from.' I was trying to make light of a difficult conversation, but I didn't think that I was succeeding.

'I guess I was just wishing.' I wasn't expecting to hear him say that about a baby, but nothing should shock me any more.

'It wouldn't bother you?' He took my face in both of his hands and looked me deep in the eyes. My body tingled at this intense moment, and I just wanted to know what was going through his head.

'Why would it bother me, Ash? We have been making love together for weeks without any precautions. If I didn't want a child, do you think

I would be so stupid? I love you. I want you in every way possible.' His sincere, loving voice had my spine tingling.

'Is this a day for getting everything in the open?' I had got a lot of my chest today, and it was nice to know what he was thinking as well.

'Honesty is the best policy, Ash. I hope this is when you say you want the same things.'

'I haven't really given it much thought. Of course, I want children with you. I just never actually gave it much thought until today.' I had given up thinking about having a relationship, that kids never really entered my mind.

'And the resignation bit? If you were telling me you were pregnant, I could let you go without hesitation. But to let you go through Rupert is killing me.' I could see what today was doing to him, and I felt bad for it. I hated that my misery was rubbing off on the people whom I cared about.

'We will play it by ear. I am not promising anything. One thing though, I don't want to hear that man's name mentioned in this house again.'

'Deal.' I didn't want to bring work home with us. When we were at home, it was our time and that man wasn't going to spoil that for me. 'We have the whole afternoon off. What do you fancy doing?'

'I don't care as long as it is with you.'

'Stay in or go out?'

'Go out.' I wanted to forget today, and the best thing that would solve that was to go out and have some fun.

'So I get the job of deciding. How is that fair, Ash?'

'Let's go and see your parents.' I couldn't believe that I was suggesting such a thing, but it was the least we could do after our last visit.

'Are you sure?'

'Yeah. I love the cottage, and your parents are there so it is killing two birds with one stone.' The cottage would be one place that would erase anything from my mind.

'OK. Let me get changed out of this suit . . . And Ashley, as much as I find you sexy in anything, you do have a closet of your own.' Now I was confused. How and when did this happen?

'I do. Where?' How did I know nothing about this? My husband-to-be was just a legend. I had to get used to the fact that I was never going to want for anything ever again. We had walked through to the room opposite our room, and everything looked the same. Nothing had changed from the last time I was in here. But we walked into the walk-in closet, and it was full of all my favourite colours. Gobsmacked was definitely an understatement. 'When did you do this?'

'Well, I have to confess, Ash. It was Rosa and Carlos who have done all the hard work.' He really did know me inside and out. Some married couples would take years to get where we were, and I still couldn't get my head around how compatible we were for one another.

'I really do love you, Mr Black.' I kissed him like I never had before. Our mouths had become one, and the electricity flowed through my body.

'You have no idea how much relief I feel to hear you say that. I thought after today, you were having second thoughts.'

'Second thoughts about working with you. Never a second thought about spending the rest of my life with you.'

'Glad to hear it, Ash. I will leave you to get ready while I jump in the shower. I won't be long, OK.'

'Don't be long, Mr black. You send me crazy when you are gone too long.'

'Join me then.' His voice was sexy and seductive, and I wanted to run with him.

'Then we will never get out. Go and get your shower before I change my mind.' I was so glad that we were both smiling again. It was horrible to have an atmosphere around, especially when it wasn't anything to do with us or our relationship. I really hoped that we could have the same working relationship because I didn't think I could spend a full day away from him. I looked around the closet in amazement. How could I pick what to wear? I went for the first outfit that came to my hands, jeans and nice cerise pink top. I went to the underwear drawer, and there had to be a set in every colour. Cerise pink lace was on the top. I couldn't have done that again if I tried. When Christine and I had sleepovers, we used to have fashion walks and used to dream about this kind of thing. But now I had it all right in front of me. I took the clothes back through to our room to get ready. Space was no option. I missed my lover when he was gone. Dale and I bumped into each other in the hallway. He looked as gorgeous as ever with his white towel wrapped around his waist.

'I promised I wouldn't be too long, didn't I?'

'It is amazing how quick you can be when you don't have me distracting you.' His cheeky laugh caught me off guard; it was so nice to have my man back. He pulled me close to his wet body, and I desperately wanted the towel to fall for a repeat performance of this morning.

'Ash, you are a good distraction. I wouldn't have it any other way.' His tone was very seductive, sexy, and soft, just the way I liked it.

'I will bear that in mind. Now are you going to let me get dressed or are you going to drip all over me leaving me wet?' I placed my head on his wet shoulder as the realisation of what I just said hit me. Only I and my mouth could say something like that without thinking.

'Well, that is a new way to get you wet, sweetie.' I slapped his arm in a playful nature and laughed. 'Ow, you have a mean slap on you, Mrs.'

'You big girl's blouse. Get ready before we don't make it anywhere.' I got a nice peck on my cheek as he walked into his closet. I walked back over to the bed to get ready, and I didn't even care that Dale could see my body any more. I slipped out of Dale's T-shirt and replaced my underwear with the sexy pink set. It did get me curious how Carlos and Rosa could pick all these lovely things for me.

'Well, Miss Malone, you certainly know how to grab my attention.' I never even heard Dale come back out of his closet; he was very quick. He has gone for the casual look as well, jeans but no top as of yet. He did look rather sexy out of a suit.

'Dale, you are going to give me a heart attack. There is only so many shocks one heart can take in a day.' I was standing in just my underwear as he paraded over the room, who would have thought that I could be so comfortable to be sitting like this.

'I could always give you the kiss of life, my love.' He could always make me smile with his witty responses.

'That would be very nice of you, babe.'

'What can I say, I am a very nice guy.' He was a nice guy, and he knew it. Every time he spoke he was nice. Every situation with him was nice. Even today at his unhappiest, he was still nice. I pulled my jeans up and turned to look at him. He had put a cream T-shirt on, and by God, he got my pulse racing. I slipped on my top that hung below one shoulder to show off my bra strap. We were a perfect couple in every sense. We could never say that we were not suited to one another. 'Why is it that you look so good in anything you wear?' My shoulders shrugged as I walked up to my fiancée. I placed my hands on his chest and looked into his twinkling eyes.

'I could say the same about you. It is nice to see you out of a suit during the week.' I went over to my dressing table and sprayed my favourite perfume, Gucchi Guilty. I slipped on my boots and was ready to roll. I swung around on my chair to face my man, and I still felt like the luckiest girl alive.

'Ready when you are, Mr Black.' Dale got up and walked back into his closet. He came out with a pair of Vans and a little black box. I was intrigued to know what was in the box, but as usual Dale kept me waiting until his shoes were all tied.

'I am ready. But first, I got you a present today. I planned to give you it in your office, but when you came in in such a state, I forgot all about it.' He came and knelt down beside me, and I was intrigued. Well, it wasn't an engagement ring because I already had one. What could it be?

'What is it?' Dale handed me the box, and I fumbled with the box to open it. I discovered a lovely diamond chain. It was gorgeous. I was speechless. I didn't know what to say.

'Do you like it?'

'It is lovely. But I can't expect this. You have already given me too much this week.'

'Ash, you need to get used to me showering you with gifts, because I want to. Not because I need to. Let me put it on for you.' I handed him the box and turned around in my seat. I put my hand over it to feel it in place on my neck. The light made it sparkle in the mirror. I had never seen something so simple yet so gorgeous. It had my name written all over it, and he would have known that when he had seen it.

'It is beautiful. Thank you.' Dale's kiss on my neck sent shivers down my spine. I turned in my seat to kiss his lips, and I would never get tired of feeling his lips on mine.

'Are you ready to go and see my parents?' I nodded and smiled. Dale pulled my hand up to help me on to my feet, and I winched my face up as I could feel my arm a bit sore. Then the realisation of what happened today came flooding back to me.

'Sorry, babe.'

'Don't be. It is fine. Let's go, and I am driving, Mr Black.' I was determined to leave today behind me and enjoy myself with my new family, and driving was the first thing that let Dale know that I was feeling more myself.

'If you say so, Ash.' We headed out of the room hand in hand so in love with one another. Who would have known that not an hour ago? I was so upset with everything. We saw Carlos and Rosa enter the hall looking very concerned about me; they were just like my family as well. 'Guys, you can take the rest of the day off. We are heading up the mountain to see my parents. You can have the rest of the day to yourself.' I was getting used to the whole nicey, nicey thing that Dale had going on with his workers. He showed them the respect that they deserved, and in return, he had a happy workforce.

'Is everything OK now, Dale?'

'Yes, thank you, Carlos. If you need to use one of the cars, please do.' Rosa handed me my jacket, and I folded it over my arm.

'Thank you, Rosa.' She was just like my mom, and I thought that is why I had come to admire her so much.

'Have fun, won't you.' Rosa was just perfect in every way. She would be a perfect mother or grandmother to anyone.

'We will, Rosa.' Dale's hand in mine was all any girl could want, and I had no plans to let it go anytime soon. We left the house and headed towards my car. It was still in the same place that Dale abandoned it not an hour ago.

'Can you remember the directions?'

'I think so. If we get lost, it will just be another adventure.' Dale and I smiled together as we buckled up to enjoy the ride. Every day was an adventure with Dale, and I couldn't wait to see what happens next.

We made it to the cottage in one piece. It was all lit up like something out of a movie. It was so welcoming and gorgeous. It did get nicer every time I came up here.

'It is even nicer all lit up . . . All homely and inviting.' I felt Dale's hand on mine as he moved closer to me.

'You really love this cottage, don't you?' What was not to love about it?

'It is gorgeous. I have never fell in love with a property like this one . . . When we were looking at properties here to move to . . . I looked at hundreds, and in the end Christine made the final decision. Nothing even came close to this.' His hand pulled my chin towards him, and I could feel my body react to his touch already. I could feel his warm breath on my skin as his lips pressed tenderly on mine. They were so soft and inviting just like the cottage, and I loved them both very much.

'This is just as much yours now, Ash. Enjoy it.'

'I don't care that you have millions, hun. You are more than enough.' I was always brought up to value the important things in life, and money and valuables were never high on the list.

'We have so much in common. It sometimes feels unreal . . .' I knew exactly what he meant. I had to keep nipping myself to make sure I was awake. 'Are you ready to face my parents?'

'You make them sound like a pack of wolves.' We were both laughing as we got out of the car. But I remembered the first time I came to meet his parents. I had been petrified to go in. Now I didn't even hesitate. We walked into the nice, warm cottage to be greeted by silence. You wouldn't know that there were three adults staying here just now.

'Mom, Dad.' Mhairi and Jake came through from the kitchen, and I immediately noticed that they didn't look themselves. 'What is wrong, Mom?' It was funny because I didn't even know them, and I knew that something didn't seem right and so did Dale.

'Nothing. We were going to drop by later, to check on you both.' Mhairi was concerned about something. I could hear it in her voice.

'We are fine, Mom. Why wouldn't we be?' I wasn't sure if it was the perfect getaway now. We have just come from one situation to another.

'Come and sit down. Jake, bring coffee through.' I don't know about Dale, but the nerves in my stomach were doing somersaults.

'Your brother called before and said that he had heard there was an incident in the office today.' News did travel fast.

'Mom, you have been worried over nothing. Yes, there was an incident . . . My assistant manager had a bee in his bonnet. He then took it out on another member of my staff and attacked Ashley.' Hearing Dale say it loud made it sound horrific.

'He hurt my arm and was rather rude. He didn't attempt to murder me.' I had to interrupt because the story sounded horrible told by a man. The room went silent as Jake handed me my coffee, and I really needed something much stronger, but it was going to have to do just now.

'Ashley dear, you must have been terrified.'

'Mhairi, I don't mean to sound rude. But I just want to forget all about today.' I came up here to escape from it all. Never for one second, did I think they would know the whole story inside and out.

'Of course, dear.' I was glad that she took my feelings on board because I didn't want to talk about it any more. My mood had lifted, and I wanted it to stay that way.

'I hope you fired this sorry ass.' Jake sounded funny when he was filled with fury.

'Suspended without salary until the hearing, but he will be fired. There is too much evidence stacked up against him this time.'

'Good.' Jake could make coffee. This was the best coffee that I had tasted in ages, and it was a good distraction.

'I know that you kids love this cottage, so your dad and I are going to head out to get some things for dinner. Nikki is away shopping, so you have the cottage to yourselves for a couple of hours. The beds are all made if you want to lie down. I will phone when I am on my way home.' Mhairi clearly wasn't good at the whole subtle gestures. I didn't know who was more embarrassed me or her.

'Thanks, Mom. But we can order food in for dinner.'

'OK. We can decide when we get back then.' I had a feeling that they were trying to get away from us for some strange reason.

'You can take my car if you need one.'

'Thank you, dear.' They really seemed to be in a hurry to get out of here. I looked at Dale as the front door shut behind them, and I was hoping that he noticed it as well.

'What was that all about?'

'I have no idea. I will hazard a guess and say it is for us to be alone together.' I thought that as well, but it just seemed a lot more than that. Maybe it was me overreading the situation, but I wasn't going to let it get in the way of me and Dale, being alone for a little while.

'They are sweet.' I really liked Mr and Mrs Black; they were the sort of people who would get along with anyone. 'Your dad can make a good cup of coffee.'

'Don't tell him that. His head will grow in size.' I laughed and laid my head back on the back of the couch. 'So, my wife-to-be, what do you have in mind for this afternoon?' I sat up and placed my cup on the table. Dale's voice was back to being soft and gentle, just the way that I liked it.

'It seems a waste not to take advantage of a couple of hours together.' I climbed over Dale's legs and sat straddling him. This couch had seen some amount of action over the last few weeks. My cheeks flushed at the thought, and I felt my body gearing up for him already.

'Is that so, Miss Malone? You can be such a tease. You know that, don't you?' I bent down and kissed him passionately, letting him fill every inch of my mouth. We were both groaning as our breathing got faster. I let my mouth go all the way down to his neck, his aftershave tickled my nose. 'Ash.' I heard my name, but I didn't want to stop. His mouth was more desirable when I was kissing it. 'Ash, let's go through to the room. It will be warmer.' I stopped kissing his neck and looked at him.

'You mean, in case someone walks in.' I was always the careful one, but today I was past caring. I just wanted to share my love and affection with this man.

'They might come back.' I shook my head in protest. We both knew that they wouldn't be back for hours.

'They won't be back for ages. Live a little, Mr Black.' I lifted his T-shirt over his head and carried on kissing his neck down to his chest. My hands were like magnets rubbing all the way down his torso. Undoing his button was easy on these jeans. For the first time in my life, I was taking control of the situation. I lay soft kisses all the way up his body until I reached his lips. I stood off him and pulled his jeans down while he was still sitting; all he had to do was lift up. I stood in front of him and took my jeans off, and I could sense that his eyes never left me. I climbed back on top of him and slipped my top off. We were both entwined together half naked. I could feel his hard penis rub against my pants. My body ached for him. His hands caressed my breasts as our mouths engaged with one another. I let my hands rub down his body to release his package from his shorts. I couldn't resist but take him in my mouth. My hands rubbed up and down the length of him. Listening to the groans escape his mouth made me need him more. My mouth slid over the top of him, taking every inch of him. His body arched off the couch. 'Oh my God, Ash.' My body longed to be invaded by him. I had waited too long. I stopped and took my pants off and hovered over the top of him, slowly inserting his penis into me. I cried out in ecstasy as our bodies became one. I slid on and off him until my body climaxed. Our bodies worked as one to make sweet love. His thumb massaged my clitoris as I rocked back and forth. Our bodies climaxed together in one final thrust. My head lay softly on his shoulder as I gathered my bearings. I felt him kiss my shoulder as he moved my hair out of the way. Our tangled bodies were full of love. I could feel him still inside me as we composed ourselves. I didn't want to move any time soon.

'Where did that come from, Ash?' I looked at him in surprise. The first thing that he usually asks after we make love is 'are you OK?'

'What do you mean?'

'You surprise me every day at something you do. Then today we have mind-blowing sex in the shower and then again here.'

'Are you complaining, Mr Black?' I pulled my top back over my head as I locked eyes with my lover.

'Of course, I am not, babe. I love you. I love to see you grow in confidence.' He got that right. My confidence has grown so much over the last few weeks. I was the type of person who would have sex in the dark. But that was before I moved here and met Dale. I was like a mouse before, and I could see that myself now.

'I don't know where that came from if I am being honest. It must have been building up from this morning.' I handed Dale his T-shirt and moved off him to curl up beside him. I watched as he pulled his shorts back into place, and I couldn't believe that I had just done that. 'I love curling up beside you.'

'Me to, babe . . . Do you fancy taking this through to the bathroom?'

'Sounds nice. Another reason that I love this cottage.' I pulled the throw off the back of the couch and wrapped it around me. I lifted all our clothes up so that there was nothing to give us away when his parents came back. The walk into the bathroom woke me up. There were candles burning already, and the smell of lavender and chamomile teased my nose. 'What have I done to deserve all this.' I loved this sensitive side of Dale. He knew everything that I wanted before I did. I placed the clothes on the chair and walked over to him.

'You are just you, Ash. Don't ever change. You are perfect in every way.' I stripped the rest of my clothes off and climbed into the bath; relaxation was just what I needed right now.

'Are you just going to stand there?' I wanted him behind me to snuggle into the hot water. He climbed in behind me and kissed my shoulder. The feel of our bodies together was magical.

'Are you OK, Ash?' Here came the concerned speech, I wondered how long it would be.

'How can I not be OK, babe? I am here with you.'

'I love to see how happy this cottage makes you. It is a shame it is not bigger.'

'I would be happy wherever I was as long as I am with you.' He probably thought that I was pulling his leg right now, but it was the truth. A cardboard box would be just as good. The roasting water surrounded us both, relaxing any aches or pains that I had.

'This has just finished off a perfect afternoon. Thank you.'

'Thank you for sharing it with me.' We lay back in the water, and Dale massaged my shoulders. I could get, too, used to this. I felt like I was in heaven. There was no other word to describe the way I felt. My eyes closed as we relaxed in the hot water and not a single memory sprang to life. I had never felt so relaxed.

We were sitting on the couch all snuggled up when Mhairi and Jake returned. I did hope that they didn't have any special powers. I didn't think I could deal with them knowing what Dale and I had been up to in here.

'Hey, kids, did you have fun?' My cheeks immediately blushed. I was a poor liar. Dale stroked his hand across my tummy as he sat up to look respectable. I was glad that he was so composed.

'Yeah, Mom, it was nice to spend time up here. I had a bath since I never had a shower after work. Don't worry all towels are in the laundry.' Dale was a gem; he had taken the suspicion away from us, and I could relax a bit. Only I knew that Dale had a shower before we left the house.

'That is fine, honey. Nikki is on her way home. I was going to send your dad out for Chinese. What do you both think?'

'Chinese is fine for me. Ash?'

'Yeah, sounds nice, at least I will be able to eat it tonight.' We all exchanged a smile with one another as we remembered my last time up here. This is what a close family unit was like, and I loved how Dale got along so well with his family. It was a good environment for bringing kids into and settling down.

'Dale, open the wine, sweetie.' Dale got up and screwed the wine open; he was a dab hand at opening bottles.

'Can I help with anything?'

'No, dear. You relax. I will just set the table.' I had a funny feeling that I wasn't going to be able to lift a finger around here. Mhairi was too busy being a mother hen.

'Enjoy it, Ashley, because in a few weeks, Mhairi will have you doing everything.' I appreciated Jake's sense of humour; it made me feel so comfortable when I was here.

'Don't listen to him, Ashley.' We were all laughing and joking together. We had come a long way from my first ever visit.

'Will I just order a bit of everything?'

'You're good with Chinese, Dad. Just you pick. Here take this.' Dale got his wallet out to hand his dad cash, but Jake wasn't for accepting it.

'Don't be silly, Son. This is our treat.' Dale came back and sat beside me. His arm went around my shoulders, and I relaxed into him. He was like my own little shell, and I couldn't imagine my life without him now. Mhairi sank into the seat opposite us. She looked worn out for a vampire. 'What a day! I will be glad to see the back of it.' Mhairi sounded really stressed; it wasn't like her.

'Mom, what is wrong? This isn't still to do with the incident at the office.' I was glad that Dale was persistent with his mom because it was clear that there was more going on.

'No, Son, it isn't . . . I am as well telling you before you hear it from someone else . . . Your brother phoned to drop a bombshell . . .' We were both glued to her, wondering what she was going to say? 'He is a dad.' I couldn't say anything because I didn't know his brother. I just waited for someone to say something.

'Are you serious?' Dale sounded shocked. I didn't understand why Dale was so shocked, so I couldn't say anything to him.

'Unfortunately I am being deadly serious. The girl dropped the baby off at his office.'

'Oh my God, the poor child.' I felt sorry for the baby without even thinking. How could a mother give her child away? 'I am sorry. I just don't know how a mother could do that.'

'No, you're right, dear. Now Callum hasn't got a clue what to do. He wanted us to drop everything and run, but we want to be here with you guys. We have told him that if he wants our help, he will have to come here.' I suppose that we should be honoured that they wanted to spend as much time as possible with us, but surely Callum should take priority over us right now.

'Mom, I am shocked. You must be happy. You always wanted to be grandparents.' Mhairi would be a good grandmother; she would do everything she could for her grandchild.

'Dale, if you were telling me now that you were going to be a dad and that Ashley was carrying my grandchild, I would be over the moon. Callum, on the other hand, he just does everything wrong. I am sure it is just to get our blood boiling. He is going to show up here, and we are going to have everything to do.' I was honoured that Mhairi thought that way about mine and Dale's relationship, but at the moment, I felt really sorry for the situation that had landed on their laps.

'When is he getting here?'

'Tonight. Why do you think that your father is flapping?' It all made sense now. No a wonder they were funny when we first arrived.

'Do you need anything for the baby? I mean this cottage isn't exactly child-friendly.' I really didn't know how much I wanted to be a mother until this very minute. Here I was offering to do anything that I could to help a child whom I had never met before.

'Well, we have a pram and a cot to build. Jake was going to stop by the supermarket for all the necessities. Nikki has had fun all afternoon shopping for baby clothes.' It seemed like they were all set for their arrival, but God knew where everyone was going to fit in here.

'Is it a boy or girl?'

'I have a granddaughter, dear.' I thought Mhairi would be more excited, but she didn't seem thrilled at the idea. 'Dale, will you help your dad build the cot and pram?'

'Of course, I will. But on a serious note. How does he know the baby is his?'

'Dale.' I snapped quickly and sharply at him, and he looked at me with dread in his eyes. I knew nothing about Callum, but I still didn't want to see Mhairi upset.

'Ash, you don't know my brother. Anyone could find out his family are wealthy. Now he has a baby to take care of with no mother.'

'We have asked all these questions, Dale. We just have to trust him.' Dale got up and walked through to the kitchen. I signalled to his mom that I would go. I followed behind him quickly and wanted to know what was bothering him. This wasn't like him at all.

'Dale, what is wrong with you?' He turned around and leant against the worktop. I didn't like to see him so worked up.

'This is just typical of Cal. He messes up, and we are left to pick up the pieces.' I could understand his concern over the whole thing, but he was just going to have to put it all behind him for his family's sake.

'Babe, there is an innocent baby involved in this mess. She never asked to become a part of this.' I walked over to him and placed my hands around his waist. 'You just have to be there for your niece.'

'What if this goes pear shaped and she turns out to be someone else's?'

'You can be the bigger person and say that you supported his decision.' I moved my hands from his waist and placed them around his neck.

'Where has this maternal instinct came from?' I moved my head from his shoulder and looked him in the eyes. My shoulders shrugged because I had no idea what to say.

'Who knows? One day this could be us. I would want to know that our child had a loving family around him or her, no matter what.'

'Our child would get more than enough love from us, babe.' I knew that we would never be in the same situation as his brother, but it was the only thing that I could think of to get him on side.

'Well, why not start with our niece?' His lips touched mine, and without any protest, I let him in. His arms clasped around my waist, and I felt his need to be with me.

'Sorry to interrupt, but your dad is back.' We followed Mhairi through to the dining table. The smell of the food was delicious. I didn't realise how hungry I was.

'Hey, guys.'

'Hey, Nik.' Nikki sat opposite me at the table, and Dale went outside to help Jake bring boxes in. The fact that he was helping his dad was a start. His mind wasn't going to change overnight, but I thought everyone understood his concerns.

'Thank you, Ashley, for bringing Dale around to the idea.' I could only shrug my shoulders and smile to his mum because I didn't feel that I had done anything.

'It is nothing, honestly.' I had only done what anybody would have done. It was no big deal.

'Who would have thought a baby needed so much things.'

'That is only the start, Nikki.' Dale and Jake joined us at the table, and I was relieved to see that everyone was still chatting away as normal. Jake poured wine into the glasses, and I thought everyone was going to need it.

'None for me, Jake. I don't want to push my luck with my stomach.' Everyone tucked into their food apart from Mhairi and Jake. They didn't really make it noticeable though. I was only being nosey to see what they were like at mealtimes.

'Well, this is nice spending time with you, kids.' I couldn't help but think how hard it was for Mhairi and Jake, having to live this secret life. They must miss spending family time together.

'It's good having you here, Mom.' The food was lovely, but I couldn't force myself to eat too much. My stomach still felt kind of funny tonight.

'Girl's clothes are just gorgeous. Ashley, I will have to show you everything that I got.' I loved hearing Nikki's excitement over her niece. I did hope that Dale would come around as well.

'There is always so much to choose from for girls. I wouldn't know when to stop.' The idea of shopping for a baby intrigued me. Our niece would never want for anything, and I would look forward to spoiling her.

'You will have all this, too, look forward to, dear.' I didn't really want to think about having children of my own right now; it didn't feel appropriate under the circumstances.

'So, Grandad, are we going to make a start on these boxes?' Dale threw a towel over to Jake in a playful protest. I was glad that he quickly changed the subject away from us having a baby. He would have known that I wouldn't want to talk about it.

'Less of the granddad, Son, but yeah, let's get started.' Dale placed a kiss on my head as he got up from the table. It was nice to feel him touch me, and I didn't mind him showing me affection in front of his family. I loved him too much.

'Can I be excused?'

'Of course, Nikki.' Nikki was a typical teen. Once the dinner is over with, it is right out of sight again. I could remember my teenage years too well. I was shy and reserved just like Nikki. Mhairi and I cleared the table away. We worked well around the cottage together, and I thought it was because we both loved it up here. 'Thank you for today, Ashley. You have made it so much easier.'

'My pleasure, Mhairi. It is good to be here a part of your family.' I didn't want to lie to her. It was nice to feel a part of this family, even if it wasn't the normal type. Only I had to get over the fact that they were vampires, and I was already.

'Mhairi, come and see the pram.' Jake was eager for her to see the pram that they bought. They have been very quick with it. I expected them to be here for hours.

'Hopefully, the cot is as easy to build.' Dale seemed relieved that one thing was out of the way, and I knew that he still wasn't entirely happy about the situation, but he was trying his best.

'It is lovely, Mhairi.'

'Yes, it is, dear. I just hope Callum likes it.' I got sidetracked as I spotted the baby clothes on the table. They looked so tiny and cute. It was hard to believe that they would fit on someone because they were so small. I jumped as I felt two arms wrap around my waist. I didn't know why I was so jumpy any more because I knew that Dale was never too far away from me.

'They look so tiny, don't they?'

'Are you OK, Ash?' I could hear the concern in his voice, but there, really, was no need.

'Yeah, I am fine. Why?'

'It is just you have got so involved in all this tonight, and it isn't even ours.' I put the clothes down and turned to face him. She wasn't ours, but she was still part of this family, and I couldn't take it out on a tiny baby.

'It is a "she", Dale. Do you want me to run a mile and let you get on with it? Our time will come. We can have fun in the meantime.'

'This conversation isn't over with yet, Mrs. I am going to build the cot, and we will head home. OK?' I walked over to the couch to be with Mhairi. It had been a very long day, and I just wanted to relax.

'It really is nice to see you and my son so in love.' I was taken aback when she started to speak about me and Dale, but I gave her all my attention and let the men get on with it.

'Thank you, Mhairi. I really do love him. You don't need to worry about that.'

'I know, dear. You two will make great parents some day.' I reached over and squeezed her hand; the coldness was there, but it didn't bother me any more.

'Our day will come. We have a long and happy life ahead of us.' I enjoyed my chats with Mhairi. She was so down-to-earth and said it how it was. There was no beating about the bush; if she didn't like something, then she just told you how it was. We both sat and watched Dale and Jake as they threw the babies cot up; they weren't even trying. Our chain of thought was interrupted by a knock on the door, and I got up to answer it since Dale was busy. It felt weird. No one has ever knocked on the door before. Dale followed me because he obviously thought that it was weird as well.

'Hello.'

'Hey, Callum, come in. You don't have to knock on the door, for God's sake.' I could tell that there was no love lost between these two brothers. Dale lifted some bags into the cottage, and Callum ran back out to the car. He brought a car seat in with a tiny bundle, sound asleep. I sat back down on the couch and watched Dale and Jake finish off with the cot. The atmosphere had changed, and it wasn't as inviting any more.

'Aw, look at her, Callum. She is gorgeous.' Mhairi was fussing over the tot. It was nice to see her excited now that she was here. 'Can I hold her, Callum?' I didn't understand why she felt the need to ask. I would never have wanted her to ask if it was me.

'Of course, Mom.' Mhairi took the tot out of the seat and sat on the sofa opposite me. This family seemed to get bigger each day. It would be even better if everyone got on with one another.

'Who is the chick?'

'Watch your mouth, Cal. The woman sitting on the chair is my fiancée, Ashley.' Callum had a smug look on his face as he held his hands up. I didn't think I liked him very much. But I had learnt never to read a book by its cover.

'Callum, behave yourself. Ashley has got everything organised for Kiara coming tonight. Don't you dare show this family up.'

'Sorry, Dad, I didn't know.' Dale came and sat on the arm of the couch beside me and put his arm around me.

'Here, Ashley, I am hoggin' her. Meet your niece.' Before I could say 'no it is fine', this tiny baby was bound into my arms. I sat looking at her for a couple of seconds. I didn't know how to react at first.

'Hello, little one, you are just lovely.' My maternal instinct kicked into full swing instantly, and I cradled her into my chest, just like she was a precious gem.

'She is just adorable, isn't she, hun?' I managed to nod my head and not say a word.

'You two look adorable with her.' Mhairi really wanted this child to be ours, but she wasn't, and I knew that it was all getting to Dale.

'Unless anything else needs built, we are going to head off.'

'Thanks for all your help, you two. Will we see you tomorrow?'

'Maybe, Mom. Depends what we have on at work.' I handed the baby back to Mhairi as Dale grabbed our jackets. It was amazing how one person could change the dynamics of a house.

'Ashley, here is your keys, dear.'

'Thank you, Jake. Dale, you can drive.' I got all my goodnight hugs and kisses from everyone, but I wasn't sure how to take Callum so I didn't bother to say a word to him. 'Good night every one.' We quickly left the cottage and headed outside. The cottage was stuffy tonight. There was no air with all the bodies crowded into it. 'That cottage was too crowded tonight.'

'You don't say, Ash. I am glad to be going home.' I climbed into the passenger side and sunk into the seat. This felt like a little piece of heaven.

'Don't you feel up to driving tonight.' I leant my head back and shook it gently. I could quite easily sleep here. I felt exhausted. We drove home in silence. There was only the radio on in the background. This had been another hectic day. My head was pounding and my body was aching. How many more days could my body take without protesting? The only good thing was that I had Dale. He was my knight in shining armour.

Chapter 11

Quiet Days

A couple of days had passed since the whole Rupert scenario, and I had been going into the office as usual. Dale had never mentioned me leaving, and I hadn't really thought about it too much since. I had had time to calm down and really didn't think that I would be happy working anywhere else. I had the taste of the good life. Today was the first day that I was in on my own, and I was a little bit on edge, but I wasn't going to let it spoil my day. Dale had meetings out of town today, and I wasn't enjoying being too far away from him. All I wanted to do was get all my work finished and get home. I was sitting at my desk filing all my files away when my laptop pinged. I had mail. The system was so slow today that it took forever to open my mail. I was very excited, and I just knew that it was going to be Dale. I was like a child with a new toy when I was around him. My body went all weak at the mention of his name, and I swore that the electricity radiated through us both when we were together.

To: Miss Ashley Malone
From: Mr Dale Black
Msg: Missing you

> Hey, babe, I hope everything is going OK in the office.
> I can't wait to see you later. I am missing you like crazy.
> I will try and get back before you finish. Love you lots.

Dale
xx

I quickly read through my mail and had butterflies from a simple email. This man knew how to get me going even when he wasn't around. I was going out of my mind today and that was because he was working away. How could I ever leave this office and move on to another job? I was going to have to grow a pair and get used to my own company again.

To: Mr Dale Black
From: Miss Ashley Malone
Msg: Missing you

> Hi, hun, everything is OK. It is very quiet today. I feel quite sick, so once I am finished, I was going to head home if that was OK. I can't wait to see you either. Don't rush I will see you at home later.
> Love you lots too.

Ashley
xx

I pushed the laptop to the side and got back to my work. Once this was done, I was going to lunch, and then hopefully after lunch, all going well I would get home. I had everything crossed that I would make it home early because whatever was making me feel so rubbish wasn't going away. My laptop pinged at me again, and I leant over to read my mail. I was never going to get finished if I didn't stop replying to Dale.

To: Miss Ashley Malone
From: Mr Dale Black
Msg: Missing you

> Ash, don't ask me if it is OK to go home. Are you OK, babe?
> I really wish you would go to the doctors. I have been worried
> about you the last couple of weeks. I will be home as soon as I
> can. Love you

Dale

xx

I knew that Dale was right. I had to find out why I was feeling so rough. The sickness was driving me crazy now. Could I give in though? Did I want to find out? I could probably count on one hand how many times I have been ill and here I was living my dream and constantly getting bugs. Even as a child, I was never ill. My mom used to take advantage of any illness because she got a chance to take care of me. I hit reply and sat for a few moments, waiting to figure out what to write. I hoped that the computer would write my reply for me. But that was never going to happen.

To: Mr Dale Black
From: Miss Ashley Malone
Msg: Missing you

> I will register with a doctor and get checked out.
> Will that make you happy? Get back to work, Dale!
> See you soon.

Ashley

xx

I knew that this response would make him happy. He worried too much about me. I knew that I should be honoured that I had found this man, and I was grateful that he cared for me so much, but I didn't like to think that I was putting him out. My phone rang and startled me, and it brought me back to here and now. I pushed the hands-free button and hoped it was nothing important.

'Hello, Black's Enterprise.'

'Hey, Ashley, it is Steph. I have Dale's mom on the other line. She is looking for Dale, but she sounds upset.' I couldn't just ignore her. She would only phone here if it was important.

'Put her through please, Steph.' I wondered what had happened now. We had spent the last couple of days in peace and quiet, enjoying our time together, and it was good just getting that time and space to ourselves. Was that the calm before the storm?

'Hello.'

'Hi, Mhairi, it is Ashley. Is everything OK?' I could hear what Steph heard now. She sounded really off, and it wasn't like her at all.

'Hello, dear, everything is going belly up. Callum walked out after he and Nikki had an argument. Jake went after him, and now I can't settle Kiara. I didn't know who else to turn to.'

'Mhairi, calm down. I will be right over. I will leave a message with Dale.'

'Are you sure, dear? I don't want to put you out.' I wished everyone would stop thinking that they are putting me out; if they didn't want my help, then why did they bother phoning me.

'Put the phone down and see to Kiara. I will be over soon.' I could hear Dale already, 'I told you this would all go pear-shaped.' My laptop pinged, and I quickly opened it. I knew that it was Dale, and I had the good job of telling him what had happened.

To: Miss Ashley Malone
From: Mr Dale Black
Msg: Missing you

It would make me happy. I don't like you feeling ill.
We will talk about it when I get home. Love you.

Dale
xx

I had to get to him quickly, and the only way that I could do that was through email. It was the coward's way because I couldn't hear how he actually felt about the whole thing, but it was easier for me.

> To: Mr Dale Black
> From: Miss Ashley Malone
> Msg: Missing you
>
> Where are you? I have to head to your mother's. She has been on the phone upset. Callum has walked out after a row with Nikki, and your dad went after him. Kiara is screaming, and your mom can't settle her. Will you get me there when you finish?
>
> Ashley
> xx

I hit send, and before I even saw or heard from him, I just knew that he was going to be angry. I cleared everything away and hoped to hear back from him before I left. Just as I finished my thoughts, my laptop pinged to life. My heart skipped a beat just thinking about his response. I felt bad for dropping this on him, especially when he was in a meeting. But I couldn't hide it from him.

> To: Miss Ashley Malone
> From: Mr Dale Black
> Msg: Missing you
>
> I am about an hour away from finishing this meeting. Can you go and sort my mother out, please? There is a hammer in the drawer if you need it. I will be back as soon as I can. This family is driving me crazy. There is never a dull moment. Ash, thank you. I am sure you will sort Kiara out.
> Love you.
>
> Dale

I quickly read my mail and rushed out of my office. I went to get Steph and explained what was to be done. I knew that my first priority should have been the mountain, but I had to make sure the office was running smoothly first. Steph would know that if she needed to get me, I had my cell. I left the building as quick as I could, and for once everything was on my side. The elevator was waiting for me, and there was no one wanting to chat. I got to the ground floor in record time and rushed out to my car. I didn't like driving fast, but I had to make an exception today. I had a fast driving. She could handle everything I threw at her. My phone was ringing already; surely, it wasn't the office. Now I knew why I was just a PA because I couldn't handle all the stress and strain of being a boss. I managed to push hands-free button and answered my call.

'Hello, Ashley Malone speaking.'

'Hey, Ash, it is only me. Did you get away from the office OK?' I was relieved that it was only Dale. I couldn't take all the extra running around today.

'Yeah, just heading up the mountain now.' Dale sounded really pissed off. His voice was dull, not his usual happy tone.

'OK, babe, I will give you half an hour, and I will phone you back.'

'OK. Are you OK?' The silence was there for seconds, but I knew that he was worried about me.

'Yeah. Just fed up that you have to run around unwell because my brother won't grow up.' I knew that he would automatically jump down his brother's throat, and he didn't even know what had happened.

'Listen, I was going home after lunch anyway. There is nothing ventured.' I didn't want him to think that I was putting myself out.

'Going home to rest. Not to look after a baby and an elderly woman.'

'I am only a few minutes away. Phone me back in a little while.' I didn't want him to get stressed out at work. He needed to keep him calm especially when he was with clients.

'OK, babe, speak soon.' I listened as the line went dead. I would do anything to have a magic wand right now. I took the fork exit to take me into the cottage and quickly grabbed my phone and headed into see what was going on. I was on autopilot. I could still hear Kiara, screaming from outside. I had no idea what I was going to walk in on, but I was here now. I couldn't turn back now.

'Mhairi. Where are you?' She came through from the bedroom with a tired baby in her arms. She looked so upset herself, and I felt so sorry for her.

'I can't calm her down, and she won't take her bottle.'

'Give me her, and you go and put the coffee on.' Mhairi handed me the baby and did as she was told. I certainly didn't like being harsh, but at the minute, someone needed to calm the situation down. I lifted Kiara up on to my shoulder and patted her back. She soothed instantly. I couldn't believe that she had screamed all that time. She had to be exhausted. Her bottle was sitting on the table in front of me, and I sat down and cuddled her in to take her milk. I never thought that I would be the one to enjoy feeding a tiny baby her milk. I guessed I never had a maternal instinct until I fell in love with Dale. He seemed to bring the best out of me. Mhairi came back through with a tray of coffee and biscuits. She was more than gobsmacked that I had settled Kiara down.

'How did you do that?'

'She probably sensed that you were stressed.' My phone was ringing, and somehow I managed to answer it without disturbing the baby too much.

'Hello . . . Yeah, Kiara is feeding just now. She has exhausted herself with all that screaming . . . No, your dad isn't answering, and Callum has put his phone off . . . Yes, I am fine. See you when you get here.' I put my phone down and lifted Kiara to break her wind. She was out for the count. 'Where do you want me to put her, Mhairi?'

'Anywhere, dear.' The pram was right beside us, so that was the easiest option. 'Come and get your coffee, Ashley.' I sat back down beside Mhairi, and any fool could see that she was upset.

'What is wrong, Mhairi?'

'I am not cut out for all this fighting and bickering any more.' I put my hand on hers and squeezed it gently.

'We all get days like this, love. Tomorrow will be a better day.' I knew only too well that two days were never the same. You just had to bounce back from it.

'I hope so, dear. Do you mind if I take your car to go out looking?' I could hear the desperation in her voice, but I couldn't possibly lose her as well.

'No, I don't mind you taking my car, but Dale will be here any minute, and he will have a better plan of action.' I didn't want to be the one to break the news to Dale that I had lost his mother now as well. That would be the icing on the cake.

'You're right, dear.' My phone rang again. It never rang for days; then, all of a sudden, it never stopped.

'Sorry, I have to answer this.' Mhairi waved her hand at me, and I quickly walked into the kitchen to answer it. 'Hello, Ashley Malone.'

'Hey, Ashley, it is Steph. Sorry to bother you, but I have Robert on the line. He needs signatures on some paperwork.'

'Can you connect him to my phone, please, Steph?'

'Yes. I think I can. Hold on.' I was relieved to see Dale standing in the living room. He looked up and smiled at me, and I was glad to have him here. Anything could happen now, and it wouldn't matter because I had him by my side.

'Hello.'

'Hi, Robert, it is Ashley. What can I help you with?'

'Hi, Ashley, I need a signature from you or Dale to confirm a few things.'

'Can this wait until morning, Robert? It is just that we have had to leave the office to deal with an emergency family thing.' I was hoping that he would understand.

'Yes, Ashley, that is fine, honey. I will fax them over just now.' Relief washed over me. Luck certainly was on my side today because I didn't think that I had the energy to run back to the office just now.

'Thank you, Robert. I will take care of it myself first thing.'

'Great. Speak soon, Ashley.' I hung up the phone and slumped against the worktop. I was glad of the support to be honest.

'What is it, Ash?' I didn't want to concern Dale with more work, but now he was asking so I had no choice.

'Aw, nothing. Robert needs signatures on some paperwork, but I have put him off until tomorrow. He is going to fax them through just now.' Dale walked over to me and placed his hands on my waist. I felt much better feeling him hold me.

'Thank you, babe. You look very tired.'

'I am, but I will be fine. What plan do you have about your dad? Your mom wanted my car to go out looking, but I managed to put her off for the time being.' I did hope that all of this would unravel itself and we could go home.

'Ash, I don't know what to do for the best . . .' Kiara's cry stopped Dale from talking any more, but it didn't make him take his hands off me.

'What about your dad and Callum?'

'I think if I am being honest, they will walk in as if nothing has happened. What is wrong with the baby?'

'I don't know. Your mom said she was like it for hours today, but she calmed down the minute I took her.' I didn't want to sound too cocky about it, but I thought that she was just stressing because she could sense all the atmosphere.

'Ashley dear, do you want to try again?' I couldn't say no. It was horrible listening to a tiny baby crying so sore. I walked over to Mhairi and took the baby from her. It felt like the most natural thing in the world for me to do, but she wasn't mine.

'Come on, Kiara, you are upsetting your grandma.' I cradled her this time, and she soothed down again. The pain in Mhairi's face was enough. She clearly thought that the baby didn't like her. I would be feeling the very same thing if I was in her shoes.

'We need to find her dad. It isn't fair on her getting attached to me.' I loved the child like my own, but she needed her own dad to be here caring for her.

'I am going to wring his neck when I find him.' I knew that Dale was mad at Callum, but that wasn't going to help anyone.

'Dale, take her.' I practically threw the baby at him. I was glad that she didn't seem to mind though. I had to run to the bathroom to be sick again, and I just made it. Could I really keep going like this? I leant up against the wall and placed my head in my arms. My body was shaking from throwing up so violently, I had never experienced anything like this before.

'Ash, can we come in?' Dale's head peeked around the door with Kiara, cosy in his arms. They sat across from me on the floor, and I reached up and placed the toilet seat down and flushed it. My body felt all weak from being sick, but seeing Dale cradle his niece for the first time was a magical moment. It brought tears to my eyes.

'She likes you too.'

'What can I say, she has good taste.' I reached forward and touched her soft hand. I was heartbroken for this tiny bundle. No one seemed to want her around, and she didn't know if she was coming or going. 'Ash, what is going on?' I shook my head curiously and sat back against the wall. I had a feeling that I was going to need to be comfortable.

'What do you mean?'

'If you knew why you were being sick and feeling terrible, would you tell me?' I couldn't get my head around him thinking I was keeping something from him.

'Dale, I haven't even seen a doctor. Why would I know? But to answer your question, of course I would tell you.' He looked down at the baby, and his look said it all. He was thinking about what to say next or how to say it.

'Can I put something to you?' Did I want to hear any of this now? Today of all days, Dale picked this moment to rake everything up.

'Go for it.' I inhaled a deep breath and waited for it.

'You are tired. You are sick a lot. You keep getting a sore stomach.' It was my body. I was well aware of how I felt. I just didn't know why.

'And where are you going with this?' The whole room was silent, even Kiara didn't make a sound.

'Could you be pregnant?' He looked down at Kiara and then up at me. I should have known that he was starting to put two and two together, but I couldn't answer his question because I didn't know. Obviously, we had been sleeping together, a lot. But that didn't mean that I was pregnant. I hated how a woman gets a sore stomach or has a bug and everyone automatically thinks that she is carrying a child.

'I don't know anything any more, Dale.' I stood up and rinsed my mouth out, and I didn't know how I felt. I slowly turned to look down at him, and he had never taken his eyes from me. 'Dale, we have enough on our plates this afternoon. Let's get your dad home and take things from there.' I didn't want to think about me being sick just now. I just wanted to forget about it.

'Ash, my dad will be fine. I am more concerned about you and the fact that you could be carrying our child.' I moved to shut the door over because the last thing we needed right now was for Mhairi to hear any of this. 'Will you keep your voice down? We don't even know if that is what the problem is.'

'We never will if you don't face this.'

'Don't push me, Dale. We will deal with this tomorrow.' I walked away from him and opened the door. I had never actually spoken to him in that way before, and I had never just walked away from him. I felt bad, but there was bigger fish to fry right now.

'Are you OK, dear?'

'Yeah, I am fine. I never ate this lunchtime, and my stomach was protesting.' I tried to make a joke out of this situation because Mhairi had enough to deal with right now. She didn't need our problems as well.

'You need to look after yourself, dear.'

'She can't look after herself for taking care of this family.' My fiancé was like a Jack Russell today, and he was really doing my head in.

'Enough, Dale.' I snapped at him again because sometimes he was just too honest. I managed to glare over at him, and hopefully, it would be enough to shut him up. His phone started ringing, and with Kiara sleeping in his arms, he managed to juggle them both. He really did look good cradling his niece in his arms. Fatherhood would suit him one day.

'Carlos . . . OK thanks.'

'What is it, Dale?' Poor Mhairi was at her wits' end with everything today. It was a shame.

'Carlos is bringing Dad and Nikki back.'

'And Callum?' She was beside herself with worry, and any mother would be the same in this situation.

'Mom, I don't know. Dad will be here in a minute. He will fill you in. He is the least of my worries at the minute. For his sake, I better not see him today.'

'Dale, you are not helping. Go home if that is the mood you are in.' I was really on the ball today; where my nippy tongue had come from was anyone's guess. I had held my tongue too long, and today was the day that I was going to answer back as I felt fit.

'Home is where we should be, not dealing with my immature brother.' You could cut the atmosphere in here with a knife. It was horrible being stuck in the middle of it. I could see Dale's point, but my heart sided with Mhairi. The door swung open and in came Nikki and Jake. They both looked as bad as each other. Mhairi jumped up and gave Jake a hug; she was in some state today, and I didn't like to see her like this.

'What has happened?'

'Callum has booked into a motel. He is refusing to come back home. He doesn't see the point in all the arguing.' Callum was right. I didn't see the point in all the arguing either, but now there was a tiny baby involved. They all had to put their differences aside for her sake.

'What motel, Dad?' Dale asked the question that I longed to know.

'Three Kings, in town.' I got up and rushed out of the door and jumped into the car beside Carlos. I didn't know where my energy came from to move so fast. 'Take me to the Three Kings in town, please, Carlos.'

'Ashley.' Dale opened the door and bent down beside me. I could see how upset and hurt he was, but I had to do this for everyone.

'Give me half an hour with him, and if I don't come back, you can come for me.'

'On one condition . . . After this we find out tonight.' I sighed, but I knew that it was one condition that I had to agree on.

'I promise.' I kissed Dale on the lips and told Carlos to go. My door closed over, and we were on our way. I wanted to keep a clear mind for meeting Callum, but it wasn't easy with everything floating about. As much as I wanted to punch him, I had to think about this from his point of view. I had no idea what I was going to say him; we were like chalk and cheese. Why couldn't Callum be like Jake and Dale? We would get along just fine. I looked out of the window as we reached the town. My mind was all over the place: Callum, Kiara, Dale, and the fact that I could be pregnant. When was I ever going to get a break?

'Ashley, it is just up there, but I can't get the car any further up.' Thank God for Carlos, interrupting my mind games because I could get lost very easily in my own thoughts.

'Thanks, Carlos. Wait here for me, and don't answer Dale's calls until I come back out.' I got out of the car without even waiting for Carlos to make any excuse. I knew that he would do as I said; he was just like a brother figure to me now. My heart was beating so fast as I rushed down to the motel. I was still dressed in business clothes and felt uncomfortable about going into a motel dressed like this. But needs must. I didn't have to look very far; Callum was propping the bar up, the very place that I expected him to be.

'Callum.' He looked very sad and down, and I didn't expect to see him like this.

'Where is everyone?' I wasn't surprised that he thought that I was here with someone other than myself.

'It is just me.' I pulled a seat up alongside him and looked at his long pale face. Anyone could see that it was killing him to be away from Kiara. 'Come back to the cottage with me, Callum.'

'I can't, Ashley. They are driving me crazy. I am never going to be perfect like you and Dale.' I couldn't help but smile at him because he had no idea how mixed up we were.

'Have you heard yourself? We are far from perfect . . . Do you want to know what I have been doing all afternoon?' I saw him look at me slowly for an explanation, but I didn't know how to tell him how upset his daughter has been.

'I am sure you are going to tell me.'

'I have had to comfort your daughter. She has been so upset and needs her daddy.'

'She will want for nothing. I will make sure of that.'

'Money and possessions are nothing without love.' My parents always used to drum that bit of advice into my head, and now with age I could understand every word. 'Come home and sleep it off, and start afresh tomorrow.' His whole body swung around on his seat, and the tears held back in his eyes.

'I want my daughter, Ash, but I don't think that I can out her through this life.' I didn't know what he meant, but I wasn't feeling shy tonight.

'What do you mean, honey?'

'She deserves better than this . . . Vampires is something she shouldn't need to see.' I wasn't surprised that Callum was seeing the negative side to his parent's being vampires, but there were worse things on this earth.

'She deserves a daddy who loves her, and the rest will work itself out.' Part of me could understand his concerns, but the other part of me knew that Mhairi and Jake would act no different to Kiara.

'I bet Dale is gunning for me . . .'

'I think that he has other things on his mind right now, hun.' I didn't really want to discuss my life tonight, but Callum needed to know that we had our own life to deal with as well.

'Now you have got me intrigued.'

'You don't want to know, Cal . . .'

'Try me . . .' He was Dale's brother all right. He couldn't drop anything.

'I haven't been too well lately, and now I think I know why . . .' He had that same look of concern that Dale always had, and it made talking to him easy.

'You're not ill, are you?'

'No . . . not exactly. I think that I might be pregnant.' I never expected to be sharing my problems with Callum of all people, but he was a good listener.

'You will be great parents, Ash.'

'Well, now you know my story. Are you coming home with me to get your daughter?'

'One bit of grief I get and I am off . . . I always knew that Dale would fall in love with someone like you.'

'Bossy and nippy.' We were both laughing together now; it was nice to break the ice with Callum. He wasn't as bad as I first thought. A baby always brings a family together, and for the second time this week, I had learnt not to judge a book by its cover.

'I was thinking beautiful and smart.'

'Should I take that as a compliment?'

'Please do. I don't give them very often . . . Is Kiara OK?' Anyone could see that he wanted to be a dad to his daughter; he really did care about her, and it was nice to see.

'She was sleeping when I left.'

'Thank you for taking care of her.'

'Carlos is out front waiting on us.' We got up and walked out of the motel, and I felt relief flood through my body and felt proud that he listened to me. We stepped into the car and sat in silence. 'Carlos, can I get your phone, please?'

'Sure.' I took the phone from him and dialled Dale's number. It only rang once, and I heard the concern in his tone.

'Hi, it is just me. Get your mom and dad to back off for tonight. I will be back in five.' I hung up without even listening to Dale; he knew that we were safe and homeward bound that was all that mattered. Now that I had dealt with everyone else's problems, I had to go home and face my own. The car was silent from the moment we left the motel, and it felt like a morgue. Cold and silent.

'What if I screw up, Ashley?' I knew that something was bothering him, and now I heard him talking to me I just wanted him to know that he could only do his best.

'You wouldn't be human if you never screwed up. You can only do your best and never let anyone tell you otherwise.'

'She deserves better.'

'She deserves her daddy. Everything else will come.' The car pulled up outside the cottage, and we all got out together quickly. 'Just be a daddy to your baby, honey.'

'Thank you . . . You better look after yourself as well.'

'Go . . . Carlos, can you tell Dale to meet me in my car when he is ready?'

'Sure, Ashley.' I walked over to my car and slumped into the passenger's seat. I knew that Dale wouldn't be too long; he would be on autopilot. I had finally given up trying to have a nice, quiet day. Are they even possible? Dale jumped into the driver's seat and turned to look at me.

'I don't know how you managed that, but thank you.' I let my head relax to the side to look at him and didn't know what to say. 'Are you OK?'

'I will be when I get home and out of these clothes.'

'Do you want to go home?'

'Please.' My body was empty. Everything that I had to give today had been given. Dale pulled away from the cottage and headed down the mountains. We would be home in no time at all, and that was all I wanted. Our car was so silent. Was this another calm before the storm? I noticed Dale taking a detour through the town, and I sat back and enjoyed the ride. I didn't want to know where we were going any more.

'I will be back now.' I didn't even have the energy to find out where he was going. I put the radio on and rested my eyes; this actually felt like heaven, peace and quiet. Dale broke the silence by banging his door shut, and he quickly started the car and drove off. He never looked twice at me, and I couldn't help but wonder what kind of night were we going to have? The roads were quiet, and the streets were deserted so we got home in no time, thank God. The car came to a halt outside the house, and we both got out. I grabbed my bags from the back seat and walked in front of Dale. The minute we stepped inside, the feel of home hit me, and for once I could actually get used to living here with Dale. 'I am going to head up.'

'OK.' Dale was quite blunt with me, and I didn't know how to feel. Was he just getting me back for snapping at him earlier? I got into our room and slumped on the bed. I lay back and stared up at the ceiling; my body relaxed into the soft covers. I felt Dale's presence as he came over and lay on his side beside me. I was glad to see him, even though I wasn't sure where this was going to go now.

'Are you OK, Ash?' I never took my eyes from the ceiling; it was my focus point. 'Are you mad at me?'

'I am not one to hold grudges, but you didn't have to snap at your mom . . . None of this mess is her fault.' I knew that Mhairi could be difficult, but she didn't deserve the last word out of everyone's mouth.

'Are we talking about Callum or what I said in the bathroom?'

'Both.' His hand gently pulled my chin around so that we were facing each other. I knew that he wouldn't want to talk to the side of my face.

'I don't class a pregnancy as a mess, Ash. I stopped by the store on the way home to get this.' He pulled a home pregnancy kit from his back pocket and waved it in front of me. 'We need to know, Ash.'

'Will it change anything?' I couldn't deal with anything that would jeopardise our relationship, and I just wanted to know where we stood with one another.

'What do you mean?' I sat up and thought about what needed to be said. I couldn't just jump in with my two feet.

'If it is positive, then what?' His hand came up and moved my hair away from my face. I couldn't resist any more; I needed to look at his face. It was the only way that I could see the truth.

'I thought that we wanted this, babe. I would be over the moon . . . me, you, and our own little bundle of joy.'

'And if it is negative?'

'Then we will just have to have more fun trying.' I sat and sighed; those were the answers I hoped to hear, but my mind was still working over time. I was so scared. The luck this family had was poor. What did that say for us? 'What are you scared of, Ash?'

'Everything. I don't want to lose you. I don't want to fail at being a mother.' After hearing Callum tonight, I knew how easy it was to feel like a failure, and I didn't want that to happen to us.

'Stop it. You will never lose me. I have never loved anyone as much as I have loved you. Seeing you with Kiara has proved to me that you will be a perfect mother. You are meant to be a mommy. I want you to be the mother of my child.'

'Why do you have to be so nice?' I held my hand out to take the test. I needed to do it now before I changed my mind. I got up and started to walk as Dale pulled my hand back.

'Whatever the result is, just remember that I love you.' My heart fluttered in my chest as I walked into the bathroom. The instructions were pretty straightforward, but I was like a nervous wreck. I went over to the toilet and did the test. Doing the test was the easy bit, but the one-minute wait was the hardest part. I put the seat down and flushed the toilet. I placed the test down while I washed my hands, and I sat back on the seat in a foetal position and placed my head in my knees. The minute had to be up, but I had frozen on the spot. I heard the door open, and Dale walked over to me. He perched down beside me and placed his hands over mine.

'Ash, what is it?'

'I don't know. I can't look.' I couldn't even look up at Dale. He took the test off the side and studied it carefully; the instructions sat beside it. The silence had me a nervous wreck.

'It is positive, Ash.' I looked up to listen carefully. It hadn't sunk in. 'It is positive, babe.' I took the test off him and saw the two lines clearly. I couldn't believe what I was seeing. I quickly stood up and leant against the washbasin.

'This means . . .'

'We are going to have a baby, Ash.' Dale's arms hugged me tight, and he seemed really happy about our news, and I was glad that he took it in his stride. I didn't know why I was so nervous earlier when he mentioned me being pregnant.

'Are you OK about this?'

'You have made me the happiest man alive.' I took his hand and brought him back through to the room. I needed a seat and quickly. I sat on the end of the bed, and Dale knelt in front of me. 'Will you start looking after yourself now?' I felt like one of those nodding dogs lately; my head never stopped nodding. 'Will you book into the clinic tomorrow and let me take care of it?'

'I will look into it tomorrow.'

'Are you happy, Ash?' Happy was an understatement. I thought that I was going to burst with the excitement of becoming a mommy. It was the best news that I had ever heard.

'Yes, I am just overwhelmed. In the space of a few weeks, we have practically moved in together and got engaged, and now we are having a baby.'

'It all seems like a dream.'

'Will you lie with me?' We hadn't even had a shower or took our clothes off, but right now that was the last thing on my mind.

'Of course, I will, babe.' We both lay back on the bed, and Dale placed his other hand on my tummy. My eyes were heavy the minute I lay down, and I felt the light flicker out like a burnt-out candle.

CHAPTER 12

Joy and Pain

'Good morning, my name is Ashley Malone. I am looking to book into one of your pregnancy clinics, but I am not sure how to go about it . . . Yes, this is my first pregnancy . . . Private care . . . Please . . . Anything between four and six weeks, but it is a guess . . . Yes, that will be great. Thank you. What do I need to bring with me? OK, thank you. See you tomorrow.' That telephone call took a huge wait off my shoulders. This whole pregnancy thing now felt real, and I just had to get my head around it all. We were going to be parents, and I couldn't be happier. I sat at the breakfast bar with my coffee in front of me, and for the first time in my life, I felt complete. I had a good upbringing with my mom and dad, and I was giving everything that I ever wanted. My mom and dad would have been thrilled at becoming grandparents, and at times like this, it made me realise how much I miss them and how incomplete my life has been without them.

'Morning, hun. How are my two angels doing?' I was glad that Dale came through and stopped me from thinking about my parents. I didn't want to think how unhappy my life had been. I just wanted to look to the future and think about how happy we are going to be. I felt like I couldn't stop smiling and someone was going to know something was going on. It was going to be hard to keep it from everyone, especially if I couldn't stop being sick.

'We are fine.' I felt his arms wrap around my waist, and his hands caressed my tummy. It was one of the most naturalist things in the world to do, and I loved him dearly for it.

'What is all this?' I had a couple of things written down on a notepad for my appointment at the clinic, and of course, Dale spotted them in front of me. He never missed a trick.

'I have an appointment tomorrow at the clinic . . . 9.30 in the morning.'

'Good. Nothing but the best for my two favourite people.' I knew that he was speaking from the heart, and we would never need to worry about a thing, but I wanted his full support not just material things.

'I know you have had a lot of time away from the office, but I was wondering if you could come with me?' I hated making him take time off from work because he never had time off until he met me.

'Ash . . . I was there before you even asked. By the time this baby is born, you will be sick of the sight of me.' I swung around in my seat to face him, and his face was full of joy. 'How did we fall asleep in suits and I get up to find you here in a robe all fresh?'

'You looked so peaceful. I didn't want to disturb you. Besides, we couldn't go into work with yesterday's clothes on. People would talk.'

'I have woken up this morning. You are glowing. You are taking care of yourself. You booked an appointment at the clinic and then spoil it by saying you are going to work.' I didn't realise that I had to be taking things easy and staying away from work. I could see that I and Dale were going to disagree on things over the next nine months.

'I am pregnant, not ill, babe.' I wasn't going to be one of those women who couldn't lift a cup because they were pregnant.

'Please take today and tomorrow to yourself. Treat yourself, sleep, and do whatever you desire. Just let me take care of the office today.' It did sound nice to spend some time by myself, but there was so much to do.

'It wouldn't be fair on you . . . Besides, I have that paperwork to take care of for Robert.' I wouldn't feel comfortable leaving everything to him; it wouldn't be fair.

'I think that I can sign it without you there. Please, babe, humour me.' I could see the exhausted look in his eyes as if to say, I was too tired to argue, but I really wanted you to take it easy.

'OK. OK. You win. I will put my feet up and relax today.' I was far too excited to argue back; it was about time that I took care of myself and forgot about the outside world.

'I love you, Miss Malone . . . Since you have had your shower, what do you plan on doing?' I knew what I wanted to do, but would he give it to me?

'That depends on you.'

'Depends on what?' The curious look on his face made me laugh. He clearly didn't think the same as me.

'If you are joining me?'

'You know that I would love to but work has my name all over it today . . . This morning at least.' He really didn't sound keen on leaving me, but needs must, I suppose.

'So this is us second best to work, Mr Black . . . We can't be having that now.' I couldn't help but use my sarcastic charm on him; he was too easy to get going.

'Are we playing that game now, Miss Malone? That is below the belt.' I screeched as he tickled me and squeezed me close. I felt alive and so in love with this man that it felt unreal. 'As much as I want to give in and spend the whole day with you, I have to get our company ready to run itself.' I was very confused. Why would it need to run itself? I turned to look at him, very intrigued. I didn't know if I wanted to know what he meant either.

'Why would it need to run itself? Where do you plan on going?' I was very nervous now, and my heart couldn't take the suspense. Was he leaving us to our own defences as well?

'I want to spend as much time with you and our baby in the first few years. I don't want to be a part-time dad who works every hour godsends.' I rested my head on his chest with relief. I really took that the wrong way. I thought that was his way of saying goodbye. Of course, he wouldn't be leaving us; my hormones were definitely playing tricks with me. 'Do I even want to know what you were thinking?'

'Blame the hormones. I thought that was you saying you were going somewhere and that you were leaving us to our own defences.' As I said that out loud, it hit me how ridiculous I sounded.

'Ash, I am going nowhere. You are carrying my child, and the love I had for you has quadrupled since yesterday. I didn't think it was possible to love someone as much.' I could understand exactly how he felt because I felt the same.

'Now that we have cleared that up, are you going to let me cook you breakfast? You can go for a shower.' I wanted to see what it would be like to be a housewife. I wanted to be the best wife and mother anyone could ask for.

'OK. Since you are going to take things easy and look after yourself, I will let you cook breakfast.' A tender kiss was placed on my lips as I watched him leave the kitchen. Today was another fresh start for us, and we had jumped over another hurdle and survived. What more could we ask for?

Daydreaming was my middle name. But lately, life was far too adventurous to dream. I was in my closet getting fresh pyjamas on and sat on my stool. For the first time in months, I could actually map out our future. I was relieved to see what Dale always could because I always felt abnormal in some way, for only seeing here and now. But now I knew that all my fussing wasn't needed, not now or ever.

'Hey, there you are. I wondered where you had got to.' I didn't realise that I had been sitting in my closet for so long, but it must have been a while if I had him looking for me.

'Sorry. I was just thinking and clearly lost track of time.'

'Is everything OK, Ash?'

'Sure. I am going to go for a lie-down and make the most of a quiet house.' I shocked myself by saying that I was going for a lie-down. I couldn't actually remember the last time that I had a day to myself, and I was going to make the most of it.

'Glad to hear it. Rosa will make you lunch if you are here.' It was nice to know that Rosa would still be here if I needed anything, but I wasn't planning on going anywhere today.

'Dale, will you go? I am an adult. I have lived on my own for a lot of years.'

'OK, I am sorry. I just care about you . . . About both of you . . . OK, I am going.' He would be as well wrapping me in cotton wool. I was like a delicate rose about to snap at any minute. 'I love you, Mrs Black-to-be.'

'We love you too.' I got a kiss on my cheek as he rushed out of the door, and everything went quiet. Peace perfect peace. I got up and walked out of the room, and I thought that I was still on cloud nine from last night. Nothing could deflate me today, so anything could get thrown at me, and I would bounce it back. The house was so quiet as I moved around. It felt nice to walk around the house and take everything in rather than just rush around the place. The kitchen was my first stop because I needed a cup of tea.

'Good morning, Ashley. Congratulations about your baby news. You will both make great parents.' Rosa knew about the baby. I didn't really want people to know yet, not until tomorrow, not until we knew that everything was OK.

'Carlos and I heard you and Dale talking last night. Don't worry, we won't say a word until you are ready.' Anyone would have thought that Rosa was going to burst with pride.

'Thank you, Rosa.'

'Let me get you your coffee.'

'I am going to have a tea this morning . . .' Her face was a picture as she turned back to look at me. I was a coffee queen, but I had suddenly changed my mind this morning. 'What? I suppose I better cut some of the coffee out.'

'Go and put your feet up, and I will bring it through.'

'I am going to go up for a lie-down.' I was so lucky to have all this extra support. Some women would do everything themselves, but here I was with a loving husband, family, and extra help around the house. Pampered princess was an understatement. I pulled the covers back on my bed and climbed in. I cuddled into Dale's pillow for added comfort while he was away. I could still smell him from it, and it eased me back into a sleepy state.

'I will place your tea here, Ashley.'

'Thank you, Rosa.' I managed to answer Rosa and no more. My eyes were closed, and my body was relaxed. The baby and Dale were in my mind until morning turned into night. I thought that I had this to look forward to for the rest of my life, and I was really looking forward to having a little person around all the time.

'Ashley . . . Ashley.' My mind was all hazy. My eyes were all fuzzy, and I didn't have a clue what time of day it was. I had been sleeping since Rosa fetched me my tea.

'What is it?' I was concerned that there was something wrong. It wasn't like him to wake me up in such a panic.

'Are you OK?'

'Yeah, why?' I sat up in bed and tried to make myself more lively. Dale's face looked very concerned, and I had absolutely no idea why.

'Rosa phoned me just after lunch and said she was worried about you because you haven't moved since this morning.' My head shook without me even thinking about it. I felt quite angry and betrayed that Rosa could do that to me.

'Hey. Hey. Hey.' Dale pulled me towards him to comfort me, but my tears were from anger. I pushed back from him and looked down at my hands. 'I was just about to come home any way.'

'That isn't the point, Dale. Is this how it is going to be now? Let's run and tell, Dale, if something doesn't seem quite right.' The nippy sweetie was back, and I couldn't help it.

'No.'

'Ashley isn't eating, let's get Dale. Ashley looks pale, let's get Dale. News flash. I am pregnant. Not dying.' I felt like a nagging old sweetie wife, but I was acting like a stupid child at the same time. I was more than angry that everyone was keeping tags on me.

'Now that you have got that out of your system, can I speak?' I looked up at him intrigued. What could he say that was going to calm me down? 'It isn't going to be like this. I will tell Rosa that she doesn't need to keep tabs on you.' I lay back into bed. I didn't know what to think any more; my head was going round in circles. I couldn't deal with this pampered-princess routine. I had always been a free spirit, and nothing ever kept me tied down. But now I felt like I was suffocating. I looked up to see Dale taking his shoes off, and he pulled his tie over his head. I loved him unconditionally and didn't want to lose him, but the added eyes and ears were going to drive me crazy.

'I think that I might go home for a couple of days.' You could have cut the silence with a knife. I desperately wanted Dale to say something, but he lay beside me on the bed, and his face was like stone. He looked like he had the weight of the world on his shoulders, and I couldn't help but think it was all because of me.

'Is that what you want to do?' His voice sounded hurt as if I had just ripped his gut out.

'I don't know what I want any more. My head is nipping with all the added eyes and ears. I was doing what I promised, and still it get backs to you.' He placed his hand on my tummy, and I could feel his eyes burning holes through me.

'Please tell me that you are not getting second thoughts about us . . . about the baby.' His voice was all shaky, and now I felt like rubbish for it.

'You and our baby are the only two things that I am sure about. I love you both more than words can describe.' I saw the relief wash over his face, and I was glad to see it. I could be such a bitch at times. Why did I even give him those doubts?

'You both mean so much to me, Ash. Tell me what I need to do. What will make you stay in our home?' I knew what I wanted to say, but I didn't want to sound like a bitch.

'I just want to be treated like a normal person . . . No fussing . . . If I am feeling rough, I can tell you myself. Rosa and Carlos don't need to go behind my back to carry stories back to you.' My hormones must be raging because my tears were like a tap lately.

'Shh. I don't like to see you like this.' I cuddled into him and sobbed myself dry from tears. 'You can blame the tears on the pregnancy.' I wished I could, but I thought that everything was just building up on me.

'There is only so much that I can blame the pregnancy for. I should have gone to work.' If I had busied myself at work, then none of this would have happened.

'This isn't just to do with Rosa, is it? Is there something else bothering you?'

'No, there isn't anything else bothering me.' His gentle hand ran through my hair, and it felt nice. It was strange lying here now. I felt peaceful and complete. My eyes closed as we lay tangled together. Love is one of the most powerful things in the world that can make or break two people. But when it is the true thing, it is unbreakable.

I came to the same position that I fell asleep. The whole room was pitch-black, and it felt very peaceful. Dale was still lying beside me with his arms wrapped around me. I moved out of his grasp and rolled out of bed to get on to my feet. I had slept more in the last forty-eight hours than I had done in years. My body felt light as a feather as I walked down the stairs and into the kitchen. I needed a cold drink, and the first thing that sprung to my mind was milk. I never drink milk, but I wasn't going to complain. At least it was healthy and good for the baby. I poured myself a glass and drunk it in one go. It got me wide awake and fully aware of everything going on in my life. Since moving to Anchorage, everything had worked out just perfect for me. I couldn't believe I was going to be a wife and a mother, and I couldn't be any happier with my life.

'Ash.' My thoughts were broken by Dale wondering where I was. I thought that I would have woken him the minute I moved.

'In the kitchen.' The breakfast bar had become my perch. I didn't feel at home, but it was comfortable.

'I thought you had run away.'

'What do you take me for, Mr Black? You can't get rid of me that easy.' Dale pulled a stool up beside me and looked at my empty glass.

'You, drinking milk, now that is a first.' He was just as surprised as I was. Pregnancy really does strange things to your mind and body.

'It is strange because I never drink milk, but it was the first thing that popped into my mind.'

'Have you eaten, hun?'

'No. I was contemplating what to have before you came down.'

'Let me make us something to eat. Or we can order something in. What do you fancy?'

'I am not fussed. What do you fancy?' We both sat for a few moments, and nothing was said. We were always doing this when it came to food; none of us could decide.

'I actually could just eat some soup.' I was going to turn into a bowl of Mhairi's soup, that was all I have eaten the last couple of days.

'My mom sent some more home-made soup over. It is in the fridge.'

'That sounds perfect for us. Let me do it.' I needed to feel like I was doing something before I sat too long and fell asleep again.

'Let me do it, Ash. Let me make it up to you for today.' I didn't argue the point. I was just so relieved that we were both here together. I really wanted to know what was going through his mind after today because I bet I opened a lot of old wounds.

'What are you thinking, Dale?' I watched my man potter around the kitchen; he was very sexy when he was domesticated. Never in a million years did I think that I would be marrying a man who would take care of me in such a way.

'I just can't believe how everything has turned out for us.'

'It still feels like a dream. I keep expecting someone to wake me up at any moment.' I enjoyed just sitting chatting about random things it flowed so easily.

'Coffee?' Coffee wasn't good for the baby, but I didn't want to turn into one of those pregnant women who watch everything they eat and drink.

'No, I will just have another glass of milk.' I got up and walked over to the fridge. I felt like I had a bounce in my step. I poured my milk out and placed the carton back in the fridge. I could feel all eyes on me and glanced over to him. He was leaning against the worktop, smiling at me like a Cheshire cat.

'What is amusing you, Dale?' I walked over to him and stepped over his legs. I placed most of my weight over him and waited for his response. Was my Dale really lost for words?

'You never seem to amaze me, Ash. But the last couple of days, I feel like I don't deserve you.' I put my glass down on the counter and placed my arms around his neck.

'What do you mean?' I studied his face, waiting for him to enlighten me.

'It is just . . . You have taken on me, my family, and work . . .'

'Eh, excuse me, Mr, but at what point was a gun placed to my head?' I interrupted him quickly because the last thing I wanted was for him to feel like any of this was his fault. His shoulders shrugged, and his arms wrapped around my waist. 'I am here because I want to be here. I am marrying you because I love you, and we are having a baby together because it feels like the most naturalist thing to do.' I was just rambling on now. But at least I was getting my point across. I was never a girl who did something out of her will. I lived for the moment and did what I wanted, and that wasn't going to change now.

'You really make me the happiest man alive. We really need to look for a house together. This is ours, but I would really like somewhere to call our family home.'

'You must have read my mind. But right now I need to eat.' We both laughed and hugged the life out of each other. I didn't want to let him go, but I really did need to eat. I broke away from him and walked around to my seat. The soup smelled as good as ever. Mhairi had a good recipe for vegetable soup, and I would never get fed up of eating it. 'Your mom is a fantastic cook.'

'She loves cooking. Just don't tell her that you have a craving for her soup, you will never look at soup again by the time the baby is born.' It was nice to be part of a family again. Since my mom and dad had passed away, there was never much of a family unit around me. Christine was as close to family that I had, and it was all that I thought I needed, until now.

'Talking of your parents. How did they take our news?' I really didn't need to ask this question, but I felt that I should be inquisitive.

'All I am going to say is I was glad I was on the phone.' We both knew that his parents would have been thrilled by our news; they were dying for us to settle down and have a child of our own.

'That's good then . . . But I am not the slightest bit surprised.' I could imagine screaming, and crying was a big part of their phone call.

'They want us to pop in tomorrow after your appointment.' Of course, they did. Mhairi was going to be the doting mother-in-law and grandma-to-be.

'I knew they would be OK about it. How is Callum and Kiara?' Dale sat with a puzzled look on his face, like he didn't want to tell me the whole story. But he was bound to know that I wouldn't let it drop that easily. 'Dale . . . How are they?'

'They are still here. My dad said that Callum and my mom can't even be in the same room together. My dad actually praised Cal. He said he has stepped up to the mark and he is providing for Kiara.' I was glad that he told me, but I felt awful that I made him go back to face the music. I knew that he could do the best by Kiara, I never doubted him for one minute.

'There has got to be something that we can do.' I hated to think that Kiara was stuck in the middle of a war zone.

'I was going to run a few things past you tonight, but then we fell asleep.' I turned in my seat to give him my full attention. I was all ears.

'Go for it. You have my full attention.'

'Well, you know that I had to sack Rupert . . . Well, there is a job needing filled, and Callum has all the qualifications and more to fill his position . . . This will also provide free time up for us to be together without work.'

'You don't need to explain any of this to me, Dale. Callum is your brother, and he does need a job. That position does need to be filled ASAP, but it is your company, and you will know what is best. You know how I feel about us working around the clock, and you know that I don't want work to come before junior . . .'

'That will never happen, Ash. You and our baby will never be pushed aside for work, no matter what it is.' I loved how keen he was to be a husband and a doting father. There aren't many men around who would be so happy about a baby.

'Has your mom never told you that interrupting a lady is bad manners?' His smile faded, and my mind wondered again. 'What now?'

'There is one last thing . . . I was going to ask him to stay on at the cottage . . . I mean he needs somewhere to call home for Kiara.' All this was sounding good, but it had absolutely nothing to do with me.

'Dale, I am flattered that you felt the need to share all this with me before you jumped in with two feet. But what you do with your business and property is your choice. I will never step in the way of those decisions.' I had been lucky to fall in love with someone with so much capital, but none of that interested me. It was the man I love, not his millions.

'One thing that I will correct you on is, what is mine is yours. If I had to make a bad choice that would hurt you both, I would never forgive myself.' He could never hurt us even if he tried. He didn't have a bad bone in his body.

'You won't hurt us, babe. If I thought for one minute you were going down the wrong path, I would say something. But you have a level head on your shoulders. We are the lucky ones.' I placed my hands on my tummy and looked into Dale's eyes. He placed his hands over mine and kissed me tenderly on the lips. I jumped off my seat to be closer to him because I couldn't bear to be away from him any longer.

'Come to bed with me, Mr Black.' His face was a picture. He certainly wasn't expecting my flirtatious seductions right now. But he didn't resist my charm. We made our way upstairs and headed into the master bedroom. I closed the door behind me and leant up against the back of it. I couldn't actually wait any longer for him.

'Are you sure about this, Ash?'

'It is too late to care about being careful.' Dale's head touched my forehead, and we both knew what he meant. I just couldn't help but get him going. It didn't matter what part of my body he touched, my heart fluttered in my chest.

'I don't want to hurt you both.'

'The only way you are going to hurt me right now is by turning me away. That would upset me, and then junior would be upset.'

'You drive a hard bargain, but when you put it like that . . .' Dale took my hands as we walked over to the bed, and I sat on the bottom and slid up towards the pillows. The feel of Dale's body hovering over the top of me sent my body wild. Our lips were sealed together as he kissed me passionately. I pulled his T-shirt over his head to feel his manly skin under my fingers. I sat up underneath him so he could slip my pyjama top off, and my body cried out for his kiss and for his touch. He laid me back down, placing gentle kisses from my lips all the way down to my breasts, down to my tummy. My body arched as he tickled me with his tongue. I felt him slip my bottoms off, and he placed gentle kisses up my thigh. I craved for this man right now, and I wanted to feel him inside me. His kisses were placed around my hips as his mouth teased my lady bits. His tongue circled around my sex, sending the electricity through my body. Groans escaped my mouth out of sheer delight. I needed him now; my body was like a lightning bolt as I climaxed. My whole body tingled, right down to my toes. He didn't stop. His tongue kept sliding in and out of my sex, circling my clitoris. I was on fire. He moved up my body kissing every inch until he reached my mouth. I could taste myself on his lips, and I couldn't catch my breath. He sat up and slid his bottoms down, and I watched his hard package spring free. I couldn't wait to feel him inside me. He hovered over the top of me and sank his tongue into my mouth. I felt him slide inside of me, and I cried out with pleasure. He felt at home inside of me, making love to me. My body would never get bored of his touch, and we both climaxed together as one. My heart was pounding in my chest. He moved to the side of me, and we lay together without a care in the world. I never wanted to care about anything ever again.

'You better make the most of my body now because in a few months, I will be like an elephant.' I wasn't looking forward to the whole bump thing. I was hoping that I would start to enjoy it when I could feel the baby move inside me.

'I don't care what size you get, babe. We will just have to be adventurous.'

'You won't be saying that when I am nippy and wobbling to and from the office.' I wanted a baby so much, but I didn't think I realised how hard it was going to be over the next nine months.

'It will all be worth it, hun. No matter what the next seven or eight months bring. We will be a proper little family at the end.' I turned on to my side to cuddle into him, and we lay in each other's arms, not saying a word. Our body language spoke volumes. I lay my hand on my tummy, and Dale placed his hand over mine. We were like overprotective parents already.

'You do realise that for the rest of our lives we are going to have someone depend upon on us.' I lay beside Dale exhausted, and I was getting ready to roll over and fall asleep because I thought he had crashed out on me.

'Ash, you can't and won't scare me away. I am in this for the long haul. Till death do us part.' He always seemed to say the nicest of things to me. I rolled on to my other side satisfied that we were in this together, and he followed behind me. His arm wrapped securely around my waist, and I felt very secure in his arms. My eyes felt very heavy, and my head was sore. I needed sleep and plenty of it. We had a busy day ahead of us, and I wanted to be as fresh as a daisy.

CHAPTER 13

Bad News

I could feel soft hands stroking my cheek as I heard someone call my name softly. My mind had been struck with a blow as I came around. 'We have slept in, hun. It is 8 a.m.' I jumped up and rubbed my eyes. I felt funny, and my stomach felt very wobbly. I quickly got up and ran to the bathroom. I just made it. I felt so rough this morning. Is this what I had to look forward to over the next few months? I placed my head on my arm on the toilet seat, and I felt like I was hungover. I heard Dale come in behind me, and his presence bent down beside me on the floor. I didn't want him to see me like this. I must have looked a right state. 'Ash, are you OK?' I didn't even have any energy to answer him. I really wished I could shake this morning sickness off because I wouldn't wish it on my worst enemy. Dale really was driving me daft, keep asking if I was OK. Did I look OK? 'I will run the shower for you.' Please yourself was my first thought. I really didn't care this morning. I knew that I had to move quickly or we would be late for my appointment, but I had no motivation. I heard the shower spring to life, and I moved my head to see if I was going to get up. But the sickness started all over again. Dale's hand rubbed my back as I retched my insides. I had never felt so weak in my life. 'I am glad that you are getting checked over today, Ash. You have me worried sick.' I was worried myself. But how could I say that out loud? It would just make Dale more paranoid, and that wouldn't help any of us. I managed to get myself up on to my feet and flush the toilet. I walked over to the sink and rinsed my mouth out, but I just couldn't come to this morning. The mirror reflected my naked body wrapped in a blanket, and I shook my head at myself in disgust because I was letting this pregnancy drain me, and nothing ever made me feel like this.

'Ash, are you going to talk to me this morning or will I just answer my own questions?' I wasn't in the mood for talking, but I could see how worried he looked.

'I am sorry. I am fine. It is just morning sickness. Millions of women do this in a year, and they get through nine months.' I felt like I was being sarcastic, but it was the truth. I wasn't any different to any other women.

'You don't have to suffer alone. I want to be here for you every step of the way.' I was gazing into the mirror looking at Dale's caring reflection. I loved the fact that he wanted to be around at the bad bits, but at this rate, the next nine months were going to be bad.

'Dale, I am flattered that you are here, sticking by me and the baby. I know that you want to be here for us, but you can't take the sickness away. There are some things that are meant to torture us, and this is one of them.' I was feeling very sick and weak, and I had no idea if this was normal.

'Let's get today out of the way, and once I know that you are completely OK, I promise that I will settle down. You mean the world to me, hun.' His soft hand stroked my face, and I turned to be in his arms.

'We are going nowhere, babe. Will you join me in the shower?' I just wanted to forget about the sickness and get this morning out of the way. But feeling sorry for myself wasn't going to help anyone.

'You don't need to ask me twice, babe.' I walked around him and let the blanket fall to the ground. I stepped into the shower and hoped that I would wash the morning away, but that wasn't going to happen. I was glad that he was coming in the shower with me because I needed his support. My legs felt like jelly, and my stomach felt like it was doing somersaults. Could today get any worse? When I first met Dale, I didn't think it would ever be possible to feel as nervous. But this morning getting ready, my nerves had reached an all-time high. On top of the nerves, my body felt very weak, and my head was pounding. I just wanted my mom around to offer help and advice, like mothers usually do. But instead, I was left wondering what was coming next.

I was sitting at the breakfast bar like I had lots of time to spare, but already I was running behind schedule for my appointment at the clinic. I could quite easily jump back into bed and forget all about the clinic.

'Are you ready, babe?' I stumbled to my feet and placed my cup beside the sink. I really didn't want to show Dale my nerves. I wanted to be composed and relaxed. This morning was supposed to be a happy occasion, but deep down I knew something was going to hit me with a bang. 'Here is your bag, Ash.' The worktop was keeping me upright. I was afraid to move too far just in case I gave Dale more cause for concern. I placed my bag over my head and looked at us both. We looked very sophisticated for a couple in their twenties. Having a baby was a big deal for us, and we were going to challenge every moment. 'Everything is going to be fine, babe.' Dale's soft hand rubbed along my face for reassurance, but at this moment, I couldn't share his enthusiasm.

'We better make a move before we end up late.' I stood and watched as Dale grabbed the keys. He took my hand and led the way to my car. There was no way that I could drive this morning, and I thought that he had realised that. Normally, he would ask if I wanted to drive, but he just took the initiative this morning that he had to drive. He was like the perfect gentleman as he opened the passenger's door and waited until I was in, before he left me. Did I look as bad as I felt? He came around and jumped into the driver's seat, and his presence beside me always made me calm down. 'How far is the hospital from here?' I didn't want to sit in silence any more because I would go mad. Dale reached over and squeezed my hand, and the reassurance was just what I needed right now. I wished that his squeeze would make everything disappear, but the reassurance was just as good.

'Five minutes. Try and relax, Ash. I won't leave your side today.'

'It will be the longest five minutes ever.' I was creating a tense atmosphere in the car, and I knew it would be just as useful to sit quiet.

'It is always the same when you want to get something over with.'
I nodded my head and gazed out of the window. The movement of the
car made me feel quite woozy, but one thing that caught my attention
was the scenery. It never failed to amaze me how beautiful and fresh
everything was. I couldn't wait to raise my family here in Anchorage. I
felt myself smiling now, and the nerves weren't so intense, but I couldn't
shift this feeling I had in my stomach. We pulled into a big car park, and
I spotted the large building in front of us. It wasn't what I was expecting.
'We just have to find a space now. Keep your eyes peeled, Ash.' I didn't
have to look very far because Dale pulled into a space not far from the
door, which was lucky for me. 'See, it is our lucky day.' We both got out
of the car, and I stood and waited for Dale to come around to me. He
took my hand and placed a tender kiss on my head. 'Let's find out where
we are going.' I followed beside Dale, squeezing the life out of his hand.
I just wanted to run a mile and forget about all the check-ups. What we
didn't know wouldn't hurt us. We walked up to the reception desk, and
this elderly woman looked up to us.

'Can I help you, dear?'

'Can you point me in the direction of Dr Ching's clinic, please?' I
don't know where my confidence came from to answer the receptionist,
but it surprised me, and by the way Dale smiled at me, he was surprised
as well.

'Yes, dear. Just down the hall on the right.'

'Thank you.' Dale and I echoed each other as we spoke at the exact
same time. My stomach was churning, and I felt sick. Was today about
to get any better? I opened the door on the right, and Dale held it until I
walked in. He seemed just as nervous as I did now, and normally, he was
calm under pressure. This place was full of reception desks; there must be
more receptionists than doctors. I had to walk over to another desk and
wait for someone to appear. Dale's hand sat on the base of my back, and
it was nice to feel his touch.

'Hello, can I help you?' The voice startled me. One minute, there was no
one there, and the next, out of nowhere there was a young lady talking to us.

'Ashley Malone, here to see Dr Ching.'

'Take a seat, doll. Dr Ching will be with you shortly. Did you bring a
sample with you?' I managed to nod and remove a urine sample from my
bag. 'Thank you. I will let Dr Ching know that you are here.' Dale and
I both walked over to the seats and sat down. We never spoke another

word. We sat in complete silence. The clinic felt like a morgue. I watched him twirl my engagement ring around my finger, and it did make me smile. Nerves do strange things to people; it really did mess with your mind. This middle-aged man came towards us, and my stomach felt like it was going to come up through my mouth.

'Ashley.' Dale and I stood up, and the doctor shook both of our hands. 'I am Dr Ching. It is a pleasure to meet you.'

'Likewise, Dr Ching. This is my fiancé Dale Black.' We all shook hands again and stood like children waiting to hear the next move.

'Are you feeling OK, Ashley?' Now I was concerned that I looked hellish because there was no other reason that a doctor would ask something like that.

'Morning sickness. I will be fine.' I didn't know who I was trying to kid. We all knew that I was standing here in a bad position today.

'Please come through, and we will get this started for you.' We followed the doctor through to his office, and the room was cool and bright. I watched him close the blinds to darken the room, and the reality of everything had hit me now.

'Ashley, do you want to take your jacket off and pop up on the bed.' I didn't say a word, but I followed orders and handed Dale my jacket and bag. 'First of all, congratulations. I tested your urine sample, and it confirmed your pregnancy. Second, I am going to carry out an ultrasound. Just to check you and baby over. Do either of you have any questions before we start?' I lay back and got comfortable. My head shook at the doctor's question, and I just hoped Dale wouldn't ask anything. I just wanted to see my baby. Dr Ching rolled my top up to show my bare tummy, and Dale stood up to see the screen clearly. He clenched my hand and rubbed his thumb over my hand. The gel was frozen as Dr Ching spread it over my tummy with his machine, and it took my attention of my hand. The scan started, and I initially looked over to the screen. I didn't have a clue what to look for, but I didn't see very much. I looked at Dale's face and then Dr Ching. Something didn't seem right. 'Is everything . . . OK?' My voice was all shaky, and my heart was racing. I was starting to panic. Dale knew me too well, and his free hand stroked my head, and his other hand squeezed mine.

'Is everything OK, Doctor?' The doctor was too busy measuring things to even notice our concern. He put the machine down and faced us. I knew at that second, this was my hard blow coming.

'There is no easy way to say this.' The doctor took my other hand, and the tears rolled down my cheeks. 'There is no baby.' I was so confused, and my head was spinning. I needed Dale to step in and take over for me because my grief had taken over every aspect of my body.

'What do you mean "no baby"?' Dale looked over at me and wiped tears away from my face.

'Have you been having pregnancy symptoms, Ashley?' I could hear the doctor speak to me, but I felt numb. The feeling I was experiencing today was similar to the one I felt on the day I got told about my parents being killed.

'Yes, Dr Ching. She has been bad with sickness, pain, and tiredness.'

'OK. Ashley, when I look on the screen, there is a growth.' He picked the machine up to show us, and it looked round like a head. 'This growth is quite large and the cause of all the symptoms and false results.' I could hear him and understand the words that he was saying, but I couldn't take it in.

'What do you mean a growth?' Dale was being my rock right now. There was no way I could do any of this without him.

'The most common causes are an abscess or a tumour, and at the moment, I would tell you it is too big and in-depth for an abscess.' His words hit me hard, and I couldn't control my tears and heartache. I couldn't even ask the questions that I wanted to.

'But you can take it away, right, Doc?' Dr Ching stood up beside me and placed his hand on my arm.

'We need to do biopsies right away. This will help us decide what happens next.'

'Am I going to die?' Dale looked at me with pain in his face and tears in his eyes. It was the first question that I could get out, and it was probably the worst. But I needed to know.

'Ashley, I can't answer that truthfully until I get your biopsy results.'

'But you're not saying that I am going to survive it.' I burst into tears, and Dale cuddled into me. I sobbed my heart out at the very thought of death. My earth was shattering piece by piece today.

'Can you excuse me for one moment? I will go and see when I can book you in for these tests.'

'Money is no option, Dr Ching. Please make it as soon as possible.' I heard the door shut over as Dr Ching left us. I sat up on the bed and went over everything that we were just told. Now I do wish it was all one big dream and that I was going to wake up at any minute and laugh.

'Why us?' I didn't mean to say that out loud, but like everything else, I didn't know what I was thinking or saying right now. Dale's arms wrapped around me like a secure blanket and as always he was my comfort blanket.

'We will get through this, Ash.' I shrugged away from him because I didn't want or need pity right now.

'Why don't you run for the hills? You have been given a free get-out of jail card. There is no baby.' Tears rolled down his cheeks, and he wiped them away to keep strong. I was hurting, and I thought that I was just trying to hurt everyone around me.

'Ashley, how can you sit there and say that? I love you regardless. If I could take this away from you, I would.' We both sobbed together as reality had hit both of us at the same moment. Dale held me in his arms until I had no more tears left to cry. The door opened, and the doctor came towards us. Everything was like slow motion. 'Sorry, I took so long. Can you come back tomorrow? I have made a space in theatre for you. The quicker the tests are done, the sooner we will know what we are dealing with.' I laid my head on Dale's shoulder and just stared into space.

'She will be here, Dr Ching.'

'If you come in for 09.30, I will get you prepared, and hopefully all going well, we will get you home for dinner time.' I felt like I was sitting in a war zone. There were bombs and guns all going off around me, and I was oblivious to everything.

'Thank you, Dr Ching.' Dale extended his arm, and Dr Ching shook it. Everything was happening too quickly for me.

'Ashley, this is my card. You can contact me day or night.' Dale took the card and placed it in his pocket and wrapped two arms back around me as the doctor left the room. He obviously knew that I needed time to digest all this information. I honestly felt like my life had been torn apart in five minutes.

'Let's get out of here, Ash.' Dale wrapped his arm around me and helped me back on to my feet. The ground felt as though it was moving underneath me, and if I never had his arm wrapped around me, I would have crumbled. The waiting room was quite busy now with pregnant women and their partners, but here was me being helped up by my partner for all the opposite reasons. We should be leaving the clinic laughing and smiling, looking at our baby's pictures. Everything seemed so bleak, and I couldn't see our future planned out any more. What good was going to come of today? We got outside the building, and the air just hit me, and my legs crumbled underneath me. Dale stopped me from going down as his tower of strength kept me upright.

'The car is just over here, babe.' I knew where the car was, but I couldn't find any more energy to keep going. The weather was cold, and I didn't want to try any more. What was the point in fighting when I couldn't win? Dale practically carried me back to the car and opened the door. I sat down in the seat, and he perched down beside me. I saw the man I loved in pain. His tears and heartache spoke volumes.

'Ashley, I am not going to sit here and insult your intelligence.' He caught me unaware, and I couldn't even guess what was coming next. 'We are going to fight this every step of the way.' I wanted to say I know we will. Everything will be fine. But deep down I knew I was drowning. I was in way too deep. I placed my hand on his cheek, and he covered it with his hand.

'I will do everything that Dr Ching throws at me, but we need to prepare ourselves for the worst.' Dale shook his head. He didn't want to hear those words, but we needed to face this head-on. It killed me to see him crying just as hard as I was, but nothing was going to take it away. 'Dale . . . when we get these results back and we find out how bad it is, I want you to promise me something.'

'Anything, Ash. Name it.' He really would go to the end of the earth to give me what I wanted, and if I was honest with myself, the only thing that I wanted was to have my life back.

'I want you to move on. Find someone to settle down with that will make you happy. Have a family.' He wiped my eyes and held my face in place to look at him.

'I am sorry, Ash, that is one promise that I can't grant you.' I took a deep breath and closed my eyes. 'I am here with you all the way. You are my life, no matter what, and I will not walk away from you. If I can't have you, I don't want anyone else.' He pulled me close to his chest, and I cuddled into him like a small child would do to his or her father. Life was so unfair at times.

'Do you want to go home and get some rest?'

'I need to see Christine. Since everything is happening tomorrow, I need to tell her.' As always I was thinking about everyone else. I would be happy if everyone I cared about was OK.

'There is an office we can use at work. Get in and I will take you. You are freezing, Ash.' Dale closed my door over and rushed around to the driver's seat. I watched him quickly start the car and get the heating on. I really was freezing. I only had five minutes to gather my thoughts and think about what to say to Christine. This was either going to go well or going to be horribly wrong. She thought I was pregnant anyway, so that bit wouldn't come as much of a shock. The tumour, on the other hand, was the shock. I still couldn't take it in myself.

'How do you want to do this, Ash?' His voice drew me to him. I honestly didn't know how to do anything, let alone tell my best friend that I could be dying.

'Just show me to a quiet office, and I will find some way to tell her.' We both got out of the car, and Dale took my hand again. It actually felt good being here; this was the only place that I could block everything out. We went into the main reception and got keys. Everywhere seemed quite busy today. The receptionist made a call over loudspeaker, and I hardly made out a single word. Dale's smile still made my heart melt after everything that we had been through this morning. Love was blooming between the two of us, and it was horrible to think that it could end very soon. I followed him over to the conference suite; it was a room that I hadn't been in before. It was a big open room with lots of light coming through the windows. I shrugged my jacket off and threw it on the table. I wished that I was invisible right about now, and I wouldn't have to face Christine.

'I will be right by your side, Ash. Anytime you need my help, just squeeze my hand.' I sat down at the big table, and if I could imagine being at work, I might just get through the next five minutes. I jumped as I heard the door open, and my heart was going so fast that I thought it would stop at any moment. 'Come in, Christine.' I turned in my seat, and Christine came over and sat beside me. Dale sat up on the table at my other side and took my hand.

'Now I am worried. You have been crying, and I am pulled into the conference suite for some talk.' Christine knew me too well. She could tell when something was wrong. She was just like Dale in many ways. 'Is it the baby, Ash?' That was all she had to say, and my tears had started; I needed to stay focused to get everything out.

'There is no baby, Christine . . .' Christine threw her arms around me before I could even finish.

'You can try for another baby, Ash.' I pushed her away because I needed her to listen to me carefully without jumping to conclusions. She sat back down and placed her hand on mine, and I had no idea how to start.

'You don't understand, Christine . . . The doctor has found something on the scan.' Christine looked just as puzzled as we did this morning, and I had to relive it all over again.

'You have lost me, Ash.' I stood up and walked over to the window, maybe if I wasn't looking at anyone I would be able to compose myself.

'I have a tumour, Christine.' You could cut the atmosphere in the room with a knife. Silence was golden in some circumstances, but right now it was like someone had already died. I turned around slowly to find Dale beside me and Christine gazing right through me.

'But you are going to be OK, right?' I squeezed Dale's arm, and his hand covered mine. 'You know as much as we do, hun. Ashley has got to go to hospital tomorrow for biopsies. We will know in a couple of days how bad things are.' Christine stood up and walked over to me.

'Ashley, you are as tough as old boots. You will be fine.'

'I will tell you the same as I told Dale . . . We need to prepare ourselves for the worst . . . I am not getting these tests to see how good things are.' Dale's hand had been my tissue more times than enough today. His eyes were so soft and sincere as he looked through me. 'I am sorry. I can't do this right now. I need to go.'

'You can't just drop this bombshell on me and walk away . . . Ash.'

'I am sorry, Christine. I just need to get out of here.' I quickly ran out of the room and out of the building. The fresh air hit me like a ton of bricks, and I stopped dead. Where was I going to go now?

'Ashley.' I heard Dale shout on me from behind, but at this moment, I didn't want to hear how badly I just handled that situation. 'Ashley, I can't help you if you are going to run away from me.' I wasn't running from him intentionally. I was relieved that I had told Christine, but now she would be a liability. I really couldn't be her sitter right now; I needed everyone to be strong for me. 'Where do you need to go in a hurry?'

'Anywhere, as long as Christine isn't involved. I can't get my head around all this, never mind trying to explain to my obnoxious friend. If you really insist on being with me, then I just want it to be us.' I knew that I was asking a lot of him, but I needed time to get my head straight.

'Well, you have me, Ashley. I am going nowhere. I have had twelve missed calls from my mom. I need to put her straight, and then we can do whatever you want.' I felt more heartache jump out of my heart. Mhairi was going to be devastated about the baby.

'Your mom is going to be so upset about the baby.'

'I can do this on my own if you want to go home.'

'No, the mountain is just what I need right now. What happened to doing it all together?' I made the first move this time and took Dale's hand. We moved slowly over to the car, and like the perfect gentleman, he opened my door. I climbed in and buckled up. This car was like my sanctuary today, and my head lay back against the headrest. I watched Dale climb in beside me and start the car.

'You look tired, honey.'

'Hmm. I feel it. But we will get this last bit out of the way first. I might feel a huge weight lift off my shoulders.' The car took off in a breeze, and my eyes closed over. My mind went crazy. All of today's flashbacks kept repeating in my head. I wanted to scream, to let it all out, and to see if that would make me feel better. But I knew that it wouldn't do much good. My eyes flickered open as I felt the car climb up the mountain, and I dreaded this bit. Dale's parents were lovely; they didn't need any more family drama.

'Are you OK, Ash?' Already I was so sick of hearing 'are you OK'. I had lost count how many times that I had heard it today.

'I will be.' The car pulled up outside the cottage, and my heart was pounding. I had to breathe in through my nose and out through my mouth. Sheer panic was rushing through my body. Dale got out of the car and came around to get me. Out of every man in the world, I couldn't ask for anyone better to go through all this with.

'You can do this, Ash. I will do all the talking if you want.' I took one final deep breath and found some confidence. The walk from the car to the cottage was going to be like a trapeze, one wrong move and we would fall. I got out of the car and Dale's arm sat comfortably around my waist. We headed into the cottage, and the first thing that I noticed was Mhairi and Jake sitting in the living room with Kiara.

'We wondered where you two were. We were going to send out a search party.' Mhairi seemed so happy, and I felt bad for what was about to happen next. They didn't deserve any more heartache.

'Where is everyone, Mom?' Dale was calm and very well presented, and I was going to let him take care of his parents. I would just end up a blubbering wreck.

'They are all out, dear. Why?' Jake got up and told us to come and sit down on the couch. He obviously knew something had happened. We both sat down, and Dale's arm wrapped around me and his other hand squeezed my hand.

'Mom, you need to sit and listen to what we have to say. OK? You can't interrupt until we are finished.' I could remember hearing the same words a while back when I was going to get the truth about his parents. That all seemed like a lifetime ago now.

'Dale, spit it out. You are worrying me.' I felt his body tense as he took a deep breath in. Even Dale was going to struggle with this part.

'We have been at the clinic all morning, and we got told some bad news . . .' I was trying so hard to keep it together in front of Mhairi and Jake, but already my eyes were filling up with tears. 'There isn't going to be a baby.'

'I am so sorry . . .' Her hands covered her mouth as she took in Dale's news. 'You can always try again.' That was it. My sobs started all over again, and Dale cuddled me into his chest. I just wanted to be invisible right now.

'Mom, please listen . . . Ashley has a tumour growing in her womb, and it isn't good. We have to go back tomorrow for biopsies. These results will tell us how bad things are.' I turned my head to see how Mhairi and Jake were taking the news. I couldn't lift my head from Dale's chest. Jake sat on the coffee table in front of us and placed a hand on me and Dale.

'Kids . . . I don't know what to say . . . Ashley, we will be here if you ever need us. You have given this family so much over the last few weeks . . . I know Dale will take care of you, but if you ever need someone to talk to other than Dale, you know where to come.' He looked physically sick, just like we did when we heard the news.

'Thank you, Jake.' Jake was such a lovely man; it was obvious where Dale got his manners and charm from.

'I don't understand, Jake. What does all this mean?'

'It means, Mhairi, . . . that I might be dying.' I could remember growing up hearing about people dying. It scared me to death. I never wanted to die. I never thought that it would be an issue until I was old.

But now it was here. I didn't feel scared. As long as I had Dale, nothing would faze me.

'But you are so young.' I let out a grin; someone needed to take my place and come out with silly things. I was just glad it was Mhairi.

'Mom, it isn't something that only happens to the elderly. We are going to support Ashley in any way possible, and from today, there are no more silly questions or responses.'

'Dale, it is OK.' I wanted to calm him down. I wouldn't be able to cope if he fell apart at the seams.

'I am going to take my wife-to-be home. We are going to spend the next twenty-four hours together, and I will call you tomorrow, to let you know how it all goes.'

'Stay for something to eat.' Mhairi always wanted to feed us, but my stomach wouldn't cope with food.

'Thanks, Mom, but we just need to get our heads around this.' We stood up, and Jake hugged me tight and kissed my cheek. The whole vampire thing didn't even faze me now. We had bigger fish to fry, and that boat had sailed a long time ago.

'Phone if you need anything, Son.'

'Thanks, Dad.' We left the cottage in a hurry. I had no idea what came over Dale. He had been so together all morning, and then five minutes with his mom, he was a state.

'Dale, what was that all about?' I stopped dead outside the cottage, but he walked over to the edge of the mountain. I followed behind him, taking in the view. It was just as beautiful. I sat on a large rock and placed my hands in my pockets. It was very chilly today, a typical winter's day in Anchorage. I was glad when he perched beside me, and I could feel his heat transfer over to me. 'Are you going to tell me what that was all about?'

'Sorry.'

'What are you apologising for? I only want to know what changed.' I never took my eyes from the town below us; it kept me calm and made me forget all about the pain and heartache that I was feeling.

'I just realised that I could lose you. I don't know how I will cope without you, Ash.' The tears choked Dale as he spoke, and for the first time today, it was me who was the strong one.

'We will get through this together . . . . It is so beautiful up here.' Changing the subject seemed the best option at the minute.

'It is beautiful, just like you, doll.' I turned slowly to look at him, and his mouth pressed gently against mine. Our tongues massaged one another's mouths as I lifted my hand and stroked his cheek. He pulled away from me gently, and I turned on to my side to look at him . . . I sat and looked at his crying eyes and felt every bit of his pain.

'I am sorry . . . I shouldn't have kissed you like that.' I felt like a knife had been drilled through my heart. Why shouldn't he kiss me like that? What had changed?

'Don't you dare . . . I need you to kiss me like that. I want us to go home, and I want you to make love to me like you did last night.' I was being honest from the bottom of my heart because we would never get through this if he wasn't going to touch me. Life has got to go on.

'But . . .' I placed my hand back on his cheek and made him look me in the eyes.

'But what?'

'I don't want to hurt you.'

'You will hurt me more by not touching me . . . I want us to live normally for as long as possible.'

'I will try, Ash. I love you.'

'I love you too. Now can we go home?' Dale's hand squeezed mine, and we walked over towards the car. I knew that whatever happened from this moment forward, Dale would be my rock. We had to have each other to lean on or we would fall apart at the seams. Life really was cruel in many ways, but we just had to make the best out of a bad situation.

CHAPTER 14

The Tests

I couldn't sleep, so I got up and had a shower. Dale was sleeping peacefully, and I didn't want to disturb him. Sleep seemed the last thing on my mind right now. I took a coffee and sat out on the veranda, and it was a very cold night, but it felt nice. It was hard to think about dying, especially now. Leaving this life behind was what was killing me more. When my parents died, all I wanted to do was join them. But now I had so much more to give. I was not ready to go anywhere. The tears started to fall down my cheeks, and I really didn't care. I felt free. My body felt numb, like someone had drained me. But sitting here in the dark with only the moon for light and the cold breeze on my cheeks, I was relaxed. No one could see me, and no one could hear me sobbing like a baby. I never thought that it was possible to feel as bad in my life, and it felt so unfair.

'Ash, what are you doing out here?' Dale threw a blanket around my shoulders and sat down beside me. I was in a little world of my own and actually quite enjoyed thinking of useless things.

'I couldn't sleep, and the night air appealed to me.' I choked back the tears when I felt Dale's arm around me. The last thing I wanted was for him to notice me upset. I didn't want to be sitting crying all the time. I wanted to be strong and face it all head-on.

'Ash, I will sit up and do whatever you want, but can you just come inside before you catch pneumonia?' I couldn't help but sit and giggle. Dale's head peered around in front of me to see what I found so funny, and I was glad that I still had a sense of humour.

'Sorry, I am just being a sarcastic bitch . . . It is just that pneumonia is the last thing we need to worry about.'

'Sarcastic is good, babe, but can we continue this conversation in the house?' He was very eager to get me into the house, and I knew that he thought it was dangerous for me to be out here in the cold. But if we were honest with one another, we knew that nothing could hurt me more than the tumour. I stood up and let the blanket fall to the ground. I was enjoying the cold air for a change. I put my cup down on the table and reached my hand out for Dale's. He was frozen, and his skin felt like his parents. Now I knew what he would feel like if he was a vampire. I knew that it was a strange thought, but my mind was all over the place. I really felt bad having him out here in his pyjamas. He should be snuggled up in a nice hot house.

'Are you coming?' I walked in front of him, and he followed behind me. Although it was the middle of the night and we should be tucked up in bed sleeping, I just wanted to spend every moment living life to the full. 'I have been doing a lot of thinking.' Dale looked anxious as I spoke, and I really didn't like making him feel like that. But if he listened to me, I thought he might actually like it. I made it to the one room that I loved in this house, and that was the snugly study. It was the first room that I had seen in the house and that would always stay in my mind.

'This sounds serious.' He walked over to me and placed his hands on my hips.

'After today, I want us to make a list of all the things we were going to do together . . .' I knew that I wasn't going to spend a lot of time dwelling on things. I wanted to live a bit of our life together while we still could.

'OK. That sounds like a plan. But where is this going, Ash?' His voice was quiet and tender, and the goosebumps rose on my arms.

'Well . . . Once we make the list, I want us to do as much as we can, ticking them off one by one.' I had watched a film once and this happened, and I could remember thinking what a good idea it was. I never thought for one minute that I would have to do the same plan in my early twenties.

'This all sounds perfect, Ash . . .' I knew that there was a 'but' coming, but I wanted him to speak in his own time without me forcing him. 'But you seem to be giving up . . . Like you already know your fate.' I took a few deep breaths and gazed up into his eyes.

'I will never give up on us, babe. I will fight this head-on and will accept whatever hand I am dealt . . . But deep down, if I am being a hundred per cent honest, I know something is wrong . . . Each day it is getting worse.' Dale's head bowed down to hide his emotions, and I pushed his head back up to see his face. I didn't want him to hide from me. I wanted us to be open with one another and share how we felt. 'You don't have to hide your emotions in front of me.'

'I can't lose you, Ash.' He buried his head into my shoulder, and we both sank to the ground. We cradled each other close. Every breath and every sob was echoed in the silent room. But I thought it was what we both needed to get through the next few days.

'We will just have to spend whatever time we have, happy and in love, just like we planned.' The house was so still. Yesterday, I could picture our children running around, making too much noise pulling all their toys out. But now that dream was shattered. It was a distant memory.

'Marry me, Ash.' I pulled away from him, to look at him closely. Did I hear him right? Or was I dreaming again? 'We can do this next week. Just me, you, and close family and friends.' I could hear the words and see his lips move, but I didn't know what to say. I didn't want him to think that he had to marry me because I was ill.

'You are being serious, aren't you?'

'I have never been more certain about anything in my life. I want you to be Mrs Black.'

'And what if I don't have . . .' The tears stopped me from getting all my words out. Everything seemed so bleak without time behind us.

'Stop right there. We could have a week, a month, or forever. It won't matter as long as we have each other. Let's start our list with getting married.' I couldn't believe that he still wanted to marry me. After everything that had happened, nothing had changed between us. We were still love's young dream with a lot of damage to cause.

'But I can't give you everything you want.'

'You are everything I ever want . . . Everything I need.'

'OK. Let's do this.' We sat on the floor of the study curled up together, and it felt good, just the two of us and nothing to do. At least some goodness had come of today. One lesson that I had learnt was that life could be sweet, but it could also turn sour at any time, and it didn't care who it crushed in its path of destruction.

I woke up with the faintest touch stroking my face. I immediately looked up to find two eyes looking through me. We were still on the floor in the study tangled together, and I immediately wondered how the hell we manage to fall asleep here?

'What time is it?' I really didn't care what time it was. I was in no hurry to move. But it was the first sensible thing that popped into my head.

'Gone seven.'

'You should have woken me.' Dale's head shook softly as he placed a gentle kiss on my forehead. How could everything bad happen to us when we were so in love together? Nothing made any sense any more.

'I just woke up about half an hour ago. I heard Rosa in the kitchen.' I completely forgot all about Rosa. What must she be thinking?

'I could stay here like this forever.'

'We could still have forever, Ash.' Listening to the pain in Dale's voice was worse than going through this ordeal. I hated what this thing was doing to us both. We had spent so many weeks living life enjoying each other's company, and then we came down with a huge bang. 'How are you feeling this morning?'

'I feel OK . . . I think.' I did feel OK this morning for a change. There was no sickness so that was a bonus. My body was aching, but that was the result of falling asleep on the floor.

'That is a good change.' I knew what he meant, but I didn't think of it as 'good'. I wanted to be going to work, getting ready for our baby, and preparing for our wedding. That would be good. But instead, I was going to get ready for theatre, to get these biopsies done. I really wanted to run and hide, but that wouldn't help anyone.

'We should move from this floor.'

'Do you want to move?' I shook my head because I never wanted to move, but that wasn't an option today. It was amazing the things that we took for granted. I would never have thought of treasuring moments like this before yesterday. 'What are you thinking about, Ash?'

'Everything . . . Us . . . Today . . . The future . . . My head is nipping.' The chandelier in the middle of the room took my attention. If I stared at it long enough, maybe everything would return to normal. 'I am so scared, Dale. I have never been frightened of anything, my entire life.'

'Hey, you don't have to be scared. I will not leave you today or any day. I will be by your side every step of the way.'

'Thank you.' I wished that I had met Dale years ago; everything seemed such a waste.

'You don't have to thank me, Ash . . . I love you. I can't imagine my life without you.' The phone rang in the background, and none of us moved to answer it. We were in a time warp, and everything was moving apart from us.

'Dale, your mom is on the phone.' We both looked towards Rosa. This small woman was standing in the archway, wondering what to do. Her face was so soft and tender, and she looked so tired and upset herself. I was shocked to see how many people were affected by my tumour.

'Tell her I will call her back in a little while.' Rosa's small legs trotted back along the hall, and I couldn't take my eyes away from where she stood. I always did wonder what it would be like to have a messenger running about after our becking call. But I never expected it to be someone like Rosa; she was a star.

'You could have taken the call.'

'Nothing is going to make me move until you want to move.' That was reassuring, but if it was left to me, I would never move.

'My bum is numb, so yours must be worse taking my weight.' We both laughed together, and it was nice to act normal and forget for a few seconds what was going on around us.

'Do you fancy a shower?'

'I could go a nice hot bath, but I will settle for a shower if you join me.'

'I don't know why I never put a bathtub in this house . . .'

'Shh. A shower is perfect.' Dale pushed himself up on to his feet and held out his hands to take mine. Every bone ached as I was pulled up on to my feet, and every muscle protested. He was so gentle and patient with me; he was just like an angel sent down to help me. His arms wrapped around me, and this embrace was perfect, just what I needed. 'Number two on our list is to get a bath put in.'

'Great minds think alike. I will get someone in tomorrow.'

'Dale, there is no hurry.' How can I be so stupid? Time was against us; of course, there was a hurry.

'Let's go and get this shower.' We headed out towards the stairs and were halfway up when the front door opened. We both turned around to see who was visiting this early. I didn't really have the strength for visitors this morning.

'Mom . . . Dad. What are you doing here?'

'I had to see you both. I couldn't let you leave for the hospital without making sure you were both OK.' I let Dale's hand go and walked back down towards them. I was honoured that they thought of me in that way because after all, they didn't need to care.

'Thank you for coming.' I kissed both Mhairi's and Jake's cheeks.

'We are both bearing up . . . We just need to get today over with.' Dale's hands were placed on my shoulders, and I felt comfortable now.

'I told Rosa to tell you I would call back later.'

'She told me, but I couldn't stop worrying about you.'

'Honestly, Mhairi, please stop worrying. I can't bear seeing everyone I care about hurting. If you want to help me, really help me, can you just treat me like normal for the time being?' I was really not out to be harsh to people, but I had to be tough if I was going to get through the next few days.

'I will try, dear.' We were all standing in the hall like someone had died already. This was one thing that I didn't want from my family.

'Mom, we were just going to get a shower.' Mhairi always brought the angry side out of Dale, and I really didn't know why.

'OK. Phone me when you know anything.' We both got a hug and kiss, and Mhairi and Jake left pretty quickly. I stood and stared at the closed door behind them. Dale's shoulder was the perfect height for me to lean my head back on, and as usual I was glad of the support.

'What have we done to deserve this?' I didn't even mean to say that out loud; my head and my mouth were not connected today, and I am sure that was a bad start.

'We haven't done anything wrong. It is just one of those things.' I wanted to believe him. I really did. But something was telling me otherwise. I really didn't see the point in being the model citizen any more. I had never been in trouble with the police before. I had never taken drugs or been abusive in any other way, and this was the thanks I got. I thought if I could go back ten years, I would, maybe, do a few things differently and live a little.

'I think that the shower is shouting on us. My poor bones are aching.' I felt like I had done ten rounds with Mike Tyson, and the longer we stood here, the worse they were getting. Dale took my hand and led the way to the bathroom. I couldn't wait to get a heat in me. I suddenly felt frozen. My whole body was shattered. I thought that I just needed a rest to take everything in, and hopefully, my head would be clearer.

Pulling up outside the hospital was one of the most frightening experiences of my life. We sat staring out of the front window, and I was hoping for a miracle. I did hope that Dale would just reverse and take me home, but that was like waiting for yellow snow to fall from the sky. My head was so mixed up that I couldn't even think straight. This kind of thing was something you read about in a magazine or heard about from someone. It wasn't something that you expect to creep up on your own doorstep. Cancer is all around us nowadays, and it was one thing that had never really affected my family or friends before. I always thought of myself as being lucky until now. My luck was slowly running out piece by piece.

'You can do this, Ash.' I wanted to believe Dale. I really did. But I didn't think I was strong enough. I was going to look for any excuse to get out of today.

'I really wish that I was back at home with you . . . on the floor . . . Not a care in the world.'

'Well, after today, that floor can be your oyster.' I was trying my hardest not to laugh because today wasn't really a laughing matter. But Dale was the only person doing what I asked—treating me the same as usual.

'Thank you, for not treating me differently.' This must be really hard for him. He thought he was going to be a father, and now he was comforting his ill partner. 'I have never asked how you are?'

'As long as you are OK, I will be OK.' I knew that he wasn't telling me the truth, but I didn't want to push him. I hoped that he could confide in me when he felt the need to. 'We really should go in.' I got out of the car and stood looking up at the hospital. My body was a nervous wreck. Nerves always got the better of me, but these nerves were different today. 'Are you ready?'

'Ready as I will ever be.' It was a lie, but I had to show a brave face, or I would run a mile. Dale took my hand, and we took a slow walk up to Dr Ching's clinic. It was weird seeing Dale casually dressed. The only time I saw him dressed in casual wear was at weekends. Today, he ditched the suit for a pair of jeans and winter cardigan. He looked just as scared as I felt. But being a man, I knew he would never admit that to my face. Walking through the clinic door was like a walk to hell. The steps got slower, and the corridor got longer, and we didn't seem to get any further forward. I didn't even know how we had managed to make it into the clinic. Dr Ching was already at the desk, talking to the nurse, and I really wanted to disappear. But the minute he spotted us, he came right over to us. I really didn't mind waiting today; there was nothing good to come out of today's visit.

'Ashley. Dale. How are you both?' The clinic was quite full, but here I was getting preferential treatment. I hated to feel that I was getting this care because we were private clients. It didn't seem fair on everyone sitting.

'I am still in shock, Dr Ching. But I just want to get today over with.' Dr Ching's warm hand touched my hand, and he seemed very considerate to our feelings, and I suppose I was grateful to him for it.

'Today will be pretty straightforward. You will probably get some bleeding after the procedure and stomach cramps. It will probably feel like a period, but it will settle down.' I couldn't feel any worse so he was as well getting on with it.

'I can go home afterwards.' I didn't like hospitals at the best of times, but when I was the patient, it was a hundred times worse.

'We will play it by ear, but I don't see why not. Let's get you into a gown and make you comfortable.' We followed alongside Dr Ching, and there was no way I could run now. The long corridor was never ending as we walked along.

'When will we get the results back, Doctor?' These were the first words that Dale had spoken since we entered the hospital.

'I hope to know in a couple of days. I will chase them up.' We went into a large room, and it was all white with a bed in the middle of the room. Dale and I looked at each other, with no expression on our faces. This was it. There was no turning back.

'I am going to leave you for five minutes. Can I get you to take all your clothes off and get you to put this gown on?'

'Sure.' I couldn't let go of Dale's hand; he was my security blanket. If I let go, I would probably fall.

'Once you are ready, pop into the bed and make yourself comfortable.' Dr Ching left the room, and the only feeling that I could describe was terrified.

'Do you want me to wait outside until you are ready?'

'No . . . Please stay.' I didn't want him to leave me. I was acting like a child, but I couldn't help it. I felt all over the place.

'I didn't want to leave, Ash. It was just in case you wanted privacy.' I loved him for his sensitivity. He always put my feelings first, and that was why I loved him so much.

'I think we have passed that stage, Dale . . . Please don't leave me.' I walked over to the bed where the gown lay, and I couldn't believe that I was going to have to wear this. Dale had seen my body more times than enough, so today wasn't going to be any different. I didn't want him to feel uncomfortable though. I started taking my shoes and jacket off, and he took everything off me and placed it neatly in the bag. My skin felt warmer than usual, but I dare say my nerves had a big part to play in that. I slipped the gown over my head and slipped my trousers and pants off. I had changed into this gown in no time at all. Anyone would think that I was in a hurry. Dale placed the bag of clothes on the chair, and I climbed into the bed. The covers felt cold underneath me, and I was glad of it. Dale perched on the bed beside me and took my hand. His soft, warm skin made me feel comfortable. I didn't know where I would have been without him by my side.

'We will be home in no time, sweetheart.' I took every bit of him in carefully. I didn't want to miss a single thing. 'I love you, Ash.' I squeezed his hand and tried my hardest to smile. Today was going to be difficult for us all.

'I love you more.' I loved him more than words could describe. I didn't realise how powerful love was until now. The thought of going to sleep and never waking up and never seeing his face again was murder in itself. The tears flowed down my cheeks, and I couldn't stop them. It was like someone had turned a tap on again. Dale's hands should be all wrinkled with the amount of tears he has wiped away lately.

'Before you go to theatre, I have something to run past you . . . I thought about swapping with my mom and dad. I was going to tell them to move into our house, and we would move into the cottage.' It seemed like a perfect idea, but the thought of all the upheaval was another matter. I loved the cottage because it felt like home. The cottage was the loveliest place that I had ever been. 'It will just be us and plenty of TLC.'

'Don't hurry them out, Dale.'

'If it is what you want, we will be in there tonight, hun. Just say the word.' It was what I wanted. I couldn't think of a better place to recover after today.

'Sounds nice.' Dr Ching and a nurse came in. I was glad that I got my answer in before it was too late.

'Ashley, this is Susan. She is your named nurse . . . Susan will be here with you from start to finish. Anything you need, just let her know.' I felt like an invalid, and all this attention wasn't necessary.

'Hi, Ashley, just like Dr Ching said, anything at all don't hesitate.'

'Thanks.' Dale never moved off the bed, and I was glad of his presence. He kept me calm.

'We are ready for you now, Ashley. Can I get you to sign this consent form?' I took the form and read through it, not one bit made any sense to me. The easiest thing to do was just sign on the cross. I took the pen from Dr Ching and signed my life away. The tears wouldn't stop, and I felt stupid now. What was I crying for now?

'Dale, I can get Susan to show you to the relatives' room.'

'No, he can't go.' It had never crossed my mind that I would have to leave him here. Dale jumped forward and held me in his arms, and I soothed into his chest.

'Can I not stay with her until she is asleep . . . ? She really is in no state to go alone.'

'I really shouldn't allow this, but under the circumstances, I am going to say yes.' I felt like I could breathe again once he had approved Dale coming with me.

'Thank you, Doctor.' Dale held me tightly, stroking my hair. 'I will be here until you are asleep, and I will be here when you wake up.' I was glad to hear that he would be here for me, but I hated the fact that he was left sitting on his own for the time being.

'What if I don't wake up?' I knew that I was sounding ridiculous, but I had it splattered all across my head and I needed to say it.

'Ashley. Trust me, you will wake up. I am one of the best gynaecologists in Alaska.' Dale got up of the bed and never let go of my hand. The bed rails were lifted up, and the brakes were taken off. I was a bit more relieved at knowing I was in good hands. But I couldn't stop the tears from falling down my cheeks.

'Let's go.' Dr Ching was at the top of the bed, and Susan was at the bottom of the bed. They manoeuvred the bed out of the room and along the corridor. I had such a tight grip of Dale's hand that it was turning blue. We made it to the recovery room, where Dr Ching and his team got me ready for my procedure. Dale stroked my face so softly, and I could feel how exhausted my body was, physically and emotionally. I was getting pricked in my hand with needles, and I was feeling anxious in every way possible.

'Ashley, we are going to place this mask tightly over your face, and by the time you count to ten, you will be in dreamland.' I couldn't speak. I was like a dumb person. My lips were sealed shut.

'Ashley, I love you. I will be here when you wake up.' I saw the tears roll down Dale's cheek, and that made me worse.

'I love you.' The words were sobbed out as Susan placed the mask over my face. I focused on Dale's eyes as my head got fuzzy and my eyes got heavier. I felt drunk until there was nothing else to focus on.

My eyes flickered open, and I caught sight of Susan changing a bag of some fluid. I still felt drunk. My head was buzzing, and my eyes were heavy. I was just relieved that I was still alive.

'Hello, sleepyhead.' I managed a half of a smile, but I didn't want her. I wanted Dale. I pulled at the mask on my face, feeling panicked.

'Dale . . . Where is he?'

'Leave your mask on, honey. Dale has just nipped to the bathroom.' My stomach felt very weird, like I had butterflies floating around. The door creaked open, but I still felt too weak to lift my head.

'How are you feeling, darling?' voice made me open my eyes to look at her. 'The first thing that she asked for when she opened her eyes was you.' The voice was confusing me, and I felt my hand getting squeezed. This time when my eyes opened, I saw Dale's eyes peering through me.

'Hey, sweetie.' His face was all red and puffy, like he had sat and cried the whole time I was away.

'Did everything go OK?' I was assuming that everything went OK because I was here alive talking to my fiancé.

'The doctor hasn't been in yet, but Susan said everything went according to plan.'

'I need a drink.' Susan handed Dale a glass of water with a straw, and it looked good, just what I needed.

'Just take small sips, hun.' Sips would be fine because my mouth felt like sandpaper. Dale held the glass to my mouth, and I sipped away at the ice cold water. It felt good. The door creaked open again, and the room went silent. It was amazing all the things that you could hear in a hospital.

'How is she doing, Susan?'

'Dale, I feel sick.' Dale quickly took the sick bowl of the table and held it in front of me. I felt like an invalid. I had to sit forward as I was violently sick. Susan came and held my hair out of my face, while Dale was my rock holding the bowl, and I had just got the oxygen mask off in time. Everyone was running about looking after me, and I hated it all.

'How long has she been like this, Susan?'

'She only woke up five minutes ago, but this is the first time she has been sick . . . Everything has been stable until now, but that is to be expected with how quick she had to move.'

'I expect that this is the anaesthetic. It will wear off. I will write you up for an anti-sickness drug. That will help it pass quicker.' I was glad that he knew what he was doing because I didn't know whether I was coming or going.

'Is everything OK though?'

'The procedure went accordingly. We will get the results back ASAP. However, when I had you in theatre, I noticed that your ovaries were still ovulating. I managed to take away several visible eggs.'

'What does that mean?' I lay back, and Susan gave me a wet wipe to freshen me up. But I was more intrigued in what Dr Ching was going to say. Dale asked the question that I wanted to, at least we were both thinking on the same wavelength.

'I saw how devastated you both were yesterday about the baby. But no matter what happens with this outcome, Ashley will either have years of treatment which will kill any chances of having a baby or she will have to have a hysterectomy. Either way she will never have a child of her own.' What he was saying hit me like a ton of bricks. The only thing that I ever wanted was a child, and now that was never going to happen. 'But these eggs that I have harvested will be able to be used by you both when the time is right. Money isn't an issue with you both, so one scenario is your sperm would be taken to fertilise Ashley's egg and then transferred to a surrogate. I just wanted to give you the option of having your own child.' I was amazed that all this could be possible, and it had given me some kind of hope. Someone was looking after me after all.

'Also if the worst comes to the worst and you don't make it . . . you can sign a form for Dale to use your eggs. This is all things that you can think about later, but all these options are possible.' I was glad that he was thinking of everything because we would never have thought about the future with or without me.

'I don't know what to say . . . Thank you.' I knew now that he knew I wasn't going to make it. I didn't have to wait for my results, and if he was honest with me, he would tell me the truth. 'You know the outcome already, and you are not going to tell me, are you?' I didn't know whether it was the thought of dying or the anaesthetic still in my system that gave me the courage to speak my mind, and I could see the look on everyone's face. They all knew that I was right.

'I can't tell you anything like that without having the evidence. It would be more than my job's worth to fill your head with rubbish.' I should have known that he wasn't going to tell me. He was a typical man who needed proof and evidence.

'It will only be a couple of days, honey. I am sure Dr Ching will be on the lab's case until he gets them.' I heard Susan, but I couldn't take my eyes away from Dr Ching.

'How are you feeling, Ashley?' I thought that he had the cheek asking me how I was feeling after blatantly lying to me.

'OK. I feel better since I was sick.'

'Good . . . We will monitor you and see how you go.'

'So I can go home now.' I just wanted to go home to my own bed. I didn't want to put a face on here. I just wanted to get home with Dale and get on with the time that I had left.

'Give it a couple of hours, and I will discharge you myself.' I shook my head and looked at Dale and then back at Dr Ching.

'No, now. A couple of hours aren't going to make any difference. I can sleep in my own bed and take pain relief if and when I need to.' The doctor knew that he wasn't going to change my mind.

'Dale, can you manage, if I agree to this?' Dale looked at me with a face that I had never seen before. I was hoping that he would agree to take me home.

'My fiancée wasn't asking for you to agree. She told you that she was going home.' Dr Ching didn't know what to say or where to look. He certainly didn't expect Dale's response and neither did I.

'OK. I will get your discharge ready . . . I will be in contact as soon as I know anything.' The atmosphere had changed in the room, and I was relieved to be going home.

'Thank you, Dr Ching.' I tried to sit up alone, but I felt very stiff and sore. Dale helped me carefully, and I swung my legs out of the bed.

'Are you OK?'

'I will be when I get out of here.' Dale smiled at me and lifted my clothes on to the bed. Susan had followed Dr Ching out of the room, and Dale and I were finally alone. They were probably going to discuss how I shouldn't be leaving here, but I had passed caring now.

'Let me help you put your clothes on.'

'I am not an invalid yet, Mr Black.' I lifted the gown over my head and placed my arms through my bra. Dale went behind me to fasten the clip, and I really did feel weak.

'You are still stubborn.'

'That will be there until I take my last breath.' How insensitive could I be. 'Sorry. I didn't mean to be a bitch.' Dale bent down to help me put my legs in my pants and trousers. I felt very uncomfortable being the patient. My fiancé shouldn't have to dress me like a child; he should be enjoying his life the way he wanted to.

'Don't be sorry, babe. I would think that there was something wrong if you thought before you spoke.' My shoes were last to get put on, and I was already to go. I finally realised what he had said and smiled softly. I was never good at thinking before I spoke, so why should I change a habit of a lifetime.

'Dale.'

'Yeah.' He stood up in front of me and placed his hand on my cheek, and I longed for his touch.

'Please tell me that you didn't chase your parents out of the cottage.'

'My mom and dad are thrilled to have our house. The cottage is too small for a baby. You said so yourself, Ash.' I did say that. For our baby. 'Ash, I am so sorry. Look who is being insensitive now.'

'You don't have to walk on eggshells around me. You're right. The cottage is too small for Kiara.' I was devastated about not being pregnant, but Kiara couldn't suffer because of it.

'You don't need a constant reminder of the baby, and I didn't do it for Kiara. I did it for us. We have the cottage to ourselves. No busy house with all the noise, and I know how much you like the cottage.' I really wanted him to be honest with me. I knew that he was struggling and the tears before theatre only proved that.

'I do love the cottage and you . . . Will you promise me that tonight you will be honest with me?' Dale looked very confused as to where I was going with this. But we were only going to get through the next coming weeks or months if we were honest with one another. 'Honesty is the best policy', so my mom and dad always told me, and I planned to keep that in my head for the rest of my days.

'I am always honest with you.'

'You keep telling me that you are OK, but I know you too well, to know that you're not.' The door creaked open and in came Dr Ching. Perfect timing as usual. What was it with doctors showing up when they were not wanted.

'These are your discharge forms.' Handing me the envelope, I looked at him carefully. For the first time I noticed that he must see a lot in his line of work. But he seemed to be hurting just as much as we were. 'This is some pain relief. It is all labelled correctly. I have also given you an anti-sickness tablet. You will know when you need it.' Dale took the bag of medication and shook Dr Ching's hand. 'If you need me, day or night, just call me.' I nodded politely. 'You're free to go. Take care.' I eased down off the bed and stumbled over. Dr Ching caught my arm and steadily got me standing straight. How embarrassed would I have been to fall over in front of the doctor? That would just be my luck.

'Take your time, Ashley. Your body has been through a lot in twenty-four hours. You need rest.'

'I will be fine, once I get home.'

'She is as stubborn as a mule, Doc. I will take care of her' I took Dale's arm and walked for the door. I left the doctor standing and never looked back. I really didn't care for what the doctor had to say. I had one mission right now, and that was homeward bound.

'I could get you a chair, Ash.' I slapped his arm, and he laughed at me. At least I saw him laugh today. I wouldn't use a chair even if I needed to.

'Don't get smart, Mr Black.' I was walking very slowly, but it wasn't because I was sore. My body seemed to have only one pace today.

'The car is out front anyway.'

'That is one of the best things you have said all day.' The hospital was like a mile from the car. The corridor was never ending today, and I got the slightest feel of cold air coming through the main doors; it felt so good. It was amazing how cold air felt so good. Never in a million years did I think that I would value the cold winter air.

'Why are you putting up with all this?' I needed to ask this question. Especially now, when he could see how bad things were going to get, this was just the beginning. He was being a saint to me, but he was getting very little in return. I didn't understand how someone would put up with all this when they could walk away and live a happy life. Silence was golden, and I thought that he was going to play deaf and dumb and avoid my question.

'I love you, Ash.' Was love enough? Could I let him put his life on hold for love? 'I will take you any way that I can get you.'

'But what happens when I am gone?' We had been over all these questions, but I needed him to know that he still had time to walk away.

'Stop talking like you're going somewhere soon . . . You could have years left.' We both knew that that wasn't true. It was about time that we accepted that fact.

'Dale, when the time comes, what is going to happen to you?'

'You have lost me, Ash.' Outside the hospital, I could see the car waiting, and I stopped dead and looked at him. The car would wait, what I had to say wouldn't.

'You need to promise me that you will move on with your life and not mope around after me.'

'Ash, stop.' I was taken by surprise. This was the first time Dale had ever raised his voice to me, and I wasn't sure that I liked it. 'I can promise you a lot of things, but don't ask me to move on without you . . .' My eyes immediately filled up with tears. Death didn't frighten me, half as much as Dale's life stopping. I couldn't bear him living in pain and heartache.

'Let's get the results back before you have yourself dead and buried . . . I am sorry for raising my voice to you. I just can't bear to think of you leaving me so soon.' I could see Dr Ching's face today, and he knew more than he was letting on, and I knew what my fate was. I could feel it inside me, tearing me apart piece by piece. 'Carlos is getting cold. Let's go home, and we can have as many discussions as you like.' Dale wrapped his arm around my waist, and we headed for the car. Carlos opened my door for me, and it took me several extra steps to reach him, but I managed it in one piece.

'Hi, Ashley. How are you feeling?'

'A bit sore, but I will be OK when I get home.' I climbed into the car slowly and swung my legs around. 'Ouch.' Dale and Carlos both bent down beside me. Their faces were full of concern, but there wasn't much need for it.

'Ash, are you OK?'

'I am fine. I was just sore when I tried to move over.'

'Don't move. I will get in the other side.' I was going to hate the next couple of days. I didn't like being a patient and certainly hated feeling ill.

'You look very pale, Ashley. Are you sure you are feeling OK?'

'The next person to ask me that question is going to get a punch. I just want to go home.' Dale got up and went around to the other door, and Carlos stood and stared at me until Dale got in beside me. You would think that I was a child needing looked after all the time. Carlos was going to be just as bad as Dale. I was sure I would lose the head with one of them, before the week was out.

'I feel terrible for shouting at you.' I laid my head on Dale's chest, and this was my comfort blanket. I did intend to get the use out of it, in the coming weeks.

'Don't feel bad, Dale. I am driving myself crazy, so I must be driving you daft.' His soft kisses on my head made up for him shouting. I had forgotten about it already. Right now the only thing on my mind was sleep and plenty of it. Who needs a hospital when you have two strapping men who care about you and a nice comfortable cottage? I had everything that I ever needed. Even if this was my last day on this earth, I had everything I needed right here.

CHAPTER 15

The Longest Forty-Eight Hours

I woke up to the sound of lovely music playing in the background. It was so soothing and relaxing. I felt very confused because the last thing that I could remember was closing my eyes in the car. Now I had woken up in this nice comfortable bed. I slowly turned on to my side, and I wanted to get up, but the sound of the piano playing was just so soothing. My body wanted to get up, but my mind was telling me to lie at peace. Dale's head peeked around the door, and his face lit up as he walked over to me. His side of the bed felt very empty without him lying beside me.

'Hey, babe, how are you feeling?' I managed to smile at him and reach my hand out to touch him. I didn't want to think about feelings right now.

'How did I get here?' I knew that I sounded ridiculous, but by God, I had no memory of moving from the car.

'You fell asleep in the car, and you gave me the fright of my life. I couldn't wake you up.' I was shocked. No a wonder he got a fright. I could only imagine what he thought. 'I phoned Dr Ching, and he said that it was normal after an anaesthetic, especially with how quick you left the hospital.' I felt like I had lost too much time, like I was sleeping my life away.

'So what time is it?' Dale glanced at his watch and smiled.

'5.45 p.m.'

'I need to stop sleeping like this.' I knew that it was good for me, but it felt very unhealthy at the same time.

'Your body needs rest, and sleep is the best thing for it.' I sat up and felt a sharp pain shoot across my tummy. It was a horrible feeling, like someone was tearing right across my lower stomach.

'Ouch.'

'Are you OK, hun?' All I was doing to this poor man was making him concerned and paranoid. He was going to have a heart attack any time soon.

'Probably just lay too long . . . I will be fine.' Once I was all comfortable sat up on my pillows, Dale came and lay beside me. His arm wrapped around my body, and we lay cuddled into one another. This was the perfect outcome of the last twenty-four hours.

'Christine called when you were sleeping.' Oh my God, I forgot to call her and let her know everything was OK.

'I forgot all about her. Is she OK?' How bad did I feel right now. How could I forget all about her?

'Yeah, I kept her up to date yesterday. She is going to pop in tonight. I told her where to find us.' I lay rocking my head like I had no cares. I really did hope that Christine was OK with everything. I didn't think that I could bear her still angry and upset. 'Do you want anything, Ash?' I didn't know if I wanted anything. I was too comfortable in Dale's arms.

'I have everything right here.'

'I bet I know one thing that I could tempt you with.' I tilted my head up to look at his handsome face. Even upset, he still looked sexy.

'What?' I really wanted to know what he thought that I would want, more than him.

'A nice, hot bubble bath, with lots of candles and nice music.' He was right. That sounded like heaven. It was my idea of a nice, quiet night in.

'You know me too well, Mr Black.' He sat me forward to get his arm back, and I wanted him and the bath so badly.

'Stay here, and I will run it for you.' He got up and went to walk away until I pulled his arm back. 'What is it, Ash?'

'Don't make me stretch up to you.' His sexy smile and gleaming eyes knew exactly what I wanted. He placed a hand at either side of me in the bed and kissed me tenderly on the lips. He stopped and looked me in the eyes, and there was that twinkle that I loved.

'I love you, Ash.'

'I know you do, babe.' I got a peck on my lips before he left the room to run my bath. I did hear him tell me to stay here, but I wanted to get up and prove to both of us that I was fine. I threw the cover back and swung my legs out of the bed. I sat for a few moments to compose myself, and for a change, I felt fine. As I pushed up off the bed, I felt a bit tender, but I felt better than I expected. I walked slowly off to the bathroom, and I could smell the bubble bath already. I met Dale in the hallway, and his face said it all.

'Ash, I told you to stay there.' I shook my head and stood still.

'I feel fine . . . Honestly . . . Please, stop fussing.' He took my arm and walked beside me to the bathroom. I sat on the toilet seat and pulled him down to my level.

'I am fussing because I want to . . . I want to take care of you.'

'I really appreciate it . . . But there is going to be times when I can't walk along this hall. Let me do things when I feel able . . . I feel really stupid as it is.'

'Why do you feel stupid?' How could I explain this to my lover without sounding ridiculous? Everything going on in my head was nothing that I really wanted to say out loud.

'I am nearly twenty-four, and I feel like an old-age pensioner . . . You are my friend, my lover, my fiancé, and now my carer.'

'But I want to be all of the above . . . You are my wife with or without the piece of paper, and I want to help you through this difficult time . . . What happened to us enjoying the next couple of days together.' We were supposed to be enjoying life, no matter how long life was going to be. Why did I have to be so bloody stubborn? I really wished that I took the laid-back approach of my mom; she didn't care too much at what life threw at her, and now I knew that was the best way to live.

'We are going to . . . I promise . . . Are you going to help me into that bath before it gets cold?'

'I thought that you were never going to ask, Miss Malone.' I slipped my slippers off, and Dale helped me slip my pyjamas off. Before I knew it, I was standing naked in the bathroom. Six months ago, I would have never let a man help me strip naked to take a bath. But I didn't feel the slightest bit uncomfortable in front of Dale. Standing naked in front of him seemed natural, like I had been doing it all my life. He knew my body inside and out, and at times like this, I was glad. He helped me step into the bath, and I slipped myself under the water. I splashed him with the water deliberately, and his face was a picture. If only there was a camera about to capture this moment, it was another favourite of mine.

'You need to come in with me now . . . You're wet any way.'

'You're a devil. You had that planned.' I put a playful look on my face and played with the water like butter wouldn't melt.

'Me. Never.' Dale didn't need asking twice; he slipped his clothes off and slid in behind me. His body fit around me like a neatly fitted glove, and I lay back and slipped down the bath a bit. 'Now, this feels like heaven.'

'Glad you think so, Ash.' Right at this moment lying in Dale's arms under the water, I felt completely normal. There was nothing to suggest that I was ill in any way. If only we could spend our entire life in a bath, then everything would work out perfectly.

'I feel secure when I am in your arms.'

'If I could only take this . . . away.' I could here in his voice that he was fighting back tears. I turned slightly to look at him, and I wished I hadn't now.

'Don't cry, babe . . .' I placed my hand over his cheek and tried to rub the pain away. 'You are already doing enough.'

'If only enough was good enough.' I wanted to scream at him, but a part of me was glad that he was opening up to me. I needed to know what he was thinking. 'I want to marry you . . . have a family with you . . . and live a long and happy life with you.' I lay very still and quiet so that he could get it all off his chest. 'Why does life have to be so cruel?'

'Life is a bitch. We just have to make the best out of a bad situation.' I quickly realised that my words were all wrong, but no matter what I said, it always sounded wrong.

'If you are feeling OK tomorrow, we can go to the church if you like. We can see when we can get married.'

'It doesn't matter how I feel. I want to do it tomorrow. Let's start as we mean to go on.' Dale leant forward and took my lips with his mouth. He made my body hungry for him. Every time he touched me, he made me tingle, and I would never understand how my thoughts and feelings surface when he was around.

'That just makes everything disappear.' His smile was just so addictive that I couldn't help but smile with him. 'Can I say something? I don't know how this is going to sound, but I need to say it now.' I sat up and turned on to my side slightly. I honestly didn't know how to put my next conversation. It would either go right or go horribly wrong. But since we were getting everything out in the open, now was the best time.

'I was thinking about what Dr Ching said yesterday, about taking my eggs away . . .'

'You don't need to talk about this now, Ash.'

'Please . . . Let me finish. If I am dying and I only have weeks left, I want to sign the form that Dr Ching mentioned . . . You don't have to use them, but it will always be an option for you. You can always have a part of me.' I looked down at the bubbles surrounding me, hoping that the bubbles would have a perfect answer for me. I wanted Dale to say something, to let me know that he understood what I had just said, but I knew that I was asking a lot of him, something that he didn't have to think about right now.

'You would do that for me.'

'Of course, I would. I know how much you wanted a child with me, and I accept your decision about not moving on. But I can't let you live alone without me. This way you would just have to find a surrogate mother to carry our child, and you would always have a part of me.' It was weird to think that I would still have a child getting brought into this world, but I wouldn't be part of its life in any way, shape or form. I just knew that Dale would give him or her the best possible life.

'You never know, you might be OK. You might be here to see our child enter the world.' I knew that was wishful thinking on both of our parts, but I didn't want to build our hopes up.

'I know I won't be, but with you as a father, I will be happy.' He placed his arms around my naked body, and I closed my eyes and let the water soothe away my pain. It just seemed so unfair that we had to go through all this. Why us? Why did we have to make all these painful decisions? 'What would you say if I said I wanted to go out?' He did look shocked, and I could see his brain ticking it over thinking about all the pros and cons.

'Where?'

'A movie. A meal. Something normal.' Anything would be normal as long as it wasn't sitting moping around thinking about the inevitable.

'When?'

'Now . . . No time like the present.' The suspense was killing me. I wanted to know what he was going to say.

'OK, let's do it.' He didn't sound convinced, but he was going along with it to make me happy. He certainly didn't need to try to make me happy, just his presence made me the happiest woman alive. We lay still in the water, and I couldn't believe how lucky I was to have Dale, not many women could say that about their men. It was like I was sent to Alaska to meet him, to have my perfect love, to have a taste of what life should be like, and to be able to say that I have succeeded in everything that I have done in my life.

I walked along the hall to the living room, and I felt like I was on a first date again. I could hear Dale talking to someone, and my initial thought was 'how dare someone spoil our plans and pop in'. But as I reached the living room, I noticed that it was just the phone he was talking into.

'Yes, Mom, we are fine. We are going out for a few hours tonight, just to have some fun for a change . . . OK . . . Speak to you tomorrow . . .' I stood and leant against the wall, and Dale turned to look at me. He looked radiant as he threw the phone on to the couch.

'You look lovely, Ash.'

'You don't look so bad yourself, Mr Black.' He came towards me and wrapped himself around me; he took me by surprise, but I liked it. I felt humane again.

'What do you want to do first?' I didn't really care what we did first, but I needed to decide something.

'Eat.'

'Good choice.' Dale went over to the stand and got our jackets, and he came and helped me into mine. He really did have a kind heart and a gentle soul.

'You are the perfect gentleman.'

'I like to try.' I picked the car keys up and walked to the door. 'Eh, I said that we would go out, but I certainly never said that you could drive.' God loves a trier. I threw the keys over to him, and he had to stretch to catch them. I watched him carefully as he placed them back on the table, and confusion washed over me.

'Are we flying to dinner?' I amused myself as I let a little giggle out, and I could see that he thought I was funny; he just didn't want to laugh at me. He opened the door, and I slowly walked out of the cottage, I could see the Mercedes sitting waiting for us. 'Carlos . . . I forgot all about him.'

'It beats flying.' He thought he was funny as he let a little laugh out this time. I wasn't going to burst his bubble tonight. He could be funny if he wanted to be. He wrapped his arm around me to help me to the car. It was a cold and frosty night, and you could just tell that we were well and truly into winter now.

'Good evening, guys.'

'Hello, Carlos. Thank you for coming up here at the last minute.'

'My pleasure, Dale.' I eased myself into the car, trying my hardest not to hurt myself. I was relieved when I was in and Dale was close by my side.

'Are you OK, Ash?'

'Yes. I am fine. Please don't ask me that again, tonight.' Everyone was like a broken record repeating over and over again.

'I will try.' I placed my hand on top of his and sat patiently, waiting to see where we were going.

'Your skin feels like . . .' I stopped dead in my tracks because I quickly realised what I was going to say and it was neither the time nor the place. Dale smiled at me. He obviously knew exactly what I was going to say. 'So are you going to tell me where we are going?'

'You will soon see. It isn't too far from here.' I actually had no idea. That anaesthetic had obviously tired my brain out.

'How is everyone settling in up at the house, Carlos?'

'Everyone is fine, Ashley.' I knew that Mhairi would make it her home, no matter how much notice she was given. 'Rosa sends her love. She is missing you both.' His words did crush my good mood. Rosa was like a mother figure to me, and I strangely missed her as well.

'What is wrong, Ash?'

'Nothing . . . I miss Rosa. She was just like a mother hen to me.'

'We can go and see her whenever you want . . . Carlos can bring her up to see us as well.'

'I know . . . I am just being silly . . . Nothing that a nice cold glass of wine won't fix.' The car came to a stop, and I noticed that we were on the harbour.

There was only one place that we could be going, and that was Maggie May's. Dale climbed out, and I eased myself out to take hold of his arm. All that I could think about was the first time I saw Dale. It was in this very restaurant. So much had happened since then, and I would say all good, apart from the tumour.

'Is this OK?'

'It is perfect, Dale.' Perfect was an understatement. If tonight worked out perfect, I would be the happiest person alive. Linking Dale's arm felt like we were united as one, nothing could harm that tonight. The restaurant was quiet when we walked in, and I looked around the room just like I did on my very first visit. I spotted Christian, standing at the bar, and he looked just as gorgeous. He immediately stopped what he was doing and ran over to me. His arms were going to crush the life out of me. 'How are you doing, baby girl?'

'I am fine, sweetie.' I could breathe once he released me. It was nice to see Christian, but I didn't want him to treat me any differently.

'Come over to the booth. It is nice and quiet.'

'No. I don't want quiet, Christian.' Christian looked at Dale for reassurance, and I could tell that he was wondering what was going through my mind.

'Where do you want to sit?' I looked around the room and spotted a table for two in the middle of the room. I walked over to it and slipped my jacket off. Dale took my jacket off me, and we sat down. Christian bent down beside me, and I immediately noticed that he didn't look his usual happy self. 'What can I get you to drink, Ash?'

'A glass of sweet white wine, please.'

'Just make it a bottle, Christian.' Dale really was going to treat me normally tonight. I half expected him to tell me not drink on my medication, but the only one thinking about my condition was me.

'Sure, I will bring it over for you. If you need anything, just give me a shout.' I watched Christian walk away from us, and I really didn't know that my condition would affect too many people.

'I am sorry. I didn't think this through. I thought that I would bring you here and sweep you off your feet. I forgot about your friend working here . . . I just wanted to rekindle that first time we met.'

'You have. This is perfect. Christian won't spoil that. He has had his moment.' I could see that Dale had really thought this through. He was so considerate. My hand reached over and took his hand. His smile would lighten a dark room anywhere. 'I love to see you smile. It remembers me of the first time I noticed you.' Christian interrupted us as he placed our glasses down and filled them up.

'Are you ready to order, Ash?' I didn't even look at the menu. I ordered the same thing all the time.

'I will have the salmon, sweetie.'

'I will take the same please, Christian.'

'Perfect choice. It won't be too long. Enjoy your wine, guys.' Christian seemed very distant with us. He wasn't his usual bubbly self, but I wasn't going to let anything get in the way of me enjoying tonight. The wine was delicious, and I had to put my glass down before I drank it all myself.

'Now we are here. I haven't a clue what to say . . . I don't want to say the wrong thing.' I sat and thought carefully about everything Dale was saying. I didn't want him to feel awkward with me. I just wanted us to be normal with one another.

'What is happening with work?' I thought if I lead the conversation, then we would flow with one another, just like we always do.

'Callum is taking care of everything, Ash. He has made Christine his personal assistant. When we spoke earlier, he said he was bored. You have everything organised well.'

'That sounds about right.' I might be dizzy at times, but I was always very able to do my work. I was missing my usual daily routine at work. That was the one thing that I wish I could still do.

'He is going to do everything he can to let us take the time off.' I took a gulp as it finally hit me that everyone was being so nice. I didn't think that it was all necessary, but deep in my heart, I knew that I was really ill.

'Everyone is being very nice.'

'He said it was the least that he could do after everything you did for him and Kiara.' I wished this was as straightforward as the situation with Kiara.

'How is Kiara?' So much had happened over the last day or two that I never gave the baby a second thought.

'She is good. My mom thinks that she is missing you.'

'Aw, the wee soul . . . We can go and do some Christmas shopping tomorrow, after we go to the church.' I loved Christmas shopping, and this year there was a baby to make it more special. I would be able to spoil my niece rotten, and that would make me feel better in myself.

'You are such a good influence on me, Ash. Normally, I run around on Christmas Eve in a mad hurry to get everyone their gifts.' I let out a little giggle because I certainly didn't expect him to do it himself, so it was music to my ears. I thought Dale was too organised for shopping.

'I like Christmas, and this year Kiara will make it special.'

'Christmas will be special because you are here. I never thought that I would find someone so special to me.' I could cry at how nice he was to me. Every bone in my body tingled when he spoke so highly of me.

'We will have a good time . . . We will make sure of that.' I couldn't take my eyes off my glass because I was focused. I knew that this could be my last Christmas, and I was determined to make it a good one. I broke my focus as Christian placed our food down in front of us. The last thing that I wanted to do was cry.

'Here we go, guys, two salmon.'

'Thanks, Christian. This smells lovely.' I didn't expect anything less. The food was the best for miles around. People come from all over the country to eat here.

'Can I get you anything else?'

'No, I think we are good, thanks.' Christian certainly wasn't himself; he normally hinged around for small chat, but today he couldn't get away from me quick enough. Maybe he was just trying to give me some space to get on with my night.

'Ash, turn that frown into a smile.' Dale was right; we were having a nice time.

'You're right, I am sorry . . . This is lovely.' I actually felt like my throat had been cut. It felt good to want food and not gag at the thought.

'It is good to see you eat.' My mouth was watering as I took my first bite. It was to die for. 'So, what do you think we should get Kiara for Christmas?' I liked how the conversation got put back to a subject that I liked. I knew how difficult it must be for him to ignore the fact that I had a tumour, but he was doing really well.

'I would like to get her a guardian angel necklace . . . I thought about it the other night when I was in bed. But I wasn't sure what else to get.' I hope that one day I could be her guardian angel and guide her down the right path.

'The chain is a lovely idea, babe.'

'I thought it was appropriate. Don't you think?' I felt the tears choke me as I thought about it. I placed my fork down and grabbed my napkin. I didn't want anyone to see me upset.

'Hey, come on, sweetheart. You have been so strong. We can change the subject.'

'No, I am enjoying myself . . . It is just . . . Everything overwhelms me at times, and I get lost in the moment.' It was a weird one because one minute I was thinking happy thoughts, but it quickly reminded me off what was going on, and I couldn't control the pain inside my gut.

'You are doing so well, Ash . . . We wouldn't be human if we didn't cry.'

'I can't have many tears left.'

'That makes two of us, doll.' After everything, we still managed to make each other smile. I lifted my glass and took a large drink, hoping that it would erase some painful memories.

'Better?'

'Much.' I couldn't face another bite. I had done well, but I feared if I took any more, I would just end up throwing it back up. I watched Dale carefully as he filled our glasses back up, and it was nice to see that he was treating tonight like any other night. 'If I didn't know you better, I would say you were trying to get me drunk, Mr Black.' He laughed out loud and sat back in his chair and smirked at me with his sexy look.

'Damn, you caught me out . . .'

'I have enjoyed tonight . . . Even though there has been tears, there has been more laughs.'

'As always, I have enjoyed your company, Ash.'

'It is weird how things plan out, isn't it?' When I thought about death, I expected to live to a ripe old age. I thought people died when they were ancient but not when they were in their prime.

'I wish that I met you years ago.' That was something that we could both agree on. But I was very grateful to have him in my life now.

'My mom always used to say to me that everything happens for a reason, and I used to believe her . . . But surely, this isn't happening to us for a reason.'

'Don't give up hope, sweetie. Have a little faith.' I liked how everyone told me to believe and have faith, but I was losing any faith that I ever had. Everyone whom I grew up with and everything that I believed in had vanished over the years.

'Are you finished?' Dale nodded at me intriguingly. 'Can we walk?'

'Sure, let's go.' We got up and walked over to the bar, and Christian gave us our bill without even being asked. We hardly ate anything, and there was still wine in the bottle, but it was just nice to be out with Dale, like a normal couple on a night out enjoying each other's company.

'Was everything OK for you?'

'Yeah, great, thanks.' I never spoke. I let Dale do the talking. I didn't feel like I had much more to say to Christian. I let Dale help me into my jacket and watched Christian walk up to me and wrap his arms around me.

'Take care of yourself, Ash.'

'I will . . . Dale is making sure that I do.' Christian let me go, and immediately I felt my lungs fill with air. Christian patted Dale on the back, and it was nice to see them getting along.

'Speak to you later.' Christian walked away from us, and I could see him wiping his eyes. I had to walk away before I broke down in the middle of the restaurant. We got outside, and Dale's hand clutched mine. I felt safe and secure now. We started walking along the harbour, and it was a cold night, but it felt good against my cheeks. I now knew what it meant when someone said, 'You realise what is important, when it is too late,' because I can relate to that saying now.

'Ashley.' I swung around when I heard someone yelling my name. Christine was running towards us, and my heart sank into my chest. I couldn't bear my friends over the top reactions tonight.

'Hi, Christine.'

'Hi. Is that all you can say?' I must have looked as stunned as I felt because Dale squeezed my hand tighter. I had no idea what had rattled her cage.

'What is wrong with you?'

'What is wrong with me? I will tell you, shall I . . . I have been worried sick about you. I went to visit you, only to find the house all lit up but no one there . . . I thought the worst.' I felt bad for forgetting that she was dropping by, but I just needed to get out of the house.

'Christine, calm down. We left you a message to say we were going out.' Dale sounded really angry at Christine, and he had every right to be.

'Calm down . . .'

'Christine, what do you want me to do? Do you want me to sit at home and wait to die? Don't you dare come down here on your high horse, giving me the third degree.' I saw red I needed all the support that I could, not my best friend being a bitch.

'Everyone needs to calm down . . . This isn't any good for, Ash . . .'

'That's right . . . Everyone walk on eggshells. Ashley is sick.' I couldn't believe that Christine was being so immature.

'Enough.' Dale really roared at Christine, and she stopped dead. I didn't know if I was more shocked at Dale shouting or someone shutting Christine up. 'You should go home and think about what you are saying.'

'Just leave her, Dale. There is no talking to her when she is in this mood.' I loved my friend to pieces, but she could create an argument in an empty room, especially when she was in this mood. Dale and I had had a lovely night so far, and I didn't want her to ruin it.

'Ash, I was worried sick.'

'Join the club, Christine . . . How do you think we feel . . . This isn't all about you . . .' Dale's arm wrapped around my shoulders; he clearly knew how upset I was. I never raised my voice. I couldn't help but notice people staring at us in the street. I really could kill Christine for making me crazy. 'I am dealing with this the best way I can, and if you don't want to be a part of that, then you know what you can do.' I turned and walked away. I had to before I hit her. I just left Dale and Christine standing. I knew if I didn't walk away, the whole situation would escalate into something huge. My whole body was shaking from anger, and that wasn't me. How dare she come here and ruin my night? I never asked for anything, but tonight was supposed to be special.

'Ash, wait.' I heard Dale running behind me to catch up. 'Are you OK?' I really wanted to know what 'OK' meant; everything seemed to be against me, and I was at the end of my tether. I couldn't take any more.

'I just want to go home.'

'Carlos is back in the car park . . . Can you manage to make it back?' I never even answered the question. I just turned and walked back towards the car park. We walked back in silence, and right now that suited me because with the mood I was in, I would end up snapping at him, and none of this was his fault. 'Ash, will you speak to me.' I suddenly stopped in my tracks and turned to look into the water. The water was calm and tranquil, and I hoped that it would keep me calm.

'What do you want me to say?'

'Anything . . . Anything is better than the silent treatment.'

'I can't take no more, Dale. This week would test anyone's patience, and I am ready for snapping . . . I saw red at Christine, I had to walk away before I hit her.'

'Ash, look at me.' I took a deep breath and turned to look my fiancé in the eye. 'Christine deserved everything you said there . . . Anyone else would have said much worse.' His soft and gentle voice brought tears to my eyes.

'Was I asking for too much? All I wanted was to come out tonight and have some fun . . . I can't even do that right.' I was shivering with the cold winter's night, and I could actually hear my teeth clatter together.

'First, let's get you in the car for a heat. Second, you never ask for too much. I wish you would ask for more.' Dale's arms wrapped around my shoulders, and I placed my head on his shoulder, I could feel the heat rise from him, and I immediately stopped chittering. I enjoyed walking back to the car in Dale's arms. Nothing was ever a bother for him. I wish that I had his patience. We approached the car, and Dale opened the door for me. Carlos never even saw us coming. The poor man jumped around when I climbed into the back seat.

'I am sorry. I never saw you coming back.'

'Carlos, shut up.' Dale burst out laughing at my response to Carlos. 'I am glad you find me funny. Carlos, can you take us to the house?' I was getting good at giving orders. As I glanced back at Dale, he was sitting looking at me, with a glint of curiosity in his eyes.

'I just want some normality.' Dale waved his hands up as if to say 'I never said a word'. He reached his arm out to me, and I shuffled up to cuddle into his chest. He felt so strong beneath me. I wish time would freeze, and we could stay in this embrace forever. It was the only time everything felt 'OK'. 'Aargh. Who need enemies when you have got friends?'

'OK . . . Now that you have got that out of your system, are you OK?'

'I am sorry about tonight.'

'What are you sorry for, Ash . . . ? None of this was your fault . . . I don't know about you, but when it was just the two of us, I had fun.'

'I did too, honey . . . Just a pity it can't be the two of us twenty-four-seven.'

'If that was the only way we could be happy, that could be arranged.'
I felt the car come to a stop, and I didn't want to move. My mind was
flickering through his last words, and it sounded good in theory, but to
be realistic, that would never happen. The short car journey from Maggie
May's was over, and we reached the house. We were lazy; if we could have
walked the short distance, it would have cleared my head for me.

'Let's go and have some fun.' I sat forward and looked around;
everything was the same as usual so that was a good sign that no one had
killed anyone.

'Fun . . . Here with my parents . . . Are you mad?'

'You never know . . . Your dad is always fun.' I loved Jake to pieces;
he was just so fantastic.

'His middle name should have been "fun".'

'I can see where you get your personality from.'

'I don't know whether to take that as a compliment.' Now this
was my idea of a good night. We bounced off one another and took
everything in our stride.

'Of course, it is a compliment.' We got out of the car, and
immediately, I felt at home. Dale's hand clasped mine, and one simple
touch made my heart flutter. I would love to know how one touch could
make me feel so alive. I felt even more alive when we walked into the hall
of the big house. I spotted Rosa walking to the kitchen, but the minute
she saw us, she ran over to me and gave me a big motherly hug.

'Hello, dear . . . How are you?' I let Rosa pull away from me, but she
never let my hand go.

'I am fine, Rosa. I was missing you, so I had to come back and see
you.' The rest of Dale's family gathered in the hallway around us, and I
thought they were all afraid to speak to me.

'I have missed you both as well. It isn't the same without you two.'

'I hope everyone is treating you right.' I smiled towards everyone, and
it seemed to lighten the mood.

'We are trying, Ash. But you take a lot to beat.' Callum was the first
to come and speak to us. He had Kiara in his arms, and her tiny face was
calling my name.

'Can I?' I signalled to him to take Kiara, and without a second
thought, he handed me her. 'Hello, baby girl.'

'Can I get you a drink, dear?' Jake was always very polite to me, and I
knew deep down that he wasn't going to change now.

'I will have whatever you have.' He smiled and toddled away to the kitchen as I walked into the living room with Kiara in my arms. Everyone followed me in one by one.

'Look at you, big girl . . . Where are your aunty Ashley's stories?' It was amazing how one baby could make you forget anything. Tonight never existed, and my tumour was gone. That was exactly what I wanted out of tonight.

'It is good to see my two favourite girls smiling.' Dale sat beside us and put his arm around me. This was exactly how I wanted to spend the next little while in his arms with Kiara.

'Tell your Uncle Dale, we are happier now he is sitting here . . . Yes, we are.' Jake put my glass down on the table and sat beside it. I knew what was coming. Jake was just like Dale. When he had something to say, he just said it.

'I am only going to ask this once tonight, I know you must be sick of all the small chat . . . How are you feeling, dear?'

'I am fine, Jake. All the better for being here.'

'That is good enough for me.' I appreciated the fact that he was respecting my decision, to act normal. It meant the world to me. 'How was your meal, kids?' Dale and I looked at one another and smiled.

'The meal was lovely, Dad, just what we needed.' I looked up to Mhairi and studied her face. She hadn't spoken one word to us since we arrived, and that wasn't like her.

'Are you OK, Mhairi?' The room fell silent, too quickly. Everyone was making himself or herself busy, even Dale was busy playing with Kiara.

'Yes, Ashley dear . . . I am fine.' She didn't sound fine to me, and everyone knew that something was on her mind. What was rattling her cage?

'Mom, whatever is on your mind spit it out.' I shuddered to think what was going to come out of Mhairi's mouth.

'Nothing, Son . . . I am just struggling to put on a brave face . . . to act normal.'

'Mom, nothing is ever normal in this house, so what is the difference? We are not asking you to sing and dance. We just don't want to sit and dwell on it . . . Ashley and I can't possibly shed one more tear . . .'

'Mhairi, what do you want to know?' I interrupted Dale quickly because woman to woman I knew Mhairi had something going on in that mind of hers.

'Ash, you don't have to do this.'

'If it is going to help your mom adapt when we are around, then it needs to be done.' Dale turned on to his side to comfort me if it was needed. After tonight's scenario, tears were on the agenda. I kept a hold of Kiara on purpose because I knew that she would keep me sane.

'I don't know what to ask dear. I don't want to sound stupid or nosey.'

'All we know is that the tumour is bigger than what the doctor expected. He won't know how bad things are until the results come back . . . We have prepared ourselves for the worst, Mhairi . . . So whatever comes back, we won't be shocked.' I really wanted to be honest and open with her. I felt that she needed it to be strong for Dale.

'So what do you want me to do?'

'I just want you to be there for Dale . . . We have promised each other that until we get the results back, we are going to have fun and enjoy what we have left.'

'You have my word that I will be there for both of you, and I will try to act as normal as possible.' I sighed a relief. It really did mean a lot hearing her say that. 'So you two, what do you have planned for tomorrow?'

'Christmas shopping.' I smiled like a Cheshire cat. I felt really excited about Christmas shopping this year. I thought it was all to do with Kiara.

'Mom, Ashley and I are going to church tomorrow.' I was pleased that Dale changed the subject to something that we could all talk about. Mhairi did have a petrified look on her face as to where this conversation was leading to. 'Since we found out about the tumour, it has made us value the time we have together . . . I have asked Ashley to marry me as soon as possible. She took some persuading, but with a long chat, she has said yes.' Now it was Mhairi letting her breath go; she looked very relieved.

'I don't know what I thought you were going to say there, but I couldn't be more happier for you . . . You both deserve this. If you need a hand with anything, just ask.'

'Thank you, Mhairi . . . Look at this little madam, she is out for the count.' We were all looking at Kiara in my arms; she made us all so happy and grateful for what we had.

A couple of hours had passed where we laughed and joked. Mhairi and Jake shared childhood memories of Dale, and we never stopped laughing. 'I have enjoyed this chat tonight . . . Thank you for being the perfect host.'

'No. Thank you both for coming down to see us.'

'I don't want to be a spoilsport, but you look exhausted, babe. Do you want to go home?' I was ready to go home and relax because I really did feel exhausted now.

'Yeah, that sounds good. Who is taking Kiara?' I placed a kiss on her tiny head and handed her carefully up to her dad. She looked so peaceful. I edged myself off my seat and a bit stiff with sitting cradling the baby. But I rose to my feet and let each and every one of my extended family give me hugs and wish me well. 'Good night everyone.' Dale took my hand, and we left the house at our own pace. The car was sitting waiting for us, and Carlos had the heating blasting; it was nice and toasty. I laid my head back on the seat and felt every bit of energy I had slowly leave my body. Dale placed the softest kiss on my lips, and my eyes flickered open to see his face peering into mine. It was a face that would never ever leave my mind.

'That felt good, Mr Black.' His touch and his kisses always felt special, like I was the most magnificent person in the world.

'Glad you enjoyed it, Miss Malone.'

'Is it so bad that I actually enjoyed myself tonight?'

'No, of course not, babe . . . It was nice to see you happy . . . I think my mom was right. Kiara has missed you.'

'It is weird how a baby can make you feel, isn't it?'

'I am grateful that she has come into our lives at this precise moment . . .'

'We can spoil her rotten for Christmas . . . Lots of dresses and pink.' I always pictured myself with my own little girl, and she would always be dressed in pink. I used to play with dolls when I was a child, and my mom used to make me lovely frilly dresses for them. I really was the girlie girl back then.

'You have everything all planned, Ash. Is there anything you haven't thought about?'

'I guess I have had so much time to think. It is scary what one person can think about in twenty-four hours . . .' We had never moved from the minute we got in the car. Dale's face was still a few inches away from me, and his aftershave had all my senses going. 'Do you know what I really want to do, right now?'

'Name it, and it is yours to do.' I managed to flash my cheeky smile as I gazed into his perfect eyes.

'You promise . . .' Dale squinted his eyes and nodded his head. I knew that he would give me the world if he could. I couldn't believe how lucky I had been to get a man like him. I leant over and whispered into his ear because I didn't want Carlos to hear me. 'I want to go home and get a nice hot bath and want to take you to bed.' His cheeky smile intrigued my mind, and I desperately wanted to know what he was thinking.

'You can take me home . . . to bed . . . to sleep, if you want.' His soft and quiet voice made me laugh. He could be such a tease when he put his mind to it. But I couldn't resist a slap on his arm.

'You knew what I meant, Mr Black.' He pulled me close to his chest, and we cuddled up on the back seat. It was good to sit back and let someone else to do all the work. If someone had told me a year ago that I would have a chauffeur, I would have laughed in their faces. Now here I was enjoying every moment.

I felt like I was in a dream. I woke up to find Dale leaning over me, kissing my lips softly, and it was the perfect wake-up call.

'Now that is a good morning wake-up call.' I moved my lips to speak, but my body felt lifeless. Something didn't seem right at all this morning. Normally, I would be bright and full of life to face another day. But something was stopping me from moving.

'I thought that you would like it, but you seem different this morning . . . Ashley, are you OK?' I felt very different this morning, but how could I tell him that I felt ill? This would be the icing on the cake. 'Ash, I am going to phone Dr Ching . . . Ashley . . .' I couldn't open my eyes as much as I wanted to because they seemed glued shut. I felt Dale jump off the bed, and everything went silent for a few moments. I actually knew what it was like to be blind. I felt helpless and stupid.

'Hello, this is Mr Black. Can I speak with Dr Ching please? It is regarding my fiancée Ashley Malone . . . Thank you . . . Hello, Dr Ching . . . I am really worried about Ashley. She isn't very responsive this morning . . . OK, thank you.' I heard Dale's conversation with Dr Ching and knew that I needed to see the doctor, but I didn't like to feel like a patient. Dale came back over and sat beside me; his warm hand squeezed mine. 'Ash, Dr Ching is coming to see you.'

'I am fine . . .' I was trying to kid myself on. 'Just tired.'

'It won't hurt to get his opinion, sweetie . . . I am just going to call my mom. OK?'

'OK.' I was worried about myself. I couldn't even lift my head to make myself look good. I was curious to find out what had changed drastically from last night. But on the other hand, if I was going to be like this until I died, my life was over. I didn't want to know what was staring me in the face; it would do us no harm to be blind on the whole situation.

'Mom, can you come over? Something is wrong . . . Dr Ching is coming over . . . OK, thanks.' Dale's conversation with Mhairi was heart wrenching. When I die, I was going to leave a huge hole in his heart. I hated listening to him flapping around like a chicken. Why us? What had we done so bad to make this happen?

'Ash, can you hear me?'

'Yeah.' I opened my eyes slightly and searched for Dale sitting beside me. I could see the tears in his eyes and the anxiety in his face, and it pulled at my heart strings. I couldn't bear to see what I was doing to my nearest and dearest; it wasn't fair.

'I want you to know that I love you. I will always love you.'

'I love you too, Dale . . . We will be fine, hun.' Was I kidding myself here? Was I really going to be fine or was I in denial? Twelve hours had passed so quickly, and I had no idea if I had twelve hours left in me. I went to sleep feeling like a woman and woke up in a lifeless state. I didn't think that things could deteriorate so quickly.

'You have got to keep fighting this, honey . . .' I was trying to fight every step, but how could I admit to the man I love that I was in too deep. 'We have a wedding to plan . . .'

'Bring the minister here . . .' I wanted to die as Mrs Black, and I didn't care how we did it.

'I will contact him today, Ash . . . Dr Ching is on his way. He will help you.' Dale stopped talking and wiped his eyes; there was someone in the cottage because I could hear them walking on the floor.

'In here, Mom.'

'What has happened, Son?'

'We are still waiting for the doctor . . . She is talking now but still very sleepy.' Dale never let go of my hand, and I felt every bit of his anxiety.

'Ashley, can you hear me, dear?' I felt Mhairi squeeze my hand, and I opened my eyes to see her concerned face leaning over me.

'I am fine.' Mhairi was holding on to Dale's shoulder as she showed comfort to us both. Dale was very upset, and that was all down to me. How could I ever forgive myself for all this?

'Hello.' I immediately recognised the doctor's voice and tried to be OK, but no matter how hard I tried, nothing seemed to work this morning.

'In here, Dr Ching.' The minute the doctor came in he lifted my spare hand and checked my pulse.

'Ashley. Can you hear me?'

'Yeah. I am not deaf. My head is sore. Please lower the tone.' I tried to sound alert, but who was I trying to pretend to? I just didn't want to feel defeated.

'Can you open your eyes for me?' I did as I was told and opened my eyes. I actually felt like a Chinese person. My eyes were only open in slits.

'Are you in any pain, darling?' Dr Ching was being very professional. His tone was very sincere, and I knew how bad I looked now.

'My head is sore . . . But I am mostly stiff.' The pain wasn't major. I had felt worse.

'What is happening, Doc?'

'I won't know for sure until I take some blood samples, but I recon it is all down to infection . . . also the possibility of the disease progressing. We won't know what is going to happen until we see how Ashley responds to treatment.'

'And the other results . . . Are they back yet? I mean you are talking like you know that it is cancer we are dealing with.' I tried to tell Dale that I knew that Dr Ching knew my fate. The day that he took the biopsies, he knew what was happening; he was just being professional.

'No. I checked before I left, but I have left my secretary chasing them up . . . Even when we get those results back, there is no guarantee of a treatment to work.' Hearing Dr Ching talk directly to Dale made me realise that time wasn't on my side; we had to use what we had left and make the most of it. The doctor wasn't stupid; he knew that something serious was going on. Dale just didn't want to hear it before.

'So what happens now?'

'Plenty of fluids and antibiotics. I am going to give her a few injections and that will give her body a kick-start . . . This is just the first setback, Dale . . . It is going to be the first of many . . . Please don't think I am being horrible or nasty. I just don't want to lie to you. It is better that you here it straight.' All I wanted to do was jump up and cuddle Dale. He was sobbing his heart out, and I couldn't do anything. Everything I was going through was easy compared to hearing Dale break his heart. 'I don't mind you staying, Dale.'

'Come through and get a coffee, Son . . . Let the doctor help Ashley.' Mhairi was right; he needed a break out of this room.

'I can't leave . . .'

'Go.' I didn't even let him finish his sentence. He needed five minutes to digest all this information.

'Are you sure?'

'Yes. I will have a new lease of life for you coming back.' I really wanted to believe that sentence myself. I wanted to bounce back from this setback, but I wasn't sure that my body would give me a chance. Dale stood up and placed a tender kiss on my lips, and normally, that was all I needed to give me a boost.

'I love you, Ash. I will be next door if you need me.' The room quickly went silent, and then there was me and Dr Ching. This was the first time we had ever been alone together. But right now I couldn't care what he needed to do, as long as he gave me a little longer with Dale.

DALE'S STORY

CHAPTER 16

My Heartache

'Mom, I can't bear this . . . I want to take it all away from her.' I had never felt so useless in all my life. All I could do was sit and watch my wife slip farther and farther away from me. It was torture, physically and mentally. Everything was out of our control, and we had to leave it all in the doctor's capable hands.

'You just have to be strong for her, Son. It is going to be hard, but your dad and I will be here for you both.' I was trying to be strong, but this morning has made it all so real. I was losing her quicker than I ever imagined, and I was going to fall apart at the seams.

'We were so happy last night . . . It was good seeing her with Kiara . . . We came home and had a wonderful night together, and then we wake up to this heartache . . . Was last night our last night together?' I had every emotion running around in my head, and I couldn't, for the life of me, shift them.

'Of course, it wasn't your last night together. You heard the doctor, honey. It is just a setback . . . Ashley will bounce back from this.' I was normally the one with all the enthusiasm, but today it had all disappeared. I felt sad and lonely and couldn't see a way forward from here.

'Until the next setback and the one after that . . . she is only going to get weaker.' There was a knock on the door, and I couldn't be bothered to answer it. My dad quickly left my side to answer it because if it was left to me, I would have left it. Visitors were the last thing on my mind today.

'Dale, we know that Ashley is sick. That is no surprise to any of us. All we can do is make the most of the time we have left with her whether it be days, weeks, or months.' For the first time in my life, my mom showed me her kind, caring side. All the walls around her were down, and she was my mom.

'Dale. There is someone here to see you and Ashley.' My hands were glued to my head, but I managed to turn around on my stool to see Christine, standing beside my dad. 'What has happened, Dale? Is Ashley OK?' I knew that I had to tolerate her for Ashley's benefit, but it was going to be hard.

'You are concerned today. That is very nice of you.' I wanted to tear her apart for everything that she said to Ashley last night. She was out of order, and I wasn't going to be nice to her.

'Dale, you have every right to be angry with me. You can't hate me any more than I hate myself.'

'Ashley is with her doctor . . . She has had a setback . . . An infection . . . She is lying in there like it is her deathbed.' I broke down in floods of tears, and both my parents came to my side. If Ashley dies, I am as well dying too; life won't be worth living.

'She is going to be OK though . . . Right?'

'We don't know, dear. We have to wait and see how Ashley responds to treatment.' My dad was nice to everyone, no matter who they were. I wish I could be like my dad in that sense, it would be so much easier to accept Christine.

'Dale, do you want to come through?' I shot off my seat and practically ran after the doctor. I couldn't believe what I was seeing when I entered the room. I stood in the doorway gobsmacked. The doctor had Ashley all propped up with pillows, and she was awake; I couldn't believe it.

'Hey, baby, how are you?' I rushed over to sit beside her, and this was like a second chance for us, and I didn't want to ruin it.

'Whatever Dr Ching has given me is working a treat.'

'It is just to give your body a boost . . . Kick it into gear . . . I am going to get these bloods back, and I will be back in a couple of hours. We will keep all these drips going for twenty-four hours and take it from there. They are disconnected again just now, but Susan will be back in a little while to give you what is needed.'

'Thanks, Doc. I don't know how I can ever repay you.'

'It's my job. I am here for you both around the clock. Call me if anything changes.' We both watched as Dr Ching left the room. I still couldn't believe the change in her; it was a miracle.

'You frightened the life out of me, Ash . . . I thought you were . . .'

'Shh . . . You can't get rid of me that easy.' If only she was right, I could see her slipping further away each day, and it was all out of our control. I never thought that I would find someone and lose them in the same breath. It was crazy.

'Can we come in?' I was glad to see my family standing in the doorway. It would, maybe, stop my mind from wondering and thinking the worst.

'Of course, come in.' My mom and dad were very eager to make sure Ashley was OK. It was nice to see them all getting along, but now I wasn't only going to lose my wife, my parents were going to lose a daughter.

'God, Ashley, you look a million times better.' My mom always had to be honest, but today her honesty was appreciated, and we all had huge smiles on our faces.

'I feel better, Mhairi. But in all honesty, I couldn't have got much worse.' It killed me to see Ashley so weak. But I knew that she would fight her way through the bad times, even if it killed her.

'Ash.'

I forgot about Christine being in the cottage, but I quickly jumped to defence and shot her a look.

'If you don't want her here, just say, babe.' I was being harsh, but Christine had made her night hell last night, and no one wanted a repeat performance.

'What do you want, Christine?'

'I came to apologise . . . I was out of order last night.'

'Now you have apologised, you can leave . . . I want to spend time with my husband-to-be . . . I don't have the energy to argue and bicker.' I was so proud of Ashley. She had handled the situation perfectly. Christine quickly left the room, really upset. Normally, I would have sent someone after her, but today was going to be all about Ashley. She needed all our support, and she was going to get every bit of it.

'Mom, I am not going to ask you to leave the cottage, but could you give us some time alone?'

'Of course. I am going to get some soup made anyway. If you need anything, I am just next door.'

'Thanks, Mom.' We watched carefully as the room emptied, who would have thought this room would have seen so many people. As the door closed behind my dad, I turned all my attentions back to Ashley. 'You look very comfortable, baby.' I thought that we underestimated Dr Ching; after this morning, he seemed very clued-up.

'I would be even better if you were in here with me.' I just loved to see her smiling; that would be one thing that I would hold on to forever.

'I thought that you were never going to ask.' I lay on my side and used my arm as a prop. I never wanted to take my eyes off her.

'I am going to contact the minister in a little while. I want you to be Mrs Black.'

'Well, you go and organise the minister. It's not like I am going any where . . . If we keep putting it off, we will never get around to it.' I had waited what seemed like a thousand years for Ashley to come along, and now I didn't care how we became Mr and Mrs. It just needed to be done ASAP.

'Will you be OK on your own?'

'I am not going to be on my own. Your mom and dad are next door . . . I will get some rest and wait for you to return.'

'OK. Promise me that if you need anything, you will call my mom or dad.' I smiled as I watched Ashley cross her fingers.

'I promise.' I got up on to my feet and leant over her. I placed a tender kiss on her lips, even though I didn't want to leave her. But in all honesty, I knew I had to get the ball rolling before it was too late. I started walking to the door, with what felt like strings holding me back.

'I love you, Dale.' I stopped and looked back, to notice the inevitable, this dying woman lying in our bed . . . My dying woman.

'I love you more, Ash.' I left the door open ajar and headed towards the kitchen. For the first time in my life, I felt dread and fear. I didn't want to lose my family; they were too important to me.

'Mom, I need to nip out. Will you keep an eye on, Ash? She knows to shout if she needs you.' She was my whole world, and I needed to know she was going to be safe until I returned.

'Of course, I will . . . Where are you going?'

'I am going to get a minister to marry us . . . It is what we want, Mom, so please no lectures.' I saw her look on her face, and it was one we saw a lot when we were younger.

'You have your mind set, Son. I will be with you both every step of the way.'

'Thanks, Mom. It means a lot . . . to both of us.' I grabbed my jacket and Ashley's keys and rushed out of the door. I then realised that before long everything I touched was going to remind me of my wife: her keys, her car, and her picture. It was all going to remind me of her perfect smile and what our life should have been like. Before long, it was all going to be nothing but memories.

I pulled up outside the church and sat in the car for a couple of minutes. My nerves were in full swing. This made me realise how Ashley must feel when she got nervous. I managed to pick up the courage to get out of the car to go and find the minister. I knew what I wanted to say, but if it came out that way, it would be a good start. As I walked through the door, I could see the aisle that we should walk down, and it suddenly hit me that we didn't need a church or an aisle; we could make our own day, and it would be just as perfect.

'Can I help you?' The voice startled me, but it brought me back from my dream. I managed to turn around and watch this middle-aged man walk towards me, and I knew that he was just who I was looking for.

'I hope you can . . . My name is Dale Black, and I am looking into marrying my fiancé Ashley . . . The thing is, she wanted to be here today, but she is ill.' It was hard to stand here and explain to a stranger that I wanted to marry my girlfriend before she died.

'Take a seat, Dale.' We sat on the end bench, and his sincere face made me feel comfortable. 'When you say she is ill, what do you mean exactly?' I took a deep breath and looked straight in front of me. I did hope that I would find the answer in the crucifix staring back at me, but nothing jumped out.

'Well, to cut the story short, we thought that we were going to be parents and went for the check-up . . . Only to find out that there was no baby growing . . . There was a tumour growing in her womb . . . We are waiting for results to come back, but she is getting weaker each day. We got up this morning to face our first setback . . .' I choked back the tears and took a deep breath before I crumbled. 'I thought that was it over . . . But her doctor has worked wonders with her . . .' I let my breath go as I finished the main part of the conversation. The rest of the time spent here was going to be background information.

'And you both want to be married.'

'We had big plans for the future, but things haven't gone as planned . . . We want to be husband and wife, more than anything in this world.'

'I would like to meet Ashley, if that is OK?'

'Of course.' I knew that Ashley would love to meet this man. He was just the type of person whom she would really get along well with.

'This should take six weeks to finalise . . .'

'We don't have six weeks.' I interrupted the minister quickly because I knew myself that six weeks was pushing it. Surely, there was a quicker way to make Ashley's wishes come true.

'I can see that you might be racing against time . . . If I meet Ashley today, I can marry you whenever you like.' I immediately felt like a huge weight had been lifted off my shoulders. I could actually breathe easily for the first time in days.

'You don't know how much this means to us.'

'I have a pretty good idea, son . . . I marry a lot of people, and I can see that they are not right for one another, but I have a duty to marry them . . . I haven't met Ashley yet, but already I can tell that you both mean the world to one another, and I will be honoured to marry you.'

'Thank you . . .' I quickly put my head into my hands. I had kept strong until the last minute, and now I am a bubbling wreck. 'I am sorry . . .'

'Don't apologise, Dale. You are being very brave. I don't think I could be as brave as you.' The feel of the minister's hand on my shoulder reinstated some of my faith in myself. I wanted to be the brave one, but the question was, how long can I keep it up for?

'I was brought up to believe in God and to have faith . . . But how can God do this to a special angel?' I was probably in the wrong place to discus about God, but I needed to get it off my chest.

'Things like this happen for no reason, and some things are just too big for God to have any say over . . . I can fully understand why this would make you doubt your faith, but just believe in yourself and your family . . . The rest will fall into place, son.'

'Thank you, for listening to me ramble on.'

'It is what I am here for, anytime . . . Can I follow you home now? And we will get everything all sorted.'

'Of course.' I stood up and shook the minister's hand. He went his way, and I went my way. I headed out to the car and felt the fresh air hit my lungs. I couldn't quite believe how easy this had been. Ashley would be so happy. I was so happy. I jumped into the car and spotted the minister pull up behind me. He flashed his lights at me, and I pulled out and headed for the mountain. All I wished for now was that Ashley was still alert enough to talk things through.

I pulled up outside the cottage, and my heart was racing. I didn't know what to expect when we went inside. Everything looked OK, and no one was rushing out to meet me, so that was a good sign. I got out and went to meet the minister and was glad that he looked just as terrified as I did.

'Thank you for doing this.' I would never be able to show this man how much this meant to us both; he was doing us a huge favour. I walked into the cottage, and no one was there; everything was calm and quiet. I guessed where they all would be. My mom would be in her glory, caring for Ashley.

'Hello.'

'In here, Son.' Just as I thought my mom was getting to be a mother hen, she would be driving Ashley crazy. I entered the bedroom and made way to Ashley's side. It felt like I had been away hours.

'Hey . . . How is she?'

'Just the same, Son. She was cold, so your dad brought the heater in and gave her your blanket.' I smiled at the blanket because it was years old. I had it when I was a child and here was my dying wife using it.

'One of the downsides of being up here in the mountain, it isn't the easiest to keep warm.' I took her hand and rubbed her cheek. It felt really warm, considering she was feeling cold.

'Ash.' I was never so glad when she opened her eyes to look at me. It was a relief to see that she was still here. 'How are you feeling, doll?'

'Better for seeing you . . . How did you get on?'

'I have the minister here with me. He wanted to meet you.'

'Where?'

'Hello, my dear, my name is Tom . . . Dale here has told me that you both want to get married as soon as possible.'

'Yes, Tom. As soon as we can.' You could tell that Tom was really used to dealing with situations like this because he was so professional.

'Depending on how you want to do this, I can marry you as quick as tomorrow.'

'Really.' Tom nodded his head towards me and Ashley. I really wanted to give Ashley her fairy tale wedding, but none of that mattered now.

'I always wanted a traditional church wedding . . .' It had dawned on me that I still couldn't give her everything that she wanted. 'When I was a little girl growing up, I and my friend always acted out our wedding . . . All white and glowing . . . Surrounded by friends and family . . . Walking down the aisle with flower petals every where . . . with our groom waiting at the end . . .' Her eyes rested on me, and her hand squeezed mine softly. She wanted me to look at her to listen to her. 'But now the only thing that matters to me is that my groom is by my side . . . I don't want to die Miss Malone.' I sat and stared into Ashley's eyes because I had never heard her speak so passionate about something before. I just wished I could give her the dream she so deserved . . . and more.

'I can come back tomorrow and marry you, if that is what you both want.' All eyes were on us now, and I couldn't take my eyes of my beautiful wife-to-be.

'You just have to say the word, Ash.'

'Tomorrow it is.' I felt elated that I was getting to marry the woman of my dreams. I kissed her hand and couldn't hold the tears back any longer. They were tears of happiness and sadness all rolled into one.

'We will say 12 is for the ceremony?' Tom was looking to both of us for confirmation, and we both nodded. I couldn't speak right now. My emotions had taken over. 'I will leave you both to organise your big day . . . It has been a pleasure to meet you both.' Tom held his hand out to shake mine, and of course, I accepted. He has been our saviour today. He bent down to kiss Ashley on her cheek, and her smile was just perfect.

'I will see you out, Tom . . . Mom . . .' I glanced around to make sure my mom would stay with Ashley.

'I will stay here until you come back.' Even my mom had a smile on her face. I followed Tom out of the room and headed back towards the living room. He stopped to face me, and his face was full of sorrow and heartache, and he didn't even know us.

'You know, Dale, I have married many people, but when it comes to this kind of ceremony, it kills me . . . It makes me doubt my own faith.' I never expected to hear that from a minister, but it must be a sad time when he doubted what he had been brought up to believe.

'I expected to spend eternity with Ashley . . . have kids . . . have a good life . . . But we have been dealt this hand . . . It just seems so unfair.'

'You just have to make the best out of a bad situation. You have a good family support unit, and that makes all the difference. I am only a phone call away, day or night.' Even strangers were touched by our story, and it meant a lot to us all.

'Thank you, Tom. We appreciate all you are doing for us.' We shook hands again, but this time I felt a connection with this man. He felt warm and supportive, just like I had known him all my life.

'You get back to that lovely wife of yours.' I stood and watched as Tom left the cottage, and I suddenly realised that up until I met Ashley, this cottage never got visitors. It was me and me alone, but now my wife had made it visitor central. I had tried for years to make it a hot spot. How was I going to manage without her by my side? I had to quickly snap out of my way of thinking and head back to my family. As I walked along the corridor, I had a sense of belonging. I knew exactly what I was going back to say to everyone.

'Hey.' Everyone turned to look at me, and even Ashley seemed very alert; she looked much better already.

'What do you want to do for tomorrow, Dale?' I knew that my mom always wanted me to have a big romantic wedding with hundreds of guests. But now, none of that meant anything. We had love and each other and that was all that mattered.

'Just use your head, Mom.' I reached into my pocket and took out my wallet, and I handed my card to my mom. I must have been mad. 'Just take this and do whatever you want.'

'I will do you both proud . . . I promise.' I didn't doubt her for one minute.

'Are you mad, giving your mother full power over your bank account?' My dad was right, but it was a small price to pay in order to marry my angel. We were all laughing together, just like any normal family would. It felt nice under the circumstances.

'She can do what she likes, Dad. She can't do much damage in twenty-four hours.'

'This is your mother we are talking about.'

'Behave yourself, Jake. I will make tomorrow perfect.' My mom was perfect for this kind of thing. She would do everything that she could.

'Dale . . .'

'Yes, hun.' Her voice was soft and sweet, just like the first time I met her. 'Will you do me one last thing?' I would do anything for this woman; even if it wasn't possible, I would make it possible somehow.

'Anything, honey.'

'Will you phone Christine and tell her that I need to see her right away?'

'Of course.' I bent over to take the phone of the bedside table and dialled the number. That was a small thing to ask; it was easy and doable. I felt nervous as I sat and waited for an answer because after our encounter today anything could happen. I would drag Christine here if I had to. But just as I was about to hang up, I heard her voice.

'Hello, Christine, it is Dale . . . Yes, everything is OK. But Ashley wants to see you as soon as possible . . . OK, see you then.' I flung the phone down on to the bed and noticed that we were finally alone. My mom and dad must have vanished into thin air because I never even felt them move.

'She is going to come right up.' For the first time in our relationship, I felt stupid. I didn't know what to say.

'You better get your best tux ready, Mr Black.' I immediately smiled at my beautiful wife-to-be because she never failed to amaze me. How could she still smile and be happy after everything that has happened?

'I will scrub up OK, Miss Malone.' I really wanted to keep this happy conversation going; these memories would stay with me forever, and I could always look back on them.

'Tom seems very nice.'

'Yeah, he was lovely, Ash . . . very friendly . . . and accommodating.' I watched in shock as Ash threw the covers back. I wondered what the hell she was doing.

'Where do you think you are going?' I was shocked beyond belief. I would never have believed it if I had never seen it with my own eyes.

'The bathroom.' she had a witty, sarcastic voice on as if to say you should have known that.

'Ashley, let me carry you.'

'I have legs . . . Just help me get up and don't let me fall.' Why did she have to be so stubborn? I did as I was told and helped her get up. 'I think that I will have a bath when I am through.' I let out a smirk and shook my head; the best part of it all was that I knew she was being serious. 'What is so amusing?' I didn't want to hurt her feelings, but I knew I had to be honest.

'Ash . . . I thought that I had lost you this morning . . . And you want to walk to the bathroom and have a bath . . . You have needles in your arm.'

'Well, excuse me for not wanting to wet the bed or smell from not washing . . .' Was I being very overprotective? Was I going too far? I was sure she was going to tell me any minute. 'When I don't want a bath, then you should worry.' I never answered her back. I just wanted to go along with her, anything for a peaceful life. We walked slowly out of the room, and all I could do was support her weight. We made it into the bathroom, and I really admired her strength, not many people could have found this strength today.

'Ashley.' I was never so glad to hear Christine's voice. Maybe she could be the big bad wolf and make her see sense.

'In the bathroom, Christine.'

'What the hell are you doing up, Mrs?' Finally Christine and I agreed on something.

'Don't you start. Dale is bad enough.' I looked up to Christine and shrugged my shoulders. I had tried to talk sense into her, but failed miserably.

'I am going into that bath whether you help me or not.'

'So is that what you want me for . . . to help you in the bath?' Christine sounded as confused as I must look.

'No. Dale is more than capable of helping me to get into the bath . . .' Christine knelt beside Ashley and placed her hand on hers. 'I am getting married tomorrow . . . Dale, can you get my bag please . . . ? Christine, I want you there tomorrow.'

'Ash, I wouldn't miss it for the world.'

'I will be back in a minute.' I got up to go and get her bag. That was an easy task. I knew where I put it when we came home last night.

'Here we go.' I handed Ashley her bag and leant against the sink. I was intrigued as to what was going through her mind.

'I want you to get me a dress . . . nothing big and clumsy . . . simple and elegant.' Ashley took her purse out of her bag and handed Christine her card. I didn't want to interrupt because I was glad that Christine and Ashley were on speaking terms again. 'I want you to be my maid of honour.' Christine wrapped her arms around Ashley and hugged her tight.

'I won't let you down, Ash.'

'I know . . . Now go so I can get my bath.' I had never really seen a strict and bossy Ash before. It was quite nice to see. Just a shame it had to take an illness to bring this side out. Christine got up and gave me a smile. 'I won't be long, Ash. OK.' And as quick as lightning, Christine had vacated the bathroom.

'And finally, the cottage is empty.' I saw the relief rose in her face, and she looked at peace for the first time today.

'This cottage is lovely when it is quiet.'

'No, it is lovely when it is just the two of us.' I couldn't agree more. She made a perfect point. I started the water in the bath and put her favourite bubble bath in. I glanced over at Ashley from the bathtub and couldn't help but smile. She looked just as gorgeous, even though she was ill. I went over to her and bent down in front of her.

'Are you going to join me in the bath?' I really wanted to say yes. I wanted to feel our naked bodies touch.

'No. You are going to relax in there yourself while I heat you some soup up.' Did I really say that out loud?

'You know how to disappoint me, Mr Black.' We both laughed together. I felt really rotten that I was disappointing her, but she needed to relax.

'I will make it up to you, doll.' I would make sure that I would make it up to her if it was the last thing I did. But right now my main concern was to get her in the bath safely.

'I will hold you to that.' I knew that she would remind me, and that made me happy. 'I was thinking before.' Did I want to know what she had been thinking about? I continued to help her take her pyjamas off and hoped that she would tell me in her own time. 'Your mom and dad are so lucky . . . Well, they don't have to worry about getting sick . . . or dying . . . They will have each other for eternity.' Her words made me freeze. Why didn't I think of all that? She was right; they would be together forever. 'It is a love story in itself. Don't you think?'

'Yeah. I never thought of it like that before.' I didn't want to tell Ash what I was thinking until I got all the facts, but my parents got changed into vampires to stop them dying completely. What if they could change Ash before she died? When I thought about it, I knew that I sounded crazy, but I would go to any extreme to keep Ashley here with me. Crazy was the new normal in the Black family.

'Are you OK, Dale?' I didn't know the answer to that without lying.

'Yes. I am fine, babe.' I helped Ashley into the bath and watched her lie back and relax. I would never get fed up seeing her enjoy silly little things. 'I will go and get that soup sorted. OK . . . ? I will be right back.' I got up and strolled out of the bathroom just like there was no tomorrow. I still couldn't believe that we had the answer staring us in the face. I just had to get my mom and dad back to figure it all out.

I was lying on the sofa when I heard the door open. I lifted my head up to see that it was my parents coming home. I had to compose myself and just spit it out. It wasn't something that I could tread lightly on. But I wasn't sure what I was talking about so that made things a lot worse for me. Maybe I should have listened all those years ago when my mom and dad tried to educate us on vampires.

'How is Ashley?' My mom wasn't even in the cottage properly, and she wanted to know everything.

'She is sleeping . . . Dr Ching was back to give her more medication . . . I was trying to catch up on some work, but I couldn't concentrate. I thought I would catch forty winks while Ashley was comfortable.' I was playing a game of chase at the moment because I was trying to do a hundred things at once, but nothing was actually getting done right.

'Well, we have had a productive afternoon. Everything will be perfect tomorrow.' Everyone seemed so happy, and here I was about to drop a bombshell. How would they take my news? I suppose there was only way to find out.

'I have been doing a lot of thinking this afternoon . . .' My mom and dad looked nervous, and they had every right to be. They came and sat on the table in front of me, and I sat up straight. 'It was something that Ashley said when she was in the bath and it got me thinking . . . You never have to worry about illness or death because you are . . . vampires . . . You are together forever . . . Would it be possible to change Ashley?' My mom and dad looked at one another. They looked scared and shocked.

'Dale. We have thought about this already, and it wouldn't be fair to put you and Ashley through more heartache . . . We are happy together, but we wouldn't choose this for anyone, especially not family.'

'But who are you to decide? If this is doable, then surely this would be Ashley's choice?' I wanted it to work, but I needed it to work more.

'Son.' My dad looked very emotional. I knew that he would be on my side if he could be. He has a strong connection with Ash, a connection that I never thought I would see. 'It would never work . . . you as a human and Ashley as a vampire.'

'Then I would change as well . . . I would rather be a vampire with my wife by my side, as opposed to be a human with no wife.' I broke down in floods of tears at the very thought of losing her. The reality of losing Ashley was finally hitting home, and I couldn't live without her. I knew if anyone could understand, then my dad would.

'Dale, I can't imagine what you are going through right now . . . If I could help, then I would.' I jumped up off the sofa into a fit of rage; why was everyone treating us like children?

'But you can help . . . You both can . . . You are choosing to ignore this.' I was shouting at my parents now, whatever next?

'What is going on?' I spun around in a daze, and Ashley was walking towards us. I immediately ran to help her to the chair. She was one stubborn lady.

'You should have shouted, hun.'

'I doubt you would have heard me . . . What is all the shouting about?' I didn't want to burden Ashley with any of this, especially when no one would even consider to help.

'Ashley dear, I am going to tell you what Dale has just put to us, and I want your honest opinion.'

'Dad.' I was mortified that Ashley was going to know what nonsense I had rattling around in my head. I would do anything to keep her here with me.

'If you want me to help you, then I need to know what Ashley will think about it all.' My dad sat in front of Ashley and took her hands in his. She looked as white as a ghost today, and it was killing me to see her so ill. I sat on the arm of the seat beside my dad and Ashley, and my mom showed her disapproval by walking over to the window. I didn't expect my mum to go with any of this; she wasn't into the whole vampire thing at the best of times.

'What do you think of me and Mhairi . . . as vampires?'

'I don't think of you any different to us.' My heart was racing, and my palms were sweating. I just wanted my dad to get to the point.

'If I told you that I could change you into a vampire, what would you think?' Ashley burst out laughing. She clearly thought that my dad was joking. But she suddenly stopped. Her face was a picture. I could have laughed at her expression.

'You are being serious, aren't you?'

'By changing you into a vampire, you would never die from this thing.' I couldn't take my eyes off her, and I was trying to read her response, but there was nothing, not even a clue.

'Did you know about this earlier?' Ashley sounded really pissed off now, and I didn't know what to say or where to look.

'It was what you said today that got me thinking . . . I can't lose you, Ash . . . If we have to be vampires to live a long and happy life together, then so be it.' The whole room went quiet as we sat waiting for Ashley to say something.

'I . . . don't know what to say.' I got down on one knee beside her and kissed her mouth, like it was my last kiss.

'Tell me that you can give up on us . . . That getting married tomorrow means nothing . . . That you can leave me alone . . . I can't live without you, Ash . . . The day you go and leave me is the day that I may as well die too.' I knew that my mom would be cringing at the way my mind was thinking, but I couldn't help it. I had to play the guilt card. It was the only way Ashley would consider all this nonsense.

'Dale, you know that I love you . . . You know that I want to marry you tomorrow, come what may . . . But become . . . vampires. Have you heard yourself?' I had heard myself, and I knew that if we wanted this to work, then we could make it work. We were strong enough to do whatever our minds wanted us to do.

'Yes, I have heard myself. You don't have to live without me . . . I am going to have the next fifty, sixty years without you in my life.' I was laying everything on the line here, and I felt like I was getting nowhere. I wanted to scream and bite her myself.

'And then what? Can you sit there and tell me that you can live without work . . . without being a daddy . . . All the things that we had planned together?'

'Yes. I can live without everything if I have you by my side. We can be a family . . . We can use your eggs and get a surrogate just like Dr Ching said.'

'You have thought about everything.' It was all I could think about this afternoon. I had gone over it in my mind that much that I believe it myself now.

'I love you, Ash. I would do anything to keep you here with me.'

'I need to lie down.'

'Please say that you will think about this?'

'I will. But at the moment, I am exhausted . . . Come with me. I feel like I haven't seen you today.'

'Sure.' It was a relief to hear that she would think about everything and that she still wanted me near her. I had to be grateful for that. I couldn't possibly ask for any more.

'Ashley. When you want to talk about it, you know where to find me.' I was proud of my dad for going to help me. It must have taken a lot to convince him to do such a thing. It isn't like vampires are a popular choice in Anchorage.

'Thank you, Jake.' We headed back to the bedroom, with my arm wrapped firmly around her shoulders. I felt at home with her. I just hoped and prayed that she would agree to the change. I had to live in hope. I knew how hard it would be to change into a vampire, but it would have to be worth it, wouldn't it?

ASHLEY'S STORY

CHAPTER 17

The Wedding and Results

Today is supposed to be the happiest day of my life. But here I was sitting looking in the mirror, crying my eyes out. It was a mixture of emotions all boiling over into one. I was ecstatic to marry Dale, but now I had all these mixed emotions about the whole vampire scenario. I really could see where Dale was coming from, but if I was perfectly honest, I was scared senseless about dying, and now I had to think about coming back as a vampire. Who would have thought that life could be so complicated.

'Ash.' I heard a knock on my door and quickly wiped my face to hide the evidence of crying, but anyone who knew me well enough would know that I wasn't myself.

'Come in.' I looked in the mirror to see who was coming through the door, and I was relieved to see Christine's face. She knew me too well, but I was hoping that she wouldn't be too pushy with me today.

'Hey.'

'Hey, Ash.' Christine came towards me and perched beside me. I was glad that we had forgotten all about our disagreement the other day. I wouldn't be able to cope if our friendship had broken up now. We had been friends since we were little girls, and we always promised that our friendship would never come under threat.

'What is wrong, honey?' I really wanted to share the whole vampire story with Christine, just to see what she thought about it. But I couldn't risk revealing Dale's parents. They had all been fantastic with me over the last few weeks, and I would never forget them for it.

'I am just being silly.'

'You are one of the bravest people whom I know, and I am so proud of you.' I wished that everyone would stop telling me how brave I was. I didn't feel very brave. I was just getting by because I had to for my family's sake.

'That really does mean a lot to me, hun. But you should be calming me down, not making me worse.' Today was going to be one of those days because I could feel it in my blood. It was going to be tears, tears, and more tears.

'Well, to change on to a positive note, what do you want to do with your hair and make-up?'

'Loose curls . . . I never leave my hair down, and today I want to be different.' I just didn't want to be the usual Ashley Malone today. I wanted to show everyone that I was OK and today was going to be special.

'That sounds nice, babe.' I knew that Christine would make me look gorgeous; she was a natural at hair and make-up. 'Have you looked at your dress yet?'

'No . . . I trust your judgement.' I didn't want to collapse in floods of tears, which was why I left the dress until I was putting it on.

'You will love it, Ash . . . Right, let's make your hair curly.' I put all my faith in Christine, and I sat and let her make me into a glowing bride. I felt completely comfortable sitting here getting ready for my wedding, although I did have butterflies in my tummy. I had planned this day for a lot of years, but I never expected it to happen overnight.

'Have you seen Dale since you arrived?'

'Yeah, his dad has got him in the other room.' Jake was the perfect person to be with him right now. They were like two peas in a pod. 'His dad is lovely.'

'Yeah, he is.' Jake was one of the kindest men I had ever met. He reminded me of my dad so much. 'I can see where Dale gets his charm from.'

'You are lucky to have a man like him, Ash. There aren't many of them about nowadays.' Christine was spot on for a change. Dale was the best thing that had ever happened to me. 'Is everything OK, Ash? You are acting kind of funny today.' I didn't think that there was a right way to act today under the circumstances, but I wasn't surprised that I was being different. I had too much going on in my head to act normal.

'Yeah. I think that everything is finally sinking in . . . if only we had a magic wand.' I did have a magic wand; What was I thinking about? Why wasn't I using it? I didn't want to die, and I wanted to live my life with my husband. What was to think about?

'Today is going to be perfect, Ashley . . . You and Dale are meant to be together. Anyone can see that.' If Christine only knew the half of it, little did she know that she was actually convincing me to take the second chance, she just didn't know it yet. 'I got you a tiara to go with your dress. Do you want me to put it in?'

'Do what you like, hun.' Christine had thought of everything. I was so grateful to have friends and family like them. I wondered what damage Mhairi had done on Dale's card? She would have thought of everything and more.

'What do you think?' I looked up into the mirror and took a deep breath in. I looked beautiful. For the first time in my life, I actually said that I looked beautiful.

'Wow. You haven't lost your touch, love.' I couldn't stop staring at myself in the mirror. I looked so different, compared to the usual me.

'If you want me to do your make-up, you will have to keep the tears under lock and key.' Christine was like Dale. She always knew how to make me smile.

'I will try . . . I promise.'

'Do you just want natural colours?'

'Yeah. Sounds like a plan.' I got up off my seat without even thinking and walked towards the door. There was something that I needed to do, and I needed to do it now. 'I will be back in five.' Christine looked gobsmacked, but I wasn't an invalid yet. I still had my independence behind me and hoped that I could have that until the end. I didn't wait for a confrontation with her. I just headed up the hallway and out of the cottage. I passed everyone on the way, and I didn't even look twice. I just kept walking before my feet couldn't take me any more. I needed to be outside in the air because I felt closed in like I couldn't breathe.

'Ashley.' I heard Dale shouting on me from behind, but I didn't want to turn around. I knew that he would follow me, so there was no need for me to stop. I walked right over to the edge of the mountain and just stood there. As always the scenery was just breathtaking, and I stopped to gather myself together. 'Ash . . . Are you OK?'

'I am perfect . . . Just perfect.' I couldn't be any better. This was the first time that I had seen or spoke to Dale from last night, and I had missed him so much. 'I missed you.' I turned to look at him standing beside me. His tall well-built frame hovered beside me like some temple 'After the wedding, I want us to sit down and discus our future . . .' I couldn't believe that I was going to say all this now, but if I didn't say it now, I never would.

'You have lost me, Ash.' His voice was soft and sweet, and it made me love him a thousand times more.

'I have spent one of the longest ten hours of my life . . . I don't want to leave you now . . . I want to marry you . . . I want a family . . . kids . . . a dog.' I wanted the whole traditional family life and wasn't ready to leave my nearest and dearest hanging around.

'Does this mean you want to think about the whole vampire situation?' My poor husband-to-be was standing beside me frightened to death at what I was about to do or say.

'Yes. I think I am ready to talk about it. I am not ready to lose you.' I looked all around me, and our mountain had been transformed into a wedding venue. I never noticed when I first came out, but there were flowers everywhere, and we were standing under an arch. It was like something out of a dream.

'What has happened out here?'

'My mom and my card . . . It can all come down if you don't like it.' How could I not like it? It was beautiful. I just couldn't believe all the trouble everyone had gone through.

'It . . . is . . . magnificent . . . She has done all this in one day . . . *Wow.*' I thought my monotone had showed how shocked I felt right now.

'It was supposed to be a surprise . . . She didn't expect you to come out here before the wedding.' I felt rotten that I had spoilt the surprise.

'Only I could do the opposite.'

'Now that you have got the runaway bride out of your system, can I get you back in the house before you catch the death of cold?' I took his face in my hands and studied his face. I couldn't believe that in a short while I was going to be Mrs Black. All my dreams were rolled into one, and I was honoured to spend what time I had left with my perfect man. 'You still have time to change your mind. You don't have to marry me. We can stay as we are.'

'Are you getting cold feet, Mr Black?'

'I have never been sure about anything my whole life. But I know for a fact that we are going to walk down that aisle today . . . I just wanted to make sure that you were doing this for the right reasons.'

'I love you, Mr Black.'

'I love you more, Miss Malone.' I placed my mouth over his and kissed his lips softly and tenderly. His lips were so warm and soft, and his smile made every part of my body come alive. I had been craving for his touch for hours, and I wanted to run away with him and make mad passionate love until we had nothing else to give.

'I can't imagine not kissing you or smelling. How good you smell . . . Or making love to you . . .' I had more to lose by dying than I ever did by changing to an immortal vampire.

'It seems like you have already made your mind up.' In my heart I knew what I wanted, but was my mind telling me to do something different?

'Maybe I have . . . It just feels like a waste to throw it all away now.'

'C'mon, let's get you back inside . . . I am sure Christine is having a fit.' I had forgotten all about everyone left inside the cottage. We started walking back to the cottage, and I was more myself now. I had Dale's arm wrapped around my shoulders, and he was my comfort blanket. 'Your hair looks beautiful by the way.' I felt my cheeks flush slightly. It was weird after all the time we had been together; he could still make me blush at the stupidest of things.

'Thank you, Mr Black. You don't scrub up too badly either.' The door of the cottage was thrown open before we even reached it, and I rolled my eyes as I saw a not-so-happy Christine approach us. She was like a mad woman possessed.

'Ash. Will you get your ass in that room . . . now?' Dale and I were so happy and in love that we both couldn't stop smiling. I didn't care that my friend was having kittens or that everyone was panicking. I was clouded by love, and my feelings were in overdrive right now.

'I better do as I am told for once.'

'Don't keep me waiting too long, Mrs.' I kept walking and ignored my husband-to-be. I didn't plan on being late, but it was the bride's prerogative to be late. I spotted Mhairi putting flowers in Jake's jacket, and I just had to stop. I turned back to look at Dale, and there he was standing in the doorway looking hotter than hot in his tux. I couldn't help but smile at him.

'Mhairi, everything is beautiful. Thank you.' For a vampire, she had very good taste, and I was using her as my distraction.

'I am glad you like it, dear.' Like it. I love it. Everything was perfect for us today, and I couldn't be happier.

'Ash . . .' I was driving Christine crazy. Patience was never her strongpoint at the best of times. I walked back towards Dale and placed my hands on his chest. I felt like I couldn't tear myself away from him.

'You do realise that Christine is going to kill you if you don't follow her . . .' Now I knew that Dale was joking because he couldn't care how stressed Christine was getting. He enjoyed winding her up like a toy. 'Are you OK?'

'I really do love you, Dale . . . I love you so much that it hurts . . .' I promised myself that I wasn't going to cry, but it was hard when I was standing here facing the man I love on what should be the happiest day of our life.

'Don't upset yourself, honey . . . I know how you feel, and I am more than honoured to become you husband . . . however long we may have together.' His arms wrapped around me, and I sunk into his chest for the sheer comfort.

'Ashley . . . What is going on?'

'Pipe down everyone . . . Just give them a break, will you?' I heard Callum speak up for us for the first time, and I realised how proud I was of him. He had come so far in such a short space of time. I placed a kiss on Dale's warm lips and left him standing before I couldn't leave his arms. I left the room quickly and left everyone wondering what was going on in my mind. I slowed down once I was out of sight of everyone.

'Christine dear, please don't let Ashley back out of the room before the wedding.' I heard Mhairi giving Christine her orders, and I wondered what else she had up her sleeve?

'I will try, Mrs Black.' Christine followed quickly behind me because I had wasted so much time on being sentimental.

'Now that you have got whatever it was out of your system, can we get back to making you into a bride?'

'Of course.' I had no plans to go anywhere else. I had said everything to Dale, and now I was ready to be Mrs Black. It still didn't feel real, that in one hour's time I would be walking down the aisle to meet my husband.

The last hour had gone by very slowly. I just wanted to get it all over with and be Mrs Black. Nothing else mattered today, apart from me and Dale declaring our undying love for one another.

'We are ready when you are.' Christine closed the door and looked at me with watery eyes. She was a sucker for weddings. It was one of the only times that I have seen her crying like a baby.

'It's time, Ash.' Christine was wearing a long cerise-pink dress with an ivory fur cardigan to cover her shoulders. Bearing in mind it was a freezing cold day out. She looked stunning with her blonde hair all clipped back, a perfect princess if ever I saw one. I stood up slowly and let my dress straighten out. I felt like a princess myself. The long white dress fell down to my ankles, and the silk and lace felt sexy as it clung to my skin.

'Will you go and get Jake for me, please?'

'Now?'

'Yes, please.' Christine left the room quickly, and I never moved a muscle. There was one final thing that I had to do before I walked down the aisle. Christine must have flown outside because she was back in a flash, with Jake by her side. They both looked worried, and I could only imagine what was going through Dale's mind.

'Is everything OK, dear?' Poor Jake looked terrified as to what I wanted him for.

'Yes, everything is or will be perfect . . . I would like to ask you to walk me down the aisle.' In the short time that I knew Jake, he was just like a father figure to me, and I could use a supporting figure walking to the groom.

'If that is what you want, dear . . . I will be honoured to give you away.' I couldn't stop smiling now. I had everything that I wanted. I walked slowly over to Jake and linked his arm. Part of me felt sad that my parents weren't here to see me, but now that I had Jake here, it felt complete. Christine opened the door, and we all walked out into the hall. I couldn't believe what I was seeing. The cottage had been transformed into a winter wonderland. It was beautiful. Flowers and petals were everywhere. Callum was standing holding Kiara in a beautiful ivory dress.

'One flower girl delivered.' I laughed at Callum's sarcastic tone. It was a nice surprise to see Kiara all ready to be my flower girl. I had no idea that all this had been organised. 'You look gorgeous . . .' I heard Callum's soft and sweet tone for the first time today, and I looked down to the floor so I didn't have to look him in the eye. 'I hope that one day I will find someone just like you.' I felt my eyes well up and quickly realised that I couldn't cry, not yet anyway.

'Thank you . . . Apart from Dale, that is one of the nicest things anyone has said to me in a long time.' I knew that Callum wasn't all bad. Deep inside him there was a loving guy just like Dale, and he would make someone a perfect husband one day.

'I mean it, Ash. You have showed me how to love my daughter, and I will never forget that. Dale is one very lucky man.' I knew that inside the old Callum, there was this loving father figure waiting to jump out, and I was pleased to see it today.

'Don't get her crying, Cal. Get back to being best man.' Christine took Kiara, and Callum quickly did as he was told. Everything was perfect.

'Cal, put Dale's mind at ease . . . He will think something is wrong.' We all knew that Dale would be very nervous right now; he would be thinking the worst.

'I will tell him that you have run away.' I didn't think I could run, even if I tried. But I knew that Cal was just trying to act normal around me.

'Go, Cal.' I was very grateful for Callum's witty charm today. It was just what I needed.

'My wife doesn't know when to stop.' We all had a little giggle with one another as Jake looked around the cottage. There was not one thing left in this cottage that was left untouched. I couldn't imagine what she could do with months of preparation.

'She is a gem, Jake. Keep hold of her.' Mhairi was one in a million. There certainly couldn't be two of her.

'Right, enough of Mhairi. Let's make you my daughter-in-law.' Christine opened the cottage door and music started playing. The soft music was pleasing to my ears.

'I will see you at the altar, Mrs Black.' Christine walked gracefully in front with Kiara; they looked beautiful. All these faces were staring at me, and I couldn't believe how many people Mhairi had managed to invite at such short notice. I looked further down the aisle and saw Dale all dressed in a tux, standing beside Tom. For the first time in weeks, I felt like a nervous wreck. Jake squeezed my arm, and we looked at one another with a smile on both of our faces. I didn't think that I would have made it to Dale if I didn't have Jake guiding me.

'Are you ready, Ashley?'

'I think so, Jake.' We started walking slowly down the aisle, and all eyes were on us. I really did feel like royalty. We reached Dale at the edge of the mountain, and Jake squeezed me tightly in a hug, and his cold lips kissed my cheek.

'Look after her, Son . . . I am proud to call you my daughter-in-law.' His words hit me hard, like a ton of bricks. The tears built up in my eyes as I watched Jake take his seat.

'Ashley. You look stunning.' I was going to be a princess for a day, and Dale was my prince. I was glowing at his comments, and I was going to accept them for a change. He took my arm, and we faced Tom as he proceeded with our wedding ceremony.

'Are you OK, Ashley?' Tom whispered down to me before we went any further. Everyone was wrapped up in making sure I was OK, but I felt like I was on cloud nine today.

'I couldn't be better.' I clung to Dale's arm for support because I was never good in front of an audience. I would never have made an actress, not in a million years.

'I would like to thank everyone for joining Dale and Ashley today. We are gathered here to celebrate these two people joining together to share their love and passion for one another. Ashley and Dale would like to say their own vows today. But before they do, I would like to do a blessing if I may.' Tom looked at me and Dale for our approval, and of course, I wanted him to do a blessing; it was very appropriate. 'Lord, bless this special couple as they are wed. May they find security and peace in their commitment to you and each other. Grace them with your wisdom as they make decisions. Give to them thankful hearts in good times and faithful hearts in hard times. Grace them a never-ending desire to love each other as you love them. May they bring out the best in each other and draw strength from their unity with each other and with you. May their happiness grow in strength and in depth as they become a witness to your love.' I had taken every word in that Tom had just said, and it was beautiful on so many levels. I was surprised that I was crying yet, but I was determined to stay strong. ' . . . Ashley.' I blocked out everyone staring at me and just thought of me and Dale standing here ourselves. This was our mountain, and it was the perfect place to share our love for one another.

'I feel like I have waited a thousand years to be here with you . . . I want to share our lives together in sickness . . . and in health . . .' I felt the tears drop down my cheeks, and Dale wiped them away with his hand. My strength gave away the minute I said 'sickness and in health'. 'I love you more today than yesterday, but I will love you more tomorrow than today . . . And I promise to honour and cherish you from this day forward . . . I love you, Mr Black.' I couldn't control my tears now. Dale put his hand on my face and stroked it tenderly with his thumb. That always calms me down, and he knew that. It was amazing how well he knew me; we were compatible on so many different levels.

'Dale.' Tom was so supportive towards Dale and me. The tone of his voice said it all.

'Ashley Malone, you are my life. I want to spend the next fifty . . . sixty years with you . . . more if possible. I promise to love, honour, and cherish you. I will be by your side in sickness and in health till death parts us . . . Darling, don't be afraid. I will be here to wipe away your tears . . . to catch you when you fall . . . And I will be the husband you deserve and more . . . I love you, Ash.' Dale stepped closer to me without moving his hand from my cheek, and his warm lips kissed me softly. My heart melted, and my nerves had faded away. 'Ashley . . . Dale . . . repeat after me . . . Ashley, do you take Dale to be your husband?'

'I do.'

'Dale . . . Do you take Ashley to be your wife?'

'I do.'

'I now pronounce you husband and wife. You may kiss the bride.' Dale swept me off my feet and devoured my mouth. Our friends and family all cheered and clapped for us. This had been one of the best experiences of my life, and I was glad that we have actually done it. We were now Mr and Mrs Black; it really did happen. We turned to face everybody, and there wasn't a dry eye to be seen. I didn't feel as bad now. I wasn't the only one crying.

I was standing looking over the mountain, listening to our wedding guests chatting and laughing. I had to escape away from everyone, just to spend a few minutes recalling my day. It truly was a day to remember. I felt the presence of someone coming towards me, but I didn't want to look away from the magnificent views.

'Ashley.' I knew the voice too well. It was my wonderful husband. 'Are you OK?' Dale was always very protective of me, even before we found out about the tumour. It was part of what made me fall in love with him.

'I am fine, sweetie . . . I just needed five minutes.'

'Do you want me to leave you alone?' I put my hand around to touch him, and he squeezed my hand tightly. I didn't want him to go anywhere.

'Please stay.' I wanted to be here with him, just the two of us. 'I just love standing here, looking over this mountain. All your cares just fade away into nothing.' Dale let my hand go, and his arms wrapped securely around my waist.

'It is a lovely view, babe . . . And with you standing here, it truly is breathtaking.'

'I can remember standing here the very first time you brought me up the mountain.' I could remember it like it was yesterday.

'We have come a long way since then, Ash.'

'I have had a lot of good memories from this cottage.' This cottage was making my last memories memorable, and I would never forget them.

'We can make plenty more memories.' I wanted to believe that, but with the luck we were having, something was going to turn sour.

'Today has been wonderful. Your mom has done us proud.' If it was left to me and Dale, we would have got married on our own, but Mhairi had given us back some of our childhood dreams. That I was entirely grateful for.

'I will never forget today, Ash . . . You look so beautiful . . . Your hair just makes you so radiant.' I felt chills run down my spine as he played with my hair. 'I have a surprise for you . . .' I tilted my head around to look up to him, and his face wasn't giving anything away. 'If you don't want to, it is fine.'

'What is it?' I didn't know who was more nervous, me or him.

'I have booked us into a hotel . . . about an hour away from here . . . I will understand if you.' I quickly stopped him in midsentence by putting my finger on his lips.

'Of course, I want to go with you . . . There is no point in getting married if we can't enjoy our first night as Mr and Mrs.' Our moment was interrupted by a car's bright headlights, and we both looked to see who it was. I didn't recognise the car at all, but then I wasn't good with cars.

'That is Dr Ching's car.' Dale's words made me freeze. Why was he here tonight? Dr Ching got out of the car and spotted us. He walked over to us, and he had a look on his face like he didn't want to be here. The same look that he had the very first day he told me about the tumour.

'Ashley . . . Dale . . . If you want me to go away and come back tomorrow, I will understand.' Oh, for the love of God, he knew the results.

'Do you have any news, Doctor?' Dale squeezed me tighter, so I knew that I couldn't fall.

'I have your results.' I just knew from the way he was talking that it was worse than what we thought. I could still here our guests laughing and joking, and I knew that only our immediate family and friends would know what was happening over here.

'Just tell us, Dr Ching.' My nerves were in my throat, and I felt like I was going to suffocate. I needed to know one way or another.

'Do you want to sit down?'

'No. Just get on with it.' I just nipped the head off this poor doctor, for absolutely no reason. I could feel my heart beating in my chest so hard that it was distracting me.

'The tumour is malignant, Ashley.' I already knew that. I just needed to know the truth now.

'If you are honest, you will now tell me that you already knew that because I did.'

'I had an idea, but I couldn't go on that. I needed proof.' I put the doctor on the spot, but I was glad that he told me the truth because now I could trust him a little bit more.

'And what now?'

'The cancer has progressed and spread to your lymph nodes.' The word 'progressed' had made my heart pound harder in my chest. I didn't want to hear any more.

'Dr Ching, stop talking to me in riddles and just give it to me straight.'

'There is no cure, honey . . . We can try to slow it down . . . Make you comfortable . . . But nothing will take it away.' I felt like I had been cut into two, and I couldn't feel my legs. Dale's arm was keeping me standing.

'How long, Doc?' I was so glad that Dale asked that question because I don't think that I could bring myself to accept this. Although I knew my fate, it was harder to accept when you get told the truth.

'It is hard to say at the moment . . . But with the way things have progressed over the last forty-eight hours, I would say weeks rather than months . . . I am so sorry.' I felt sick. I just wanted to throw myself off the mountain and end it all now. 'I will come back tomorrow afternoon and discuss everything with you.' The doctor walked back to his car, and I broke down sobbing. I couldn't breathe. I felt like I was hyperventilating. Dale let us both slide to the floor, and we both sat there crumpled and broken together. My beautiful white dress was lying all over the ground, creating a blanket for me.

'Just take a few deep breaths, Ash. Let it out.'

'Why us, Dale . . . ? What have we done that is so bad?' I wanted to scream and shout and smash something, just to let the anger all out of me.

'You haven't done anything, baby girl.' Why was this happening to me? This was something that happened to old people . . . strangers . . . not a twenty-four-year-old, who had her life to lead.

'Let's get you inside . . . It is freezing out here.' I couldn't feel how cold it was because my body was numb with the shock.

'What about everyone?' I couldn't face a hundred faces right now.

'I will get rid of them all.' Dale helped me up on to my feet and tightly wrapped his arm around me. I couldn't stop crying. I buried my head into his shoulder and hoped that no one would notice us. We passed Christine, and she followed behind us, then Mhairi and Jake. It was like a game of follow the leader.

'Mom, send everyone home please.'

'But . . .'

'No buts, Mom. Just do it.' Dale really startled me by shouting at his mom, but I had no energy to lift my head. We got into the cottage, and Dale sat me down on the couch. I was chittering with the cold or nerves

242 | K M L o w e

or both. 'Christine, grab the thick blanket off the bed, please.' Christine didn't even hesitate. She ran off to get the blanket and came back and wrapped it around me and perched on the floor beside me. She looked at Dale and me, with great concern. Christian handed me a glass with some spirit in it, and I didn't even care what was in it. I just downed it in one go. I felt my body heat up immediately. I handed the glass back to him and looked up to him with so much sadness breaking my heart.

'Keep them coming, Christian.' No one dared to argue with me right now. They knew to leave me be. I heard the door open and the rest of Dale's family gathered around us. Christian did the right thing and brought the glass and a bottle back to me.

'Ash, that isn't going to solve anything.' Christine had the cheek telling me to watch what I was drinking. She could drink like a fish.

'That is good coming from you . . . Tell me what is going to solve everything, Christine . . . I am dying . . . Nothing can get any worse.' I really didn't want to just blurt it out, but right now it was the only way I could tell everyone. The drink was giving me the Dutch courage that I needed. 'I have weeks to live, so if you can wave a magic wand, feel free.' Dale took me in his arms and stroked my hair. It felt nice and soothing, but the alcohol was more appealing.

'Dr Ching came by . . .' Dale addressed everyone so that I wouldn't have to. 'The tumour is cancerous, and it has spread to lymph nodes . . .' I felt his tears drip on to my head, and I couldn't comfort him the way I wanted. 'They can try to slow it down, but they can't cure it . . . Dr Ching said that with the progression over the last couple of days, we are looking at weeks.' The room was silent, and all I could hear was my breathing.

'This can't be happening.' Christine was also very emotional now, and I was so wrapped up in the alcohol that I didn't feel a thing. Dale stopped my hand from filling my glass back up again, and I couldn't help but push him off. 'Ashley, Christine is right, that isn't going to change anything.'

'Well, it is helping me now, so don't push me . . .' I had never felt as nippy in my life, but tonight I could kill someone.

'Ashley dear, is there anything that you want?' Jake was always so caring and compassionate to me. I tried to be nice and let everything else run out of my head.

'Peace . . . and another bottle of this.' I lifted the half empty bottle and heard Dale take a deep breath. I looked down at his hand twirling his wedding ring. I just knew that he had a lot to say and he was just biting his tongue.

'I can give you all the peace in the world . . . I could be a good bouncer and empty the cottage, but I don't think another bottle would do you any good.'

'We have a hotel reservation anyway, so peace will come on its own.'

'Ash, we don't have to go now.' I shook my head and lifted his head up, just enough for him to see my face.

'You either come with me or I get Carlos in here to take me.' I wanted to spend my wedding night in style, and I didn't want to do it without my husband. But I would if I had to.

'Ashley, stay here and let us help you.' Christine wanted to help me, but I didn't want help or pity. I wanted to spend my wedding night the way I should be spending it, if I wasn't ill.

'I don't want help, Christine.' I filled my glass again and went to drink it when Christine snatched it off me. She was very brave the way I was feeling tonight because I was ready to snap.

'You can do what you like, Ash, but you are not drinking yourself into oblivion.' I saw red and jumped up with the bottle in my hand.

'Goddamn it, Christine, what is your problem?' Dale jumped up behind me very quickly. I thought that he was frightened to see what I was capable of.

'No, Ashley. We have little time with you as it is, without you doing stupid things to make it worse.' Could things get any worse? I couldn't help but laugh at my friend. She had tickled my funny bone.

'Just get out of my way, Christine.'

'No.' I threw the bottle off the wall and stormed the opposite way past Dale. I shocked myself. I couldn't believe that I just did that. I didn't have a bad bone in my body. I spotted Carlos standing at the car and rushed over and climbed in.

'Carlos, just drive . . . *now*.' But he was deliberately not quick enough. Dale was opening the door before I could say 'boo'.

'Ashley, you are not going anywhere without me, so don't waste any energy trying.'

'Dale, give it a rest . . . You are all driving me crazy.' I realised how selfish I must sound, but I couldn't shift the way I felt right now.

'We all care about you, hun.' I felt really bad because I was deliberately pushing everyone away from me. What was I thinking about? Did I really want to be on my own?

'Tell him to drive then because he sure as hell ain't listening to me.' I was even snapping at Carlos, and he had done nothing to me.

'We are not moving from this spot until you calm down and stop pushing me away.' I put my head in my hands and realised how I just behaved; it was so out of character for me.

'I am sorry.'

'Ash, you don't have to apologise.'

'I just behaved like a spoilt teenager, for no reason.'

'You have taken everything so well, babe. It has only been a matter of time before you snapped.' This thing had turned me into a monster, and I didn't like what it was making me do. 'I still think that we would be better off staying here tonight.'

'No, please. I just want to spend tonight alone.' Stuck here would make me think about everything, and I would torture myself to death.

'Ash, I can't let you go anywhere on your own in this state.'

'I don't want to go alone. I want you to come with me.' I put my hand on his face and stared into his eyes. 'Please, Dale . . . I don't ever ask for anything . . . But I want this . . . I need this.' I couldn't even read Dale's expression, so I didn't have a clue what he was going to say.

'OK . . . Let's go and get some things together and get out of these clothes.' I was so relieved to hear that he would come with me, but I couldn't face anyone. I felt ashamed of what I had just done.

'Can I stay here?'

'No, come with me . . . You don't have anything to hide in here for . . . Everyone in that cottage loves you, and they don't care about your outburst.' Dale opened the car door and got out. He stood and waited for me to exit the car, and I wasn't sure what to do. I realised that I had to do this now or I would never face them. I got out, and Dale held his hand out to me; of course, I accepted it, and we walked back over to the cottage. Everything outside had changed from a wedding venue to a morgue in the space of ten minutes. Everyone was still in the living room, and they all looked sad and lost.

'I want to apologise to you all. There was no need to behave the way I did.' Callum walked over to me and took my hand. I was more surprised than anything else.

'You have nothing to apologise for, Ash.'

'Thanks for understanding, Callum.' I thought everyone was frightened to approach me, and they all kept their distance.

'Ashley dear, you can scream, shout, and smash what you like.' I was very grateful for their understanding. It meant a lot. Christine sat with her back to me and never moved an inch. I let go of Dale's hand and went to sit beside her. 'I am sorry, Christine.' Christine couldn't look at me, and that hurt me more. 'I am going to go away tonight, and I don't want to leave things the way they are.'

'You're running away more like.' Her tone was cold and harsh. I feared that we weren't going to build any bridges tonight.

'I am going to spend my wedding night with my husband . . . I am not running away . . . If you want to be here tomorrow when Dr Ching comes back, you are more than welcome.' I was trying to offer her an olive branch and hoped that she would accept it. But in all honesty, we were as stubborn as each other.

'I will make sure she is OK, Christine.' Dale was trying to help ease the situation, but she was having none of it. I got up to go and get changed, and I felt really sick. I had to run to the bathroom. This hadn't happened for a few days, and I had got used to no sickness. I leant my head over my arm on the toilet and sobbed. The realisation was there. When there were no symptoms, you could ignore the fact that you were ill. But when you felt unwell, it was impossible to ignore.

'Ash. Baby.' Dale came over and rubbed my back. 'Are you OK?'

'Yeah, I am fine . . . I better get used to this.'

'You had been doing so well.' I was glad that he had noticed the sickness had vanished for a couple of days. I really hated being sick. I wouldn't wish it on my worst enemy.

'I probably didn't do myself any favours, drinking like that.' I stepped up and walked over to the sink to rinse my mouth out.

'Christine has packed you a bag, so you just have to get changed.' What had made Christine change her mind?

'Is she OK?' I really cared about Christine. I didn't want to leave things the way they were.

'Yeah, she is fine, hun . . . Come and get changed.' I was determined to make the most of our night together. Nothing was going to ruin our wedding night, not even cancer.

'This is gorgeous, Dale.' Our hotel room was a honeymoon suite, and I had never seen anything as nice in my life. The room was huge with all different rooms that branched off. I was overwhelmed by it all.

'I am glad that you like it.' Dale felt very distant, and that isn't what I wanted tonight. I didn't want him to be walking on eggshells.

'Can we just forget about the cancer for one night and just enjoy what we have left of our day.' Dale never said a word to me, and my heart was breaking. He had leant himself up against the bar, looking very out of place. I walked over to the fridge to distract myself from the atmosphere, but I wasn't succeeding. I could have had any drink that I wanted, but the water had my name all over it. I wanted to spice things up a bit, so I walked over to Dale. The water was nice and cold, just perfect for drinking. 'Will you say something, Dale?'

'I really want to give you a night to remember, but I am not sure that I can.' I felt the life drain from me as he spoke. The distance between us wasn't normal, and I didn't like it one bit.

'Apart from the results, we are the same two people in love with one another. Let's not let it ruin things between us.' I lifted the bottle of water over his head and poured it over him. He jumped out of his skin, and I couldn't help but giggle.

'You have lost your mind tonight.' I couldn't stop laughing. I had amused myself. 'That is one I owe you, Mrs Black.' He came and wrapped his arms around me and swung me around. 'I love you, Ashley.'

'Prove it, Mr Black.' I had a sexy, playful tone about my voice, and he put me down on my feet.

'Ashley, I want to make love to you every minute of every day.' He had my face clasped in his hands, and my body was crying out for him. 'The way you looked today with that dress on and your hair hanging loose . . . I planned to bring you here tonight and make love to you that many times that we would need a day of rest in each other's arms . . .' I felt a but coming. 'But . . . I am not sure I can now.' He had just put another nail in my coffin, and it hurt me so much.

'I am damaged goods . . . You don't want me.' I could hardly stutter the words out. I felt nauseated.

'Of course, I want you, Ashley.'

'So what then . . .' This was why he wanted to stay at home tonight. He would have had the perfect excuse to just lay with me and cradle me in his arms.

'I want you here and now, but I can't block out how sick you are.'

'Just go home, Dale.' He shook his head at me, and I pulled away from him. 'I will come home in time for Dr Ching coming.' I went over and lifted a bottle of wine from the fridge and grabbed a glass. My next port of call was a long soak in the bath with my bottle of wine.

'That is really going to help.' I came back out from the bathroom to get my bag, and I could quite easily have said a lot of things that I would regret.

'Tonight just gets better and better . . . I found out that I am dying . . . I get married to someone who has now finally realised his true feelings and now he can't bear to be around me . . . So I think that I deserve a glass of wine in the bath . . . Close the door behind you, Dale. I will see you tomorrow . . . maybe.' I quickly walked into the bathroom and closed the door behind me. In all the time that I had known Dale, I had never locked a door. But tonight, I just needed that time to myself. The bath was huge, and it would help me ease a lot of my tension. I was planning on spending a while in here with nothing and no one to annoy me. Feeling alone was a new thing for me, and I wasn't sure that I liked it very much. The only person whom I wanted here was my mom, and I couldn't have her. Everything was certainly testing my patience today, and it was only a matter of time before I lost everything either through me pushing them away or death. Either way I felt alone.

I had to leave the bathroom, and part of me wanted the hotel room to be empty. Christine had only packed me sexy silk pyjamas, and I didn't want Dale to see me in them. He had made himself clear enough before, and we were going to struggle to get over that now. I stepped out of the bathroom, and the whole room was quiet, no one but me in it. For the first time in months, I didn't know if I wanted to laugh or cry. I went over to the bar and got another bottle of water. I felt dehydrated, and my head was sore from all the tension.

'I hope that you are going to drink that one.'

'Jesus Christ, do you want me to have a heart attack?' I didn't know how much more my poor heart could take. 'I thought that you had gone.' I should have known that he would be lurking somewhere. He had changed into shorts and a vest top, so he wasn't planning on going anywhere.

'Why are you here? I mean it won't be much fun watching me sleep or be sick . . . I will pass you covers through, and you can sleep on the couch.'

'It is our wedding night, Ash . . . I don't intend on letting you spend it alone.'

'You are going to have a long night then . . . Once I am finished this, I am going to bed. Alone.' I was doing it again. The nippy bitch was back.

'Dressed like that is going to prove a problem.' Because I was standing here in sexy pyjamas, he thought that he could change his mind.

'Well, I am sure the couch will be comfortable.' I was cutting my nose off to spite my face, but he hurt me.

'Ashley, please . . .'

'Please what, Dale? Please sleep with me . . . Please be the dutiful wife . . . Please don't be a bitch.' I was getting fed up of being a bitch, but it was just falling off my tongue tonight.

'Please. Let's see what happens.'

'Dale, we have had sex that many times we shouldn't have to see what happens.' My words seemed to tear a strip off him; he had gone quite pale. 'Was I OK to sleep with when you thought that I could give you a child?' I couldn't believe that I had just said that; it was below the belt for even me. I had hurt myself by saying it, but it was what I was thinking.

'I can't believe that you think that.' I heard the pain in his voice and hated myself for it. 'If you are trying to hurt me, then you are succeeding . . . I love the bones of you, Ashley. When are you going to wake up and see that?' I walked over to the corner sofa and sat down and put my feet up. Dale came over and sat at my feet, and I laid my head back and just stared at him. What has happened to us tonight? 'Is that what you really think, Ash?' Of course, it wasn't, but did I want to keep acting like a new bitch in town?

'No, of course, it isn't . . . not in my heart any way.'

'It is bad enough that I have given you any cause to think that . . . I am so sorry, Ash.' Why was he apologising to me? It was me being a bitch.

'Don't apologise. You don't have anything to say sorry for. I am just in one of those moods.' I swung my feet back on to the floor and sat forward to get up. I was all over the place and couldn't think straight.

'Where are you going?'

'To give us some space. I will pass you covers through.' I didn't want space from him, but I thought that we needed it.

'Don't go to bed, Ash . . . Please stay.' Dale was practically on top of me with the way that he had positioned himself, and I felt my breathing getting harder, and my heart began to race. I didn't know how I managed to squeeze away from him, but he caught my hand as I stood up. 'I love you, Ashley.'

'Is it enough, Dale?' I loved him as well, but right now I wasn't sure if love was enough to get us through how we felt. His mouth hungrily took mine, and my body immediately jumped to attention.

'Don't do this out of guilt.' I could hardly breathe with how fierce he had just kissed me.

'I have never thought of not sleeping with you, Ash. I just didn't want to hurt you . . . But with all that has been said, it looks like I have hurt you in other ways.'

'Don't make yourself feel bad.'

'Also, I married you today because I loved you weeks ago, and I love you now. I haven't figured out any other feeling for you because you are sick.'

'What?'

'Before you went to the bath, you said, "You married someone who has figured out his true feelings." My feelings will never change towards you.' He kissed my lips slowly and softly, totally different from a minute ago. I couldn't push him away even if I tried. I felt him lift me so my legs wrapped around his waist. Our hands tangled in each other's hair as the heat and passion soared through us. I was laid back down on to the couch, and his hand moved up my chemise to caress my breasts. My body was alive as we shared the passion between us.

'Dale, are you sure about this?' I let out a cry because my body craved his touch. I didn't want him to stop, but I didn't want him to continue out of guilt.

'You are my wife. Of course, I am sure.' I pulled his vest off and rubbed my hands over his body. Another cry escaped my mouth as he bit my nipple through the silk fabric. I felt like I was in some kind of dream as I squeezed every inch of his body. I sat forward slightly to get his mouth, and he slipped my chemise off, leaving me in just my silk pants. Our bodies didn't even have to try to react to each other. He got me to lift up so that he could slip my pants off, and I wanted him inside me already. He kissed all the way up my leg, leaving every spot tingling. His lips felt so good. I felt like electric as his mouth slid on to my clitoris; his tongue was so soft and warm, and I couldn't believe how my body felt like a temple. Every inch of my body shuddered as I climaxed with his mouth. Why did I doubt this man's feelings? I felt him move as he took his shorts off, and his whole body slid over the top of me. His mouth made love to my mouth so soft and sensual. We were both hot and bothered and wanted each other in every way possible. I felt his hard package slip inside of me, and we both let out a groan of pleasure. He pushed inside me harder with each thrust, and my body was like a quivering wreck. His warm mouth on my breasts sent shock waves through my body until I felt him tense and explode inside me. We both lay there puffing and panting, taking in what just happened. I could feel his heart beating against my chest. It was so strong just like him. I let my hand run through his hair as his head lay on my shoulder. I could lie like this forever and never move.

'I love you, Ash.'

'I know you do . . . I love you too, hun.' He lifted off me, and I moved over slightly so that he could lie beside me. We lay beside each other, with our naked bodies on fire.

'I am sorry, Ash.'

'Shh. Don't bring any of it up . . . Don't waste it.' I had just made love to my husband for the first time as Mr and Mrs, and it felt good. It felt really good to feel human for once.

'I hope that you are not tired, Mr Black.'

'What do you have in mind, Mrs Black?'

'Food for starters.' I felt hungry, but I just hoped that it would stay down. 'Then let's see what happens.'

'It is good to have my Ashley back.' I laughed and looked up to the ceiling because I was glad to be back.

'What compared to Ashley the bitch?'

'I wouldn't call you a bitch . . . just a Jack Russell today.' I had never been called that before; it was another first. 'You better watch out then. I could bite.'

'Sounds good. I think I could handle that.' It was nice to be lying here flirting with my husband; it was good to be acting like a normal married couple. 'I will call room service. What do you fancy?'

'Surprise me.' Dale always knew what I liked, and after today, I really don't care what I ate. He got up and put his shorts and vest back on. I was enjoying the view. We were dressed in record time, and I got up to go to the bathroom. Tonight had seen our first disagreement, and I prayed that we would never exchange words again. Hopefully, it would be the first and the last. I would just have to keep the Jack Russell locked away. I came out of the bathroom to hear someone knock on the door, and Dale was nowhere to be seen. I had to open the door in my pyjamas. Now that would give the staff something to talk about tonight.

'Mrs Black?' I couldn't even speak; the person in front of me was handing me the biggest bouquet of roses.

'Thank you.' I accepted the flowers and closed the door; the smell was just divine. I took the card out and opened it. But I knew who they were from before I looked at the card.

To my darling wife,

I will honour and cherish you from now until forever.

I love you, Mrs Black xxx

'I had forgotten about those.' I wiped a tear from my eye and walked over to my husband. After our rocky start tonight, everything was working itself out nicely.

'I love them, hun. Thank you.' Roses were one of my favourite flowers. 'How did you know that I liked roses?'

'Well, if I am being honest, I asked Christine, and she said that you loved lilies. But I didn't think that they would be appropriate . . . It was a pure guess that I went for roses.' I had to kiss him, just to show him how much he meant to me.

'Lilies are my all-time favourite, but you have done well to pick roses.' All I could smell now was the roses on the table. Dale had wrapped himself around me, and I felt safe and secure. I didn't ever want to move. But the door went again.

'*Ggrrr*, don't they know that this is a honeymoon suite?'

'I will get it, hun. It will be our food.' I let Dale get the door this time, and I went and curled up in the corner on the couch and made myself comfortable.

'I hope that you are hungry.'

'I have lost my appetite, but I will give something a go.' This was one thing that I hated about this illness . . . I was hungry, but I didn't feel like eating. It was driving me up the wall. All I wanted to do was eat what I wanted.

'There is soup here, Ash. Do you want some?'

'Please, that sounds like the safe bet.' I was going to turn into a bowl of soup; it was all that I seemed to enjoy now.

'One positive thing about becoming a vampire, I wouldn't need to worry about eating food.' Dale about choked on his bread. I didn't think that he was expecting me to talk about vampires.

'What do you mean, babe?'

'I have been sizing up all the pros and cons of changing, and that was a pro.' I was actually considering going through with this . . . Was I mad?

'What other pro have you came up with?'

'I get to be with you forever . . . I never age . . . We get to live the life we planned.' When I said it out loud, it all didn't sound so bad.

'And the cons?'

'We get stuck in a fantasy land . . . I never get to be a mommy . . . We get fed up of each other . . .'

'Ashley, I could never get fed up of you, even when the Jack Russell is out.' That was reassuring to know, I suppose.

'I am not ready to die, but I am not sure changing into a vampire would be any different from dying.'

'I am not ready to lose you . . . I am being selfish, I know . . . But as I have said a million times now, I won't be able to live without you.' I didn't want to leave him on his own; he is my everything.

'I know that if the tables were turned and it was you dying, I would be begging you to change . . . There is family, friends, and work to consider in all this . . . Can you give it all up?' I wouldn't want him to give up his entire life for me. I would think about it every time something wasn't quite right, and it would haunt me all the time.

'To keep you . . . I would give up everything . . . I won't have anything without you.'

'Jake said that he would get his friends involved in changing me . . . I think that we should meet them to discuss the whole process.' This all felt like a nightmare now. We shouldn't have to involve mythical creatures to help us stay together. But if it was the only way, it had to be considered.

'I will say to my dad tomorrow. But right now you look really tired.' I felt physically and emotionally drained.

'I feel tired.'

'Do you want to lie in bed?'

'That sounds nice.' My soup had filled a hole, and it just needed to stay down now. I wanted to go and curl up in bed with my husband and sleep like a baby. There was a huge part of me that wanted to wake up in the morning and realise that this had all been a bad dream: that I didn't have cancer and we were living our life, if only things could be so simple.

Chapter 18

Meeting the Experts

Dale and I were curled up on the couch back at the cottage. Our night away was just what we needed, and we were both fresh and relaxed, ready to face the day ahead. The cottage was so quiet with just me and Dale in it. It wasn't meant to host big parties. Mhairi must have cleared up after the wedding because everything was gleaming. The only thing that stayed was all the lovely flowers. The cottage smelt like a florist's.

'This is the life, isn't it?' The silence was broken by Dale's soft voice.

'It is bliss . . . It is hard to believe that all those people fit in here yesterday.' We had about thirty maybe forty of our closest family and friends in here yesterday. It hardly seemed possible.

'It couldn't have been any more perfect . . . until the end . . . But we managed to finish it off in style.' Dale bit my ear, and we were like two love birds so in love together. 'Our peace will be shattered soon.' Did he really have to remind me? I really just wanted it to be me and him spending the day like we were doing.

'I know . . . if only time could stop.' I really didn't know how much my head could take today. Mhairi and Christine could both give a painkiller to a sore head. But putting them both into the same room together was a recipe for disaster. 'I hope that we can get some time with your dad before anyone arrives.' I really wanted to get the whole talk of vampires out of the way before Dr Ching arrived.

'We will make time, babe.'

'Hello.' We had spoken too soon. Mhairi's voice could be heard at the bottom of the mountain.

'In here, Mom.' Dale and I never moved. We didn't care how lazy we looked. We were officially on our honeymoon, and we were enjoying spending this quality time together.

'Are we interrupting? We can come back later.'

'No, Mhairi, you are fine. We have been lying here for ages. It is about time that we get up.' Their timing was bad, but no time today would be good. I sat up and could feel Dale clenching on to my top, and he got me smiling from ear to ear. As much as I wanted to stay in that embrace, I was sure that everyone would have something to say. 'We have all night for lazing around.'

'I will put the kettle on then.' Mhairi always had to be busy in the kitchen. It was like she couldn't sit still. Jake came walking in with Kiara in his arms, and they were both so happy under the circumstances. It was nice to see their happy smiling faces today.

'Hi, kids, how are you all today?'

'All the better, for seeing this little princess.' I held out my arms to take Kiara from Jake, and he handed her to me without thinking.

'Hello, my princess . . . Look at you all lovely in pink . . . Tell your uncle Dale to get up and talk to you.' I knew talking to Kiara like that would get Dale up. He couldn't resist her charm. He had a soft spot for his niece, and anyone could see that now.

'Dad, can we talk to you before anyone else comes in?' Jake knew what this was going to be about before we even started.

'Sure, what is it?' I looked at Dale, and he looked at me. I didn't think either of us knew how to start.

'We were talking last night about changing, and we want to meet your friends to discuss everything.' Dale's voice was really low and soft. I couldn't help but notice how secretive he was.

'OK . . . I will get in contact with Lelland and Lavina . . . I will see if they can come over, ASAP.'

'Thank you, Jake.'

'You're very welcome, dear.' Jake patted Dale on the shoulder and walked into the kitchen. I dare say Mhairi would have something to say about this revelation. But it wasn't about her right now. It was all about how I felt and how I wanted to spend my life.

'Where is Uncle Dale's princess?' I just loved watching Dale with Kiara; he was so sweet. It was times like this that killed me to think that I would never carry a child of my own. 'Where is my stories?' Kiara goo gaad away, and we were both smiling at her. It was another perfect moment that I would never forget.

'She is a wee cutie.'

'Just like her aunty . . . Yes, you are honey pie.' I really didn't deserve how nice he was being to me today because I had been a bitch with a capital 'B' last night. I just hoped that I had got it all out of my system because I hated hearing myself like that.

'Anyone home?' Christine had finally arrived, and she seemed a lot brighter. I just hoped that she would stay like that for the time being.

'Hey.' I really didn't know how to act around her until I knew what mood she was in. She really could be like a jekkel and hide. One minute she was lively and full of life, but the very next minute she could be pulling the hair out of someone's head.

'How long have you been back?'

'We got home about eleven.' So far so good. Christine seemed OK for now; hopefully, it would stay that way as today progressed.

'Here we go.' Mhairi brought a tray full of tea and coffee through and placed it on the coffee table. She moved my roses over to the window and had a quick smell before she placed them in the light.

'Someone has been spoilt.' Mhairi loved flowers as well, and she couldn't help but admire any flower she came across.

'Only the best for my wife.' The atmosphere was a lot calmer today. Everyone wasn't walking on eggshells around me, and that was what I wanted. Life would be so much easier for us all if they treated me like they had always done.

'Kiara is due her bottle, dear. Do you want me to give her it?'

'No. Give it to me, love. I don't mind giving it to her.' Mhairi handed me her bottle, and I got comfortable to feed my little angel. I didn't want to miss a single second with her because I didn't know when that was all going to end.

'What time is Dr Ching coming over?' Then the normality is shattered by one simple question.

'He phoned earlier to say it would be about two.' Dale was like my knight in shining armour; he answered when I didn't. He seemed to know when I switched off to everyone.

'Someone is a hungry monster.' I quickly changed the subject, and although it wasn't a great topic, it felt appropriate. Dale would be the only one who knew I didn't want to talk about Dr Ching.

'You are the only one that she takes a bottle like that for.' Mhairi seemed surprised that Kiara felt comfortable around me. Babies are supposed to sense tension. But then, when I have Kiara in my arms, I never felt stressed or tense. I fell relaxed and honoured to be around such a happy content little angel.

'You're just jealous, Ash . . . Kiara can eat more than you.' Dale was making a joke of my lack of eating, and I appreciated the way he was treating me. I was like Ashley who was OK, and he was right; I probably was jealous of how well she was eating.

'Yeah, too right, hun.'

'How can you two sit and joke?' Here it came. I wondered how long Christine would take to start.

'Christine . . . I had my tantrum last night . . . We spent last night getting everything out in the open, and now we are going to start this roller coaster as we mean to go on . . . I am here with family and friends, and I am the same Ashley that I always have been . . . I don't want to be seen as Ashley who has weeks to live.' Everyone was sitting quiet, waiting for the next outburst, but I wasn't in the mood for any arguments today. I sat Kiara up to break her wind, and I didn't even have to try. 'Clever girl.'

'I don't know what you want from me, Ash?' That was it. I didn't want anything from anyone. I just wanted them to act normal around me, and I didn't think that I was asking for too much.

'I am sick of arguing . . . I don't have it in me to be screaming and shouting . . . Smashing things and running out . . . Just be my friend and go with the flow.' I surprised myself at how calm I had been. I didn't even raise my voice once.

'I can't promise you anything . . . You seem to be shutting everything out though.'

'Dale, go and put Kiara down for a sleep.' That was probably the wrong thing for Mhairi to say because this little angel was keeping me calm, and judging by Dale's reluctance to move, he knew exactly that.

'Trust me, Christine . . . I am not shutting anything out. Dale and I got everything out in the open last night, and we know where we stand with one another. I have came back today ready to face anything.' I kept telling myself that I would do anything the doctor asked me, just as long as I got time to spend with my family.

'OK. I will try. But don't push me away.' Why did everyone think that I was pushing them away? It wasn't in my nature to push anyone away. I loved each and every one of them in some way or another, and I was happy that they were all in my life.

'That will never happen, honey.'

'I am going to change the subject because I am sick of all the animosity. How was your hotel, Ashley?' I could have kissed Jake for changing the subject, but I felt my cheeks flush as I reminded myself of our night of passion, tears, and laughter.

'The hotel was lovely, Jake . . . We had the honeymoon suite.' Dale came and sat back beside me and smirked at me getting all embarrassed. 'It was perfect in the end.' We had a rocky start to our night, but we managed to fix it all out and enjoy our time together.

'With the look on your faces, you had a nice night.' I hated how Jake knew what we were thinking; he was like a mind-reader.

'We had a good night, Dad . . . We laughed and cried, but it was good.'

'I will stop there because I don't want all the glory details.' I curled my legs up beside me and cuddled into Dale. His body was like a temple when I cuddled into him. His strong frame was just what I needed wrapped around me today.

'That sounds like the safe option, Dad.' Dale's arm around me was just like a safety net. It felt good to feel comfortable in his arms.

'You look tired, dear?'

'I feel it now, Jake.' I hate feeling so lifeless; how it crept up on you when you really didn't want it to?

'Once the doctor has been, we will leave you two on your own.' Jake just finished his sentence when someone knocked on the door. My body froze and my heart pounded at the thought of it being my doctor. Mhairi went to answer it, but we all knew who it was before she even came back.

'Hi, everyone.' Jake got up out of his chair so that the doctor could sit beside Dale and me. One good thing about this doctor was his timekeeping. He was never late. 'How are you both?' I never moved from Dale's side. If I was cuddled into him, I would be fine.

'Bearing up . . . Better than last night.' I would never forget how that destruct button was pushed, and I crumbled to pieces in front of everyone. It was horrible.

'I am sorry if I ruined your day.' It was a bit late for sorry, but I would have been angrier if I knew that he knew and never told us.

'You didn't ruin anything, Doc.'

'Before I start, do you have any questions for me?' Where would I start? There was a million and one things rattling around in my head, and I had no idea where to begin.

'You said last night that you can slow it down . . . How?' Thank God Dale was listening last night and that he was on the ball today. Everything that was said last night was a blur in my mind.

'There is a medication that Ashley can take, but I have to warn you that the side effects are not nice.'

'What time difference will it make?' I picked up the courage to speak because I needed to know the answer, before I couldn't take any more.

'A couple of weeks, maybe longer.'

'I don't want it . . .' I could feel everyone looking at me for an explanation, and I felt like I owed them that much. 'I would rather have six weeks with little or no side effects as opposed to twelve weeks feeling worse than I already do.' My body felt cold and numb sitting here talking about dying. I thought that I would have years before I would ever have to make decisions like these.

'What happened to facing this, Ash?'

'I am Christine. You have no idea how I feel right now . . . The sickness and pain . . .' I couldn't imagine how much worse I was going to get, but dragging it out was only going to make it worse. 'I don't want any more side effects.'

'I understand what you are saying, dear.' Jake was my rock today. It meant a lot to hear him on my side. I knew that I wasn't making a harsh decision when he agreed with me.

'We can help with the sickness and pain if and when it is needed.' I felt like a nodding dog; all I could do was sit and nod my head.

'You must have some idea of time, Doc?'

'Dale, all I can say to you is that I reckon you will get Christmas and New Year . . .'

'Is that it?' Christine was crying as she jumped up and cut the doctor off. 'That is only five maybe six weeks.' I hated hearing how much pain and upset she was going through, and I couldn't take any of it away from her.

'I am trying to be honest with you all.' Dr Ching sounded heartbroken. This must be just as hard for him.

'I need you to be honest with me . . . No beating about the bush.' Lies and deceit would just make me worse.

'How can we help, Ashley?' This was the first time that Mhairi had ever asked a question, and I immediately lifted my head up to look at her. I knew that she was behind me, but I didn't realise how close she was.

'I am sure Ashley will tell you what she needs . . . But in my experience, all you can do is be there for her when she needs it . . . There is going to be highs and lows and everyone reacts differently.' I let out a little laugh at Dr Ching's last comment because we had already seen me have one tantrum last night.

'I think everyone saw me at my lowest last night . . . But I have promised myself to enjoy what I have left . . . And anyone in this room who can't expect that . . . Well, we can say our goodbyes now.' I sat waiting for someone to get up and walk, but no one did. Everyone seemed to understand my thoughts and feelings, and no one was ready to say their goodbyes just yet.

'So what happens now, Dr Ching?' Did I really want to know the answer to this question?

'That depends on you, Ashley . . . I can be here daily or when you need me . . . I will put you in touch with palliative care, and they will help you all the way.'

'We can call you if we need you.' I looked to Dale for his opinion. I had to remember that I wasn't on my own any more. I had a husband to consult.

'Of course, that is fine, babe.'

'OK. You have my numbers . . . Day or night, just call me . . . Dale, do you have anything on your mind that I can clear up for you? In my experience, the partners often have lots to say, but they are not sure what to say for the best.' I felt relieved that Dr Ching asked this question because Dale needed to know that he could ask anything that he wanted.

'I just want to be there for my wife, Dr Ching, and at the moment, she is more than capable to tell me what she wants or needs . . . That might change in time, and then I might need a helping hand . . .'

'You are both lucky to have one another . . . If you think of anything that you need to ask, please don't hesitate.'

'Thanks, Doctor.' Mhairi put a hand on my shoulder, and I squeezed it tight.

'I will leave you with your family . . . It is far better when you have a good support network around you.' I had a lot of people around me who cared about what happened and that I would always be grateful for.

'I will see you out, Doctor.' Jake was the perfect bouncer. I just hoped that he could bounce everyone else out as easy. Dale tightened his grip around me and buried his head in my hair. My head and my eyes felt heavy, and I felt a headache coming on. There was only so much that I could take in one day, and I had seen and heard enough in one twenty-four-hour period. I watched everyone potter around us, but I just wanted them all to go.

'I am sorry everyone. I am going to go for a lie-down.' Dale let me get up, and I felt really horrible that I couldn't be more company.

'Don't be sorry, Ashley. We were just leaving now anyway.' Jake kissed my cheeks and gave me a hug. I was very grateful to have a family unit around me. I walked into my room and curled up in the middle of the bed. I knew that Dale would be right behind me. I couldn't even think straight. My head seemed all scrambled. The last couple of months had been an all-time high, and now it was going to end. Anchorage was my new beginning, and now it was my end. I couldn't help but think that my destiny brought me to Anchorage, to meet Dale and his family.

'Ash babe.' I turned slightly so that he knew I wasn't sleeping, and he climbed on to the bed beside me and kissed my head tenderly.

'Is everyone gone?'

'Yes. Home alone at last.' That was music to my ears. As much as I loved everyone, I just loved time alone with no one to answer to. Dale and I could get so much more out in the open when we were together, and neither of us was afraid to say how we feel.

'I don't know about you, but I have been dreaming about jumping into this bed all afternoon.'

'Tell me about it. Great minds think alike, babe.' I couldn't keep my eyes open, and now that I have Dale beside me, I could sleep safe and sound in his arms. I had taken a lot for granted over the years, but now I was able to see what was important in my life, and I would never take anything for granted again.

I got woke up by the sound of voices and realised quickly that Dale wasn't beside me. It must be late because the room was black. I climbed out of bed and went through to the living room. It felt really cold tonight. I saw Dale and Jake, but the other man and woman, I didn't know who they were. They looked elegant and beautiful. I didn't think that I had ever seen two people look so flawless.

'Ash.' Dale got up and came over to me. He didn't quite look himself. 'Come and get a seat . . . This is Lelland and Lavina.' Of course, it was; why didn't I guess?

'Hello, Ashley . . .' Lavina sounded very polite and sweet. Her voice was like an angel. 'We have heard so much about you.' I was terrified about being in this room. There were more vampires than humans. I didn't really want to piss anyone off tonight.

'I didn't want to disturb you, doll.' I didn't know how he couldn't wake me? Did they plan to bite me when I was asleep?

'I am sorry to hear about your illness . . .' Lavina really had heard a lot about me. 'Jake has told me that you want to consider changing into one of us.'

'Yes . . . considering.' Nothing was set in stone yet. We were just weighing up all our options.

'It isn't easy at first . . . especially to become human friendly . . . We don't want to create you to kill humans . . . If you want this, I suggest that you leave the change to the very last minute . . . Let the cancer progress . . . It will be easier to let people think you have died.' I couldn't believe that I was hearing all this nonsense. I felt like I was in a nightmare and was going to wake up screaming at any moment. Lavina's tone was soft and informative, and I couldn't take my eyes off her.

'How does it all happen?' I knew that I was sounding ridiculous, but I thought that vampires were mythical, so what actually happens in the land of vampires was anyone's guess.

'It all starts with the bite. The venom in our saliva burns your human cells and turns them into vampire ones. The cells are capable of holding blood without the need of human food. The change takes about a week. It is a very painful process, and you may wish that you had died.' I knew that I asked, but I didn't expect it to all sound so horrific. I was even more distracted because it was Leland who was telling me all about it. Anyone would think that he was trying to put me off the idea.

'Ashley dear, you look like you have seen a ghost. Are you OK?' Jake never took his eyes off me the whole time Lavina and Leland were talking. I felt like I had seen a ghost. My mind and body wasn't connected tonight.

'It all just seems . . . unreal.' I tried to find the right word, but my head was pickled. 'It is going to be hard to just disappear . . . I thought I would just carry on life as Ashley Malone.' I might have known it was too good to be true.

'We can take care of everything for you, Ashley . . . From changing, to getting you away from the funeral home unnoticed, to helping you make a smooth adaptation to your new life.' I hadn't thought of any of that. I thought that one bite would solve everything. How naive could I be?

'How can I carry on as a vampire and not be noticed as Ashley?'

'You would move and start afresh where no one knows you.' This was all proving to be difficult. Did I really need all this extra hassle to spend extra time on this planet? Dale had never spoken one word to Lelland or Lavina since I came through. What was he thinking?

'Why have you gone all quiet all of a sudden?' I addressed Dale quite harshly, but I needed to know what was going on in his head.

'I am just listening . . . Taking it all in.' I didn't think that he had thought about everything either. It was becoming real as we sat here and discussed everything.

'What about the business you have built up from scratch?'

'I won't actually need to disappear, but Callum is going to run things from this end . . . I can run things from wherever we are.' He had been thinking hard about everything. Work had never crossed my mind until now.

'Am I the only one who thought this was going to be easy . . . ? So once I have days left, the change would take place? I have to deteriorate before anything can get done?'

'It would be for the best, Ashley . . . I could bite you now, and then we would all have added pressure of hiding you and making excuses about your disappearance.' How can these vampires be so nice? They are supposed to be vicious and unfriendly.

'Who would change me?' I asked this question purely out of curiosity because it wouldn't make any difference who did it.

'We both are more than capable of changing you . . . You can decide.' So there is one decision that I could make on my own.

'You don't have to decide anything now.' Jake clasped my hand and looked into my eyes. I couldn't decide anything now. Not until I spoke with Dale properly. But the longer I left it, the harder it was going to be.

'We are going to leave you to discuss this . . . Jake can get us any time, and we are more than willing to help if that is what you decide.'

'Thank you.' Dale stood up to shake their hands, and Jake gave Dale a hug. I knew that Jake would always be around for Dale, and that was one thing that was keeping me going. He would never be on his own.

'I will see you both tomorrow . . . Try and get some rest.' I watched closely as the three vampires left the cottage. What were we thinking? We had to be barking mad to consider any of this.

'Dale, you can move on with life after me . . . remarry . . . have kids . . . run your business without hiding in another place . . .' As I said it all out loud, I realised how hard all that must be for him.

'I couldn't get married again . . . You are the only woman for me, and I don't want kids if it isn't with you . . . If you don't want to do this, I will respect your decision. But don't ask me to move on after you.'

'There is only one decision to make . . . I can't leave you to drown your sorrows and to never have a life.' I couldn't believe that I was saying this. I must be mad as well as stupid.

'What are you saying, Ash?' I took his hand and got him to sit beside me.

'We have to do this . . . We have no other option.' Dale squeezed me that tight in his arms that I thought I was going to suffocate.

'I love you, Mrs Black.'

'I will do this, but you have to help me organise my funeral.' I choked back the tears because either way I was dying. I was never going to live a human life again, and that was hard to comprehend. Ashley was going to die one way or another.

'Shh . . . Don't cry . . . We will do everything together . . . I promised to be by your side from now until the end.' Now our end was going to be forever.

'Will you get Tom to come back? I want him to do my service.' Tom was the perfect choice. He gave us closure by marrying us, and now he could give us new beginnings by doing my funeral. 'I don't want anyone to wear black. My favourite colour is pink.' I had given a lot of thought to what I wanted. 'Since you are not losing me, I would like to go home and be with my parents.' Dale was taking everything in like a sponge. Listening to my every word like it was my last.

'You have everything planned.' His voice was in pain and very shaky.

'Deep down, I knew that it was coming.' You shouldn't have to plan a funeral at twenty-four years of age; it seemed so unfair.

'We will get it all sorted tomorrow, Ashley.' I was grateful to have Dale here to help me. I couldn't imagine not having him in my life.

'Now, I am going to send Carlos for some food. Do you want to take a bath?'

'Where is Carlos?'

'He is at the house, but he wouldn't mind coming up here . . . I think my mom is driving him daft.' I could only imagine what Mhairi was like with Carlos and Rosa. I couldn't bear to think about it.

'He will get some peace then.' I got up to go and run a bath. It was just what I needed after the day we had had. 'Just order me anything.' I felt very hungry for a change. That was a first in weeks. 'Are you going to join me?'

'I will be through in five.' That was just what I liked to hear. I walked into the bathroom and started the water. I quickly had to sit down because my stomach was all sore, like cramps soaring through me. I took a few deep breaths and sat to see if it would pass.

'Ash . . . What is it?' Dale rushed in very concerned. I had hoped it would pass before he came in and noticed.

'I am OK . . . just a few pains in my stomach.' Was this all the symptoms going to start one by one? I could never cope with pain very good, and I didn't like taking tablets, but something was going to have to give.

'Do you want me to get Dr Ching?'

'No, I will be fine . . . If it is still the same tomorrow, then you can phone him . . . The bath will help.'

'OK. Just sit there, and I will finish it off.' Dale always knew how to fuss over me; he was probably going to drive me daft over the next couple of weeks.

'I am OK, you know.' I was as good as I was ever going to be and didn't want to be a burden to him.

'It won't hurt you to let me take care of you.' I had always been stubborn when it came to being looked after. My mom always used to have the last word when I was ill. 'I am your mom, sweetheart. I am meant to look after you.' Dale reminded me so much about my mom. They both were kind and caring and would do anything for me.

'That's it ready, Ash. Do you want any help out of your clothes?' My look must have said it all. I didn't feel that helpless yet.

'Go and get plates ready for dinner. I will manage fine.' I got a kiss on my head like I do every time he left me in a room.

'Just shout if you need me.' I rolled my eyes at him because I knew that one thing he hated was someone rolling their eyes at him.

'Go.' All I wanted to do was soak in the nice hot water and wash all my thoughts and feelings away. The last three days had had so many highs and lows, that I felt as if I was drowning. Could the next few weeks get any better?

Chapter 19

Getting Ready for Christmas and New Year

'Let's get out of here today . . . Let's escape before anyone arrives.' I really wanted to see what it would be like to disappear without anyone knowing where we were, and after meeting Lavina and Lelland last night, anyone would want to disappear.

'Sounds good . . . Where do you want to go?' I was shocked that Dale was going along with my suggestion because he was so wrapped up on giving me as much rest as possible.

'We can go and see Tom, and then we can go shopping for Christmas.' I love Christmas time, and since this was going to be my last-living Christmas, I wanted to make it special. I wanted to make it one to remember with everyone whom I loved.

'Let's go and get ready, Ash . . . Fresh snow has fallen, so wrap up warmly.'

'Yes, Mom.' I was being sarcastic because he sounded just like my mom and not my husband. My mom always used to say 'Ashley, you will catch a death of cold going out like that'. I and my mom had many disagreements about the way I dressed as a teenager, but as I got older, I grew up and dressed more appropriately. She would be proud of the woman I had become. When I looked in the mirror, I could see her in me all the time. I just wished that I had her around a little longer, to share some of my life experiences with her.

'I didn't think that you would have worn those boots.' They were brown and beige fur snow boots, ideal for a winter in Anchorage. I actually felt really comfortable in them, and it made a change from wearing heals or sandals, which was the ideal footwear in Florida.

'Why? They go with what I am wearing today.' They were very comfortable; my feet wouldn't get cold anyway.

'Here, before you forget to put them on.' Dale threw my hat and scarf over that I left on the table. 'It is freezing out there today.' For someone who had lived in Anchorage for a few years, he really hadn't got used to their winter months. I put my winter warmers on and grabbed my jacket from the stand. I was actually looking forward to getting out in the cold. I was always used to warm weather so it was a nice change for me, a different scene for me to take in.

'I am ready. When you are, Mr Black?' I was very pleased with myself because I was normally last to be ready. I was always running around at the last minute, but today I was happy to be getting out for a little while. 'Can I drive?' I hadn't driven my car very much, and it seemed a waste.

'Do you think that it is a good idea?'

'I am not on any medication . . . I know that I feel OK today . . . I want to drive.' I was shocked when Dale threw me the keys over. I honestly thought that it would be a topic that I wouldn't win. But I thought that he realised now that it didn't matter how much he wrapped me up in cotton wool, it wasn't going to change my illness.

I pulled up outside Tom's parish, and I spotted him getting out of his car. I felt very calm about organising my own funeral. It didn't feel nice, but it needed to be done. I certainly didn't want to leave it to anyone, and this way I got what I wanted and no one needed to argue over what they thought I would want. We stepped out of the car, and Tom spotted us right away, and he immediately came over to us. He seemed really pleased and surprised to see us both out.

'Well, well, well, this is a nice surprise.' Tom gave me a cuddle and kissed both my cheeks. 'What can I do for you both?'

'I want to know if you will conduct my funeral service . . . I thought, since you married us you . . .'

'I would be honoured, my dear.' I didn't get a chance to finish what I had to say because Tom had given me his answer. 'Come in to the warm, and we will chat some more.' Dale and I followed Tom into the church. This was going to be my first visit here, and I was looking forward to seeing where he worked. As I walked through the main doors, I gasped. Everything was beautiful.

'It is beautiful in here . . . very peaceful.'

'A lot of people come here just to get some peace and quiet. But a lot of the time people come to rekindle their faith and to receive some kind of motivation in life.' I could see why. I could picture myself sitting here, escaping from the world. 'Please, come and have a seat.' Dale and I sat down, and Tom pulled a chair over to sit in front of us. 'I take it you have had your results back?'

'We got them back on our wedding night.' I will never forget that moment Dr Ching told me the news. I could have died on the spot.

'Not good timing.'

'Dr Ching told me that I could have waited, but once I knew that he knew, I couldn't find out.' That was like taking a child to a sweetie shop and telling them they couldn't get a sweetie. I had to know whatever the price was.

'How long are we talking, sweetheart?'

'Weeks . . . They think that I will see Christmas and New Year but not much after that.' I promised myself that I wouldn't cry, and I was determined to see today through tear free.

'I am so sorry to hear that . . . You both must be heartbroken . . . I can't imagine what you are going through.' Even this poor man who deals with death every week was struggling to come to terms with our situation.

'We have had our highs and our lows over the last forty-eight hours, but we have promised each other that we are going to enjoy what we have left.'

'So you want me to do your funeral service?' All I could do was nod my head and smile towards Tom. 'Do you have anything in mind?' I was surprised at how much I had already planned in my head. It was amazing what crept up at this kind of time.

'I don't want anyone to wear black . . . My favourite colour is pink, and I want everyone to wear something bright to represent what I believe in . . . I did want to go with my parents, but I don't want to leave Anchorage.' I looked at Dale because this was a new decision. It was totally different to my first choice. 'My life started when I came here, and I don't want to leave.'

'What music do you like?'

'I like any music . . . We played "Amazing Grace" as one of the songs at my parents' funeral.' There wasn't a dry eye on that day. Did I really want that at my send-off?

'That is a popular song, Ashley. You can have a think about another song . . . What are your favourite flowers?'

'Lilies . . . or roses . . . I love flowers.' I sat smiling as I remembered my mom and dad's anniversary. My dad had flowers everywhere. The smell was exquisite. My dad was a romantic man; he always made my mom happy, and that was what mattered most.

'What are you thinking about, dear?'

'My mom and dad's wedding anniversary . . . We woke up one morning to flowers every where . . . kitchen, bathroom, living room. There wasn't a room untouched. Our house was like a florist's.' Dale and Tom were listening to me carefully, just in case they missed anything. I never really spoke out loud about my parents before. It was amazing what a deadly illness could do to one's brain.

'Your dad seemed like a nice man.'

'He was . . . Dale reminds me a lot about my dad . . . Kind, caring, romantic, loving, and always putting me first.'

'You are a lucky lady to have a husband like Dale.'

'I know, Tom.' I looked at Dale and took his hand; he was my everything. 'So what happens now?'

'We can get everything organised so that when the time comes, Dale won't have anything to do . . . Based on everything you have told me, I can go ahead and start all of the preparation . . . I will keep in touch with you, and if anything pops into your mind, just call me.'

'Thank you for making this easy . . . I thought that I would run a mile when this day came.' This had been a lot easier than what I had thought, and I managed to stay tear free.

'It is getting more popular to arrange your own service, but it doesn't get any easier. I think what has helped you is that we have had a connection from day one and I married you. You don't feel like you are sitting talking to a minister or arranging your final farewell. But I will always be here for you both.' I could relate to everything that Tom had just said, and he was right. It would have been a lot harder for me to talk to a stranger.

'Thank you, Tom.'

'You are very welcome, Ashley.' Dale and I stood up, and Tom followed our lead. I got my hug and a kiss on each cheek, and I felt like I had known him for years.

'Before we go, I have something for the church . . .' Dale reached into his pocket and pulled out an envelope. 'You wouldn't take anything for marrying us, and we just want to show our appreciation . . . Please take this and add it to your funds.' Tom did me the honour and accepted the envelope. He looked very sad as he stood in front of us, and I knew if we were here much longer, we would all be in tears.

'Thank you . . . I am sure that there will be many causes that this will help.' We left Tom standing with the envelope, and we walked out of the church, hand in hand. I wished that I had been here before today because it was such a beautiful place to be. Everything was so tranquil and relaxing. You could probably hear a pin drop if you listened carefully enough.

'I need retail therapy now.' We both held on to one another as we headed back for the car, and shopping was going to be the perfect end to a perfect sort of day.

'Let's enjoy the rest of our day, honey.' That sounded like a good idea. All I wanted to do was have fun and enjoy myself. I don't think that I was asking for too much even under the circumstances.

For the first day in about a fortnight, we had followed our plans. I loved Christmas shopping, and I thought Dale would regret coming along after today was over with. I didn't need much of an excuse to shop, but when it came to Christmas time, I always went overboard.

'Are you enjoying yourself, Ash?' We were walking hand in hand through the mall, just like any other couple were. It was nice. No one knew me as Ashley who was dying, and it was good to feel the same as everyone else.

'I am, honey. Are you?' No one made me feel awkward, and that was just what I wanted.

'I am enjoying seeing you happy.'

'The joys of Christmas . . . Come on, let's get Kiara her guardian angel.' I wanted this little girl to have her own special angel to look after her. One day I wanted her to look at it and knew that I would never be far away.

'You took the words out of my mouth.' I thought that he would have forgotten all about my present suggestion, with him being a man. We walked across to the jeweller's shop and walked in. We seemed very underdressed to be here today, but none of us seemed to care.

'Mr Black . . . what a pleasure to see you again.' This tall man in an elegant suit shook Dale's hand gracefully.

'Hello, Randolph . . . This is my wife, Ashley.' Randolph took my hand and kissed it. I felt like royalty.

'How can I help you today?' Randolph was very polite and helpful, just what I imagined for a place like this.

'We are looking for a guardian angel pendant for our niece.' Randolph walked over to a cabinet, and we followed swiftly behind him. He took a huge set of keys out of his pocket and opened the door. I would never know how he knew what key was for what. I was bad enough with two keys. He held out this gorgeous gold chain with an angel on the end. It was perfect, just what I wanted for her.

'What do you think, Ash?'

'It is perfect.' It was just how I pictured it.

'We will take it, Randolph.' This elegant man nodded politely and closed the door. He went behind another counter and started gift wrapping our present. 'I have that other gift to pick up as well, Randolph.' I wondered what other gift he had, but I didn't want to ask. It could have been for his mom or his sister. Randolph came over with both gift bags and handed them to Dale.

'Let me get Kiara's, please.' I expected him to refuse point-blank, but I got another surprise.

'If you must.' I smiled at him and handed the assistant my card. Today was my lucky day.

'What is wrong with you today? I haven't been told "no" once.'

'You can do and say what you like today.' He shouldn't have told me that; now I was going to take advantage of it, and he couldn't go back on his word.

'That is nice to know.' Dale had a look on his face that said 'what did I just do'. Randolph came back over to us and handed me my card. I was glad of his timing because it didn't give Dale time to explain what I could and couldn't do.

'Thank you, Randolph.'

'Thank you for all your help today.' Dale shook his hand, and we walked out of the jeweller's like a pair of love-struck teenagers.

'Where to now, Mrs Black?'

'I don't know. What do you think?' We had certainly shopped until we dropped today.

'Do you want to go home or we could book into a hotel?' Choices. I knew what I wanted to say, but could we possibly make everyone suffer any longer?

'Everyone will be going crazy, wondering where we are.'

'And . . . are you having fun . . . ? Coz I know I am.' Dale was right; I was having fun. I didn't want to think about anyone else today.

'I am enjoying today . . . It has been nice being here with you, acting like a married couple . . . What the hell? Let's do it . . . Let's book into the hotel.' We were going to get an earful for disappearing anyway, so we may as well make the most of it.

'Let's go then, Mrs Black . . . Do you want me to drive?'

'Yeah, you can drive back.' I was exhausted now. I could use the passenger's seat to recoup. 'We don't have any clothes at the hotel.'

'I will get Carlos to be discreet and drop by the cottage to pick some things up for us.' Of course, Carlos. I would never get used to having hired help. Poor Carlos got dragged into all our scams. I was surprised that he didn't tell us where to go.

'You just have everything under control, don't you?'

'When it comes to spending time with you, I would manage to sort anything.' My husband knew all the right things to say, to melt my heart. We started walking back towards the car, and the most amazing thing had just happened. The snow had started falling again.

'Today couldn't get any better. It has been perfect.' I held my hand out to catch the snowdrops falling from the sky. I felt like I was in a nice dream and never wanted to wake up.

'You like snow?' Dale looked curious to what I meant by my comments.

'No, not really. But watching the snowfall is just magical. It is like a winter wonderland.'

'Next, you are going to tell me that you don't want to get into the car.' His sarcastic tone was just what I needed to hear.

'I might just make you sit out here for hours and let you freeze.'

'Get your ass in that car, Mrs Black.' We had had such a lovely day today, and I hoped that my last few weeks were the very same. I really wanted to pack as much as possible into my last few weeks. We had so much to look forward to, and our first Christmas as husband and wife was going to be spectacular. It was good to be back at the car. My feet were killing me. When we were shopping, it never entered my mind how tired I was. It was a good distraction from everything going on in my life.

'My, My, Mrs Black, you can take a telling.' I did know how to follow orders. I just didn't always choose to follow them.

'My mom always used to say that I was the law to myself.' I was always the model student and daughter, but if I was told to do something, I generally did the opposite.

'I would have liked to meet your parents.' I looked at my husband out of pure curiosity as he started to drive. 'We all want the same for you.' They were all very similar, maybe that was why I fell in love with him so quickly.

'Loving, caring, possessive control freaks . . . Do I need to go on?' I really enjoyed pulling Dale's leg because it was so easy to do.

'Is that so, Mrs Black? Do you want to repeat any of those?'

'Not really. I am not a parrot.' We were both having a laugh and a giggle together, and I suddenly realised that I could let him see my parents. I bent down and took my purse out of my bag and handed him a photo of my mom and dad. 'This was my parents at a New Year's party the year before they died . . . They liked throwing parties at Christmas and New Year.' I could remember this party like it was yesterday. We were all so happy surrounded by family and friends, just how it should be at this special time of year.

'You are very like your mom . . . Your dad looks like a very proud man.'

'He always liked to show us off . . . Any chance that he could.' I had never really spoken about my parents since the day that they died. Today was a strange day because everything I had done made me think about them, and Dale was more than happy to listen.

'He sounds like a man whom I would have got along with.' That would have been without a doubt. My dad would have loved Dale.

'Yeah, you would have . . . My dad liked a man who could care for his family . . . He would have valued everything that you are doing right now.' My dad always wanted me to marry someone like Dale, 'My prince charming' as he always used to tell me. Never did I think that I would find him.

'I have never heard you talk much about your family before . . . It has been nice hearing about them today.' Dale switched off the car and turned to look at me. 'We are here.' I looked surprised. It had been the quickest journey ever. 'C'mon, you can share more stories when we are inside.' My mom always liked to reminisce, but I was the one who liked to forget the past . . . But since I moved to Anchorage, and I met Dale and his family, it has made me think about fond memories, memories that I blocked away, memories that would live with me forever. But my illness has made me realise that bottling things up was never a good idea because it would kill any chance you had of being happy.

Today had been perfect. I could take my last breath and would be happy. I was even happier now that Carlos was on his way with clothes for me. I couldn't believe that we had managed to sneak away today and still no one knew where we were.

'Hey, Carlos . . . Come in.' I was never so glad to see Carlos because all I wanted was my pyjamas.

'Please tell me that you haven't been followed.' I was having too much fun to be interrupted by family and friends. Carlos put the bags down and kissed my cheek.

'I was careful, Ashley . . . No one has followed me.' I sighed a relief and went to get a seat. We had all been sneaky, but it had been worth it for a day of relaxation.

'Thank you for this, Carlos.' Dale was always polite to his staff, especially Carlos. No a wonder Rosa and Carlos were not talking to their new guests in the house.

'No problem, Dale. I am just glad to be doing something for you and Ashley.' I could hear that dig, and I couldn't help but smile to myself.

'I bet my mom is driving you daft?' That was a silly question to ask. We all knew the answer before Carlos answered.

'She is OK . . . But she isn't you or Ashley.' That was a nice thing to say. I would definitely miss Carlos when I was changed. I just hated the fact that I wouldn't see them all again. 'Can I do anything else for you?'

'No. I think that it is all for tonight, Carlos . . . If my mom or anyone asks, will you just say that I got you to take files to Robert, but you haven't seen me or Ashley?' Carlos smiled cheekily like he would take great pleasure lying to Mhairi.

'Sure . . . Take care, Ash.'

'Bye, honey.' Dale stood behind the closed door, and he looked so relieved.

'We have succeeded in being deceitful to my mom . . . Now, that is a first.' Even Dale sounded pleased about that.

'I am sure she will forgive us.' Dale's wide eyes said different, but we didn't care too much.

'Do you care? I know that I don't.' Today I didn't care. I had had a day to remember without any interference. I shook my head and walked towards my husband. This was my idea of heaven.

'I don't care about anything right now.' I got my big bear hug, and that made our deceit worth it.

'Let's go and get a bath and get comfortable . . . Order dinner and book a movie to cosy up on the sofa.' My husband knew me so well; that all sounded perfect.

'Lead the way.' Dale knew more about me in our short time together than some men knew about their wives in twenty years. 'You amaze me.'

'Why, babe?'

'Because you always seem to know what I want before I even know myself.' Did he have special powers that I knew nothing about?

'What can I say . . . ? I know you better than you do yourself.' I couldn't argue with that. I didn't think that I did know anything about myself any more. 'It is all because I love you dearly.'

'I love you too, Dale.' The smell of the bath oils were going for my nose. 'Hmm, that bath smells luxurious.' I couldn't wait till it was ready. I started stripping my clothes off piece by piece until I was completely naked. I climbed into the shallow bath and let it fill up while I was in it.

'I have never met someone who loves a bath as much as you do.' I was a bath freak. I could sit in a bath all day if I could. My mom and dad would always call me a water baby. I loved anything to do with water.

'It is relaxing . . . soothing . . . And it washes away any cares you have.' I was just missing one thing right now, and that was Dale's naked body behind me. 'Are you just going to sit there or are you coming to join me?' We were back in the honeymoon suite so the bath was huge; you could probably fit another four people in it. Dale never even answered my question. He just smiled at me. I couldn't resist but to pull his arm of the side of the bath, and he fell in beside me. We were both laughing and giggling as Dale found his balance in the water.

'You are going to pay for that one.' I let out screams as he tickled my naked body with his bare hands. I felt like a child again.

'I give in. I give in.' I had to surrender before I had a heart attack with all the excitement.

'I was planning on coming in with no clothes on . . . But no, my darling wife had a brighter idea,' he said in a playful tone, and I was very amused at myself.

'You can take them off now.'

'I might not come back in.' I knew that my husband was joking. I would just have to pull him back in. I watched him carefully as he stood up like a soaked rat. He carefully peeled all his clothes off, piece by piece. His body was so elegant and sexy. 'Are you enjoying the show, Mrs Black?' Dale sat back down in front of me, and the bath finally felt complete.

'It was . . . OK. I am sure it could have been better.' Dale reached forward and tickled me again until we were squirming around in the water, laughing and giggling. Dale took my mouth, and suddenly, the playfulness had turned into a sexual nature. It felt so nice. He certainly knew how to take my breath away. I couldn't let his mouth go. I wanted it all night. We had got out of breath so quickly with the passion and the heat of the water. Dale's hand came up to caress my breasts, and it felt electrifying. I let out a whimper as he bit my nipple. My heart was beating so fast that I thought it was going to jump out of my chest. I could feel him in between my legs, and my sex was crying out for him here and now. I suddenly let out a cry as I felt him inside me. The water against my clitoris just made my body tense immediately, and I couldn't stop myself from climaxing so quickly. His muscular body against mine was a pleasure in itself, one that got me on cloud nine. The pleasure lasted and lasted until I felt Dale's body shudder inside me. We lay in the water tangled together, gathering our breath. This had been a nice surprise, one that I wouldn't forget in a hurry. 'Well, that show was better, Mr Black.' Dale splashed me again, and this time the water went in my mouth and I coughed and sat up quickly.

'Ash, I am so sorry.'

'Don't be silly . . . I am not.' I had enjoyed myself, and a little water wasn't going to hurt me. 'Dale, quick get the tap.' The water was nearly over the top, and I would never have noticed if I didn't sit up. Now that wouldn't be good if we flooded the honeymoon suite. I would rather choke as flood the hotel.

'That was close.' Dale came back and lay beside me. His body fit perfectly beside me no matter where we were. 'You are a bad influence on me.' I couldn't help but laugh at that comment. I thought we were both as bad as each other.

'Yeah, right, Dale . . . More like the other way about.' We cuddled up in the nice hot water and enjoyed one another. 'What more could a girl ask for . . . Her two favourite things, right here.'

'What a bath and bubbles?' I slapped Dale's chest and looked up to him.

'A bath and you.' I reached up and put a peck on his lips. Who would have thought I would fall in love because I still found it hard to believe?

'My only favourite thing in the world is . . . you, Ash.' I just knew that he was going to say that; one thing about my husband was his predictability. He ate and slept me, and that wasn't going to change any time soon.

'If I asked you that same question six months ago, what would your answer be?' The room went quiet, and I studied Dale's face closely.

'Probably work.' I should have known that answer because he already told me that he loved work more than life before me. 'What about you, Ash?'

'I honestly have no idea . . . I never really thought about it before . . . a bath.' We both laughed at my final response, only I could make a joke out of a serious conversation.

'We were both sad before we met each other . . . You made me realise that I didn't need to be in the office twenty-four-seven to succeed.'

'Sad . . . Is that what you call it?' That was a new meaning to our pathetic lives.

'As much as I love you, we need to get out of this bath and eat.' I hated that word lately. It always had to come between good moments, moments that we would never get back.

'If we must.' My voice must have said it all. I must have sounded like a child not getting his or her own way. I stood up out of the water and pulled a nice fluffy towel down off the shelf.

'Is my wife in the cream puff?'

'No. I will get my own back on you, Mr . . . I will just drag you off for a Christmas tree and decorations, tomorrow.' I really expected him to say that will be right, send Carlos.

'Sounds like fun. We can make it a Christmas wonderland for Kiara.' I looked at him in disbelief. When was he going to hate one of my suggestions?

'I will keep you to that.' He looked all smug and pleased with himself. One of those faces that you could screw off. I watched him carefully as he walked out of the bathroom. What was he up to?

I quickly got dried and put my fluffy bath robe on. Curiosity got the better of me. I just had to go and see what he was up to. I was more than gobsmacked when I walked into the living area. There was a large bouquet of flowers in the middle of the table and a bottle of champagne that Dale was filling our glasses from.

'Have I missed something?' He walked over to me with a glass and that same cheeky smirk that he left the bathroom with.

'Can I not spoil my wife?' I accepted the glass and took a drink. It was nice and refreshing. 'I have got you a present.' I immediately recognised the bag from the jeweller's and wondered what he had got me. 'Call it an early Christmas present.' I did an exchange; he got my glass and I got the gift bag. I took the box out of the bag and opened it carefully. I couldn't believe what I was seeing. It was a gorgeous gold locket pendant with a guardian angel on the front. 'It is beautiful . . .

Thank you.' For the first time today, I started to cry. All my emotions had boiled over, and I couldn't contain my tears any longer.

'I didn't give you it to upset you, babe.' Dale came and put a hand on my cheek, and the warmth was just what I needed. 'Look at the back.' I turned the locket over and read the writing.

All my love
Dale
x

'It has room for four pictures inside . . . I got four pictures to put in, but you can change them if you like.' I opened the locket, and the first two pictures was one of me and Christine at graduation and the second one was of Kiara. Dale wiped my tears away softly as I revealed the last two pictures. One was of me and Dale at the wedding, and the final picture was my mom and dad. I wrapped my arms around him and cried so hard that it hurt. 'Ash. I didn't mean to upset you.' All I could manage was a shake of my head. 'If you don't like it, you can change it.'

'No. I love it. No one has ever given me a gift and put so much thought into it.' I had done well all day and never cried.

'Do you want me to put it on?' I handed the locket to Dale, and he walked behind me and put it on. I could feel it close to my heart. Dale wrapped his arms around my waist, and I could feel every bit of emotion run away from me. 'We are going to eat before that champagne bubbles your stomach and makes you sick.'

'I actually feel quite hungry tonight . . . But no soup.' What did I fancy though? I was sick to the back teeth of looking at soup that the thought of it made me feel sick.

'That is good to know . . . What do you fancy?'

'I never eat fast food, but I could just eat a burger.' I had no idea where that came from. It was a weird choice for me.

'A burger it is then.' Dale actually looked pleased that I had an appetite tonight. He walked over to the phone and called room service. I suddenly heard a vibration on the table, and as I walked over to the table, I could see Dale's phone vibrating. I half expected it to be Mhairi or Christine but was surprised to see the call from the office. I debated whether to answer it or not, but I thought it might be important. This was my husband's livelihood after all.

'Hello.' After I answered it, I immediately regretted it; whatever it was, was going to ruin our time together. It could of waited. 'Steph . . . Yeah, sweetie, we are fine . . . Shopping and now booked into a hotel . . . No, honestly we are fine. We just wanted some time alone . . . Pop in and see me in the week, and we will organise something . . . OK, sweetie, speak soon . . . Bye.' I hung up the phone and felt a weight lift off my shoulders. We were still in hiding. I knew that Steph would say that she couldn't get us and we were left to carry on with our night.

'Who was that . . . ?' I jumped out of my skin. I forgot all about Dale being close by. I was getting too carried away with being deceitful to our family that I completely forgot about here and now.

'Steph . . . Callum and Christine were on her case all day to get a hold of us . . . But she hasn't heard a thing if they ask.' Steph had made me feel really comfortable when I started work at Black's Enterprise, and we had become really close over the last few weeks. I really didn't want to say goodbye to everyone just now. I wanted to have a long and happy life ahead of me.

'What are you organising, Mrs Black?' I did sense that he thought I wasn't telling him something. But he was barking up the wrong tree this time.

'A girls' spa day . . . Is that OK with you?' I didn't mean to sound sarcastic, but it just came out. I felt like I couldn't do anything lately without the whole world knowing what I was going to do, and it wasn't just Dale who was being overprotective; it was everyone who knew me.

'I wouldn't have asked if I knew it was a girl's day . . . I thought you were planning on going to work.' That never even crossed my mind, but now he had mentioned it. I didn't think it would be the worst idea that I had going on in my mind.

'Like you would allow me to work.' The Jack Russell had got out of the cage tonight. It was becoming quite funny because I knew that I was doing now.

'You're right there, Ash . . . Girl's day . . . Shopping . . . Spas . . . Are all fine . . . Work . . . And doing too much is a definite no.' I lifted my glass of champagne and finished my glass. I was having too much fun to discuss what I could and couldn't do.

'Now that we have got that cleared up, can we get back to our night?' Although it was only Steph on the phone, it had still got us off par. I was sure that we would quickly find our feet again if we put the call to the back of our minds.

'Of course, babe . . . Come here.' I quickly did as I was told and stood centimetres away from him. It was a pity that I didn't do as I was told like that all the time. Life would be so much easier for us all. 'I only fuss a lot because I love you . . . And I don't want anything to happen sooner than mother nature intends.' I crept up on my toes and kissed his lips. I could understand his point of view. I would probably be ten times worse if the shoe was on the other foot and it was Dale who was dying.

'No more fussing tonight . . . I mean it, Dale.'

'I will try.' I raised my eyebrows because deep down I knew 'try' meant nothing. 'OK. OK. I promise. No more fussing tonight.' Parents fuss. Old people fuss. Husbands were not supposed to be as bad. I would just have to put my foot down and get the Jack Russell out of the box. Now, that was something that no one really liked to see.

CHAPTER 20

Facing the Music

We pulled up outside the cottage, and already we knew we were going to be in trouble. Carlos was in the Mercedes, and Christine's car was parked beside it. 'What have we done?' I actually felt like a criminal, and we were in serious trouble for committing a crime.

'Ash, we are two consenting adults, and they will get told that.' Carlos came walking over to my car, and we got out to meet him. Dale didn't seem in any kind of mood to be dealing with his mother right now. They could clash at the best of times so I could imagine what today was going to be like.

'You are keen going in there to face the lions.' Carlos had seen them; he knew exactly what mood they were in.

'Just be ready to leave, Carlos, because they will all need a ride home.' We all shared a smile together, and Dale took my hand. I was a nervous wreck as we headed into our cottage. I wouldn't like to see me if I had actually committed a crime, I would be in a right state. All eyes glared on to us the minute we walked in, and I tightened Dale's hand to keep him close to me. They were like a pack of wolves preying on their kill. We couldn't understand a word any of them were saying as they were all shouting over one another. It was like some kind of competition between Mhairi and Christine, to see who could shout at us the most.

'Enough.' I had never really heard Dale shout like that before. He startled me, never mind them. 'We are two consenting adults . . . We do not need to ask any one's permission to go shopping . . . or to spend the night away.' Dale was very harsh, but they both shut up and listened. 'Anyone who doesn't like that . . .' Dale opened the front door and looked back to everyone. 'There is the door.' The cottage was silent, and no one muttered a word. The silence was only broken by Carlos, bringing our bags and my flowers in from the car.

'Just stick the bags in the room please, Carlos.' I took my flowers out of his hand and placed them down on to the table. I needed any excuse to not look at everyone.

'Ash, we were worried sick.' Christine sounded terrified, and for once in my life, I didn't let her guilt trip me. I didn't feel at all bad.

'We went to see Tom yesterday . . . Afterwards, we went shopping, and it got late, so we booked into a hotel . . . It is our honeymoon after all.' I really didn't know why I was explaining myself because it had nothing to do with anyone.

'But you could take clothes?' Christine always noticed the finest detail, and I cringed inside.

'Actually . . .' All eyes peered around to Carlos, like they were getting ready to attack him. 'I took them their things last night.' Carlos didn't have to stick up for us, but he did, and it took guts in front of this pair.

'I asked you several times last night if you had heard from them and you said no.' Mhairi was very angry, and I didn't know how to take her when she was angry. She was bad enough when she was in a normal kind of mood.

'Dale and Ashley asked me to say nothing, and no offence, I do work for them.'

'How dare you speak to me like that, young man?' Mhairi was like a mad woman tonight, and we had made her like that.

'Mom, enough . . . Carlos is right. He works for me and Ashley, and I told him to say nothing . . . Behave.' This whole situation had been blown out of proportion for no reason. I swung around from the table and banged my hand down to get their attention. I had heard enough.

'If you all don't shut up and stop this nonsense right now, I will walk out of that door and not come back . . . I am sick to the back teeth of it all now . . . I am dying . . . With weeks left to live . . . do you want to spend that time arguing amongst yourselves?' I felt really bad that I just shouted at Dale's mom, but they were doing my head in.

'Ashley is right . . . I am sick of it all, and I am just listening to you all.' I had never really heard Jake answer Mhairi back, and by the look on her face, she hadn't either.

'Everyone out. Now. Let these kids settle back home . . . And from tomorrow, no one better step over that door if they can't be nice.' Christine, Mhairi, Callum, and Jake picked up their things and headed for the door. I couldn't believe how quickly they all followed orders. It was unbelievable.

'Thank you, Jake.' I appreciated everything Jake just did for us. He could have sat back and let the wolves descend, but he did the decent thing and stopped them from attacking us.

'Don't mention it, dear . . . I will see you tomorrow morning with breakfast.' I got my hug and kiss on each cheek before he left. I just wished Mhairi and Christine could take a leaf out of Jake's book.

'Do you need anything done before I go?' Carlos stayed behind to make sure there was nothing he could do. But he had already done too much for us.

'No, thanks, Carlos . . . And don't take any nonsense from my mom.' Carlos patted Dale on the shoulder before he left as well. Why do we keep finding ourselves in deep water? We didn't have to go looking for trouble; it would just find us.

'Thank God for you and your dad.' I went and slumped on the sofa and put my feet up on the table. The fire was blazing, and I just loved how cosy this cottage was. It took away all the cares of the world and left me feeling fresh and relaxed.

'I don't think my dad has ever spoken back to my mom before . . . It has only been a matter of time though.'

'Has she always been like that?' I was curious to know what Mhairi was like in her younger years because I didn't know how Jake put up with it all at times.

'Yeah, if something wasn't going her own way . . . But this is one thing that she isn't going to get her own way with.'

'I don't want you to argue with your family over me.'

'You are my family, Ash . . . It is only my mom, and she will back down, especially now that my dad has told her what he thinks.'

'That just leaves Christine.' Hopefully, she would back down now as well. She was just like Mhairi, always used to getting her own way.

'Can we forget about them all and get back to planning Christmas . . . ? We can have a New Year's party, if you like.' He took on board how my parents liked throwing parties. It would be nice to start 2013 on a high, and it would give me a sense of family tradition back in my life.

'Sounds like a plan.' I couldn't stop smiling. I felt at peace, just me and Dale having fun together and no mention of cancer or death.

'So what about this Christmas tree?' I was amazed he remembered. 'Do you want to go and get one?'

'Do babies cry . . . ? Just try and stop me.' I was up and wrapped up before Dale could say 'OK'. This day was just getting better and better, and I didn't want it to stop. We headed out to the car, and I jumped into the passenger's seat. I fancied a rest while I was all excited. I was just like a child tonight.

'We will need to get lights and decorations . . . Kiara will love them.' Kiara was the perfect excuse to get all giddy. Children make Christmas feel special and worthwhile.

'This will be our first Christmas together. We will make it one to remember, babe.'

'Where do we go for a tree?' I had been in Anchorage for a few months, and I still had no idea where anything was. I was too used to getting taken wherever I needed to go.

'Just outside town. There is a yard that sells all shapes and sizes, and there is a general store in town that stocks all kinds of decorations.' Christmas is the season to be jolly with friends and family. Have a laugh and a good time. Forgive and forget. My mom would never let a Christmas and New Year go by holding any grudges. She would say it was a time for fresh starts. 'What are you thinking about, Ash?'

'Just family and Christmas . . . I had a good upbringing, and my parents always made Christmas special . . . I always thought that I would follow in my parents' footsteps and show my kids . . . a good Christmas.'

Not having kids would be the hardest thing. I would have to do as a vampire, and I thought that it was going to haunt me.

'We can spoil Kiara, even more.' I would love and care for Kiara, like she was my own, but my maternal side would never be satisfied. It would always have thirst for what it couldn't get.

'She will be one spoiled little princess.'

'I like listening to your stories about your family.' I put my hand on my husband's leg and squeezed it. He was my family now. We could make our own stories together.

'I am sure you will get fed up of them.'

'Never.' We pulled into this small car park, and I could see real Christmas trees of all sizes everywhere. The fresh dusting of snow made them look traditional and beautiful.

'It is beginning to look a lot like Christmas.' We got out of the car, and Dale came around to me and took my hand.

'You can have any tree you want.' I gripped his hand and walked into the yard.

'Dale Black . . . Good to see you again.' This older man came and shook Dale's hand. He looked too old to be in this line of business, but who was I to judge him?

'Bob . . . Nice to see you again . . . This is my wife, Ashley.'

'Ashley, I have heard a lot about you.' I looked confused. Why did this stranger know about me? 'I take it you are looking for a tree.'

'We wouldn't be in your yard if we didn't want a tree.' I couldn't help my sarcastic tone. I just didn't feel comfortable if everyone was talking about me behind my back.

'Yes, Bob. We are looking for a nice big tree.' Dale jumped in after my sarcastic outburst. He must have known something was on my mind.

'That one is perfect.' I pointed to a nice bushy tree standing on its own. It had our name on it.

'We will take that one, Bob.'

'Delivered to the house, Dale?'

'No, the cottage in the mountain.' Bob looked a bit surprised, but he never questioned our choice. 'We are going out for a while, but you leave it at the door.'

'Sure, no problem.' I already started walking to the car. I didn't like Bob much, and I couldn't hide my feelings. I climbed back into the car and waited for Dale to join me. I felt annoyed.

'Are you OK?'

'What did he mean, he had heard a lot about me?'

'This is a town, doll . . . News travels quick . . . I don't think he meant any harm by it.' I had never thought about the locals knowing all about me. 'Don't let it get to you, Ash.'

'Let's get the decorations.' This was one of the joys of living in a community with a man who owns more property than he knows what to do with. 'Dale, stop the car.' The sudden urge to be sick crept up on me, and I needed out. Dale pulled over, and I jumped out. I just got out when I was sick so much that I hurt myself. I thought that my insides were going to come up as well. My loving husband was out in a shot, standing beside me rubbing my back. Just when I was thinking that it was all a mistake, I got another setback, and it made it all feel real.

'Are you OK, sweetheart?' That was the worst sickness I had ever felt.

'It is getting worse . . .' I was helped to sit back in the car, and my body felt very weak and I felt cold from head to toe.

'Do you want to go home?'

'No. Definitely not . . . A drink of water and a mint and I will be fine.' I got my legs in the car, and Dale shut my door behind me. I felt everything inside me boil over, and I was overcome with everything flooding into my head.

'We can stop at the store and get water . . . Put your seat belt on.' I hated it when Dale got concerned and panic; he was like an old sweetish wife. I lay my head back on the rest and waited for the car to stop. It felt like forever, but it was only a few minutes. I hated what this illness was doing to my husband because it just wasn't fair.

'Wait here, and I will be back in a minute.' I didn't even lift my head to acknowledge him. My stomach was in agony from pulling muscles when I was sick. I could feel muscles that I didn't know existed. This had to be the worst that I had felt in all of this. Even when I had my first setback, I didn't feel like I did today. It was a different sort of feeling.

'Here you go, babe.' Quick as a flash, it sprang to mind. The water was really cold, and it did the trick. 'I got you some mints as well.'

'Thanks.'

'We will quickly get the decorations and get you home.' The shop was just along the street so there was no more travelling. 'Will you be OK to walk?'

'Of course, I can.' I unlocked the belt and got out of the car. Dale was by my side in a heartbeat. We took a slow walk up the street to the store, and I felt like I was floating along. There was Christmas lights in the window, and I wanted to get excited all over again, but my body was running on empty. The minute we walked into the store, I heard the Christmas music and could smell cinnamon. It was very Christmas in here, and I would have normally loved everything that I was seeing.

'Hi, Moira.' Was there anyone in this town whom Dale didn't know? It didn't matter where we went someone always knew him.

'Dale, hello, sweetie . . . How are you doing?'

'I am good. Thanks . . . I would like you to meet my wife, Ashley.' I should have been honoured that he wanted to show me off to everyone, but I couldn't shift the feeling that everyone was talking about me.

'Hello, my dear . . . Congratulations on getting married. You really make a lovely couple.' I managed a smile, but I didn't feel much like talking. 'How can I help you today?'

'We are looking for decorations . . . Just give us a bit of everything you have.' Dale was in a hurry to get me home, and now I was wishing that I was tucked up in bed.

'Give me five minutes, and I will have it all ready for you.' Moira seemed really nice. She probably knew all about my cancer, but she didn't make it obvious like Bob did.

'Ash, are you OK? You are very pale.' I leant my head into his chest to compose myself.

'I am not going to lie because if I look how I feel, you will know the truth . . . I haven't felt like this before.' I owed him the truth, and that is what I was giving to him straight.

'We will call Dr Ching when we get home, just for the once-over.' It wasn't necessary. He wasn't going to tell us anything we didn't already know. But I didn't want to protest in the middle of the store, and if it made Dale feel comfortable, then it was a must.

'Dale, I have mixed it all up for you.'

'Thanks, Moira.'

'I hope you enjoy putting it all up.' I felt very rude in the store because I never spoke one word to Moira. She must have thought that I was a right ignorant bitch.

'Paul will give you a hand out to the car with it all.'

'Thanks.' I didn't think Dale remembered that we had my car. Where were we going to put it all? We headed back along the street to my car, and I just hoped that they could fit it in, but I was doubtful. The way I felt right now, I just couldn't care as long as I got home.

'Nice car.'

'It is Ashley's. She likes it as well.' Everyone was obsessed with my car. It didn't matter who saw it. They loved it.

'It is a dream to drive.' It was a good car. It was just a shame that I didn't drive it much. I couldn't really remember much about my time before the cancer; it was all a distant memory now.

'Thanks, Paul.'

'No worries.' Paul seemed like a nice kid. He had done us a huge favour, helping us to the car. Dale would have had to struggle on his own if he didn't give us assistance.

'Right, Mrs, let's get you home.' Home was a nice word to hear when you felt rotten. The cottage was my home, and I loved every inch of it. I felt comfortable when I was there, and nothing would ever feel the same to me.

'Home is where the heart is.' Dale just caught the end of my sentence when he got in the car. I didn't mean for him to hear me say it out loud, but I guessed that is what happens when you are not thinking straight.

'What was that?'

'Home is where the heart is. My dad always used to say it to us.' I didn't mean to say it out loud, but my mouth ran away with me. But now I could see what it meant, and my heart was here in Anchorage, in our cottage. I closed my eyes and let my husband drive us home. I had never felt as bad as I do right now, and it was probably only going to get worse. Animals get put to sleep for less. It was unfair how we get to suffer in such a way; humans certainly get the short end of the straw.

'Ashley, darling, we are home.' I must have fallen asleep. But now I felt a hundred times worse. My head was bursting, and my body was aching. 'Are you going to manage or do you want me to carry you?'

'I should be fine . . . Just don't let me fall.' Dale came around to help me into the cottage, and I felt like an old person with his or her carer. Whatever had happened over the last hour had certainly floored me.

'Just take your time, babe.' As much as I wanted to say, I could run a marathon. My legs could hardly carry my weight. We reached the cottage, and I made my way to the couch. This couch could make anyone feel better, but I thought it was going to take a little bit more tonight. 'Sit there and I will phone Dr Ching.' Dale quickly ran over to the phone and dialled the number. Everything went quiet for a few seconds, and it was bliss. I just wanted to curl up and fall asleep.

'Hello, Dr Ching, this is Dale Black, Ashley's husband . . . I am not sure. Ashley isn't right at all . . . Bad sickness and not steady on her feet . . . She also said that she has never felt as bad . . . OK . . . Thank you.' Dale took his jacket and threw it on the chair. He was like a flapping bird again.

'What did he say?'

'He is going to come over.' Of course, he was. Why did I think he wouldn't? 'Let me help you with your jacket.'

'It is OK now. I feel quite cold.' Dale picked his cell up, and I wondered whom he was calling now. Everything was happening too quickly, and I didn't feel like I was getting a chance to breath.

'Hey, Carlos, can you come over and help me please?' I was surprised that Dale could have phoned any number of people, and he chose Carlos. 'Ashley has taken unwell, and I have a fire to go on and a hundred-and-one decorations to sort out . . . Dr Ching is on his way . . . Thanks, Carlos, you are a good friend.' The phone got thrown on to his jacket, and he came and sat on the floor beside me curled up on the couch. 'Can I get you anything, Ash?' I felt his warm hand stroke my cheek, and it was the only comfort that I needed. The heat from his hand gave me a sense of belonging, and it was nice to feel him close.

'I am fine.' Anyone could see that I wasn't fine, but it sounded good all the same.

'We have done too much, babe . . . I should have put my foot down and made you rest.'

'These things are going to happen whether I rest or not . . . Don't beat yourself up about it.' I certainly didn't regret a thing that we had done over the last couple of days. If I had my time all over again, I would do it all again and maybe more.

'Dale.' I recognised the voice immediately. Carlos must have flown up the mountain.

'In here, Carlos.' I could see the fear in his face the minute he sat in the chair opposite me.

'Your parents are following behind with Callum . . . Your mom heard me speaking to you.' That was all we needed, round two with Mhairi. Perfect.

'Great.' I really didn't mean to sound horrible, but I could do without Mhairi right now.

'Sorry, Ash.' Carlos sounded guilty, and it wasn't even his fault.

'Hello.'

'In here, Dr Ching.' Dale jumped up like a jack in the box to greet the doctor. 'She is on the sofa, Doc.' The doctor came and sat at my feet, and I just didn't want to hear any more bad news. I just wanted peace to let it all pass.

'Carlos, can you chop wood for the fire, please?' Carlos was up and out before I could say boo.

'You look hellish, Ashley. What has happened?' All the times that I wanted him to be honest with me and he lied, and here he was giving it to me straight at how hellish I look. I couldn't win.

'I had to get Dale to stop the car. I was that sick that much I have hurt all my tummy muscles . . . And now I just feel so weak and powerless.' He looked very concerned as he opened his case. I just wanted to get everything all done and dusted and have time to sleep.

'OK, Ashley, we will get a few checks done and take it from there . . . OK?' I didn't get much chance to speak when my worst nightmare had just happened. Dale's family walked through the front door.

'Do you want to go into the kitchen?' Dale still sounded off with his mum, and it was uncomfortable to hear. But whatever had changed? They all followed his orders.

'What could it be, Doc?' I was getting all my vital signs checked, and Dr Ching never answered Dale. I looked at Dale, with concern of my own, and he came and sat on the arm at my head and took my hand. I was glad that he could read my mind at times like this because it saves me sounding like a baby.

'Blood pressure is on the low side . . . Temperature is quite high . . . Heart rate is high, but that is to be expected if you are sore . . . I am going to give you an injection for the sickness . . . Drink plenty of fluids to keep you hydrated . . .' My head was spinning back and forward with him throwing everything at me. 'Do you want something for the pain?'

'Please.' I couldn't fight the pain any more. I had to take some pain relief. Maybe if the pain went away, I would feel a little bit more human.

'I can put a line in your arm and give you some morphine through it.' I hated the thought of taking morphine, and my body tensed at the thought of it. 'I will take some blood as well, just to compare them to previous results . . .'

'So what do you think it is, Doc?' Dale was eager to get to the bottom of what was wrong, and I was glad that he was asking because if it was left to me, I wouldn't ask.

'Do you want me to be honest . . . ?'

'Yes, of course, we do.' In a way, I didn't want to be in the dark about anything, but in another way, I felt like what I didn't know wouldn't hurt me.

'It is just the cancer progressing, and the body is trying to fight it off . . . Unfortunately, it is only going to get worse as time passes . . . But now that Ashley is willing for me to give her pain relief and anti-sickness, it will help her cope more.' I felt like a huge blow had hit me. My time on this earth was slowly running out, and no one could stop it. 'You can leave if you are funny with needles.'

'No. I am not moving.' I knew that Dale was going to say that and was glad because I hated needles.

'Can I get you to sit up and take your many layers off?' Dr Ching held his hand out to help me get up, and I could see Mhairi and Jake in the kitchen. I took my jacket off and then my jumper until I was just sitting with my vest top on. 'Perfect.' Dale squeezed my hand to reassure me that everything was going to be fine, but I couldn't share his enthusiasm. 'Getting this line in can be very sore, sweetheart. I will do it as quick as possible.' Why did he have to tell me that? My nerves were in full swing now, and my stomach was doing cartwheels. Our coffee table was like something out of theatre. Everything was sterile and felt totally unnecessary. 'Sharp scratch.' I squeezed Dale's hand that hard that I felt bad; he must be in just as much pain as I was.

'Ouch.' I felt like a big wimp, sitting with tears in my eyes.

'That is the line in . . . I will stick it in place before I administer the morphine . . . I will give you the anti-sickness in the other arm.'

'Why me? What have I done that is so bad that this has had to happen to me?' I was feeling sorry for myself tonight, and I couldn't shake it off even if I tried.

'Unfortunately, sweetheart, this disease doesn't care where it pops up.' If only we had a choice, it was my initial thought. 'I am going to put the morphine through now . . . She can't be on her own after she gets this.' I let out a snide snigger, like that was ever going to happen.

'No chance of that happening, Doc.'

'Aaahhh.' My arm was in agony. I felt like someone was cutting it off, and the circulation was restricted.

'It is going right into the muscle. That is why it is sore.' Dr Ching didn't even flinch to do all this. If I was the doctor, I would be in tears with the patient. My head went all fuzzy, and my body felt warm. All I could do was lay my head back on the sofa and close my eyes. The only good thing was that it made me feel nice and warm. 'The funny feeling will pass.' Thank God for that because it wasn't nice. 'I am just going to take some bloods, and that will be all for tonight.' I felt like screaming 'just get on with it', but the Jack Russell looked away.

'Will this stay in?' I indicated to the tube hanging from my arm. It wasn't very nice looking, and it was just going to be another reminder that I was ill.

'Yes. It can stay there . . . It is easier to give you morphine . . . Even more so now that you need it.'

'Ash . . . Dale.' Now this was all I needed, Christine as well as Mhairi. Could no one knock on a door?

'In here, Christine.' Dale sounded just as furious.

'What is going on?' I couldn't even lift my head up; the morphine had floored me.

'Christine, do you want to go into the kitchen with my family? I will explain to you all when Dr Ching is finished.' For once, Christine never argued; she just did as she was told.

'OK, Ashley, that is us all done, for now.'

'Thanks.'

'Remember, plenty of fluids . . . Rest when you can and don't overdo things. I will come back in four hours to see how you are, and if any medication needs repeated, I will do it for you . . . Although, if I feel that the morphine should be done regularly, I will get your nurse to pop in and give you it.'

'Thank you, Dr Ching. We really appreciate all you are doing.' I could hear the appreciation in Dale's voice.

'It is what I am here for . . . I will see myself out.' Dale shook his hand, and Dr Ching packed all his things up. 'If you need me before I return, don't hesitate to call.' Dr Ching hadn't even left the living room and everyone was coming out of the kitchen. Even Carlos came in from outside, with the logs for the fire. I would be glad to get the fire on because I felt frozen to the bone.

'Right . . . Before you all start, I am sure you all heard Dr Ching say that Ashley needs plenty of rest and no stress.' Dale was a typical man; he could exaggerate a lot when he wanted to.

'What did he say, Son?' Jake came and sat on the table in front of us, and I managed to straighten my head up to look at him.

'The disease is progressing, and Ashley's body is trying to fight it off . . . He has put a line in for morphine and gave her anti-sickness medication. It will help Ashley cope with it all a lot better.' Dale was good at repeating; he should have been a doctor. There was no expression in anything he was saying. He was dying inside as well, and no one could take it all away from him.

'Are you going to listen this time, Ash?'

'It looks like I have no choice at the minute.' Christine came and sat beside me and placed her hand in mine. We both shared a smile, but if she was waiting for me to apologise, she was going to have a long wait.

'Please, Ash . . . Let us get Christmas and New Year with you.' Christine hugged me softly, and my body accepted her like it was so natural. It felt nice to have my friend back in my arms.

'I promise to see Christmas and New Year.' This was one promise that I was determined to keep. Nothing was going to take me away before then.

'Who wants to help me turn the cottage into a wonderland . . . ? We have so many decorations that we could decorate Anchorage.' I smiled at Christine because I knew that she also loved Christmas, just like I did.

'Where do you want me? I love Christmas.' I knew that Christine was doing all this for me, but it was a memory that would last forever. My husband and my best friend were getting along, without any argument. I felt like I was in some kind of a dream.

'Carlos, will you get the fire going? Dad, will you bring the tree in? Callum, will you help me unload the car? Mom, you keep Ashley drinking! Christine, you can tell us where to put everything.' Everyone was up and doing their jobs, no huffs or puffs. Dale came down to my level and kissed me so softly. It was like I was going to break. 'You can enjoy the show, babe.'

'Thank you.' I sat back and watched my family working together to make Christmas magical. I felt like I was a child again. Every year when I was growing up, we came together as a family to celebrate Christmas. The house always used to smell like a bakery with my mom's baking. I should be like a beach whale with all the cookies I ate. I didn't know how anyone could hate Christmas. Even now on my last few weeks, I loved the thought of celebrating Christmas with all my nearest and dearest.

Three Weeks Later

CHAPTER 21

It Is Christmas

Christmas Eve had approached us very quickly. The last three weeks had been tough, but I had enjoyed having my family around me. I had had a long ride on a roller coaster and just hoped that it would end very soon. Everyone had been on their best behaviour, and there was no fighting or arguing amongst themselves. It felt like everyone was doing it all because I wanted them to, not because it was the best thing to do. I had reached Christmas Eve, and it is a time for celebrating and appreciating what we have. I didn't want to give up what I believe in because I was ill. I had spent most of my last couple of weeks curled up on the sofa with a big woolly blanket. It kept me warm when Dale wasn't curled up beside me. This cancer has taken everything from me, but I wasn't going to let it take Christmas from me as well. I looked around the cottage, and it was very quiet and peaceful. The tree was big and beautifully decorated. The decorations were dazzling; it was perfect. My family had done me proud, and I couldn't ask for any more. I knew that I was failing fast and that it was only a matter of time before my body gave up all together. But I was still ready to face our first Christmas as a proper family, no matter how bad I feel.

'Here we go, doll.' I was so wrapped up in Christmas and family that I forgot all about Dale cooking me breakfast. He handed me a tray with freshly squeezed orange juice, fresh fruit salad, and pancakes, my favourites. I was trying to eat as much as I could recently because I knew that was one thing that everyone noticed, and they also noticed how much weight that I had lost in such a short time. I wasn't gravely thin, but I noticed it in myself because I was always curvy and cuddly. It was always a joke between me and Christine because I hated how I looked when I was younger.

'You are spoiling me.'

'Only the best for my wife.' Dale had always treated me like a princess, and I was surprised at how much I liked it now. 'My mom is coming around in a little while to start the preparations for tomorrow . . .' I knew that Mhairi was coming over, and she didn't bother me when she was here, as long as she was in a good mood with everyone. 'She will give you your space, babe.' I was enjoying my food too much to even say anything. 'Rosa is coming to lend a hand.' Now that was music to my ears. I haven't seen Rosa for weeks.

'It will be nice to see her.' I really enjoyed Rosa's company when we lived in the house. It was going to be nice seeing her.

'I knew that you would like to see her . . . I have asked Rosa and Carlos to join us tomorrow.' I sometimes had to pinch myself, just to make sure that Dale was real. He was so kind and thoughtful that sometimes you felt like you were in a dream.

'I love you, Mr Black . . . It means a lot to me that we will all be together tomorrow.' Carlos and Rosa were as good as family anyway. It made perfect sense to have them here with us. One year ago, it was me and Christine, facing the world together. But here I was now with an extended family and friends around me, and I was grateful to have each and every one of them in my life.

'I love you more, Mrs Black.' I sat enjoying my fruit. It was so fresh and juicy every time I ate it, that I was sure Dale picks it fresh every day.

'So what needs to be done today?' Dale about broke his neck as he shot a look in my direction. I actually couldn't stop myself from laughing at his expression.

'You won't be lifting a finger, that is for sure . . . There is enough helpers at hand.' I really didn't like sitting watching everyone work around me. It made me feel very awkward. I liked to help and be kept busy; it made the day pass quicker.

'Can I ask you a favour?'

'You can ask, but don't count on getting the reply you want.' If he thought that I was going to do too much, the answer would be no. I had learnt too well over the last few weeks that he was running a tight ship, and I wasn't given too much rope to hinge myself.

'Can we go to midnight mass at church tonight?' I was looking at my fruit, cringing at his response.

'Sure.' I looked up slowly, thinking that the morphine had messed with my ears. 'We should go. It will be nice to see Tom.'

'Thank you.' I hadn't been to mass since I was a child, and it felt appropriate to go tonight. I was going to have to face a lot of people, but I felt ready. As long as I had Dale by my side, I would get through anything.

'Our peace is shattered.' As usual you could hear Mhairi before you saw her.

'Hellooo.' She was too loud and cheerful for this time of morning.

'Hey, Mom.' Kiara's crying was coming to greet us. We hadn't seen her for ages so that was a nice surprise this morning.

'Aw, what is wrong with princess Kiara?' Dale took my tray and placed it on the table. 'Let me see her.'

'Are you sure, love? She is very heavy now.' I felt really hurt that Mhairi could say such a thing. I was more than capable to hold and care for Kiara.

'I wouldn't have asked if I wasn't sure.' I wanted to tear a strip from her, but I thought that I better bite my tongue. Everything had been so calm lately, and I wasn't going to be the one to spoil that.

'Here we go, my dear . . . She knows that she is in Aunty Ashley's house.' Jake sounded very angry at Mhairi, but I was glad that he gave her to me.

'Hello, my princess . . . Look at you in your lovely dress . . . You have got a big girl.' I was in my glory now that I had Kiara. Nothing else mattered. Everyone could do what they liked because I had my distraction.

'Mom, a word . . . now.' Dale was very angry as he stormed out of the cottage in a hurry, and I cringed at the thought of him having words with his mom. Jake and I watched as Mhairi followed behind him like a naughty child.

'She is never going to learn.'

'Jake, please don't let them argue . . . She doesn't mean it.' I couldn't take any tension in the cottage, especially at Christmas. I was sticking up for Mhairi, but I knew that she didn't think before she spoke. She probably had my best interests at heart.

'I will give them five minutes, and I will go and rescue them.' Jake was such a lovely man. He and Mhairi were two different characters. It amazed me how their marriage had survived all these years.

'Is Santa Claus coming to you tonight? Yes, he is beautiful.'

'You are a natural with her . . . She adores you.' My heart melted when I heard Jake say those words to me. I felt very proud to have any part of her in my life, even if she was only my niece. She had got me through some of the difficult times, and when I thought that I couldn't go any further, I thought about her little face and she saw me through.

'I adore her, Jake . . . I always dreamt that one day I would have a daughter and she would be just like Kiara . . . But you are one lucky girl to have a big family that loves you.' I picked her up to my shoulder to give her a cuddle, and tears rolled down my cheeks. 'You all better look after her, or I will come back and haunt you all.'

'You and Dale would have made perfect parents . . . It kills me to watch you both go through this terrible ordeal. If I could only exchange places with you, I would.' Jake sat down beside me, and I placed my hand over his. This was the first time that he had ever expressed any feelings to me over my cancer, and I didn't think that it had affected him in such a way.

'It has been an honour to get to you guys, and I just hope that when I am gone, you can all continue to be one big happy family.' I knew that I was asking a lot because this family held too many different characters, but it was the only thing that I had ever asked of Jake.

'Leland is the best, Ashley. I know that you might think that he is letting you die deliberately, but he will be here when the time comes . . . I have faith in him.' I was glad that Jake had faith in Leland, because I certainly didn't.

'Dad, can you give us a minute?' I didn't realise that Dale was standing there. Did he hear everything I had just said? I was actually enjoying my little chat with Jake too much that I never realised that anyone had come back in.

'I will go and gather wood for the fire.' Dale came and sat beside Kiara and me on the couch; he looked in pain, like something had happened. I knew now that he had everything that Jake and I were saying, and it was playing on his mind.

'What is wrong, sweetie?' I just knew by his facial expression that he heard it all, but now I was worried as to what he was going to say.

'I wanted to give you everything you ever dreamt of . . .' His head bowed down, and I felt hurt and awful for making him feel inadequate. 'But no amount of money is ever going to give you the one thing you need . . . I can never give you a child . . . That maternal instinct is never going to get weaker.' The tears were rolling down both of our cheeks, and Kiara was quite happy playing with my blanket. I felt dead inside. I just wanted to say that he was wrong and that everything would be OK, but he knew me too well. He knew that I longed to be a mother and that wasn't going to go away over night.

'Where is this going, Dale?' I wanted to know what he was thinking? What was going on in his head? Would he be able to cope without a family or have I hurt him too much? I could go on all day thinking about the negative things that I had caused in this man's life.

'When we are settled as . . . You know . . . We can use your eggs . . . We can have a baby of our own.' He wanted me to be happy, and he would go to any lengths to make my dreams come true, but I didn't think it would feel the same as an immortal.

'Dale, please stop. You are going to drive yourself crazy . . . I have you and we have our niece. We can watch her grow up . . .' His eyes never looked at me once, and I could feel how heartbroken this poor man was. 'Yes, I wanted to be a mom. I wanted to carry your child and believe me that is killing me . . . But I will never carry our baby, and I will always have a part of me that doesn't feel complete . . . But I am happy to be a part of Kiara's life, for as long as I can . . . We have each other to guide us through the good and bad times.' Nothing was ever straightforward for us. We always had a mountain to climb. I really wanted to turn the clocks back and have our time over again, to feel the love that we shared all over again. I thought that we held back on a lot of thoughts and feelings because we thought that we would have had a long and happy life together. Little did we know that it was the start and the end, all rolled into one.

'I just don't like to see you do without something you want.' I could understand exactly how he felt because he wanted to give me everything that I had dreamt of. He was a proud man who wanted to give his family everything. But in my eyes, he had given me a life that I thought I would never have, and I was truly thankful to him.

'I have you, Dale, and that is all I ever need . . . Let's have a nice Christmas, for Kiara's sake.' I turned Kiara around to face us, and Dale put his arm around me. I would never want for anything as long as I had him, and I just wanted him to realise that. We had a relationship that would survive anything, and I wasn't ready to let go of everything yet. 'Where are all those stories . . . ? Tell your uncle Dale those stories.' Kiara was such a happy baby. It was such a pleasure to sit with her. I had loved watching her flourish and grow into a beautiful little girl. I just hoped that I got to see her grow into a beautiful young lady.

'I better tell everyone that they can come in before they freeze.' I couldn't help but giggle. Everyone was outside in the snow and ice, and we were sitting putting the world to rights. We should have, maybe, left them out there for a while longer. It would teach them all a valuable lesson—not to get in my bad books.

'We thought that you had forgotten all about us out there.' That was wishful thinking; chance would be a fine thing. I was surprised that Mhairi stayed out there as long without making herself heard.

'You can get back to your kitchen, Mom.' This was going to be a funny sort of day. I could feel it in my blood. Mhairi and Dale were acting funny around each other, and they were both like a ticking bomb waiting to go off.

'Ashley . . . Oh my, look at you.' Rosa hadn't seen me for a while so she would notice a difference in me. I didn't know if I was pleased or not to hear someone notice how poor I looked. I knew it how ill I probably looked, but it was different when someone made it obvious to you.

'Rosa.' We gave each other a hug, and she started to cry. Everyone that I knew just couldn't hold their emotions in around me. It was like I brought their tears and sorrow out of them. 'Please don't, Rosa . . . I am fine.'

'I think that you are an amazing woman, Ashley . . . So courageous.'

'Thank you, honey, that means a lot.' I could feel the tears well up in the back of my eyes, and I tried my hardest to keep them locked in.

'I am sorry, Ashley . . . No more tears. I promise. We will have a nice Christmas.' Rosa headed into the kitchen to be beside Mhairi. This was a recipe for disaster, to have two strong women in the kitchen, who were both more than capable to organise a Christmas dinner. I would love to be a fly on the wall today. I knew that Rosa needed to go into the kitchen because she wouldn't contain her tears sitting with me. She was such a lovely person, and I loved her for how well she took care of me and Dale. Not many housekeepers would come highly recommended by me.

'Christine has just pulled up outside.' Christine had been great over the last couple of weeks. I didn't know what I would have done without her support. I didn't like putting my foot down to everyone, but it was clearly needed for them all to get along together.

'Hey, guys.' Christine was back to her bubbly self, and it was nice to finally see. All the anger and rebellious behaviour had faded away, and I had my best friend back. I knew that the next week was going to test everyone's patience, but we were all going to have to be strong for one another.

'Hey, yourself.'

'Budge over, you two, stealing all the couch.'

'Tell your aunty Christine to sit on the chair.' We were enjoying the banter with one another, and it felt like an ordinary Christmas Eve or as ordinary as it could be under the circumstances.

'Your aunty Ashley is getting too big for her boots.'

'Christine, take her.' I quickly had to get up because I knew that I was going to be sick. I hated the feeling that just came out of nowhere. But I stumbled over Christine's feet and banged my head on the table. I felt really embarrassed over the whole situation.

'Ashley . . . Dale, quick.' Everyone came running at Christine, screaming like a town crier. Everything had happened in slow motion, and I couldn't save myself. Even if I wasn't ill, I would have found it hard to save myself after the way I tripped up.

'Ashley, are you OK?' Dale was in a state, and there was blood on the floor that made it look worse.

'I feel OK . . . Just a cut . . . I need the . . .' I was sick on the floor, and the embarrassment soared right through me. I just wanted the ground to open up and eat me.

Mhairi and Jake disappeared with Kiara, and I wondered what was wrong with them, but I had more important things to deal with right now.

'Here, put this on her head.' Callum handed Dale an ice pack, and they helped me on to the chair. If I didn't feel like an invalid before, I certainly did now.

'Christine. Dr Ching's number is by the phone. Tell him it is an emergency.' The sheer panic in Dale's voice had everyone jumping to orders.

'I am fine, Dale . . . Honestly.'

'Cal, sit with Ashley now while I clean this up.' Everyone was fussing over nothing. It was only a small cut on my head. If I was fit and well, there would have been none of this fuss. Callum's hand took mine, and his soft smile crept on to his face.

'Are you OK?'

'I am fine, Cal . . . There is no need for all this.'

'He is on his way.' Everyone was flapping like birds for no reason, and I was fine. I could have quite easily screamed at them all, but I thought twice about starting something I probably couldn't finish.

'Christine, can you help me get into fresh clothes?' I had sick and blood on me, and I didn't feel comfortable with any of it.

'Sure . . . Sit there, and I will bring them through.' I felt like a helpless little child, and I was going to end up telling everyone to leave me alone. I couldn't be doing with all this extra fussing around me.

'I will be outside with mom and dad if you need me.' Even Callum was showing all the signs of concern. I had everyone like nervous wrecks, and I couldn't deal with it all any more.

'Right, honey, let's get you into these warm fleece pyjamas.' It did feel good to have another woman's help, and it was giving Dale a reprieve for a little while.

'I can manage.'

'Stop being stubborn, and let us help you, doll.' Between Dale and Christine, I had no chance of winning this one. I was wasting my time and energy even protesting.

'Is your mom and dad OK . . . ? They disappeared quick.' Now that I was coming around to the whole embarrassing incident, I was concerned if his parents were OK. It would give me something to talk about other than myself.

'Yeah. My mom isn't good with blood.' Of course, they weren't; what was I thinking about? Vampires live on blood, that would be like, taking a horse to the well and telling it not to drink. I didn't know why I never realised before I had to get told.

'Thanks, Christine.'

'You don't have to thank me, hun.' Christine was enjoying helping me, and I just couldn't get my head around the whole idea of getting weak and helpless.

'Hello.'

'In here, Doctor.' Dale should have been a woman. He certainly knew how to blow something out of proportion.

'What have you been up to, Ashley?' I didn't know why he felt the need to ask me that question. Christine would have given him my life story when she called him.

'I felt sick . . . So I got up and tripped over Christine's feet. I banged my head off the table . . . I am fine.' I was fed up of telling everyone how fine I was. I was dying, and everyone was concerned about a bump on my head. It wasn't going to cause any more damage unless it knocked the cancer out of my body.

'Let me be the judge of that . . .' Now I had a sarcastic doctor to contend with. 'I can glue the gash. There is no need for me to stitch it up . . . You did feel sick first, but that didn't come after the bang?'

'That's what I said.' I thought Dr Ching was just trying to make me contradict myself, but the bang to my head had only caused a mess.

'You have been very lucky, Ashley. I don't know how you never knocked yourself out.' I didn't think I was lucky. If I was lucky, I wouldn't be getting ready to spend my last Christmas with my family.

'I am made of steel.'

'Let's get this fixed for you . . . You might get a sore head, but I would expect that to happen.'

'Do you all want to do me a favour and stop fussing?' I felt myself getting nippy because I had enough of them all treating me like a child.

'We just care about you, doll.' Dale was now sitting beside me looking very down. All I could smell was disinfectant. I actually felt like I was eating it.

'Did you leave any cleaning fluid in the bottle? That smell is awful.' I wasn't really interested in how everyone cared about me. I was just interested in getting on with the time I had left.

'Sorry.'

'That is all your clothes in the machine . . . Apart from that gash on your head, you would think nothing has happened.' Christine was a godsend to me today.

'Thanks, sweetie.'

'Right, Ashley, do you think that you can stay out of harm's way for a few hours?' Dr Ching was really getting on my nerves this morning.

'I am sorry. Am I being too much trouble?'

'Ash.' I thought if Dale was honest, he knew that I was getting annoyed this morning, and it was Dr Ching that was just going to cope it all.

'What . . . Did I ask for cancer . . . ? No . . . Did I deliberately trip and fall . . . ? No.'

'I will leave you to it, Ashley.' Dr Ching knew that I was angry; he had never packed up as quick in all the times that he had been here.

'Thanks, Doc.' Dale stood up to see the doctor out, and it was the best thing that had happened all morning.

'All right, nippy sweetie, what is wrong?' My friend made me laugh because I could think of a lot of things to call me other than a nippy sweetie.

'Christine, that doctor was doing my head in. How dare he come into my house and make me feel uncomfortable.'

'So he has annoyed you . . . Is that all that is wrong?' Christine knew me better than I knew myself, and she knew that it wasn't just the doctor who was getting to me.

'Where would I start, Christine?' Everything was getting to me, this cottage, everyone fussing treating me like a child, the cancer. I could go on all night.

'The beginning would be a good start.'

'Stuck in this cottage is driving me up the wall . . . I want to go out and do something.'

'Likes of what?' Christine shocked me. I thought she would have told me that the cottage was for the best.

'Last Christmas Eve, we went for something to eat and a few drinks . . . or a few too many . . . We started Christmas as we meant to go on.'

'So what, you want to go for lunch?'

'Like you and Dale would let me.' I slumped back into my chair like a stroppy teen being told they were grounded. Everything was getting me down today, and nothing was going to shift the way I felt. I just wanted to run and jump off the mountain and end all this misery for everyone.

'I am going to take you . . .' I wasn't sure if I heard her right, but I looked at her through a glare in my eyes. 'We are going to have some Christmas fun.' The biggest smile crept over my face, and I sat forward to hug my best friend; this would be the best present ever.

'Is everything OK?' Dale. Now he would be a different story. My bubble was about to get burst any second.

'Ashley wants to go out for lunch and a few drinks.' Silence was golden for what felt like hours. 'Some girl's fun.' Could Christine use her charm to win Dale around? That I was doubtful of.

'Are you mad? Anything could happen?' Dale was furious. I had certainly never seen him like this before.

'Anything can happen, anywhere . . . I have been in here for weeks and still manage to hurt myself. I am not asking your permission, Dale.' If I was healthy, there would be no questions asked. I stood up to go and get myself ready; you could cut the atmosphere with a knife. I felt awful for speaking to my husband like that, but being nice wasn't going to get me anywhere. 'Dale, I am giving in sitting here. I can't take any more.' I knew that wasn't what he wanted to hear, but it was the truth.

'I will help you, Ash.' Christine always liked an excuse to do my hair and make-up, and I was starting to enjoy getting made over. I suppose anything was better than the pale skin I had now. I hated looking like a ghost, and I was looking forward to get out in the nice, cold winter's air. It would either kill me or cure me, and right now I didn't care either way.

'Ashley, I will be here all day. Just come and get me when you want to go home. Or better still call me, and I will come to you.' Even Carlos was concerned about me going out with my friends, but I just wanted to be normal for a couple of hours.

'Thank you, Carlos.' Christine and I got Carlos to bring us into town to meet Christian. I was determined to not let Dale ruin my day. He never spoke one word to me before we left, and that was the first time he had never spoken to me. He hurt me more by ignoring me than he did on our wedding night when he didn't think he could sleep with me. I really thought that he would understand why I wanted to do this today, but I was wrong. I would have loved for him to join me today. For us all to let our hair down and enjoy our day together, but who was I kidding, that was too good to be true for my life.

'Right, Ash, Christian is in Maggie May's.'

'My favourite.' I loved Maggie May's. The food was delicious. The atmosphere was good, and the wine was even better. It was the perfect venue for today.

'Dale will come around, honey.'

'I don't want to think about Dale. I just want to have some fun with my friends.' We got into Maggie May's, and Christian was sitting in a booth with a friend of his. They looked good together.

'Hey, honey.' I got a bear hug from Christian. I thought that I was going to be crushed by his muscular frame. 'How are you?'

'Right, I am here to have fun . . . To let my hair down . . . There is going to be no mention of my life. OK?' I didn't want to speak about me or cancer today. My head was clear of it all, and I was here to have some fun.

'Deal.' Christian was a gentleman. I knew that he would try to do as I asked. 'Ash, meet my George, my partner.' George looked similar to Christian, very well-dressed and good-looking.

'Hey, George, nice to meet you.' This lovely man stood up and placed a kiss on my cheek. It was nice to be surrounded by good company.

'Nice to finally meet you, Ashley.' I knew that he would know all about me, but I wasn't going to let it put a damper on things.

'Now that all the introductions are finished, can we sit?' Christine just had to get her neb in. It wouldn't be like her.

'Hi, Kev, can we get a bottle of white and a bottle of red, please?' Christian knew our waiter with working here himself. We were going to be treated like royalty, and I was going to enjoy every minute of it.

'Of course, buddy, can I get you anything else?'

'Not now, Kev, give us a few minutes.' Christian and Kev had a good chemistry. If I didn't know better, I would say that they had had a past together. They had that aura coming from them.

'I have been looking forward to this wine all day.' Nice, cold, crisp wine to quench my thirst. It wouldn't be long before wine wasn't going to be the only thing I was thirsty for so I wanted to make the most out of today.

'Check the alcoholic out.' I loved hearing the sarcasm coming from Christian; he was the only one who could be sarcastic and fun all in the same breath.

'Oh, ha ha, Christian.' I needed this today. I had been away from them all for too long.

'You know me, Ash. I like to joke.'

'I would think that there was something wrong with you if you didn't joke.'

'Try living with him . . . He drives you crazy, right, George?' Christine loved Christian, and I knew that they would be good for one another without me.

'We wouldn't change him though.' George was smitten with Christian. You could see the twinkle in his eyes. They were like two young love birds, and I couldn't stop smiling at them.

'Not much, George.' Christine was enjoying annoying Christian, and I was enjoying the banter between them. It was nice to know that Christine would still have good friends around her when I was gone because she was going to need a good support network.

I looked at my watch, and it was saying 6.45 p.m. We had been out all day. Dale would be losing his mind, but for once I was being selfish. I didn't care what anyone was thinking. I was having fun. I had spent my whole life caring about what Tom, Dick, and Harry thought, but now I was going to think about me for a change.

'Here, Ash, cocktail time.' Christian was going to get me hung, but I couldn't say no to a cocktail.

'Thanks, hun.'

'Are you OK, Ash?' I was enjoying my cocktail so much that I didn't want to put it down.

'This one is lush . . .' I didn't want to think about how I felt, so I changed the conversation to what I liked—cocktails. 'I am a tad tipsy.' The alcohol had gone right to my head. At least tomorrow I would have an excuse for feeling ill.

'As long as you are OK, and you are having fun, who cares?' I loved Christian's out-take on life. He didn't give a flying monkey what anyone thought of him. He enjoyed life, and that was how it was suppose to be. I wished that I met him years ago; maybe I could have followed in his footsteps.

'Ash, we need to go soon.' Christine had never said that statement before closing time before; she must be getting old.

'Maybe . . . When did you become a party-pooper?'

'You have had too much to drink, and so have I . . . Do you want to be dying of a hangover on Christmas Day?' I burst out laughing because Christine clearly didn't realise what she had just said. Now, I knew that I had drunk too much.

'What is so funny?'

'Dying of a hangover.' I couldn't control my laughter, and then Christian and George started laughing with me. We were having so much fun that I didn't want it to stop.

'Right, help me get her to the car.' Christine was laughing now as well; her stupidity had finally sunk in, and she was laughing at me being silly.

'Ash can walk better than you, Christine.' We all stumbled out of the club in a line. None of us could walk straight or even talk properly. Today was just what I needed in every way possible.

'Dale is going to be so mad, Ash.' I wished that Christine would stop thinking about my husband; he would just have to be OK.

'He will come out of it, the same way that he went into it.' Christian and George were enjoying me as the rebellious thug. It was better late than never I thought.

'I am glad I am leaving you here.' Christian didn't like arguing or bickering, so he would be very glad that he wasn't coming back to the cottage tonight. I thought that air was going to be blue by the time we all got a lot of things off our chests.

'You . . . can cope it tomorrow.' I felt like I was floating since we came outside. The air had gone right to my head. 'Carlos . . . My Carlos.' I put my arm around him, and he opened the door to let us in. He was always waiting for me, no matter where I was.

'Christine, do you have a death wish, taking her home in this state?'

'Carlos, you worry too much.' I just knew that he was right, but Dale couldn't stay mad forever. We were in the back of the car, and Christian and George wished us a merry Christmas.

'See you tomorrow, chicks.' Carlos closed us in so we couldn't escape, and Christine and I looked at one another. We knew that we were done for, but Christine worried more than I did.

'We are done for. You do know that, Ash.'

'Put the music on, Carlos, and turn it up.' I didn't want to hear Christine moaning about us going to be in trouble. 'It is Christmas, Christine.' We sat in the back of the car singing 'It Is Beginning to Look a Lot Like Christmas'. We sounded like strangled cats. But it was good fun.

'Can you two not sober up in a few minutes?' Carlos sounded serious, and I found it rather amusing. I didn't have a serious bone in my body tonight.

'We will behave, sweetie.' Christine knew as well as I did that 'behave' wasn't in our vocabulary tonight. I felt the car turn, and the cottage was lit up beautifully. My heart skipped a beat because we were done for.

'C'mon best.' Carlos came and opened the door, and I stumbled out, and he caught me before I ended up on my bum. I couldn't stop laughing at myself. At least I found myself funny. 'My saviour . . . what would I do without you?' Christine linked my arm, and Carlos was at my other side. We started singing 'Frosty the Snowman', and neither of us was in time with one another.

'This isn't behaving.' We opened the door of the cottage, and Jake rushed to help me. I was glad that it was him and not Dale. He wouldn't be angry as much as Dale. Or if he was, he wouldn't show it.

'Jake, I am fine.' Dale came through from the room and threw his glasses on to the table; his face was like stone.

'What are you all about, Christine?' Obviously, the first person to get it off him was going to be Christine, but I wasn't going to let him bring her into all this.

'I am an adult, Dale . . . I have had fun.'

'Mom, make coffee please.' I slumped down on the sofa and bent down to take my boots off, but I didn't think I could even see what I was doing. Dale sat in front of me and helped me. I couldn't stop giggling. It was like I was on laughing gas or something.

'Do you find yourself funny, Ash? I have been worried sick.'

'Oh, stop fussing . . . You are suffocating me.' Everyone stopped and looked at me yelling. I could certainly get everyone's attention when I wanted to.

'Ashley, drink this coffee, love.' Mhairi handed me a strong coffee, and immediately, it was turning my stomach, but I just had to drink it.

'Suffocating you . . . Ashley, you are dying or have you forgot about that?'

'Don't be stupid. How can I forget . . . ? I never get a minute to forget . . . Well, today I did forget, and I am not going to apologise.'

'Well, let's see what state you end up in tonight when I am not here to help you.' Dale stormed off into the kitchen like a bat out of hell, and I was too drunk to even care.

'Ash, do you want me to stay?' Christine sounded drunk, but you could still hear her concern.

'No, get Carlos to take you home. I will see you in the morning, honey.' We said our goodbyes, and I stumbled to my feet.

'Ashley, do you need a hand?'

'No, I am fine, Jake . . . See you tomorrow.' I walked into the bathroom and slumped down beside the toilet; at least if I was going to be sick, I didn't have any where to go. The worst part was, if I could do it all over again, I would. There would be no doubt about that.

'Ash . . . Can I come in?'

'No. Go away.' I couldn't face Dale right now without telling him exactly what I thought. But just as I thought, he didn't listen; he just came in and kneeled down beside me.

'Let me help you into bed . . . I am sorry.' I knew that he felt bad for shouting at me, but he didn't have to apologise to me.

'I can get myself into bed, Dale. I am only sitting here because I feel sick.' I didn't want his help right now. I could manage on my own. I had to kneel up and throw my head over the toilet to be sick, and Dale rubbed my back, like he always did. I shrugged him off to stumble on to my feet. I walked over to the sink and rinsed my mouth out, and I was starting to sober up and feel the drink hit me.

'Do you mind leaving me alone to get my pyjamas on?' I watched him leave through the mirror, and my body felt empty. I hated myself for treating him like this, but I didn't feel like I had anything to apologise for. I managed fine by myself to get my pyjamas on and left my hair down because I had no energy to tie it up. I stood and looked at myself in the mirror, and I could see my reflection stare back at me. I was the same old person, but I didn't quite feel like me any more. I went through to the bedroom, and Dale was sitting on the end of the bed with his head in his hands. I didn't want to give in so I pulled the covers back and sat on the bed to swing my legs around. I was always told never to go to bed on an argument, but I couldn't bring myself to give in.

'What do you want me to say, to make this OK?' His voice made me look at him, and I didn't know what to say for the best.

'I don't want you to do or say anything. You feel strong about your opinion, and I feel strongly about mine. We are never going to agree on this one.' Dale stood up and came around to sit beside me. He had tears in his eyes, and I was the cause of more of his pain.

'I don't want to fight with you, Ash . . . I am sorry for yelling at you in front of everyone . . . I love you so much that it hurts, and I am not ready to lose you.' I sat forward on to my knees and took his face in my hands.

'I am sorry for arguing with you in front of everyone . . . We don't need to argue. It isn't what we do . . . I love you, Mr Black.' I swung my leg over him to hold him in place. 'I might be dying . . . I might have had one too many to drink, and I may be slower and weaker . . . But I do know that I want you to make love to me.' I didn't want to go to sleep on an argument. My dad always used to say to me, the recipe for a long and happy marriage was to never go to a sleep on an argument. Always sort your differences out.

'Are you sure, Ash?' I kissed him passionately with everything that I had to give. Our mouths became one, and my body came alive.

'Does that answer your question?' He slipped his hand up my top, and his hands were so cold that he made me jump.

'Sorry, babe . . . Cold hands, warm heart.' I knew that he had a warm heart. No one could be warmer than my husband. I took my own top off and kissed his neck slowly. 'Ash. I love you.' I looked into his eyes full of hurt and pain and kissed his mouth. It was like a breath of fresh air.

'I love you more.' I slipped his shirt off and ran my warm hands down his chest. I had never felt as compatible to someone in all my life. I stood up off him and slid my bottoms off slowly. I wanted it to be a tease tonight, just to make him feel what he used to when he saw my naked body. I was standing naked in front of him without a care in the world. I took his hand to stand up because I wanted him naked with me. I felt him suck my neck, and it felt earth blowing to feel him devour me in such a way. My sex was throbbing for him, here and now, and it was just getting stronger at every touch. I slid his jeans and boxers off and pushed him back on to the bed. His face was smiling happily at me, and I was relieved to see that he was enjoying himself, just as I was. I climbed over his lap to straddle him, and his cold hands caressed my breasts as our naked bodies sat entwined together. I raised myself over his package to allow him access, and we both cried out with pleasure as we felt our bodies meet as one. I slid on and off him, enjoying every thrust. His lips on mine caressing my mouth with his tongue was enough to send my body into oblivion. I couldn't contain my pleasure any longer, and my body convulsed as I hit a climax. I bent down and bit his neck out of sheer pleasure. His body tensed tighter around me as I felt him cum after me. I held on to his neck tightly, inhaling his aftershave. I didn't want to move from this position ever. Every piece of anger and hurt had vanished, and it was replaced by love and passion.

'Is that what they call make-up sex?' I never moved a muscle. I felt safe and secure in his arms, and I wanted it to last forever.

'As much as I enjoyed making love to my husband . . . Let's not make a habit of falling out.' I wanted to spend as many intimate moments with Dale before my time run out or before my body was repulsive and I couldn't bear to look at it.

'Agreed.'

'I don't want to move.'

'Don't . . . We have all night . . . It is Christmas after all.' I was relieved that I had made it our first Christmas. It was one milestone that I wanted to reach, and now I could mark it off my list.

'Our first Christmas together.'

'Our first Christmas as husband and wife.' I pulled my dressing gown off the bottom of the bed and wrapped it around me. It felt comfortable and cosy, just like my husband did. 'Where are you going?'

'Bathroom . . . Don't worry, I am not going anywhere ever again.' I stood up and kissed Dale's mouth softly before I left the room. I had never really had a sex life before I met Dale. But now I knew what it felt like to have a kind and loving lover. I never wanted it to stop. I felt like a woman for the first time in my life.

'Merry Christmas, sweetheart.' Dale and I had woken up in the same position that we fell asleep in. It felt nice to wake up in his arms.

'Merry Christmas, hun.' My head was banging, and my stomach was off. I didn't dare show any signs of a hangover because I didn't deserve any sympathy.

'Our first Christmas together has arrived.' Dale was softly spoken this morning, and I thought it was because he knew that I was fragile. Or could it be because we were another step closer to the end of my life?

'It will all be perfect.'

'Right, Mrs Black, let's get up. I have got a few surprises for you.' I was excited. What did he have for me? I was like a child at Christmas, and I was grateful to get the chance to share one with my husband. 'I will go and make coffee . . . Will you manage?'

'Yeah. I will be through in a few minutes.' I slowly got up and placed my hands on my head. 'Ow.' I slipped my slippers on and threw my robe around me. The walk to the kitchen felt like a million miles away, and I was feeling very under the weather. 'Remind me never to drink again.' Dale's cheeky smile said, 'I told you so.' I climbed up on a stool beside him as he poured the coffee, and I knew that a cup of his coffee would straighten me out. We were practically sitting naked in the kitchen, and it felt nice. We used to sit like this all the time before Mhairi and Jake came to stay with us.

'Mrs Black, when will you ever learn?' I wrapped my arms around his neck and placed my legs around his legs. 'You are a bad influence on me, Mrs Black.' We embraced ourselves together, not fighting the urge that was telling us to have sex here and now. We kissed each other like it was our first kiss and like we could never get enough of one another. We have christened every other room so why not put our mark on the kitchen as well.

'Hello.' Dale and I jumped out of our skin when Mhairi and Jake stepped into the kitchen.

'Sorry.' Mhairi backtracked and walked into the living room. I felt embarrassed, so she must be feeling really uncomfortable.

'Why are they early?' I managed to whisper out of sheer embarrassment. We managed to compose ourselves, and I followed Dale through to wish them a merry Christmas. I was very conscious about only having my robe on, but what the hell.

'Merry Christmas, Mom . . . Dad.' Jake walked over to us and kissed my cheek. I was just hoping that he didn't make a joke about our encounter in the kitchen; my body wouldn't take it today.

'Merry Christmas, dear.'

'Merry Christmas, Jake.' They looked just as embarrassed at walking in on us about to have sex on the breakfast bar, but nothing was said, and we never mentioned it either.

'Merry Christmas, Son . . . Ashley.' Mhairi sounded off with us this morning, and I wondered if it was all to do with last night's shenanigans or our floor show this morning.

'Same to you, Mhairi.'

'We were just going to exchange gifts. Do you want to join us?' Dale's face was all flushed when he tried to explain what we were going to do. I couldn't help but smile at him. We all went to take our seats in the living room, and I noticed a very large bouquet of flowers in the middle of the table. 'Those are for you, doll.' I reached over and took the card out. I tried to read it carefully, but my head was rather tender this morning. That served me right for drinking myself to an oblivion yesterday.

Merry Christmas, Ash
Love you always and forever
Dale
xx

'Thank you. They are beautiful.' I placed my hand on Dale and leant in to kiss him. I had to remember that we had company before I got carried away. 'My first gift for you is over there.' I pointed to a huge square package wrapped in brown paper. Dale looked very surprised as he walked over to open it. 'I know that you like your art.' He started opening the package, and I suddenly saw him smiling; it was all worthwhile to see that gorgeous smile.

'Ash, it is beautiful.' It was a large painted canvas of me and Dale on our wedding day. 'Thank you.'

'It is lovely.' Mhairi liked art as well, so I knew that she would appreciate it.

'Mom . . . This is from us.' Mhairi accepted the gift and started opening it. The look on her face said it all.

'It is perfect. Thank you, kids.' It was a painted canvas of me and Dale, Mhairi and Jake, Callum, Kiara, and Nikki at our wedding. 'When were all these photos taken?'

'My friend Christian. He did a course in photography, and he showed me a couple of pictures that he had taken.' Christian had a talent, and the pictures were fantastic.

'Dad, this is for you.' Jake started opening his present, and Dale handed me a box. 'Merry Christmas, sweetie.' I opened the box carefully and was stunned. It was a gorgeous ring. 'It is . . . beautiful.'

'It is an eternity ring. It was my grandmother's, but I got it cleaned up . . . My grandmother would have loved you.' I threw my arms around Dale and kissed his neck. It was a wonderful gift, and it was a perfect surprise.

'Thanks, kids . . . just what I needed.' We got Jake a new fishing rod because he never shut up about it. I handed Dale a small box, and I watched him open it like it was going to break. Exchanging gifts with everyone was a magical moment, and it would live with me forever.

'It is lovely, Ash. Thanks.'

'Turn it over, it is engraved.' I got Dale a Rolex watch because his watch was always breaking, and he was going to need a good timekeeper if I wasn't around.

Love you always
Ash x

'We have got gifts for you both.' Mhairi sounded nervous as she interrupted us, and I laid my head on Dale's shoulder. 'I don't know if we have done the right thing or not.' Mhairi handed us a large envelope, and Dale opened it. Curiosity got the better of me, and I had to sit up straight to be nosey. Dale took out pictures of a cottage for sale in Canada and handed them over to me. It looked beautiful. But I didn't understand what they were for.

'I don't understand, Mom.' Dale was just as confused as I was, and I was glad I wasn't the only one.

'We thought that you would need somewhere like this after the change, and your dad found this online . . . So we bought it for you.' I looked at Dale, and he looked at me. I didn't know what to say.

'Thanks, Mom and Dad . . . This was very thoughtful of you.' It wasn't very often that we were lost for words, but even Dale was surprised.

'Thank you both, it is lovely.'

'You are very welcome, dear . . . Only the best for my son and daughter-in-law.' It meant a lot to finally hear Mhairi accepting the changeover because she was never fully on our side. It was always Jake who supported our decision.

'Right, I am going to get in that kitchen and get today's celebration's started . . . Give me a shout when Callum and Kiara arrive.' Mhairi toddled off to the kitchen, just like that was her heaven. She felt at home when she was in a kitchen.

'And I am going to get logs for the fire.' Jake always kept the fire going; he was a natural.

'Then there were two.'

'I am going to go for a bath and get ready. What are you doing, Mr Black?' I planned on having a bath with him this morning, but Mhairi's and Jake's early rise had put a stop to that idea.

'I will get ready for Kiara coming . . . I better get clothes on first.' I lifted my coffee and got up to go for a bath; it was weird going alone.

'Don't be gone too long, Mrs Black.' I didn't want to be away from him at all, so there was no chance I would be long.

'Ashley. I knew that you would want a bath, so I started it for you.' That was very thoughtful of Mhairi. I was getting spoiled today.

'Thank you, Mhairi.' I walked into the bathroom, and the bath was run enough for me to just climb in. My bathrobe was the only thing that I had on, and I slipped it off and climbed into the hot water. It was that hot that my skin was tingling. I wanted a quick bath, but this water seemed too good to be in and out. I relaxed back in the water and felt grateful for everything that was going to happen today. Family, Christmas, and friends were all I needed.

I sat and looked in the mirror thinking about how I looked. I had a knee-length black dress on with silver sandals. All I thought about was, was it too much? I put my hair up into a roll and went for simple make-up. I wanted to look like me before I was ill, and I thought that I had succeeded in some way.

'Ash, are you OK?' Dale came in and stood at the door. He had a shirt and tie on, so I didn't feel too overdressed now.

'I am fine . . . just coming out.' I slowly got up and turned to face him. I never felt awkward with Dale; everything felt natural.

'Wow, Mrs Black, you look gorgeous.' I was glad that he still thought that I was gorgeous. It made me feel a little bit more relaxed in myself.

'Thanks, you don't look too bad yourself.'

'You do realise that I have got to keep my hands off you until tonight.' The feel of Dale's hand on my waist made my body tingle all over again.

'I am sure that you won't want a repeat of this morning's antics in the kitchen . . . You will survive.' I leant around him to open the door, and his face was a picture. I wished that I had a camera handy. I heard more voices in the living room, and that only meant more excitement.

'Merry Christmas, Ash.' Callum came towards me with Kiara, and I got a kiss on the cheek.

'Merry Christmas, Callum . . . Merry Christmas, princess.' I took Kiara from Callum and went to sit on the couch with her. Today was perfect now.

'Ash. This is Sophie . . . Kiara's mom.' I froze when I heard those words. How could a mother abandon her child and then show up on Christmas day? I looked up to see her standing there with a huge smile on her face, and I could have ripped her head off. Everyone's eyes were on me, wondering what the hell I was going to say. They probably thought that I would be the one to welcome her with open arms, but I just couldn't be nice to her.

'Dale, bring Kiara's presents over, please.' I couldn't even acknowledge the so-called mom. Everyone came and got a seat, and Dale sat beside me and Kiara. 'Santa Claus has left you lots of presents, angel . . . Yes, he has.' I was talking to Kiara in a funny voice, just like anyone does to a baby. The fact that her mother was sitting here didn't make the slightest difference to me.

'Have you two left anything in the shop?' Callum was always the joker, and I knew how to take his humour now.

'You can open them for her, smart alec.' Everyone was laughing at my comeback to Cal. Sophie was perched on the arm of the chair, next to him, and I could sense that she felt out of place. She wasn't what I was expecting.

'Do you want to open this one first?' Dale handed Cal the jeweller's bag first. 'Ashley picked this one for her.' I turned Kiara around so that she could watch her dad open her gifts.

'Ashley, this is gorgeous . . . Thank you.' Cal got up and gave me a hug. 'Dale, I am sorry, but I have got to kiss your wife. She is an angel.' I felt Cal's lips on mine, and I could have cried at how he showed his appreciation. He passed the chain around to his parents, and I was just glad that they all liked it.

'It is a good job you are my brother, Cal . . .' We were all laughing at Dale and Callum had a laugh and joke with one another; it was a nice feeling for once.

'This little princess is worth it.' We all sat around while the presents were opened, and all Kiara was interested in was the Minnie Mouse teddy.

'Kiara, do you want to give this to Aunty Ashley?' It was the cutest moment ever because Kiara put her hand out for the bag, and my heart melted.

'Thank you, my little princess.' I handed Kiara over to Dale while I opened my present. I took the box out of the bag and opened it. There was a lovely gold chain with Aunt written on it. 'This is lovely, thank you . . . Thank you, my little munchkin.' I took Kiara back of Dale and gave her a cuddle.

'Uncle Dale's turn now.' Callum handed Dale a bag, and Dale opened it. He got a silver dog tag chain with Uncle Dale engraved on it.

'Thanks, guys, I love it.' It was all the silly priceless gifts that made Christmas special, and these were things that Dale and I would cherish forever.

'Callum, we have got you a gift, and we want you to accept it for you and Kiara.' I made it perfectly clear that Sophie had no part in this gift. 'Dale, can you pass me that envelope, please . . . ? You know, when I pass away . . . Dale is moving to a small town in Canada, and you are going to run things from here. Well, we wanted to give you and Kiara some stability. I need to know that you will both be OK.' I handed Callum the envelope, and we watched carefully as he opened it.

'I don't believe this . . . Are you being serious? You guys, thank you so much.' I was relieved that he was happy and willing to accept it from us.

'What is it, Callum?' The suspense was killing Mhairi.

'It is the deeds to Dale and Ashley's house in Anchorage.' It was only a house, and we were not going to be needing it any more. It was as well getting kept in the family.

'Just look after it and treat Rosa and Carlos right.' I knew that he would take care of everything that belonged to me. I really had no worries there.

'Hello.' Christine had just arrived, but I bet that she was petrified to come in here after last night.

'Hey, Christine.'

'Is it safe to come in?' Christine looked stunning as usual, and Dale got up and went over to her. 'Merry Christmas, honey.' They shared a hug, and it made my day that they could forget about last night. 'I am forgiven then?'

'Merry Christmas, Christine.' I put my hand out to her, and she came and gave me a cuddle.

'Merry Christmas, princess.' Christine lifted Kiara from me and gave her a shuggle about in her arms. 'I have a present here for you.' Callum got up and went over to Christine. 'Merry Christmas, darling.' I had never noticed it before, but there was a connection between my best friend and my brother-in-law. They looked good together.

'Merry Christmas, honey.' I watched Sophie watching Callum and Christine in jealous.

'Christine, we have put your presents on the table.'

'Thanks, chick . . . Dale let me sit down to hand these out.' Dale moved to give Christine his seat, and I took Kiara back. 'This is for you princess . . . Has she got gold today?'

'Yeah, we got her a gold guardian angel pendant.'

'Well, this can be your second bit of gold, angel.' Christine handed the bag to Callum to open, and I sat back and watched everyone get on so well together. 'Dale . . . Ash . . . Callum . . . where is Nikki?'

'She isn't here yet.'

'Mr and Mrs Black . . . these are for Christian and George when they arrive.' We were going to have a day of giving and receiving presents, and it was a beautiful moment. I had been able to share a precious moment with each and every one of my family members.

'Christine, Kiara's bracelet is lovely. Thank you.' I had seen the bracelet already. It was lovely, perfect for a little princess.

'Ash, I didn't know what to get you, so I got Christian to help me.' I took out the box and lifted the lid off, and there was a pink album that I carefully lifted out.

'Thanks, Christine.' Dale was leaning on the back of the couch behind me. 'Christine, take Kiara now.' I was very intrigued to find out what was in the album.

'Where are the tissues?' Christine obviously knew that I was going to be in tears, so it must be something special. I opened the album carefully, and there was a baby photo of me to start with, and Callum sarcastically put the box of tissues on the table.

'Where did you get all these?' This was great, the perfect present.

'I had to rake.' There were pictures from school and college, prom, graduation, and right up to moving here, my engagement in the office, the wedding, Kiara. The tears were rolling down my face. It was a good job that I had waterproof mascara on, or I would have a black face.

'Christine, this is fantastic, thank you.'

'I didn't mean to make you cry, but I am glad that you like it.' It was perfect in every way possible.

'Right, open yours now.' Christine handed Kiara up to Dale, and she took the large envelope first. 'That is from us.' Christine opened the envelope and looked up at Dale and then over to me. She looked stunned.

'Am I reading this right?'

'I wanted to make sure that you had no worries when I . . .' Christine threw herself on top of me, and I felt like I was getting crushed.

'I don't know what to say. Thank you.'

'Just don't cry, Christine.' I had the cheek to tell her not to cry after my outburst, but I didn't want everyone crying today.

'Dad, get the champagne out.'

'I don't know if I can stomach that today.' Christine's cheeky smile said it all.

'Yeah, right, Christine.' She could drink like a fish seven days a week.

'After the state you two rolled in here last night, singing "Frosty the Snowman", I am surprised that you are both sitting here at all.' We were all in hysterics after hearing about 'Frosty the Snowman'. At least we could laugh today.

'We were up from the crack of dawn . . .'

'Too much info, Ash.' I slapped Christine's arm for lowering the tone, only she could get away with it. We all got handed a glass of champagne, and already my stomach was bubbling.

'Can I say a few things?' I raised my eyebrows and sat listening carefully to what Dale was going to say next. He wasn't a fan of speaking, but I knew that whatever he was going to say would be important. 'I would like to thank you all for coming today. Christmas is a time for family and friends to come together and celebrate what we have. This family has expanded this year. I gained my beautiful wife, a niece, and a lot of new friends. Thank you all for being here to make this Christmas extra special . . . to family.' We all raised our glasses 'to family'. I couldn't sit back any longer. I got up and walked around to Dale; his little speech was lovely. I placed a kiss on his lips, and I didn't care who was here.

'You two get a room.' I knew that it would be Callum who would make a remark about our public display of affection; he couldn't help himself.

'Callum, do me a favour . . . Build Kiara's chair.'

'You fell for that, Cal.' Today had been such a lovely day. I couldn't have wished for any more. There would only be one thing that I would change, and that would be to get Sophie out of my cottage. She hadn't even looked at Kiara. I didn't even know what she was doing here.

'Ash, who is the woman beside Cal?' I wondered how long it would take for Christine to notice a new face.

'Kiara's mother.' Christine went quite pale, like she was going to be sick.

'They are not together, Christine.' Was I missing something? Why was my husband reassuring my best friend that nothing was going on between Cal and Sophie?

'Am I missing something?'

'Don't tell me that you haven't noticed Callum and Christine together.' I was surprised that I never noticed it before, and I was doubly surprised at Dale not saying something to me.

'Together.'

'Ash, just keep it quiet.' Mom's the word. I wouldn't breathe a word to anyone. It was nice to see Christine with someone, but she looked hurt at the moment.

'I won't say a thing.'

'Right, little miss, let's see if you like your chair.' Callum took Kiara and placed her in the chair; she seemed to like it. She was making all the right sounds and showing all the right signs.

'Why is she here? She hasn't looked at Kiara, and she hasn't spoken to anyone.' I was getting annoyed at her lack of enthusiasm. It was Christmas, and she wasn't interested in her daughter.

'She showed up last night.' I handed Dale my glass and went and sat beside Sophie on the chair.

'Hi, Sophie.'

'Hi.' She was only a child herself. She couldn't be older than nineteen.

'I am going to be straight with you. OK . . . ? I don't know why you are here. Enlighten me.' I was trying to be nice, but she was going to have to give me something good to keep up my Mrs Nice Act.

'I wanted to see Kiara . . . I missed her.' I wanted to laugh, but I had no idea what was going through this kids head.

'You haven't looked at your baby, so what is the real reason?'

'I don't know how to act with her . . . Watching you with her made me feel inadequate . . . You are a natural.' I actually felt sorry for this girl. My maternal instinct had kicked in again, and I felt like I wanted to help her.

'Why did you abandon her like that?'

'I wanted her to have a life that I couldn't give her.'

'You had your reasons, I get that . . . I don't know how you could just give her up like that, and I never will. But if you want to be a part of her life, you need to start now.' I placed a hand on hers, and I got up to pick Kiara out of her chair. I walked back to Sophie and handed her Kiara. Whether she needed to realise that she was her baby or she needed a push in the right direction, I didn't know 'I would kill to have what you have got.' I walked away from them and went through to my room. I was glad that I didn't have far to go because my body felt empty. I slumped on to the edge of the bed, and I felt really bad that I had judged Sophie.

'Ashley, are you OK?'

'Yeah, sweetie, I am fine.' Dale came and bent down in front of me, and his hands were warm on my cheek.

'I know you better than that, babe.'

'I judged Sophie before I even spoke to her. She is just a kid herself.'

'Ash, Sophie isn't our problem . . . We are there for Kiara . . . You just did a great thing . . . More than anyone else has done.' I wanted to believe that I had just given her a chance, but I couldn't get out of my head how I judged her.

'Let's go back in . . . I just came through for my anti-sickness tablet.' The drawer was easy reach to take the bottle out of and that was my perfect excuse.

'Are you OK?'

'Yeah. Just feeling sick and a bit sore, but we are going back through to enjoy the rest of the day.' He took both of my hands, and we walked back through to the living room, just in time for Nikki walking into the cottage.

'Hey, Merry Christmas, Ash.' I got a big hug from my sister-in-law, and we joined together like two peas in a pod. I loved this girl to pieces. It was just a shame that she didn't come by much.

'Merry Christmas, babe.'

'What the hell is she doing here?' Dale and I looked around to see who she was talking about. 'Do you want to be a mother now? How dare you show up here at our family Christmas?' I pulled Nikki's arm back so that she was standing beside Dale and me. Christine came and stood at the other side of Nikki. I thought we were all curious as to what has rattled Nikki's cage because she wasn't the argumentative type, unless your name was Callum.

'Nikki, what is wrong?' I wanted to know what had got Nikki so upset because this wasn't like her at all.

'Her . . . Here . . . she only slept with Callum to get at me . . . Then she abandons her baby and shows up here to act like a mom . . . Ashley has been more of a mom to your child, and before long, she is going to lose the only mother figure she knows . . . You are not welcome here.' For the first time today, I felt heartbroken because Nik was right; Kiara was going to lose me, and she wouldn't understand.

'Enough.' I raised my voice at both of them. I had heard enough. 'Nik, she is Kiara's mother, and it is Christmas. Whatever she has or hasn't done, this isn't the time or the place . . . I don't agree with her abandoning Kiara either, but no one knows what goes on in someone's head . . . Please, let it go for today and come open your gifts.' The only noise we could here was Kiara, talking to her animals on her chair.

'She better stay away from me . . . Oh and by the way, if you are here for Cal, you are wasting your time. He is with Christine now.' I could have gagged Nikki; no one knew where to look.

'Nik, come and open your gifts.' Dale distracted her by shoving an envelope in her direction. It seemed to be working; thank goodness. Nikki took the envelope and started opening it. 'This is from us, but Ashley picked it.'

'Driving lessons, thanks, guys . . . What are these for?' Nikki held up a set of car keys, and I took her hand and took her outside.

'She is yours, honey.' A red sports car just like mine. I saw her reaction to mine, and I knew that she would love it.

'Oh my God. Thank you so much.' Nikki ran and sat in the car; her expression was fantastic. Hopefully, this would distract her from Sophie for a little while. I had to go inside and sit down. My stomach was in that many cramps that I could have cried. I very rarely got period pains so this was a new experience for me. I fell back on the couch and laid my head back. I didn't want anything to ruin Christmas.

'Ashley . . . are you OK?' Dale was sitting beside me in a flash; he obviously watched me coming back in from outside. The poor man was all concerned about me again.

'No . . .' I fought back the tears as I laid my head on Dale's chest. 'I am in agony.'

'What with?'

'My stomach, it feels like a knot.' I didn't want sympathy because I knew that I have brought this on myself after drinking so much last night.

'Can I get you anything?'

'Can you phone the nurse to come and give me some pain relief.' This was the first time that I had ever asked for pain relief, but to get through today, I knew that I needed it.

'Of course, I will, babe.'

'But I don't want anyone to know. Can you say to the nurse to say that she was just popping in to see if I was OK?' I didn't want everyone to be concerned about me, and I didn't want to be the centre of attention today.

'I will see what I can do. Will you be OK sitting here?'

'Yes, I will be fine.' Dale got up casually, and Christine came and sat beside me. She wasn't stupid; she knew something was wrong.

'What is wrong, chick?'

'I am getting Dale to get my nurse to come in and give me some morphine, but no one has to find out. Please, Christine.' I was begging her not to say anything.

'No one will find out from me.'

'So you and Callum . . . is it serious?' I needed to keep my mind occupied to take away the pain, and my friend's life story would do the trick.

'I really do hope so. I just hope that it doesn't go pear-shaped now that everyone knows.'

'I will die happily if I know that you are with Cal.' Christine laid her head on my shoulder, and it felt like old times. We had spent many times in this embrace over the years. We were always there for one another for the good and bad times, but now I felt really guilty that I was going to be leaving her to face the future without me.

'I don't want you to go anywhere . . . I will miss you like crazy, Ash.' I haven't had a conversation with Christine about me dying, and I was intrigued to know how she actually felt.

'I will always be here somewhere. When you get down, just look at your hand and I will be there.' It was hard to hear how hurt she was inside.

'I don't want to let you down, hun.'

'Just do me a favour and look after Dale for me.' I knew now that my time was getting shorter, and I needed to know that if it all ended badly, someone would keep an eye on Dale.

'Of course, I will. He will never get shot of me now . . . He is my only connection to you.' Christine and I were sitting blubbering like two babies, and no one even battered an eyelid at us.

'No more champagne for you two.' Cal sat on the table in front of us and put a hand on each of our legs. That table had seen some action over the last few weeks. 'Come on, you two, you will start me off.'

'We are just being silly, honey.'

'It is only natural . . . I am surprised that I haven't seen you both like this weeks ago.'

'We pick our moments, Cal.' Christine was right; these types of conversations couldn't just happen. The moment had got to be right.

'Here is Christian and George coming.' That was the perfect distraction that we all needed. Christian could make the light of any situation.

'Merry Christmas, everyone . . . Are you two hung-over?' Of course, our drunken night of fun was still topic of conversation.

'Too much champagne today, Christian.' I was pleased to see that Cal was giving us our excuses for the tears.

'No more for them then. All the more for us.' Everyone was laughing, and I, for one, was glad to see them here.

'Ash.' I turned around to see Dale standing behind me. 'Susan is here to check on you.' I was never so glad to see someone in all my life. I left the bubbly Christian and George mingling with everyone.

'Come through, Susan.' I took her through to our room, and Dale followed behind us. 'Thank you for coming up here on Christmas day.' I sat on the bed, and she sat down beside me. I really couldn't wait to climb into my bed tonight; I felt exhausted.

'No problem at all. That is what I am here for . . . What is the pain like?'

'A bad period pain, but it gets really sharp and eases off to leave me aching.'

'That sounds like a normal kind of pain for this condition, honey. If you were pregnant, this is what a contraction would start off like, and in your case, your uterus is contracting because of the tumour. I can give you morphine now, and we will try four hourly after that. You have the line in already, so the rest will be straightforward.'

'Thank you.' Who would have thought a tumour could cause so many problems? I cringed as the morphine got pushed through my line; my arm was aching.

'Have you had any bleeding yet?'

'No, nothing. Dr Ching is a bit surprised I think.'

'I am myself . . . Normally, at this stage, it would be expected. But maybe that is why you are getting really uncomfortable, so don't worry if and when that happens.'

'I keep thinking that I will have longer to live if I don't have all the symptoms.' I knew that I was sounding ridiculous, but it was something that was keeping me sane.

'I am not going to burst your bubble honey. If that is what you want to think and it is getting you through the days, then it won't do you any harm.' I was glad that she let me go along thinking the way I was because I was getting through it just fine.

'I hate this feeling after I have had morphine.' My body felt warm; my head felt fuzzy, and I felt like I was floating.

'It isn't pleasant, but it will get you through a couple of hours.' Dale's hand rested on top of my shoulder, and I rested my head to the side to feel his hand on my face. 'That is you all done, honey. I will call you in four hours to see how you are, but if you need me, just get Dale to call me again . . . Don't drink any alcohol now though.' I couldn't face any alcohol right now. I felt drunk with the morphine. 'Enjoy the rest of your day.'

'Thank you, Susan.' Dale was back by my side in no time, and I felt like I was being a pest today.

'Are you OK? Do you want to go for a lie-down?'

'No, the quicker I get back through, the better.' I had to go now, or I could end up in bed for the rest of the day, and that is something I didn't want.

'If you need anything, just ask.' Dale had his arm around me as we walked back through to the party. I spotted my seat still empty beside Christine, and that is where I was heading for.

'Is everything all OK?' Christine spoke quietly to me, not to draw any attention.

'All done.' The pain was gone already. It was amazing how quickly the morphine worked. It was just a shame that the side effects had to be so bad.

'Ashley, I have your present here for you.' Christian handed me a gift bag with a box just like Christine's. 'Dale, you will want to see them as well.' Dale put his phone in his pocket and came behind me on the couch. His arms rested around my neck, and his mouth kissed my ear tenderly. It was an album of our wedding. All the pictures that Christian had taken were in it. They were all so beautiful.

'Christian, they are . . . stunning . . . Thank you.' I couldn't stop looking at them; they were breathtaking.

'Thank you, Christian. I will treasure them forever.' We looked so happy and in love, and no one could take that away from us.

'Thank you to everyone. Your gifts have been wonderful . . . I feel blessed to have you all in my life.' I felt very emotional now, and I couldn't help myself.

'We have been blessed to have you, Ash.' Dale's voice echoed in my ear, and it sent shivers down my spine.

'Everyone take your seats at the table. We are going to start serving dinner.' I hadn't heard a peep out of Mhairi all day. She had made herself busy in the kitchen with Rosa. We all took to our feet and headed to the lovely set table. Everything was beautifully set, and it was perfect.

'Someone better get Nikki from her toy.' I had forgotten about Nikki being outside. It had been her perfect distraction.

'I will go.' Callum put his glass down and gave Christine a kiss on the cheek. He went out into the cold with no jacket on; he must be daft. I took my place beside Dale, and he put his hand on my leg. It didn't matter where he touched, my body never protested. I slowly looked around the table, and everyone was so happy; their faces were full of glee, and the laughter was magical. I had never had a Christmas like this since my parents were killed.

'I love it, Ash.' I was brought back from my moment with Nikki's arms around my neck.

'You're welcome, honey.'

'Someone can move because I am not sitting next to her.' I didn't want to stand up and be a referee again, simply because the morphine was in full swing, and I didn't want to seem out of sorts.

'Nik, behave and sit down.' Dale tried to be discreet about the whole situation. But I was getting worked up because it should never have been like this today.

'I am sorry for ruining your day, Ash, but I can't sit beside her.' I took Nikki's hand to try and calm her down, but it was going to take a lot more than my reassurance to work.

'You haven't ruined anything, hun.' Carlos stood up and kindly sat beside Sophie. 'Thank you, Carlos.' I was glad that I had Nikki at the other side of me. I would be able to keep her calm here.

'You know, Nikki, you need to grow up.' I closed my eyes and took a deep breath in; that was the worst thing that Sophie could have said.

'That is good coming from a twisted, evil cow like you.'

'Enough . . . I have had enough . . . If you two want to bicker like kids, go outside and do it.' I looked at Dale and smiled at him; he had taken the right attitude with them.

'I might throw her off the mountain.' I wanted to laugh at Nikki, but I wasn't going to encourage her behaviour.

'Nikki dear, give it a rest.' Mhairi was very calm and polite about the whole thing, and I got the feeling that something was going on that I didn't know about. I could sense the tension between them all.

'Nikki, what is going on and don't lie to me?'

'I can't, Ash.' Well, now I knew that I was right; I needed to know.

'Do you know what is going on?' I swung around and questioned Dale, and he about choked on his drink.

'What do you mean?'

'What is the secret that Nikki can't tell me?'

'Ash, I have no idea. I swear.' I could see that Dale was telling me the truth, and he was just as curious as I was.

'Nikki, tell us. Or I will make a scene.'

'Nik.' Dale was even in the dark. Surely, it couldn't be that bad.

'Kiara might not be Callum's . . . That is why she is here to get a paternity test.' I was shocked, to say the least. What else was going to come out today? I was so angry that no one told us, and I was ready to crack.

'Who else knows, Nik?' Dale sounded furious.

'Mom, Dad, and Callum.' I saw red. I didn't know who I was more angrier at?

'You . . . get outside now.' I needed to hear this from her after her lies to me a few hours ago.

'Ash.'

'Get off me, Dale. This isn't finished with in here either.' Everyone looked at me just as worried as I followed her outside. Dale followed me, and part of me was glad after having the morphine. I felt very weak as I got outside and hit the air, but hopefully, the morphine would keep me standing pain free. 'Tell me what Nikki has just said isn't true?'

'I can't . . . I am sorry.' I slapped her face so hard that I hurt myself. My head was spinning from the morphine, and my heart was racing through anger.

'Ash, she isn't worth it.'

'You sat in there this morning and lied to my face . . . I felt sorry for you.' I should trust my first instincts; they were generally right.

'She isn't yours. I don't know why you are so bothered.' I felt like a huge knife had sunk through me, and Dale pulled me back from her.

'Just go back in, Sophie.' Dale wanted her out of my sight before I did something I regretted. But I did follow her back in. I actually did have something to say in front of them all. All eyes shot up to us when we walked in, and I had never felt as betrayed in all my life.

'Sophie, you are right, she isn't mine . . . But who has been around for her all these weeks? You don't deserve to be a mother . . . As for you,

Jake, I expected more from you . . . I didn't think that I would ever feel hurt by you. Why keep it from us? . . . And I might have known that you were too quiet today for some reason . . .' Mhairi, bowed her head as I addressed her in a very harsh way. 'Nikki was the only decent one not to treat us like kids . . . I am going to sit here and enjoy the rest of my day, but don't expect me to be happy about any of this . . . You stay out of my way because the next time, Dale won't stop me.' I sat back at my seat and started eating my soup in silence. Christine and Christian kept everyone laughing and joking, but my spirit had vanished. I just wanted the day to end. Kiara was one of my main reasons for changing at the end, and now she was going to be going away before me. Dale was right weeks ago when he had doubts about Kiara, and I pushed him to bond with her. Now I could see why he had doubts, and I feel bad for being pushy.

'The soup was lovely, Mrs Black.' Christine always did love a bowl of home-made soup.

'Thank you, dear . . . I made it because it is Ashley's favourite.' I finished off my soup and put my spoon down. I couldn't even acknowledge Mhairi's comments. I felt hurt with all the lies because there was no need to keep such a big thing from us.

'Ash, do you want a refill?' Christian was doing what he did best, serving everyone their alcohol.

'Yes, please, hun. But could you give me a glass of ice water?'

'Sure, darling.' Dale sat back and looked at me with fear in his eyes. I laid my head on to his shoulder and tried to forget about today's shenanigans.

'I am not going to drink the champagne.' I managed to whisper into Dale's ear so that no one knew what I was saying.

'Are you OK?' That was a good question, and I honestly couldn't answer it; all I could do was shrug my shoulders. 'Has the pain eased?'

'Yeah. Pain free from the cancer.' My heart was breaking inside though. Kiara started crying when she woke up, and no one was in a hurry to get her, not even her so-called mother. I really wanted to get up to her, but I wasn't able to move. My body had frozen to the seat. I was surprised when Dale got up and picked her up from her pram. He came and sat back at the table with her, and I couldn't help myself. I had a bond with this baby, and I wasn't going to break it because her mother was a twisted cow.

'Did you smell all this lovely food, princess?' Kiara gripped my finger, like I was her favourite person in the whole world. 'She will be looking for a bottle . . . and to be changed.' Dale looked at me for help in what to do. But I couldn't do anything now.

'What will I do?'

'I can't do it, Dale. I have had that morphine . . . Give her to Callum or Sophie.'

'Cal, Kiara needs changed and her bottle.' With the look on Cal's face, he didn't want to do it either, but he got up and came to take her.

'Don't push her away, sweetie. Look how far you have come since she arrived.' Cal put his hand on my shoulder as if he agreed with every word, and I felt a relief seeing him take care of his daughter. Mhairi wasn't happy that she didn't have a clue what I just said to Cal, but that was the way it was going to stay. Rosa started serving the Christmas dinner, and it all looked gorgeous.

'Dale, do you want to carve the bird?'

'No . . . Dad, you can do the honours.' Dale was very off with his mom, and she knew with his tone that this whole situation wasn't finished with yet. Jake got up and started carving away; it was the first time since I met Jake that I hadn't seen him with a smile on his face.

'Who wants to say a few words?' Mhairi was trying like a bear to get Dale to do something, but he never took her on.

'I will.' Christine stood up with a glass in her hand, and with a beautiful smile on her face, she began. 'I would like to thank Dale and Ashley for having us today. Everything has been perfect. Thank you for a lovely day . . . Ash, you are my friend and my sister, and I love you to pieces . . . Thanks to Mrs Black and Rosa for this lovely feast they have served. It looks delicious . . . So everyone raise a glass, to Christmas.' We all raised our glasses and settled down to eat. Dale and George were getting on like a house on fire talking across the table. Everyone was laughing and joking and enjoying their meal, apart from me and Nikki. I was stuck in some kind of slow motion watching everyone, and they were all doing what I wanted, getting along with one another. But now, I couldn't care if they were killing each other.

'Are you OK, kiddo?' I nudged Nikki with my arm, and I couldn't help but notice that she looked upset.

'I am sorry for ruining your day . . . I could kill myself for it.'

'You have nothing to apologise for, sweetie. I appreciate you telling us the truth.' I put my knife and fork down, and she turned to give me a hug. If I ever had a daughter, I would be proud if she turned out like Nikki.

'Thanks, Ash.'

'Now eat your dinner, young lady.' We laughed together and got back to eating our dinner. I really wanted to do well with my meal, but the sickness was going to take over if I ate any more.

'You have eaten more than I expected, babe.' I sat back on my chair sipping away at my water. 'Do you need anything?'

'My tablet. But eat first.' Dale was up and out of his seat in a flash. I might have guessed that he would be off like a shot.

'Thanks, honey.' I really hoped that it would work because I hated the sickness more than any pain.

'You're welcome, but you don't have to thank me, Ash.' Dale sat back on his seat and put his arm around me; his shoulder was a good rest. I noticed that Dale hadn't eaten much either. This all felt like the calm before the storm, like something was going to erupt. I just hoped that it could wait until today was over with.

'We have had an amazing day. Thank you for having us.' Christian and George had been great company the whole day. It was a pleasure to have them.

'Thank you both for joining us.' I got a kiss and a cuddle from both guys. I was so lucky to have friends like them. 'Roll on New Year.'

'Can't wait, honey.' Both men shook Dale's hand and left with Carlos. I loved seeing everyone, but I just hated saying goodbye. I didn't know if I was going to wake up tomorrow, and that was the worst feeling in this world.

'They are two lovely guys.' I knew that Dale got on really well with George; they were very alike apart from their sexuality.

'Yeah, they deserve each other.' The best two guys had now left; the hardest job was to get everyone else home.

'Thanks for today, Ash. It has been a blast.' Christine was putting her jacket on, and she looked as fresh as a daisy. I would always be jealous of how she could drink alcohol the way she did. I just had to sniff it, and I was ill the next day.

'Glad you enjoyed it, hun.'

'I hope you two have a nice night.' We had a group hug, and everything felt OK, but was it going to be OK?

'How are you getting home?' I was concerned about her getting down the mountain since Carlos had taken Christian and George home.

'Mr Black is taking Callum and me home.'

'What about Kiara?' Poor Kiara was getting pushed away already, and I certainly wasn't going to stand for it.

'Sophie is going home with Mhairi and Kiara.' I was so angry about the whole situation, but it really was none of my business. I walked over to my couch and sunk in to it. If the couch didn't wash my mood away, nothing would.

'Thanks for today, guys. I will be back tomorrow to see my car.'

'Look forward to it, kid.' I was so happy that Nikki liked her gift and now that it was at the cottage, I would see a lot more of her.

'Mom, Dad, we won't be here for a while tomorrow. I am going to take Ashley away for a few hours. I will call when we are back.'

This was the first I had heard of this plan, but I wasn't complaining.

'Oh, OK. Have a nice day . . . Are we all ready?' Everyone started walking towards the door, and I never even moved. I didn't want to waste any more energy on them.

'Have a nice night, Ash.'

'You too, Callum.' Dale played the dutiful husband and walked everyone out. The peace and quiet was amazing. I slipped my shoes off and curled my legs up beside me. I was comfortable at last.

'I didn't think that they were ever going to go.' My husband sounded a lot happier now that it was just the two of us.

'Tell me about it . . . It was a lovely day.' It was a lovely day after all the bickering stopped. If only we knew the truth to start with, there would have been no arguing.

'Apart from my family drama.' Dale sat down beside me, and I turned around and laid my head across his legs. I had been dreaming of this moment all afternoon.

'This family should have had drama as its middle name.' Dale played with my hair, and it felt so nice feeling his fingers run through my hair. 'I am sorry for hitting that witch today.'

'Don't you dare say sorry . . . If you weren't ill, I would have left you to it . . . She deserved a slap.' I didn't like violence. It wasn't needed in any situation. I didn't know what came over me, something inside me snapped.

'What do you have planned for tomorrow?' Curiosity was going to kill me if I didn't find out.

'Not sure yet . . . I just want you all to myself for a little while, with no interruptions and nobody to annoy us.'

'Sounds nice.' It was nice to hear that he still wanted me. After everything that we had been through, he should want to run in the opposite direction. Our love for one another was still as strong and unbroken, and I clung on to the fact that we could still have a fantastic life together if everything would go on plan.

CHAPTER 22

Counting the Days

Only forty-eight hours had passed since Christmas day, and already my time was running out hour by hour. I only had one more milestone to conquer, and that was our New Year's party. Around about 4 a.m. this morning, Dr Ching had me rushed into hospital because I felt like I was suffocating. I couldn't breathe and thought my time was up. I had never felt as frightened in my life, and the question that was on Dale's and Jake's minds was, do we phone Dr Ching or do we phone Leland? No one knew what was going on, and no one certainly knew what my outcome was going to be. They both knew that if I was in hospital, Leland had no chance of helping of me, but I thought that they both thought that I still had time left on this earth.

'Dale.' I could hear my doctor's voice, and I managed to open my eyes to see what was happening. Dale lifted his head off my hand and noticed right away that I had woken up.

'Hey, sweetheart . . . You had me worried sick.' I lifted my hand up to his cheek and rubbed a tear away. I didn't want to see him upset over me.

'How are you feeling, Ashley?' This was the first time I had seen Dr Ching since I snapped his head off, and I still felt kind of embarrassed about the whole thing.

'A lot better now. I can breathe.' The mask on my face drowned out my words, but Dr Ching and Dale understood me clearly enough.

'You gave everyone a fright, including myself . . . You have taken a very bad chest infection, and hopefully, now that you have had a rest and the antibiotics take control of it, you will start to feel better . . . I want to keep you here for a day or two, just to make sure you are OK . . . Everything will work better if we give you it thorough intravenous drips.' I hated hospitals, but I knew if I wanted to see New Year, then I would need to do as I was told.

'Is this all because of the cancer, Doc?'

'I am afraid so . . . Ashley's body can't defend the same as ours, and any weak spots will be an easy target for infection . . . Some people don't actually die through the cancer. It is the infections that cause the final blow.' I squeezed Dale's hand as tight as I could, just to let him know that I was still here. I needed to touch him, to let him know that I was going to fight till the end. 'I will be in and out all day, and I will keep you updated.'

'Thanks, Doc.' Dale leant down beside me, stroking the hair away from my face. 'I love you, Ash.'

'I love you too, Dale.' My love for him was still as strong as the day we met, and it was the only thing keeping me going right now.

'Just rest as much as you need, hun. I am not going anywhere.' The door opened, and Dale looked over his shoulder to see who was there.

'Can we come in?' I recognised Christine's voice, but who was 'we'?

'Sure.' Dale never moved from my side so I couldn't see who was with my friend.

'Hey, sweetie . . . You are looking much better already.' Christine's face was all pale and puffy from crying. I hated what I was doing to everyone whom I loved.

'How is she doing, Son?' Jake and Mhairi were standing at the bottom of my bed, and Dale turned his head slightly to communicate with everyone, but he never took his eyes from me.

'Better . . . Dr Ching said he is keeping her here for a day or two. The antibiotics will work quicker going through her vein . . . But he is pleased with her response, so far.' I felt like I was invisible, like I wasn't here. Everyone kept talking about me like I was still sleeping.

'You gave us all a fright, dear.' Jake touched my feet through the cover, and I managed to look down to him.

'I gave myself a fright.' My body felt so weak, and even just talking was taking everything out of me.

'It is good that you are feeling better, dear. We just wanted to see you before we went home.' This could have been my deathbed, but I wasn't ready to forgive and forget what Mhairi and Jake had done on Christmas day.

'Dad, will you bring me a change of clothes?'

'Of course, I will, Son . . . Does Ashley need anything else in?'

'No. I packed a lot of things while we were waiting for the ambulance.' I couldn't even remember leaving the cottage. It all must have happened so quickly. My head was in a blur, and the only thing that I could remember was Dale waking me up because he heard me breathing funny, and it all pretty much faded from there.

'OK . . . If you need anything, just give us a ring anytime.'

'Thanks, Dad.'

'Take care, Ash, you will be home in no time.' I couldn't bring myself to speak much so a smile was all I managed. Jake patted Dale on the shoulder, and my in-laws left my room. Mhairi never said a word; perhaps she was still worried about Christmas Day. She would have known too well that I wasn't happy with her.

'Do you mind if I stay a while?' Why Christine was asking that question, I would never know.

'Christine, you don't need to ask that, stay as long as you like. I could use the company when Ashley sleeps.' I loved Dale so much. It meant a lot to me that he made Christine feel a part of all this. They had had their differences, but they had managed to put them all to one side for my benefit.

'Thanks, honey.' Christine pulled over a chair and took my hand. I had my two favourite people here with me, and I was happy. Anything could happen now, and nothing else mattered. Life or death, and I was ready for it.

'Just you get as much rest as you need, Ash . . . Dale and I will be here when you need us.' I was happy to see my husband and my best friend working together to make my last days special. This was one moment that I would never forget, no matter what happened.

'Dale.' I jumped as I woke up. Everything was so quiet, and I forgot where I was. I felt terrified until I saw some sign that I was still alive.

'What's wrong, babe?' Dale and Christine jumped to my side. They looked just as terrified as I did.

'I just got a fright.' I gripped both of their hands like they were going to vanish.

'You're OK, babe. We are still here . . . You have been sleeping on and off from yesterday.' No a wonder I didn't know what I was doing or saying just now. Sleep had overtaken everything, and I was left in a whirlpool of thoughts and emotions.

'That's why I feel really fresh.'

'Dr Ching took you off the oxygen earlier this morning to see how things would go.' I put my hand up to my mouth to make sure that it was gone, and it was a relief to see that there was some improvement.

'When can I go home?' I must be feeling better. I wanted to go home.

'Dr Ching is going to be back soon. We can ask him what he thinks.'

'You must be feeling better, Ash. That is the first you have asked to go home.' Christine knew me too well than I knew myself sometimes.

'I feel OK . . . Better than what I can remember, anyway.' Everything was a bit of a blur, but I could remember thinking that it was the end of the road. 'We have a party to organise.'

'That is the spirit, chick.' I would be at that party, even if I was on my deathbed. I didn't make a promise and then break it. I never had before, and I wasn't about to start now.

'Have you heard anything about Kiara?'

'Dr Ching sent a paternity test away, so we are just waiting for the results.' That was also a relief that something had been done. The longer it was left, the harder it would be for everyone.

'Where is Kiara now?'

'Still here . . . She has a pretty dress for Aunty Ashley's party.' My heart melted to know that she was still here, and I could still spend some time with her.

'Hi, everyone . . .' I was glad to see Dr Ching for a change. 'It is nice to see you awake, Ashley.'

'Dr Ching, when can I go home?'

'Well, that is a good sign that you are on the mend that you feel ready to go home. I can change your antibiotics to tablet form now that you are stronger . . . I don't see why you can't go home today.' If I had the energy, I could have kissed this man right now.

'Thank you.' Christine and Dale were smiling like Cheshire cats. They were just as happy as I was to be going home. It mustn't have been much fun for them keeping a vigil at my bedside.

'Susan will come in and get you off everything, and I will go and organise the paperwork . . . Oh and Ashley, you will be leaving that bed to go into a wheelchair just until I am satisfied that your chest is strong enough to cope with walking again.' A wheelchair. Was that necessary? I wasn't going to argue. I just wanted to go home. But I wasn't happy about the thought of spending my last days in a damn chair.

'If I must.' My husband found my sulky tone very amusing. I was glad that I could amuse someone.

'Right, Ash, I am going to head up to the cottage, and I will see you there.' I was glad that Christine would be at the cottage for me going home because I wanted to spend as much time as I could with everyone.

'OK. Thank you for everything, Christine.'

'What are friends for? Just do as you're told.' Christine picked up her things and kissed my cheek. She looked at me with wide eyes to get me to promise.

'OK. I promise to do as I am told.' This was the one time that I had no intentions of arguing or doing something that would hurt me.

'Phone me when you leave, Dale, and I will get the coffee and lunch organised.' I played with the sleeve of Dale's cardigan, and it was nice to appreciate the silly things in life. It was just me and Dale in the room now, and it was nice to get him to myself. I used to love snuggling into that cardigan he was wearing; maybe that was why I couldn't wait to get home.

'You are going to do as you're told, aren't you, babe?' I smiled at him and looked down at our hands joined together. I had no idea why everyone thought that I wouldn't listen.

'Don't worry, I am not going to be difficult.' Dale leant over and placed his soft, warm lips over mine. I had missed him so much.

'Hi, Ashley.' As usual someone walked in on our kisses. 'You look so much better, darling.' I wished that everyone would stop saying that to me.

'I feel it.'

'I have your needles to take out and your catheter. I will be as quick as I can, honey . . . Dale, do you want to stay?' Susan knew now that Dale would never leave me if he didn't have to.

'If Ash wants me to?'

'I would like you to stay, but go if it will make you feel uncomfortable.' It couldn't be nice for men to sit through intimate procedures.

'Don't be silly. I will stay with you.' Dale sat on the bed facing me, and he never took his eyes off me. Everything would feel so much easier with him beside me.

'I will do the worst bit first, Ashley . . . If you can open your legs and relax, it will be over in a few seconds.' My face must be bright red with embarrassment. Lying there with my husband and nurse, and my legs are sprawled open. It was a good job Susan knew what she was doing, and she left the cover over for privacy.

'That is it all done, honey. You have got some bleeding, but that is only to be expected at this stage.' Tears rolled down my cheeks, and Dale rubbed them away with his hand. 'You are going to get symptom after symptom, but we can help with most of them . . . If the bleeding gets too heavy, say to Dr Ching, and he can give you something to slow it down, possibly even stop it.'

'It just all feels real now.' My heart was aching at the thought of all the symptoms starting. I didn't know how I was going to cope now.

'I hear that a lot, Ashley . . . People can block out a lot when there isn't any symptoms to remind them . . . That is everything all out, honey. Dr Ching will bring the paperwork in just shortly. I can help you get your clothes on if you like.'

'Thanks.' I was going to let Susan help me to get organised, just to let Dale have five minutes on a chair away from me.

'Christine has brought you in a jogging suit for comfort.' My friend was the queen of comfort; she always knew what to wear for comfort. 'I will just nip to the little man's room since Susan is more than capable to help you.'

'Don't be long.' I got my kiss on the head before he left. I hated to be apart from him so I could only imagine how he felt at the thought of losing me forever.

'How are you both coping with all this, honey?' No one had ever asked me this question before, and I had no idea. How could I answer it correctly?

'We have got through every hurdle . . . I mean I don't know how other people cope, but Dale has been a tower of strength . . . We have had tears and laughter . . . How he copes when I am gone, now that will be a different story.' If everything went badly, I just knew that Dale would crumble to pieces.

'We have a bereavement counsellor who will help him get through the tough bits, and I will always be here to answer any questions that he has.' That was nice to know, but Dale was a private man. He wouldn't open up to a stranger.

'Now that my end is near, I am not sure I am ready to leave.' Susan stopped helping me put my bottoms on and looked up to me.

'I shouldn't tell you this . . . But from working here for a lot of years, a lot of my patients have said the very same. But come their last hours on this earth, they can tell me that they are ready to go because they have crammed that many things in to their last weeks, months, or years that they are satisfied. They are ready to lie at rest.'

'I only have one milestone left, and that is a New Year's party . . . We have planned a party on New Year's Eve for family and friends . . . I just want to see this year out with a bang.'

'Good for you, honey . . . Do you think that you can stand?'

'Yeah, of course.' I felt fine today, so standing shouldn't be a problem.

'You have a lovely family, Ashley. That makes all the difference.' I edged my way off the bed while Susan was helping at my side. Never in a million years did I think that I would need help to get clothes on. 'Just stand up, honey, and I will pull them up for you.' It was nice to have a conversation with someone who could answer any concerns I had. 'You can sit back down, Ashley, and I will go and get a wheelchair.' I hated the word 'wheelchair' already, and I didn't even have one. Susan left the room, and seconds later, Dale came back in.

'You look like a new person sitting there, babe.'

'I feel a lot better sitting up.' I just wanted to get home because this room was driving me crazy.

'Here we go. Your own set of wheels.' Dale and I watched Susan and Dr Ching came back into the room with my new friend.

'Here goes, Ash.' Susan positioned the chair beside me, and Dale took my arm to help me swing into it.

'I feel like an old lady using this contraption.'

'I have your antibiotics here, Ashley. You have got to take them three times a day, and I will call in tomorrow to see how you are.' No one was even taking me on about the wheelchair. I had to use it, and that was that, end of story.

'Thank you, Dr Ching.' I felt free again. I was leaving the hospital to go home with my husband, and it felt very good. Dr Ching opened the door, and Dale pushed me out. I wanted to run out of the hospital, but under the circumstances, I didn't think that would be happening any time soon.

'Dale, do you need a hand out to the car?'

'I should be fine. Thanks, Susan. I have my driver out front.'

'Take care, both of you.' Susan was such a lovely person. I certainly wouldn't like to do her job though; it had to be tough watching people that you have been looking after die. Dale pushed me through the hospital, and I sat in silence taking everything in. Every time I came down this long hall, I felt relieved that I was getting another day with my family.

'It is good to get you out of here, Ash.'

'It is good to be leaving here.' We went through the main doors, and I spotted Carlos standing by the car. He moved quickly to open the door. Everyone was on autopilot lately, and it had to be done yesterday.

'Hi, gorgeous.' Carlos was pleased to see me as we stopped at the car, and it was good to still have a banter with him.

'Hi, handsome.' I really appreciated the banter; it made a difference to everyone treating me like a dying person.

'How do you want to do this, Ash?'

'I just want to get up and walk. Don't let me fall, and we will be fine.' The sarcasm and the nippy sweetie was there, but I was more than capable to get into a car without thinking about it.

'I think that we will manage to keep you standing, babe.' My heart was racing right now. I knew that Dale and Carlos wouldn't let me fall, but I was frightened to show them how weak I was. I pushed out of the chair, and Carlos caught my arm as I stumbled.

'Thank you, Carlos.' Dale pulled the chair away and held my waist as I swung around and sat in the car. 'Ow.' I flinched when I got a sharp pain in my lower stomach. This car hated me sitting in the back. Every time I came out of the hospital, I got the same pain sitting in the back of this car.

'Are you OK?'

'Yeah, I am fine. I am in the car in one piece. Thanks to my two strapping helpers.' Dale and Carlos smiled at me, and Dale closed my door. I heard them fighting to get the chair in the car, but to my amazement, they managed perfectly. What would I do without them? They could have left it for all I cared.

'Let's get you home, honey.' I reached over and took his hand in mine. Home sounded good right now. The feel of the cottage was just what I needed. I placed my head on Dale's shoulder and rested my eyes. I realised how lucky I was. I had more time as a human, and I planned to make the most of it.

'Ashley, we are home.' I sat up and tried to compose myself. I only meant to rest my eyes, but as usual, I closed my eyes and my body thought that it was time to sleep. 'Carlos has got the chair out already.' I looked over to the open door, and there sitting in front of me was the dreaded wheelchair. Dale got out of the car and came around to my side; both of these men were going to drive me crazy. 'Just take your time, hun.' I edged my way out of the car and gripped on to Dale's arm; both Dale and Carlos helped me swing round into the chair. My mind and body didn't feel like they were working together any more. 'Are you OK, Ash?' If Dale asked me that question once more, I was going to crack up.

'I just want to get inside.' Carlos wheeled me away before Dale could reply, and I was glad that he used initiative to get me away.

'Welcome home, Ashley.' I thought that I was coming home to Christine, but everyone was here: Jake, Mhairi, Cal, Nikki, and Kiara. This was great, just what I needed.

'I was so worried about you, Mrs.' Nikki was the first to come and hug me, and out of everyone in the cottage, she was the only one whom I wanted to see, apart from Christine.

'I am fine, kiddo.' I was shocked to see the whole living room had changed around to make room for the chair. I didn't like it much because it wasn't my living room any more. 'What has happened in here?' No one answered me so I guessed they knew that I wasn't happy. 'Dale, can you help me into bed, please? I feel shattered.' I had great intentions to come home and sit in my living room and get cosy, but now I could have quite easily screamed in all their faces.

'Sure. Christine, do you want to give us a hand?' Dale knew that I wasn't happy, and I thought that was why he got Christine to help us, to find out what had happened. I got wheeled right into my room, and I sat with my hand on my head at least my room hadn't changed. 'Christine, what the hell is going on?' Dale was furious, but for some reason, this had Mhairi's name all over it.

'Don't ask me. They were here before me, and the cottage was already changed before I could say Ash will hate it.' Why did everyone think that they could treat me like a child?

'Ash, it will all be back to normal in the morning.' I really couldn't care at the moment. I just wanted to curl up in my own bed. I tried to get myself out of the damn chair when Christine jumped to my aid. I needed to realise that I wasn't alone, and I had lots of people who wanted to be here to help me.

'Thanks.'

'Do you want pyjamas, chick?'

'No, I will keep this on just now.' I had been in pyjamas long enough, and I was comfortable enough just now without using energy I clearly didn't have. I got helped to swing into bed, and I immediately felt ten times better. This was my room, my bed, my sanctuary.

'I have offered Christine the spare room for the time being if she wants it.' I thought how thoughtful that was. It was a pity that other family members weren't as thoughtful to other's feelings.

'Only if that is OK with you.' Christine was trying to see what I thought before she accepted Dale's offer.

'Of course, it is. I would love nothing more.' I squeezed Christine's hand as she sat beside me.

'I will nip home and get some things while you are resting.' I watched carefully as Christine left the room. Today couldn't get any better even if they tried. I lay back and curled into a ball on my side. I was comfortable relaxing in my bed, and I didn't care what happened with anyone else right at this moment.

'I will be back in a few minutes, honey . . . I will get my interfering mother put straight.' We both knew that she was interfering, but could anyone put her straight? The room went silent as Dale left me in bed, and I had time to think about everything. That wasn't a good idea right now.

I had to put any bad thoughts out of my mind and think positive about my party in three days. The phone startled me, and without hesitation, I picked the receiver up from my bedside table.

'Hello . . . Yes, Dr Ching. It is Ashley. I am in bed before you say anything . . . No just me. Why? Just tell me and I will pass it on . . . Are you sure . . . ? No, thank you . . . Bye for now.' Dale was standing in the doorway intrigued about my phone call.

'It was Dr Ching.' I couldn't help but smile. I had just won the lottery. 'Kiara is Callum's daughter . . . She is our niece.' The smile on Dale's face was priceless. This was the best news that we have had in a long time, and I thought today couldn't get any better. Who would have thought that a piece of news like that would make my day?

'About time this family gets some good news . . . I should tell them.' Dale left my door open as he told them the good news, and everyone seemed so happy. It was just what Cal needed. I could finally rest at peace and close my eyes.

'Someone wants to see Aunty Ashley.' I opened my eyes to see Kiara in Dale's arms. It didn't matter how tired or horrible I felt, this little angel could make me feel a hundred per cent better.

'Hello, princess.' Dale came and sat beside me with her, and I couldn't ask for any more today.

'Callum has asked if we will have her for a couple of hours until he sorts things out with Sophie.'

'It will be nice to have her all to ourselves.' I couldn't stop watching Dale with her; he was a natural. 'You are so good with her.'

'It is just nice to know that she is a Black.' I knew that he would love for her to share the Black's name, and now he had his wish. It was just a pity that his luck wasn't always in.

'You can make sure she gets everything she ever wants or needs.'

'We can, you mean.' I noticed that Kiara had her dress on that we had got her for Christmas. She looked very girly in pink.

'She looks tired.'

'She is due her feed and a sleep . . . She has just been changed.'

'Can I feed her?'

'You don't need to ask, babe. She would love for you to feed her and get a cuddle.' Dale handed me her, and she cuddled right in. She obviously knew that she was in my arms. 'I will go and get her bottle.' I was grateful to see what it would be like to have a baby. Kiara eased my craving to be a mother in a lot of ways. I never realised how much I would have wanted a baby until I fell in love with Dale. I just had to live with the idea of never carrying a child of my own.

'Here we go.'

'She is nearly sleeping already.' I laughed at her face just before she sucked her bottle. She was a wee cherub. 'I wonder if she will still love me when I am cold and hard like steel?' It was a stupid thought, but babies could sense a lot.

'She won't care, Ash. You are her guardian angel, and she will love you no matter what you are.' I really hoped that he was right. I couldn't bear her hating me. She could devour a bottle quicker than anything I had ever seen. I didn't know why she wouldn't take a bottle like this for anyone else. 'When I put her down, we can cuddle up if you like?' Did I like? Of course, I liked. I couldn't take another hour, not cuddled up beside him.

'Sounds nice.' Kiara was sound asleep before I even took her bottle away. I sat her up slightly to break her wind, and it came from her toes. I didn't even have to try. 'Bring her pram in, Dale.' Her little face was the cutest thing I had ever seen. Dale took her carefully from me and placed her in her pram.

'She looks so peaceful.' Dale came and climbed in beside me and dulled the lights down. It felt nice to be lying here with the love of my life. 'I missed this, Ash.'

'Me too, babe. I sleep like a baby when I curl up beside you.'

'That is nice to know, honey. I will only move if Kiara moves . . . Just rest, sweetie.' His voice was soft and tender, just like he needed this moment as much as I did. I closed my eyes and listened to his heartbeat until I couldn't fight sleep any more.

I woke myself up screaming, and Dale was hovering over the top of me. 'What is it, baby?' I had just had the worst nightmare, ever.

'Just a nightmare.' Dale climbed in beside me and held me tightly.

'I am here, honey. You don't have to worry about anything.' My body was trembling from the nightmare because it felt so real.

'It was horrible . . . I was buried in a hole alive, and all the soil was in my mouth . . . I couldn't breathe.' I started to cry softly into Dale's chest; it was a good job that he was waterproof to the amount of tears he has been surrounded in over the last few weeks.

'It is OK. Ash. You are safe . . . It was just a nightmare.' Dale's big hand running through my hair gently calmed me down. I could finally breathe easily.

'I actually feel quite hungry. I should have a nightmare more often.' We both found me amusing as I sat forward and wrapped the covers around me.

'Well, that is a good sign. What do you fancy?'

'Pizza.' We both laughed together, just like it was natural for me to say 'pizza'. I had no idea where my weird cravings were coming from because I hadn't ate a pizza since I was at school.

'Do you want to come through? And I will order one, or do you want to stay through here?' I was glad that he was giving me choices; it didn't make me feel like I wasn't here.

'I will come through. Where is Kiara?' I had forgotten all about her being here until I spotted her empty bottle on the side.

'She has had her bath, and I just fed her, so I put her down for the night.' Mr Organised sitting here. I didn't know why I was surprised. I knew that he would be a hands-on kind of dad.

'Is she staying the night?'

'Yeah, Christine and Cal have gone for something to eat, and Christine is going to go back with Cal tonight.'

'What happened to Sophie?' My body cringed deep inside, but I needed to know.

'She has agreed to leave Kiara here. They are going to get papers drawn up, so she can't just take her back when she feels like it.'

'Good. I am glad everything has worked out for the best.' It was about time things worked in this family's favour. Dale got up, and I sat up slowly.

'I will get your chair.' That definitely wasn't necessary.

'Dale, I can walk if you help me. We can eat pizza and curl up with a movie.' I could see Dale thinking about this one carefully. He didn't want to cause me any more problems, but the chair was my biggest problem.

'OK. But if you can't manage, just say.' All I wanted to do was show him that I was stronger than I looked. 'Just take it slowly.' I couldn't run a marathon, but I was walking come what may.

'Just two days ago I felt 100 per cent, and now I am walking as slow as a snail.' How could things get so bad, so quickly?

'We knew that it was going to be a tough ride, honey.' I didn't expect things to deteriorate so quickly; it had been a shock to my system. 'You are doing well, Ash.' I looked ahead when I got to the living room, and everything had been put back in its original place. No one would have known a thing had been moved if they hadn't seen it.

'Thank God, everything got put back.' I didn't want to sound ungrateful, but nothing looked right when we came back from the hospital.

'I didn't like it either . . . My mom put it all back after our talk.' Now I was worried. Dale and Mhairi couldn't just talk. 'Don't look so worried. We didn't kill each other.'

'That is something I suppose.' I sank into the couch to catch my breath and recharge my batteries. The least little thing used whatever energy I had left. 'You would think I just run a marathon.'

'Baby steps, Ash.' Dale grabbed the phone and returned to my side as quick as lightning 'What kind of pizza do you fancy?'

'Meat feast.' I couldn't help but snigger to myself. 'Don't ask where that came from.'

'Hey, Carlos, could you bring us up a meat feast pizza, please . . . ? Yeah, she is fine, buddy. Just hungry for pizza . . . Thanks, Carlos.'

'You could have gone yourself. I would have been fine. Kiara wouldn't have budged.'

'Absolutely not, Mrs Black. You heard Dr Ching.' How did I know that answer was coming, my shadow wouldn't leave me in a month of Sundays. 'What film do you fancy?'

'Anything as long as it isn't sad.' I turned my back on Dale, and he placed his arm around me. 'I actually don't care about a film. Sitting like this with you is all I need right now.' It was amazing how much this illness had brought me out of my shell because six months ago I would never have told any man what I wanted from them.

'I am sure that it can be arranged, Mrs Black.'

'I am going to be sentimental right now because you need to know this . . . I just want to thank you for changing my life for the better. We have had lots of good times in such a short time, and I will never forget anything you have done for me.' I needed to share how I felt before I burst with holding everything inside.

'You don't have to thank me, babe. You are the only person whom I have ever felt complete with. From the very first moment I laid eyes on you . . . your smile melted my heart. I just wish that I could have met you a few years earlier.' That made both of us. Life felt complete when we were together. Nothing could compare to our feelings that we share as one.

'Whatever happens, Dale, you have to promise me that you will take care of everyone, including yourself . . . I will rest at peace knowing that Christine is with Cal and Kiara is still a part of this family. But most of all I need to know that you won't fall to pieces.' This was a big ask, but I needed to hear him say it.

'I can't promise that, but I will try to keep everything together . . . But Lavina knows what she is doing, honey. Please don't give up.' I was being so brave right now that I didn't want to shatter it all into pieces. But I knew that each day I was losing more of my battle to live.

'I won't give up on purpose. I just felt that it was time to tell you how I feel. My body is failing fast . . . Our time is running out.' I tilted my head back to look at my husband, and his eyes were closed. He was clearly in pain from everything I just said. 'Dale, look at me . . . We are going to have a perfect New Year's Eve . . . We . . .' I got stopped from going any further by Dale's lips on mine. I could feel his need to be with me and the pain of losing me forever.

'We are going to enjoy what we have left, Ash.' A huge weight had been lifted from my shoulders with just sharing my feelings. But my relief was Dale's burden. The only joy that I could bring from this terrible illness was that I could pass away in the arms of the one I love.

Chapter 23

Nearly Time

I must have been the most kindest man in the world. He always aimed to please, and by God he certainly pleased. I lay here relaxing in a nice, hot bubble bath surrounded by luxurious-scented candles. It felt so nice just lying here. The weather was so cold outside, and the water felt like heaven. My skin was starting to get all wrinkled because I had been lying in the water for so long. I thought Dale had forgotten all about me stuck in the bath. I didn't want to put him out by shouting on him. I knew that he would come back in for me when he was ready. This time just gave me more time to think about everything in general. If I could go back to live my life over, I would grab it with both hands and enjoy every single minute of it. Life is too short and you never know what is around the corner. I had spent my life worrying what everyone else thinks so that I had lost the biggest part of it, and it seemed such a waste. The day Dale came into my life was the day that I started living, and I would be forever in his debts because without him, I would have missed so much happiness and joy.

'Hey, Ash, sorry I took so long.' *He* sounded out of puff, like he had been working too hard. Now that was something that I would like to see.

'What have you been doing?'

'My mom had me and my dad bringing everything in for tomorrow night. I think that she thinks we are feeding the five thousand.' Mhairi knew how to throw a party. She could quite easily cater for five thousand if she wanted to. 'The more the merrier' was her motto.

'She is at her happiest when she is being a hostess.' I pushed up out of the bath with a lot of Dale's help, and I realised how much harder this task was becoming.

'That wasn't so bad, was it?' I really wished that Dale didn't like helping me so much. I detest being a burden on him, and it just made me sound ungrateful when I moan. The hardest part was stepping out and keeping my balance. I didn't want to end up on the floor. 'Sit here, honey, and I will help you get your things on.' I felt like there was nothing that I could do on my own any more. It was hard being me right now. I wished that I could curl away and hibernate until it was all over. 'I have taken you some warm things out to wear. My dad was going to rekindle the fire for us going back through.' Feeling like you were useless was a big thing for me. I had always felt independent, but now I just felt inadequate all the time. I could understand why people use euthanasia in many situations now. I was always against any form of euthanasia, but since I became ill, I had felt like a huge burden on my family and I had hated every minute of it. If anyone asked me now, what I thought about euthanasia, then I would say favourable. Not just because I felt like a burden, but I was slowly dying and no one was going to stop that. It would, however, stop me being in pain.

'The cottage is always toasty when the fire gets going. Jake is a master at starting the fire.' I tried to get myself back on track and forget about all the negative things going on just now because one good thing was I had a good loyal family behind me.

'Don't tell him that. We will never hear the end of it.'

'Dale . . . Ash. Do you need a hand with anything?' I didn't even know that Christine was back; it was nice to hear her voice again.

'Come in, Christine.' I was all ready, but my hair needed put up out of the way. There were some things that a man couldn't do for a woman.

'Hey, how are you doing today, chic?'

'I am fine, honey. Can you put my hair up please?'

'Sure, I can. Dale, your mom is driving everyone crazy in there, including your dad.'

'What part of that is suppose to shock me?' I loved how we could all still laugh together; it was good not to be so serious all the time.

'She is some piece of work . . . But mind you she is well organised.' Organised should have been her middle name. She just didn't know when to stop once she got started.

'Control freak, more like.' Dale was getting good at speaking up about his mom. When we first met, I thought that he would be the type of son who would do anything to keep the peace. How wrong could I have been? They were like two peas in a pod, and they just clashed over the stupidest of things.

'Are you ready to face the wolves, Ash?' I actually laughed at Christine's comments because Mhairi was harmless. She just didn't know when to stop most of the time.

'Wheel me through.' Dale opened the door, and Christine wheeled me through. They could work well together when they both wanted to. I could feel the heat of the fire as we went down the hall. You could just tell that it was a winter's day.

'Hello, dear, how are you?' Mhairi was always so polite to me, even when she was in a mood with everyone else. We had bonded so well together when Kiara first arrived, so that even now when she drove me crazy, I still had a close bond with her.

'I am feeling as good as I should be.'

'Let me get you a coffee and something to eat . . . Is there anything you would like?'

'Coffee sounds good, but I am into everything that isn't good for me. I am not sure I fancy anything to eat.' Mhairi was a bit of a health freak. Everything that she cooks would be good for you, and I wasn't into the whole idea of eating healthily.

'It is a good job that I made strawberry and white chocolate muffins last night.' My mouth was watering at the thought of them. I wasn't expecting them, so it was a nice surprise.

'Sounds delicious.' Mhairi ran along to the kitchen, and I smiled at Dale; she really did mean well.

'I hope Kiara wasn't any bother last night, Ash?' I knew that it was Callum behind me, but I never saw him when I came through.

'She was a little angel. She slept all night. We will have her any time.'

'How was your night out, bro?' Did Dale really need to ask that question? We didn't really need all the glory details.

'Perfect. We just went into town and were home by twelve.' I couldn't be happier that Cal and Christine were an item; it felt right when they were together.

'It was a pity they couldn't keep the noise down.'

'We said sorry, Mom. You don't have to tell the whole world.' Cal's face was a picture, beetroot red sprung to mind.

'Here you are, my dear . . . I don't want a dozen grandchildren run around. You hear me.' It was normally Jake who would be the joker when it came to intimate situations, but I couldn't help but laugh at Mhairi; I was shocked, to say the least.

'You don't have to worry about that, Mrs Black.' Poor Christine was a funny shade of red. I was quite amused because she never got embarrassed easily.

'Thank you, Mhairi. The muffins look lovely.' Home-made baking was always the best. The fresh scent just reminded me of my kitchen while growing up. My mom was a perfect baker; she always baked for stalls for the community charities. My mom and Mhairi would have got on so well together. It was a shame that they didn't get a chance to meet. 'Hmm, delicious.'

'I am so glad that she can't hear you say that.' Dale was right. I would turn into a muffin if she knew that I liked them.

'Dr Ching has just pulled up.' Christine always knew how to spoil a moment, and I suddenly lost my appetite. I couldn't win; they told me to eat, but it was them making me lose interest in food.

'Hi, Doc, come and get a seat.' Our living room had never emptied quicker. Suddenly, it was just Dale and me sitting waiting to hear what he had to say.

'How are you doing today, Ashley?'

'I feel OK.'

'Good. How is the pain?' I was getting so fed up answering the same questions over and over again. I was going to record my answers and just put it on play when the doctor came around.

'It is OK . . . I have felt worse.'

'And Susan told me about the bleeding. How is that today?'

'Just the same.' I always felt uncomfortable talking to Dr Ching. I didn't know why. I meant this was his job after all.

'Have you had any new symptoms occur over night?'

'Nope.'

'It is good to see you using the wheelchair.'

'I have no choice. My balance is very poor.' As much as I wanted to get on without it, I just wouldn't manage.

'Eating and drinking?' I sarcastically pointed to the cake sitting on my knee.

'I have weird cravings for things that I would never have eaten before.'

'You could be living off takeaways every night, and I wouldn't care as long as you were eating.' Most things that I want was fast food; it was so strange. 'Well, I am happy to leave you in Susan's capable hands, but if anything changes, do not hesitate to phone me.' That was the best news. I really liked Susan, and she really understood me.

'Thanks, Doc.'

'I hope that you have a nice New Year, and I will try and pop in tomorrow night.'

'Thanks, Dr Ching.' I got back to my muffin as soon as the doctor was leaving the cottage. I always liked to see the back of him.

'That was a flying visit.'

'He was just checking that I was OK, Christine . . . And making sure I am doing everything I should be.' It was kind of hard not to be doing what I should be with everyone fussing over me every minute of every day.

'All is OK, though, isn't it?' I heard the concern in her voice, and she really didn't need to be worried today.

'Yes, honey.' I was already so sick of talking about me today. I really wanted everyone to change the subject.

'Mrs Black, do you fancy taking a trip out with me?' I heard Dale's voice, but he couldn't be talking to me, could he? 'Ash.'

'Me?' I was shocked and surprised all at the same time. I thought that I would be grounded until I took my last breath.

'Don't sound so shocked. You are Mrs Black, aren't you?'

'Sure, I will come. Where are we going?' I actually got quite excited because I never expected to be leaving the cottage again.

'I don't know yet, but it will get us out of here.' He must be a mind-reader because my head was nipping with everyone going on.

'I will grab your things, Ash.' OK. Now I was worrying. Christine was helping me get out of here; what was going on? I must be missing something somewhere. 'You can take my car if you like, which will save you taking the big Merc for the chair.'

'OK. What is going on?' Why was no one moaning or fighting that I was going out?

'You are going with your husband. We know that you will be safe.' I still wasn't convinced. I could smell a rat. I enjoyed putting my winter warmers on. Anyone would think that I won a million dollars just by getting the opportunity to get out of here.

'Are you ready, babe?'

'Yep.'

'Have a nice day, you guys.' Christine followed us out to the car, and I felt like I could breathe just getting outside. I didn't feel like a prisoner any more.

'I have left Ashley's key on the bedside table if you need a car.'

'I am not going anywhere.'

'I will manage to get myself in.' I wanted to help myself. I was sick of being a burden to everyone.

'OK. I will be right beside you.' Dale was like me security net; nothing could happen when he was around. I felt stronger in myself today, so I pushed up out of the chair and held on to the door to walk into the car. I was never so glad to sit down. 'Ash, are you OK?'

'Perfect.'

'Enjoy your peace.' Christine's sarcastic tone made us all laugh; we knew that she meant Mhairi was going to drive her crazy.

'See you later, Christine.' She shut my door and walked back to the cottage. I felt bad leaving her to cope with Mhairi, but I had to think about my own sanity for a change. 'So where are we going?'

'I have no idea. I just wanted to have you all to myself without my interfering mother.'

'It will be nice to spend some quality time together, but there is the small matter of that damn chair.' The chair stopped me from thinking about what we could do.

'What about a movie?'

'Sounds good. I can't remember the last time I went to the movies . . .' I was a teenager the last time I was at the movies, and we watched *Dante's Peak*. It did feel really nice doing things like a normal couple would do. 'It feels weird being back in this car.' I was so used to the Merc or my own car now.

'It is even weirder driving it . . . I would choose your car any day. It is a dream to drive.' That was a weird one for me to hear because I thought that Dale loved his own car.

'I didn't think you would enjoy driving my car.'

'Neither did I . . . She is yours, so I guess that is why I like her.' I loved Dale's honesty. For a millionaire, he didn't beat about the bush. Honesty is the best policy.

'Where is the movies about?'

'Just along here.' I didn't know where anything was around here. I was glad Dale knew where everything was or it would be the blind leading the blind. I looked out of the window, and although everything was white from the snow, it was still so beautiful. I had never seen as much snow before. In Florida, we very rarely got snow, and if we ever got a flurry, it never stuck to the ground. I spotted a big building surrounded by blue lights, and I guessed that it was where we were going. Dale pulled into a very big car park, and it looked very busy. I suddenly felt very nervous about using my chair in front of a lot of people. I clenched my hands into the seat and took a deep breath as Dale pulled into a space. 'I will get your chair out first.' I felt very embarrassed already, and I wasn't even out of the car. I hated the thought of using that chair in a public place. I would have rather stayed in the cottage. 'That's us waiting, Ash.' I sat looking straight ahead in front of me, and Dale obviously knew that there was something bothering me. 'What is wrong, babe?'

'That.' I pointed over to the wheelchair without even looking at it. I hated it with a passion.

'Ash, don't let it bother you. No one will even notice the chair.' We both knew that wasn't true, but I decided to stop acting like a baby and get it out of the car. It was harder getting out of the car compared to getting in. Life was too short to sit and dwell about silly little things. I had to do this because it would probably be the last time that I would get out alone with Dale.

'It is a good job I married a strong man.'

'Is that a compliment, Mrs Black?'

'Yeah, I suppose it is.'

'I have never been here before. All the years that I have lived here, I have never been to watch a movie.' A part of me was surprised that he hadn't been here before, but there was another part of me that knew he was a workaholic before he met me.

'Please tell me that you lifted my bag?'

'What do you need a bag for? I have my wallet.' I needed to get used to having everything. It was weird being out without a purse, but I knew that I didn't need one when Dale was around.

'So where did you go on a date?'

'What?'

'You said that you haven't been here before, so where did you go on a date?'

'I never really did dates. It was mainly something to eat and a few drinks and that was very rare. Then I met you, and I realised what I had been missing all these years . . . You bring the best out of me, Ash.' It all felt like a waste. This was our first and last movie together, and it made me feel quite emotional.

'I will take that as a compliment, shall I?'

'Of course . . . We are going to go in here and pig out on everything that we don't normally eat.' That sounded like heaven. My taste buds were in full swing.

'Sounds good.' We walked through the main doors, and everything got me so excited that I completely forgot about my chair.

'So what do you want to watch?' There was so much to choose from that I couldn't make my mind up. *'Ice age 4, Batman, The expendables 2, Ted, Arthur Christmas, . . .'* The list was endless, and nothing was jumping out at me.

'Do you fancy anything, Dale?' I really didn't care what we watched because I was just glad to be here having some fun with my husband.

'Anything you like, honey.'

'What about *Ted*?'

'OK. Let's get tickets and stock up on lots of goodies.' This felt so nice. Never did I expect to be here today. It had been a spur of the moment decision, and it was going to be a good day. Everyone was having too much fun to even notice me sitting in a chair, and I realised now that I was just overreacting before. 'We have thirty minutes until show time, so where to first?'

'The biggest pick 'n' mix ever.' My taste buds are watering for junk. I just loved a pick 'n' mix. I was pushed over to the stall, and we both filled our containers up. We were like children. Who would have thought that we were adults?

'We will have sore jaws by the time we are finished.'

'I must say that you are a good chauffeur.'

'Another compliment.'

'What can I say, I am in a good mood today.' This had been the best day that I had had in a long time. I was glad that he suggested we go out; it was just what we both needed.

'Do you fancy a big hot dog with lots of onions and tomato sauce?' I was learning today. I would never have thought that my hubby would be into hot dogs. I would never have guessed in a million years.

'Sounds delicious.' If I could run to the hot dog stand, I would have. It was good to release the inner child for a change.

'Do you want a drink, babe?'

'We'll have a coke.' I sat patiently while Dale went into the queue. He looked back at me, and I was still in love with his smile. I hadn't seen a smile like that since day one. Who would have thought a day at the movies would rekindle our time. I was that happy that I didn't want today to end. Everything was perfect in more ways than one. I saw my hubby walk back over with a tray full of goodies, and now the best part was to eat it.

'I got us some nacho chips as well.'

'We only have an hour-and-a-half movie.'

'Well, we better get started.' Dale moved a chair at the table, and my wheelchair was able to go up to the table. I had actually passed caring about my chair. I was having too much fun to worry about anyone else.

'How good does it all look?' I lifted my hot dog and took a bite of it. 'Hmm, It taste even better when you haven't had one in so long.' This took me back to my childhood days at parties or a family barbeque. It was amazing how a simple sense took you back to the good old days of growing up. Where you lived for the moment and had no cares of the world.

'You cannot come to the movies and not have a hot dog.' What a mess we were getting into! The sauce was around our mouths and in between our fingers. I had to act like a child and wipe some on Dale's nose. I couldn't resist acting like a toddler. 'That is war, Mrs Black.'

'Is that a threat, Mr Black . . . ? Bring it on.'

'You might regret what you just said.' My hubby made me giggle with his sexy charm, and he had a cheeky schoolboy look on his face. He actually suited it. 'Well, we can always say that we had fun eating a hot dog.' I didn't think that I had ever had as much fun. 'And that is before the movie.'

'Speaking of movie, shouldn't we go and get our seats?' I sat still and watched Dale take our tray away. He looked really happy, and that was all I could ask for. I hadn't noticed it for a while, but I felt so relaxed watching him glow.

'Can you get anything else on your knee, Ash?'

'Yeah, plenty of room.' I had sweets, nachos, and juice all on my knee. We were going to leave the movie later and go home to crash out. There was a queue to get in to the movie, but the minute the security guard saw my chair, he came over to let us in the side door.

'Come this way, sir.' I felt my face go scarlet; the heat was rising from me.

'That isn't necessary.' I needed to try and stop us from receiving a lot of attention.

'No, mam, wheelchairs go this way.' This was one war that I was never going to win, and I wasn't going to let this ruin my day. I sat back and let Dale follow the security guard. What harm could it do? 'Enjoy the movie, sir.'

'Thank you . . . Are you OK, Ash?'

'Yeah, I am fine.' If I was the one pushing Dale, I would say enjoy the attention. But it was hard when you were the one sitting in the chair being pushed. 'I suppose I better get used to the attention.' I was relieved when I saw another wheelchair enter the room. I was glad that I wasn't the only one.

'Listen, Mrs, stop your moaning and get the goodies cracked open.' My hubby should have been a bouncer because he knew how to make someone smile in any situation. I handed him a tub of sweets and watched him settle back in his seat. He took my hand, and I placed my head on his shoulder. We were loves young dream sitting in the movies, munching on comfort food.

'Aw, I don't think I have ever laughed as much.' My sides were aching with all the laughing.

'It was good to see you enjoy yourself, babe.' I took Dale's hand and guided him around to the front of me, and he bent down to my level.

'Thank you for a lovely day. I have had a blast . . . Here . . . with you.' I had sat and watched a movie today, and I had forgotten about everything. It was just me and Dale, and nothing else mattered.

'I am glad that you have had as much fun as I have had . . . I love you so much. It was just nice to see a sparkle back in your eyes.' I leant forward and placed my lips over his. They were soft, warm, and tender. I wanted to kiss him all day. 'What do you want to do now?' That was a good question. What did I want to do now?

'I don't know. You picked the movies, and it was a good choice. What do you think we should do?' Dale stayed very still and looked through my eyes, just like he was studying my mind.

'Are you hungry?'

'Are you mad? I have eaten more today than what I have eaten in a month.'

'I don't know what to suggest.'

'I have one suggestion.' Dale's eyes were wide with curiosity. 'We could go to the boat. We haven't been there in a while.' I would never forget my first time in Dale's boat; it was magnificent. It was the first time that we told each other that we loved each other, and we haven't stopped since then.

'Ash, have you seen the weather? It is freezing.' I had never thought about that. Why did we have to be here in the middle of winter?

'The house. It seems like a million years since we were last there. Rosa might be there, that's if your mom hasn't got her busy at the cottage.'

'Let's go.' It isn't until you get sick that you realise what you take for granted. You think that you are lucky with a good job and a nice home. But what is luck? None of the nice things mean anything without all the people in your life. Luck really does come in a lucky bag, and it is your Donald Duck what you are going to get. I had been dealt my fair share of bad luck over the last few years, but I had made the best out of a bad situation. Now that my time was running out, I thought that I was lucky for what I had. Not many people can be dying and say that they have everything that they ever wanted.

DALE'S STORY

CHAPTER 24

New Year's Eve, 31 December 2012

When I was growing up, I always wanted to be a business man and marry the woman of my dreams. Well, I could safely say that I had succeeded in all my childhood dreams. I was standing looking out of the window at the front of the cottage, realising how lucky I had been. My wife was in the room getting her hair and make-up done by a top stylist from town, and I couldn't wait to see her. I knew that our time together was running out, but I intended to make the most of whatever time we had left together. A fresh flurry of snow was falling, and I knew that Ash would love that tonight. I would never understand how anyone would like snow, but it made my wife happy and that made me happy.

'Dale son, it is 6.30. People will be arriving soon.'

'It is OK, Mom. Ashley will be out soon.' I loved my mom to pieces, but having her here continuously the last few weeks had driven me crazy.

Roll on our move, was all I could say. I was looking forward to get some peace and quiet.

'Dale.'

'What's up, bro?' When Callum never answered, I turned away from the window to see my gorgeous wife being wheeled towards me. Her hair was all pinned to the side, and it came down her shoulder in ringlets. She didn't look sick, not one bit. The pale white skin was gone, and her hair was all bouncy and full of life. If she was walking towards me, I wouldn't have known that she was ill.

'Are you OK?' Ashley's voice brought me back out of the clouds. I thought that I was dreaming.

'Yes. You look beautiful.' Not that she never looked beautiful before, she just looked radiant tonight. I looked like I hadn't made an effort, jeans and a shirt open at the chest. I thought that I had gone overboard, but my wife had bet me and went two steps better.

'It is weird seeing you dressed casual. It suits you. You look rather dashing.' It was nice to hear my wife pay me a compliment. I couldn't care what anyone thought about me, as long as my wife approved. 'Thank you for coming at short notice, Sandra.' It amazed me how Ashley was still so polite to everyone. I thought if it was me going through what she was, I would give everyone a life of hell.

'You are very welcome, honey. Just call me anytime.' It made me so happy to see Ashley smiling from ear to ear. It was amazing what a little pamper session could do to someone.

'I will see you out, Sandra.' I didn't want to leave my wife too long with my mom; she was enough to darken anyone's mood.

'Ashley, you look stunning, my dear.'

'Thank you, Rosa . . . It is weird seeing you without work clothes on.' It was nice to see Rosa in casual clothes. It made her feel part of the family. 'If Mrs Black had her way, I would have had a waiter's suit on.'

'But I wouldn't hear of it.' My mom liked to be centre of attention, but over my dead body would she turn my staff into waiters.

'I should think not.' Ashley sounded shocked that my mother could have suggested such nonsense. 'You enjoy yourself tonight, Rosa. Tonight is our party. Our rules.' I was glad that Ashley was laying the law down; it would give my mom a run for her money.

'I will, Ashley.' Rosa touched Ashley's hand so gently. It was very touching to see how Ashley and Rosa had bonded in such a short time.

It seemed like every person whom my wife speaks to was instantly connected. We were all very honoured to have met such a kind and loving person.

'You are very quiet, Mr Black.'

'Sorry, babe. I am just taking everything in.' The door went just in time to save me from explaining what I was thinking.

'Come through.' Carlos was being the doorman for some strange reason, but I managed to see past Carlos and spotted Lavina and Lelland. They looked like the perfect couple as they greeted us.

'Hey, you guys.' Lavina was so bubbly and so normal, considering that she was immortal. Ashley looked shocked to see them, but she still welcomed them with open arms. Lavina bent down to give Ash a kiss on the cheek, and Lelland shook my hand. It still seemed bizarre to shake hands with a vampire.

'Hi, this is a pleasant surprise.'

'We didn't think that we were going to make it. We were called away, but we couldn't miss a wonderful night.' Lelland never normally spoke much, so it was a surprise to hear him break into conversation. I had noticed that he was the informative one. He only spoke when something needed explaining to us in detail.

'We are glad that you are here. My mom and dad are in the kitchen.'

'We will go and see them. You kids have a nice night.' I looked at Ashley, and she looked at me. Both of us had no idea that they were invited.

'Who else has your mom invited?' Ashley was very discreet as she whispered in my ear. I could sense her sarcastic tone.

'Only time will tell.' I took a large drink of my wine, frightened to see who was going to walk through that door.

'Yes, they are through here.' Carlos made me cringe; who was asking for us now?

'Hello, there.'

'Hello, my dear, you are looking divine.' Robert and Renee were supposed to be out of town this New Year. It was a nice surprise.

'Still the charmer, I see.' Robert and Ashley hit it off the very first moment that they met. Even much so that when he phoned the office, it was Ashley he asked for.

'He will still be a charmer in heaven, my dear.' Ashley laughed at Renee's comment, and by the look on Renee's face, she felt bad for what she said. 'Ashley, I am so sorry. I didn't think.'

'Don't you dare apologise, sweetie. It was nice to see someone didn't think before they spoke to me . . . Not many people talk to me like Ashley, any more.' It had dawned on me that we probably did think before we spoke, and it was only to spare her feelings. But now I could see that she had noticed and we were all doing her head in.

'Would you like to follow me? And I will get you drinks.' Rosa was the saviour to divert this conversation away.

'Oh yes, please.' Robert was rubbing his hands together as he followed Rosa. He was a typical man, and I loved him for it. He was just a big softy.

'Callum, can you pass me a drink through, please?'

'Sure, babe.'

'I thought that you had got lost through there, Christine.' Christine had been getting ready for ages that I completely forgot all about her.

'I know. I didn't realise how long it takes to get a baby ready.'

'Aw, look at the lovely princess.' Kiara was happy kicking her legs around as Ashley spoke to her. It was good to see both of my girls laughing and smiling.

'Here we go, Ash.'

'Thanks, Cal . . . Tell Daddy to look at you in your gorgeous party dress.' Callum took Kiara from Christine and took her through to the kitchen. We heard everyone making a fuss over her. 'That actually tastes really nice.' I knew Ashley wasn't suppose to drink alcohol, but I wasn't going to question that tonight.

'I am just going to grab one . . . and kick everyone out of that kitchen.' Ashley and I both laughed at Christine's witty response. We both knew that she was going to do exactly what she said.

'Hey.' I jumped out of my skin at Ashley's raised voice.

'Hey, baby girl.' Christian and George were two lovely guys, and they always made Ash happy when they were around.

'How are you doing?'

'Even better for seeing you.' George handed me a couple of heavy bags, and by God they were heavy.

'Christian insisted that we brought some goodies.'

'Thanks, you two . . . Help yourselves to whatever you like in the kitchen.'

'We will be right back. Don't go anywhere.'

'Oh, ha ha, Mr.' I bent in front of my wife and smiled at her. I was ecstatic at how happy she looked.

'You look so happy.'

'I am, and it is all thanks to you, honey.' I felt something spark inside of me when Ashley bent forward and kissed me so tenderly. Her mouth was divine, and it got every nerve in my body tingling.

'I have wanted to do that from the minute I saw you standing at the window, looking all sexy.' Her soft voice made me go weak at the knees. It was going to be impossible to keep my hands off her all night.

'Well, the next time just scream at me.'

'Sorry, are we interrupting?'

'Hi, Steph. No, come in. My husband is just being a big softie.'

'I hope you don't mind, I fetched my friend Scott with me.'

'Of course, we don't. The more the merrier. It is nice to see you.' I knew how much Ashley and Steph got on at the office. I was just glad that she could accept my invite.

'I know it seems like forever since you were last in the office.' I didn't realise how much Ashley connected with people from work. She was going to be a loss to a lot of people. I knew that Steph had become a close friend of Ashley's, but there was a lot more people at work who would miss her keeping them right.

'Did you have a nice Christmas?' Everyone was making tonight special in its own way, and it was perfect.

'Quiet, but it was nice.'

'Good . . . Listen, all the drinks are in the kitchen. Please make yourselves at home and help yourselves.' Everyone was now coming out with a glass in their hand, and it was good to see everyone getting along enjoying themselves.

'Callum dear, get the music started.' My mom thought that a karaoke would be a good idea, so I hope that everyone could sing, or we would have a headache very soon.

'Tom. Nice to see you.' Ash was more and more pleased at every face that came in.

'Ashley, we couldn't miss your big party. How are you?'

'I am fine, thank you.'

'You are such an inspiration, darling. You look wonderful.' Tom was the only one whom Ashley would let make that remark. He knew her, and he knew what she was losing. But here she was putting on a brave face on to everything and being a perfect hostess.

'Thank you, Tom. That means a lot.'

'Tom, drinks are all in the kitchen. Please, help yourself.'

'Thanks, Dale.' Everyone was laughing and joking together. We couldn't ask for better. Tonight was going to be a huge success. I couldn't take my eyes of my wife. She was an inspiration to everyone who had this disease. It was just a shame that she couldn't survive it and show people what it was like to stand up to cancer.

'OK, everyone, since this is Dale and Ashley's party, who agrees with me that one of them should start the karaoke off?' Everyone was in agreement with Callum, and I wasn't drunk enough to sing, but I couldn't make Ashley sing. I watched my wife carefully as she whispered to Cal. He looked happy at whatever she said to him, and I was intrigued to know what was going on. Cal handed the microphone to Ash, and she smiled sarcastically at me.

'I haven't sung for years, and with my chest, I have no idea what it will sound like but here goes.' I had no idea that my wife could sing, but I sat intrigued as the music started. Whitney Houston—'I Will Always Love You'. I looked around the room, and everyone was smiling. Ashley had a voice like an angel; she was not perfect. I couldn't take my eyes away from her now.

'The last time I heard Ashley sing that song was at her mom and dad's funeral. There wasn't a dry eye in the room.' Christine had her hand on my shoulder, and it was nice to have someone close that knew how I was feeling. Christine loved Ash, just as much as I did, and we knew how each other felt inside, the heartache, the pain, and the misery. The thought of losing her forever was a nightmare. Everyone was clapping and cheering as Callum wheeled Ash over to me. She was fantastic.

'I had no idea that you could sing, babe.'

'You do now.' I could see how much that singing had taken out of her, but she was still smiling and showing the world how eager she was to have fun.

'You have a voice like an angel.' Christine had to walk away before Ash saw her tears. But I wasn't going to say anything.

'I will sing a song, but I can't sing to save myself.'

'Callum. Dale said that he will sing.' I couldn't believe that my darling wife had just done that to me.

'I meant later.' I wanted a few drinks inside me first. I needed some Dutch courage.

'You never said that. Too late, now get yourself up there, Mr Black.' I felt all eyes on me, and my heart was pounding. What was I going to sing?

'What are you singing, bro?' I looked around the room again, and everyone was enjoying themselves. Then I looked at my wife sitting in her chair talking to Christine. Her bright brown eyes were staring through me, smiling brightly.

'Savage Gardens—"Truly Madly Deeply".' I could remember hearing this song years ago and thinking that the words were lovely. The music started, and my spine tingled, I looked at the floor and just started singing; all I could think was, every word meant something. I picked up the courage to look at my wife, with tears rolling down her cheeks. I walked over to her and bent down beside her. I clasped her hand in mine and sang to my angel. I just couldn't wait for the song to end to let someone else take the limelight. I couldn't finish the last few words. I just put my arms around my wife and took her all in.

'That is one of my favourite songs.' I pulled back to look at my wife. I couldn't believe what I was hearing. What were the chances of me singing Ashley's favourite song.

'Really.' I couldn't believe that we both liked the same song. We were still learning about each other, and it was nice to share these moments together.

'You really didn't know?'

'No. I didn't know what to sing, and I remembered that song.'

'Well, I have never heard my brother sing before, but way to go, Dale, you have everyone in tears.'

'First and last, Callum, first and last.' I looked around the room and saw everyone rubbing their eyes. I had no idea that I would have had that effect on everyone.

'Who is next up on my karaoke machine?'

'Me. I will go next.' I wondered how long it would take Christian to get up and sing. 'I hope that you have "It's Raining Men".' Christian made Ashley laugh so that made me happy. 'I was about to say no more sad songs, but you have excelled yourself, mate.' Everyone started clapping and cheering as Christian parades around to his song. It was about time that this cottage saw some exciting action.

'There is only two hours left of 2012.' I hadn't looked at the time since seven o'clock. Didn't time fly when you were having fun!

'Apart from you being ill, this has been the best year of my life.' I was a little bit tipsy, but I knew everything that I was saying, and I could say it all without having a few drinks in me.

'Snap . . . Moving here and meeting you has changed my life, and tonight has been lovely.' I didn't expect tonight to go so well because there were so many different personalities under the one roof. But everyone was enjoying themselves mingling with one another.

'I love you, Ash.'

'I love you more, Mr Black.' That was impossible. I loved the bones of this woman. The sound of a lovely sweet voice took Ashley's attention, and I was stunned to see Lavina singing a beautiful song that represented her life perfectly. '"Hey Ho" by the Luminners.' Ashley knew the song well, and I hadn't ever heard it. How had I never heard of it? 'It is a beautiful song, don't you think?' I couldn't stop looking at Lavina sing; she was a natural.

'Yeah, it is lovely. I haven't heard it before.' I really didn't think that I knew as many beautiful singers.

'Do you want a refill, Ash?' Callum was being the perfect host to my wife, and I loved to see the bond that Cal and Ash have got.

'Yes, please, honey.' My whole family had bonded with my wife, and that was all I ever wanted out of life. I couldn't ask for any more.

The rest of the night had gone by so smoothly, plenty of food and drink, good music, and good company. What more could we ask for?

'Right, everyone, we have five minutes left of 2012. Will everyone get a top up ready for midnight?' Callum sounded rather tipsy over the microphone so much so that he made me sound sober.

'Mr Black, it is a good job that you just have to crawl into bed.' I liked to hear my wife's voice, even if it was sarcasm.

'The joys of having a party in your own house.'

'Does everyone want to make their way outside?' My mom had something planned for midnight, and I had no idea what it was, a perfect surprise for everyone. Christine put a thick cover around Ashley to keep her warm, and we all made our way outside.

'What has your mom got planned for tonight?' I really wished I could tell her, but her guess was as good as mine.

'I honestly have no idea, doll.'

'I will start the countdown when it is time.' Callum always did love a mic. He should have been in showbiz. '10, 9, 8, 7, 6, 5, 4, 3, 2, 1. Happy New Year.' Everyone was hugging each other and shaking hands wishing each other a happy New Year.

'Happy New Year, Ash.' I wrapped my arms around my wife from behind her chair and kissed her head. Suddenly, the sky lit up with fireworks. Everyone was 'oh' and 'ah' as they banged and cracked. The sky was a blaze, and it was a lovely surprise.

'Happy New Year, hun.' Ashley's voice was different with the crack of fireworks in the distance. I continued to hold her in my arms and enjoyed the show. 2012 had gone out with a bang just like we had planned, and it had gone off without any hitches.

'My mom has put on a good show, don't you think?' There was no answer from her. I knew that she would be amazed by this stunning moment. But I moved around to face her, and her eyes were closed. 'Ashley.' I screamed her name as I realised that my worst nightmare had come true. There was no life in her at all, and I couldn't get her to wake up.

'Dale.' Christine got down beside me still smiling. 'I will help you put her to bed, honey.' Christine was so naive. She thought that she had just got so tired and fell asleep, like she had been doing over the last few weeks.

'She has gone.' I was sobbing uncontrollably now, and I couldn't breathe. My world had just collapsed, and my life had ended.

'Dale, let Lavina and Lelland take Ashley through to the room. They are doctors.' I didn't want them to take her anywhere, but I knew that they had to.

'She can't be gone. She was so happy.' Christine was in denial, and I couldn't blame her. But I couldn't deal with her right now. I couldn't deal with myself never mind anyone else. I sat back on the ground and watched Lelland wheel my wife away. My mom and dad were bent over me, trying to calm me down, but my heart was aching. Why tonight? Why couldn't we get one more day with her? I heard everyone's tears in the background, and that just made me worse. Ashley had touched so many people's hearts that it was unbelievable.

'I phoned Dr Ching. Dale . . . he is coming right over.' Callum's voice registered, but I couldn't respond. My body was in shock at the whole thing.

'Dale . . .' Lelland's voice made me rise up on to my feet. Was she just sleeping? Was my beautiful angel just sleeping? 'I am so sorry. Ashley has gone.' I sank to my knees like I had been punched in the gut.

'No . . . No . . . No . . . She can't leave me. You have got to help her. You said that you could help her.' I sank back down on to my knees, and my head rested into my hands. I just wanted to disappear and let tonight be a distant memory.

'Come and be with her.' My mom and dad helped me up to my feet, and I walked on to follow Lelland. I felt empty. My head was pickled, and I couldn't even think straight. I stood at our room door and looked to Lelland for some support. 'We have put her on the bed. Lavina will leave you with her.' I opened the door and saw my beautiful beloved wife on the bed. She looked like she was sleeping. I walked over to be beside her, and I fell to my knees and took her hand. I sobbed my heart out. I knew that our time was near, but I never thought it would be tonight. 'I can't live without you, Ash . . . You are my world . . . It wasn't time to go.'

'Dale.' I knew Dr Ching's voice well, but I couldn't even look up to him. 'Can I come in to check over Ashley?' I watched as he took a stethoscope out to listen to her heart and shone a light in her eyes. 'I am so sorry for your loss.' It felt final now. My wife was gone forever. 'I will make arrangements for Ashley to get picked up . . . But it might not be for a few hours since it is New Year's Eve.'

'Where will they take her?' I didn't want to leave her, and I didn't want them to pick her up. I wanted her to stay with me forever. This wasn't supposed to happen.

'They will take her to the funeral home . . . You will be able to bring her home as soon as they have got everything all done.' He was talking about my wife like she was a project to get finished. 'I will go out to the car and get everything all organised. If you need to ask me anything, please do not hesitate.' I stumbled up on to my feet and pulled Ashley's favourite fur blanket off the bottom of the bed and placed it over her. She always felt comfortable with it wrapped around her.

'Would she have known that she was going to die?' It was probably the silliest thing to ask, but I needed to know that she wasn't in any pain.

'I doubt it very much, Dale . . . I think that Ashley's heart is what gave in first, and it would have been quick and painless.'

'I knew that this was coming, but I . . .'

'Even though you expected it, it is still a huge shock to you all.' That was an understatement of the century. I climbed on the bed and lay down beside her. I had never experienced as much pain in my life, and I just wished that my heart would stop with hers. What was I going to do without her?

'Dale . . . can I come and sit with you both?' I couldn't say no to Christine. She would be hurting just as much as I was. 'I can't believe that she is gone . . . She was so happy . . . I thought that she had weeks left.' I looked up to Christine and reached over for her hand; her make-up was all over the place with crying, and her body was shaking.

'We will just have to help each other through this.' I was trying to be strong for her, but I thought that we were going to need each other to get through this sad time.

'What happens now?'

'Dr Ching is away to organise everything.' Life is a bitch at times. It made me think what was the point of building up a life? What was the point when some disease was going to rip it all apart? 'Will you stay with Ashley while I go and see Tom.'

'Of course, I will.' I was hoping that Tom could clear a few things up for me, and I needed to ask the questions now before I forgot. I kissed Ashley's cool lips and climbed off the bed. I could have sworn that I had strings attached to me. I felt like every step away from her was a struggle.

'It is OK, hun. I will look after her.' I opened the door and walked down the hall. Everyone was standing with pain in their eyes.

'Dale, Son.'

'Not now, Mom.' I couldn't bear my mom's pity at this moment. I would end up giving her a few home truths. 'Tom. Can I have a word?'

'Yes, of course, you can.' I walked into the kitchen with my head bowed and took a seat at the breakfast bar. 'Dale. Son, I am so sorry for your loss. I know that it was expected, but it won't make it any easier.' Tom sat beside me and handed me a whisky. One wouldn't be enough tonight; I thought that I would need a bottle.

'It just isn't fair, Tom. I thought that we had weeks left . . . We had the most amazing forty-eight hours ever.' My tears were like a tap. I couldn't control them at all. 'What I wanted to talk to you about was the funeral. What happens now? I know that Dr Ching is arranging the funeral home to collect Ash, but how long will it take to have her funeral?'

'Well . . . I can have it arranged for the fifth, providing the funeral home is fine with it . . . You and Ashley had everything else all organised and paid for . . . The last song was to be arranged though.' The last song was going to be easy after tonight's karaoke; we both had a favourite song, and it was appropriate.

'It isn't a church song, but I know that it was a favourite of Ashley's . . . "Truely Madly Deeply".'

'Perfect.'

'I feel empty, Tom.' I was always fulfilled when Ashley was around, and now my body was completely drained.

'It is only to be expected. You were soulmates.' We were soulmates. We were lovers and friends. We were everything to one another, and I had lost everything. 'If you need me for anything, you know where I am.'

'Thank you, Tom. I don't know how to thank you enough for everything that you have done for me and Ash.' This man had been our God, our saviour, and everything that he did for me and Ash would never be forgotten.

'You don't have to thank me, Son . . . Just think about now, and what Ashley would want you to do.'

'She told me many times that she wanted me to remarry and have kids, but that is never going to happen.' Not in a million years could I move on without Ashley, by my side. I could never have kids with anyone else; it just wouldn't feel right.

'Give it time, Dale.' I drank my whisky and felt it heat my entire body up. Tom pulled me close to him and patted my back.

'I suppose I better face everyone.' I dreaded this bit, listening to everyone saying how sorry they were. It wasn't going to bring her back, but I took a deep breath and walked back into the living room with Tom at my side. 'I would like to thank you all for coming tonight. It meant a lot to both me and . . . Ashley . . . I know that Ashley meant a lot to each and every one of you in some way . . . She was just that kind of person. Fun. Loving. Kind and caring . . . You are all welcome to stay as long as you like, but I want to spend what time I have left by her side.'

'Dale . . .' I turned around to look at Christian, and his face was full of pain. No more happy, cheerful, and full of life. 'Can I see Ashley for a few minutes, just to say goodbye?'

'Of course, you can, buddy.' I saw my dad walk towards me, and even he looked heartbroken. I have never seen my dad without a smile on his face.

'Are you OK, Son?'

'I feel empty, Dad.' My dad threw his arms around me, and I crumbled in his arms. His strong frame kept me standing. I had given up trying to stop crying because it was no use.

'I know how you feel . . . I am here for you anytime, day or night . . . We are all going to miss her. She was our angel sent to change our lives.' My dad was a nice man, but I had never heard him say such a nice thing about someone.

'I just can't take any of this tonight.' I stepped back from my dad and wiped my tears away. I tried to compose myself as I walked up the hall to our bedroom. The door was open slightly, and I could see Christine sitting in the exact same position that I left her, and I entered slowly. Seeing Ashley in bed, so peaceful, it made me realise that all her suffering was now over. Her pain was gone, and she was at peace.

'Dale, if you need any help with anything, please just ask me . . . I haven't known Ash long, but she was like a sister to me.' Christian came and put his hand on my shoulder, and my eyes filled up again. I couldn't take my eyes off my wife.

'Thank you, Christian . . . Don't be a stranger now.' I had met a lot of nice people over the last few months, and it was all thanks to Ashley.

'I won't. Just take care of yourself.' I could hear the pain and tears choke Christian as he left the room.

'I have sat here trying to take it all in, but I can't accept that she has left us. I keep squeezing her hand, hoping that she sits up and laughs at me.' I sat on the bed down from Christine and put my hand on hers. I knew exactly what she meant because I had done the same thing.

'She is at peace now, hun . . . No more pain or suffering . . . No more battling to survive . . . We will get through this together. It is what Ashley wanted.' Christine put her arms around me and sobbed so hard that I could feel her pain.

'Dale.' I opened my eyes but didn't let Christine go, holding Christine just reminded me how much I was going to miss Ashley's cuddles. Dr Ching was standing in the doorway, and I didn't want to hear what he had to say. 'The private ambulance is here for Ashley.'

'You said it would be hours.'

'They are quiet just now.' This was it. My wife was leaving me forever, and I would never have her beside me again. I felt like the whole world had stopped and nothing else mattered. It was like a huge part had been taken from me, and I would never get it back.

'Can we have five minutes?' I needed five minutes, but I knew that wasn't going to be enough.

'Just come out when you are ready.' My head was floating in the clouds somewhere, and I was too weak to deal with all this grief.

'We should just let them take her now . . . Then we can grieve and get ready to give her the send-off that she deserves.' Christine did have a point, but I wasn't sure that I could let them take her away from me. I watched as Christine rose to her feet and bent over Ashley and placed a kiss on her head. 'I will never forget about you, chick.' Christine moved towards the door, ready to leave.

'Christine, will you wait . . . ? I don't think that I can leave her on my own.' Christine never moved another muscle. I got up and stroked my wife's hair; she was perfect, not a hair out of place. 'I will always love you, sweetheart . . . We will meet again one day, and I hope that you will wait for me.' I placed my kiss on her cold lips, and I felt Christine take my hand. I just knew that it was time to leave her. I got out of the room and froze. I could see Dr Ching and the men waiting to take Ashley away, and it all hit me. 'Look after her.'

'Come and get a drink, Dale.' I followed Christine through to the living room and plonked myself down on the couch. This was Ashley's favourite seat, and now it was going to be mine. No one spoke to me and that was for the best right now. Callum handed me a drink, and Christine sat beside me. Her body convulsed as she sobbed her heart out. I wanted to comfort her, but I just couldn't bring myself to move.

'Has everyone got a drink?' I didn't really care about anyone else. I just wanted to get through the next few hours. 'Could you all raise your glasses . . . to Ashley?' I heard all the voices follow Callum's lead, while Christine and I sat nursing our drinks.

'Happy New Year, everyone.' I immediately recognised the voice to be my dippy sister. I looked around to see Nikki and Carlos in the doorway. 'What is going on with everyone?' My dad rushed over to Nikki to fill her in, and I cringed. I just knew that this was going to break my sister into tiny pieces.

'Nikki . . . Ashley passed away, shortly after midnight.' The room fell silent again. It was very good at doing that tonight.

'No . . . she can't have.' Nikki never cried, not even when my mom and dad passed away. I put my drink down and went to comfort my baby sister. She threw her arms around my waist and burst into tears. 'I never got a chance to say goodbye.' Her sobbing broke my heart all over again.

'Dale.' I turned around slightly with Nikki in my arms, and I could see Dr Ching, leading the way with Ashley. I kept my arm around Nikki, as we all moved out of the way to let them through. 'I will be in touch tomorrow.' Dr Ching carried on walking, and the men followed slowly behind.

'No. They can't take her. Dale, tell them.' The screams and the sobs out of my sister was breaking my heart, and I had no idea how to help her.

'It is OK, Nik . . . They need to do their job.' My wife was bypassing me taking my heart and soul with her. There wasn't a dry eye in the room. Callum caught Christine before she sank to the floor, breaking her heart, and I kept Nikki in my arms. Was our life ever going to be the same again? Could we move forward without this special person in our lives? Only time was going to tell. If only we had a magic wand to wave, everything would work out just fine.

THE END OF PART 1

Continued Reading

I hope that you have all enjoyed reading this novel. It touches my heart strings every time that I read it. Part two of this novel will be available very soon. *The Smile—A New Beginning.*

Author's History

Kelly 'Mcmullen' Lowe was born on 19 March 1986, to the proud parents of Christine Greenlees Beaumont Steedman and Hugh Patrick McMullen. My parents taught me the true value of life, and they showed me how to succeed in anything that I wanted to do. I married my husband David Lowe on 30 December 2006, and we have two wonderful Children, Dylan and Tianna. Over the last couple of years, I was unwell, and I put all my time into my family and books. However, in 2012, I wanted to commit myself to writing my own novel. I have put a lot of time and effort into this novel, and I hope that you all will enjoy it, as much I did writing it.

This is a Trilogy Book